REBIRTH

HELL ON EARTH BOOK 6

IAIN ROB WRIGHT

ULCERATED PRESS

WANT FREE BOOKS?

Don't miss out on your FREE Iain Rob Wright horror pack. Five bestselling horror novels sent straight to your inbox at no cost. No strings attached & signing up is a doddle.

For more information just visit the back of this book.

Dedicated to politicians everywhere; the true authors of horror.

Also, cheers to Stephanie Hardy, always the first off the blocks to catch my mistakes!

"Bravery is being the only one who knows you're afraid."
   Franklin P. Jones.

"Everybody fights demons. Some are worse than others."
   John Daly

"What the fuck does WTF mean?"
   Gary King, World's End (2013),

FOREWORD

So... this is the 6th and final book of the Hell on Earth series. That's a concrete promise. There will be no cliffhangers, no unanswered questions, and no dangling plot threads. After sticking with me for more than half-a-million words, you deserve a proper ending. This book is my solemn attempt at providing one. I hope you reach the final page satisfied and entertained. Give me Hell if not!

I am releasing this book during the 2020 coronavirus lockdown crisis. Some might think my choice of topic crass in the current climate, but I know that my true readers find apocalyptic fiction to be an escape — a way of facing their fears head on. This book is for them; and for you.

I have no idea what our future is going to look like. Things will undoubtedly be different, and while change can be both frightening and painful, it inevitably leads to progress. The human race has evolved from cave dwellers to space farers. Whatever happens in the days ahead, we will continue to evolve and get better. The lessons learned today will educate us to face future challenges. The world is scary, but I promise tomorrow will arrive the same as it always has. The sun will continue to rise and we, as a people, will continue to learn.

In the meantime, turn the page and let's watch the world burn together. Enjoy the final chapter of Hell on Earth.

Love,

Iain

"And so you see, Hitler's great mistake was going to war with the Soviet Union. It split his forces in two and spread them too thin. Even more grievous was the German leader's underestimation of Russian winter and the country's poorly maintained roads. The Nazi forces froze to death without ever making it back home." Mrs Malone looked at the clock on the wall and then at her watch. "Okay, you lot, that's it for today. Tomorrow, we'll talk about the things World War Two gave us, like the jet engine and penicillin."

The class – six children aged between four and twelve – filed out of the room while Mrs Malone used a tea towel to clean the whiteboard. In the months leading up to the demon invasion, St Catherine's Primary School had completely phased out whiteboards in favour of obscenely sized multimedia screens, but the new dark age had rendered that technology useless. They didn't completely lack power at the school – they possessed batteries, hand-powered torches, and a small supply of petrol to power a small generator salvaged from a nearby builder's yard – but they just needed to be conservative. Once a week, they put on a movie from the school's DVD collection. This week, they were watching *Flubber*.

They had survived the last twelve months by first hiding in the school's basement, living off supplies taken from the cafeteria and drinking from a rusty sink, and then cautiously spreading out into the school, keeping careful watch for demons. There hadn't been any lately – possibly not for months. Maybe it was finally over. Was that too much to hope?

With the chaos of the classroom tidied, Mrs Malone headed out into the playground. Winter would soon attach itself to everything, so everyone was making the most of being outside before the weather turned nasty and forced them to hunker down inside the gym, which was the only space large enough to contain a fire. Its high, narrow windows would draw out the smoke, while its high ceilings would provide enough clean air to keep them all from suffocating. They'd survived one winter already, losing only the elderly Mr Granger. The cold had been too much for the former geography teacher's delicate frame. They had buried him in the playing field beneath the rugby posts.

Mr Bradford, the school's ex-maths teacher, spotted her standing by the nature pond – a square-framed box of water inhabited by newts, frogs, and boisterous insects. "Hi, Stella, how was your lesson?"

"Good, thanks. I think they're starting to pay attention. Perhaps the horror is finally leaving them."

Mr Bradford squeezed her arm playfully. "You still teaching them about Hitler?"

"World War Two, and yes I am."

Mr Bradford perched on the edge of the box-frame and peered across the playground to where the children were happily rushing around. They did so quietly, obeying the cardinal rule of not attracting attention. "Why not teach them something they can actually use? I'm teaching them to tie knots and make snares."

"I'll leave the practical skills to you, Mr Bradford, but I'm teaching them something equally important."

"What? How to outflank an enemy?"

Stella smirked but didn't laugh. "I'm trying to help them avoid the mistakes of the past. One day, these children will inherit what's left of the Earth. I'm trying to show them the futility of war."

"That's very noble of you, Stel. I just hope we survive long enough for any of it to matter."

"I'm certain we will. You were right; I've taught them how to outflank an enemy. We are studying military history, after all."

"Ha! Then perhaps there's hope."

For a while, they sat and watched the children play '*stuck in the mud*'. A gentle breeze carried leaves across the playground. The sun beamed.

Mr Bradford turned to her. "It's been a while since we last saw any demons. Do you reckon we might be safe?"

She'd been asking herself that question a lot lately. It would be so tempting to rush back out into the world and see what was left, but it would be foolish too. "John wants to go looking for supplies in the weeks ahead, so I'm sure we'll find out." John was the school's headmaster and one of the four adults living at the school. Miss Perrins, the school nurse, was the fourth. They were the only ones – along with the deceased Mr Granger – who had stayed behind with the schoolchildren when their parents had never arrived to pick them up. They were an odd sort of family, but they had survived together for a whole year.

"I hope John finds us something to eat," said Mr Bradford, licking his lips. "I can't survive on flour and water much longer."

Stella laughed. "We ate cabbage this morning, so what are you complaining about?"

Mr Bradford reached out and gave her a tiny shove, then smiled at her a moment longer than was comfortable. A kaleidoscope of butterflies took flight in Stella's stomach. She still considered herself married – still very much in love with her Dominic, who might still be alive somewhere – but the burden drifted away. She blushed, hot in the cheeks. "You know what I would love, Mike?" She dropped the school day formality; the kids weren't near to them.

"If it's a big juicy steak, I'm right there with you, Stel."

Her hand moved to her mouth as she chuckled. When she removed it, she let it fall onto Mr Bradford's thigh. "I would love to go for a walk. That's it, just a walk. I want to take my shoes off and splash in a stream, or pick the prettiest flower I can find. I want to see what's become of the world before my memories of it fade completely. I haven't stepped outside the front gates in a year."

Mr Bradford stared down at her hand resting on his thigh, and Stella grew horrified for a moment, fearing he might remove it in disgust. Instead, he placed his hand on top of hers. "That sounds like a great first date. What exactly are we waiting for?"

She laughed, then realised he was serious. "Are you mad? We can't go walking around outside. The only reason we're alive is because we barricaded ourselves in the basement."

"But we came out of the basement and everything was fine. Maybe we should spread our wings again. Like you said, there hasn't been a demon spotted in months."

"That's not so long, Mike."

"Long enough to risk a stroll in the park, surely? You remember the little one on Pratt's Lane? There's a gazebo and benches, a nice little stretch of grass. It's a five-minute walk. Imagine if we could make it safe? The kids could experience a slide again. They could sit on a swing."

"Sounds wonderful, but it's too dangerous."

A cheeky grin spread across his square face. "It's not dangerous at all, Stel. I've already checked it out. Once last week and again last night. Like you, I've been getting a little stir crazy."

She gasped. By leaving the school, Mike had risked them all. Yet she wasn't angry. She was excited. "You've really been out? What did you see?"

"Why don't you come look for yourself? It's safe, I promise. I saw nothing aside from a pack of wild dogs, and they seemed pretty well fed and docile. The danger has passed."

"I can't... The children..." Her insides sloshed all over the place. She had to take a deep breath of fresh air.

Mike continued staring at her. "The children are fine, John's with them, and we'll be back in ten minutes. I just want you to see that the world is still out there waiting for us. It changes everything, trust me."

Stella shocked herself by nodding. Everything about this felt wrong and irresponsible, but she needed to leave this prison. She needed to get out. A ten-minute break from being a teacher, parent, protector, and nursemaid to six children who were not even her own would, like Mike said, change everything. "Okay, but we have to be quick. Take me to the park, but we head straight back. It'll be fine, right? John is planning to leave soon anyway."

"Exactly." Mike stood from the edge of the pond and offered his hand. She took it, grinning from ear to ear. The touch of his skin was electric, the thought of leaving the school ecstasy in her veins. For the first time in a year, survival gave way to living.

She was going on a date.

Is this real?

Mike's hand felt real in hers. The warmth in her cheeks felt real.

Despite committing to taking a cheeky jaunt, Stella wasn't about to broadcast it. She whispered to Mike and asked if he had a plan. "There're three sets of keys for the main gate," he replied, "so I didn't think anyone would notice when I took some. We just unlock the padlock and squeeze around the minibus parked in the way."

"There's a gap big enough to squeeze through?"

Mr Bradford patted his flat stomach under his grubby white shirt. "I wouldn't have made it through a year ago, but it's not too difficult anymore. Nobody will see us leave."

There was something frightening about that. If no one saw

them leave and something were to happen, the children would be forever left wondering. Her feelings of irresponsibility increased to a level that almost changed her mind. Almost.

"Okay, let's be quick." She kept hold of Mike's hand and pulled him into a trot.

They exited the playground and used a side path around the school that took them to the front of the main building. The gate stood twenty feet away at the edge of a small staff car park. It was an area rarely visited as no one wanted to reveal themselves through the open bar fence that ringed the front of the school.

The staff minibus parked outside the gate was more brown than white nowadays, covered in a year's worth of dust, crud, and bird droppings. It summoned memories of museum trips and days at the zoo. She supposed all the captive animals in England were now dead – the lions, giraffes, meerkats, and reindeer. Such a waste. Endangered animals now fully extinct. That hurt more than she would have thought. Enough to stop her feet moving.

"What's wrong?" Mike asked.

"What's it like out there, really? Are there bodies?

"A lot of bones and old clothes mostly. Nothing... *fresh*. You stop noticing it after a while. I think the dogs and birds took care of the worst."

"I don't think I can do this, Mike."

He grabbed her by both arms and looked at her, piercing her with his light green eyes. "Hey, this is a date – and I always look after my dates."

"Go on a lot of them, do you?"

"Not recently. Come on, I promise it's not as bad as your imagination is telling you."

She took a deep breath and wiped her moist palms on the hips of her trousers. It took a moment, but she was able to swallow down her fear and stifle her doubts. "Okay, but I don't give anything up on a first date."

"Noted. Let me get the padlock."

Stella waited while Mike used his key to open the gate. She

knew it was her imagination, but she felt a rush of air leaping at her like a gasket had burst.

"Relax," said Mike. "I've done this before, remember?"

Stella nodded and took his arm, then allowed him to guide her towards the gap at the front of the minibus. He slid through first but kept his arm out so she could continue to hold it. She pushed herself into the gap, and suddenly the sanctuary that had kept her safe was behind her. Her veins filled with ice. She wanted to dash back inside. Then she was past the minibus and standing firmly on the pavement outside the school. It sent tingles through her toes.

"I'm outside," she gushed, barely able to control her mad grinning. "It really is safe, isn't it?"

Mike was grinning too, her joy apparently contagious. "I'm not saying we should skip around singing '*All Things Bright and Beautiful*' at the top of our lungs, but I think it's safe to explore a little. We won't have a choice soon, anyway. We've performed miracles with what little food we have."

Stella grinned a little wider, knowing the credit belonged to her. She'd been the one to ration the supplies from the school cafeteria, using the most perishable items first, and stretching out the flour, pasta, and sugar for almost an entire year. The school's vegetable garden and greenhouse had helped a little too. If not for her, they might have all starved. Not bad for a history teacher.

The first step, from the pavement to the road, terrified her, but that fear quickly faded as she took the second and the third. She could barely contain the emotions coursing through her and felt harassed by her own beating heart.

Then she saw the bodies.

As Mike had said, the corpses were more bundles of cloth and bone than anything that had once been human. A terrible thing, but the sight of them was surprisingly tolerable. It might even be possible to ignore them. Less easy to ignore was the torn apart cat in the gutter. Its corpse was fresh and half-eaten, a clear victim of the dogs Mike had spoken of. Mankind's rule no longer existed. Only nature remained – and dog ate cat.

"The park's just down here," said Mike, leading her to a small access road running beside *Marty's Salon*. Stella could still vividly remember the haircuts she had received there. Seeing the place again was surreal. The world was an echo, an echo spoiled by dead cats and piles of old bones. It took an effort to stay focused on the positive, on the fact she was outside for the first time in a year. That she was holding hands with a man.

On a date.

I'm being so silly.

They walked in silence down the access road, passing behind shops that had once traded seven days a week. The only sound now was the clip-clop of their shoes – a noise that would never have competed in the days of grumbling car engines and *ch-chinging* tills.

"It's right around here," said Mike.

Stella nodded. "I remember. It's like I was here yesterday."

"Weird, isn't it? I can still remember every detail, even the graffiti on the wall behind the Chinese."

Sure enough, bright orange letters on the wall behind the Chinese takeaway still read: MY NAME AIN'T COREY, BITCH.

She giggled.

Mike frowned. "What is it?"

"I don't know. Everything is different... but the same, you know? I can't figure out whether I like it or not."

"Nothing wrong with being reminded of how things used to be. It might help us get back to where we were."

"Perhaps."

They exited the access road and strolled across a zebra crossing – not that such pedestrian aids were necessary anymore. Abandoned cars lined the kerbs, some with their doors hanging wide open. Some with decaying corpses behind the wheel.

But the park was perfect.

The aluminium slide glinted in the weak sunlight while a

pair of swings swayed back and forth gently in the breeze. Leaves covered the ground inside the gated enclosure, but it only made things more unspoiled and grotto-like. Despite her age – she must have had her fortieth birthday by now, she thought – Stella yearned to climb the colourful bars and descend the slide, to have a carefree moment after so much desperation.

Mike seemed to read her mind, because he let go of her hand and raced ahead, hurdling the low metal railings and leaping up the stubby ladder that fed the climbing frame. From up top, he waved, a joyful grin on his face. "Who's the king of the castle?"

With a roll of her eyes, followed by a laugh, Stella pushed through the gate and hurried to join him. He reached down and helped her up the ladder, and by the time she made it, she was cackling with laughter.

Then Mike kissed her.

He did so suddenly and with no warning, leaning in while she was still giggling. It was an awkward thing and his aim was off, but once the shock abated she worked with him. They held one another and smooched like teenage lovers. When she broke away, she was awash with emotions. Mike took it as a bad sign because his expression grew crestfallen. "I-I shouldn't have done that. I'm sorry."

She put her hand against his chest and smiled, albeit sadly. "No, it was lovely. It just feels like the end of my marriage. I know we've been trapped at the school for a year, but I still think about—"

Mike nodded and cut her off. "There's no need to rush anything. The one thing we have plenty of is time, so I just want you to know that I'm here. I'm here when you're ready."

She smiled again, a little less unhappily. "I hope it's not because of a lack of options, Mr Bradford."

He seemed annoyed by that, despite her having meant it as a joke. He shook his head. "Do you really believe that, Stel?"

"No, I suppose I don't. Come here!" She leant in to kiss him again, but the corner of her eye caught movement. The two swings were gyrating back and forth like Latin dancers.

Mike was puckering up, and he frowned when he realised she wasn't kissing him. He glanced at where she was staring. "What is it?"

"Something disturbed the swings."

"Just the wind."

"There isn't any wind. Only a breeze."

"An animal then. Stella, don't worry. It's just us out here."

A creaking noise from the far side of the playground alerted her, and she whipped her head around like a bird. What she saw was a small metal roundabout spinning by itself.

"Something isn't right," she said. "I want to go back."

Mike nodded, blessedly taking her seriously. "We can go right now. Come on." He took her hand and started for the ladder, but then he leapt back and yelped.

"Mike? What the hell are you...?" Stella's words fell away as her eyes focused on the demons gathered at the railing. They stood in a line, four of them. They seemed hungry, and one of them was drooling. Bigger than all the others, it wore a filthy striped jumper and was naked from the waist down, a distended scrotum between its thighs.

Stella shrieked in terror. The demons chittered like monkeys, excited by the noise – by her fear

Mike grabbed her and held her close. "Quiet! Don't do anything. Don't move."

"Y-You told me it was safe. You told me they were gone. You bastard."

"I'm sorry."

As much as she wanted to strangle the life out of Mike, she was paralysed by fear. She prayed for him to get her out of this so that she could forgive him, but she didn't see how.

Mike squeezed her hand and whispered. "Okay, after three we make a run for it. Head straight for the access road and back to the school, okay?"

"No! No way. We can't risk leading them back there. The children."

Mike stared at her for a moment, his eyes bulbous and white. "Damn it, you're right. Okay, let's head to the shops across the road. Maybe we can barricade ourselves inside."

The demons leapt the railings.

Mike shoved Stella in the back. "Go!"

Stella raced across the climbing frame and threw herself down the slide, nearly going head over heels at the bottom. Mike was right behind her and they rushed for the gate.

Demons filled the entire playground, more and more emerging from behind parked cars and alleyways. They hooted and screeched like taunting bullies. Their stink was awful.

Mike looked back and forth desperately. "They're everywhere. Stella, I'm so sorry."

Stella felt strangely numb. A demon moved in front of her, one eye missing and the other full of hate. There was no way to avoid this. No way out. "I'm glad I got to come here with you, Mike."

"Hell of a first date, huh?"

"Don't think there'll be a second." Stella reached out and took his hand, then closed her eyes and waited. "At least the children are safe."

A crushing weight threw her to the ground. Strips of flesh were torn away from her body. Mike's hand fell away from hers, leaving her alone in a writhing sea of monsters. The last thing she heard was distant screaming. The screaming of terrified children.

BEING an estate agent had its perks. You got to wear a suit; you met lots of different people; and when the apocalypse arrived, you had keys to two dozen properties. Zolten – or Z as his colleagues had used to call him – chose to take cover inside a gated mansion in the heart of Warwickshire. Served by a single country road, the contemporary abode sat on the edge of a steep grassy hill, with a two-metre-high brick wall surrounding the front. A heavy iron gate kept out unwanted visitors. The security alarms and cameras stopped working as soon as the power grid had failed, but a panic room in the master bedroom sat behind a mechanical lock. The mansion was the safest place he had been able to think of when the demons had arrived. It had worked out perfectly.

Z was proud of the fact he had kept his head during those first days of panic, thinking rationally while everyone else was running around screaming. Rather than risk the chaos of the supermarkets, he had hit a handful of corner shops, emptying his account to buy as much pasta, tinned food, bottled water, and toilet rolls as he could shove in the cavernous boot of his beat-up Freelander. Then he had floored it to Samdean Cottage – although the word 'cottage' was a misnomer seeing as the orig- inal structure had been extended to add an additional four bedrooms, three new bathrooms, a billiards room, and twin garages. It had belonged to a Mr Paul Standing, but that man was now almost certainly dead.

During the first days of the apocalypse, Z had witnessed cars flying down the country road and had heard endless sirens in the distance, but it didn't take long for the world to go quiet. He'd been alone for almost a year and was in no doubt about the effect on his sanity. Instead of silence, Z spoke to himself constantly, even making himself laugh with ridiculous jokes. His beard had grown so long that it touched his chest even when he was looking up. He knew he stank, but he didn't care. Water no longer came out of the taps, so to have a wash he resorted to standing outside in the rain. The garden was full of buckets and containers used to capture drinking water, which saved his life seeing as how the bottled water had lasted less than two months. Food was becoming an issue; there were only stale crackers and two jars of honey left. Soon he would have no choice but to go out into the wild and see what he could find. He had seen no demons since the early days but assumed they were still out there somewhere. If mankind had survived, the power would have come back on. There would be cars on the road again. He would have heard those sirens.

Often Z saw rabbits, and even deer, from the upper windows of the house. He could try to hunt them, which would be safer than venturing into town, but he didn't know where to start. His lack of survival skills would disappoint his father back home in Romania – if he still lived – for there, many men knew how to hunt. It was not uncommon to live off the land in Romania. In the UK, people were fat and lazy, and Z had happily become one of them.

And yet I am still alive, Papa. Are you?

Part of me hopes so.

Part of me does not.

Z had left Romania mostly to get away from his father, who was an unaffectionate man who cared more for his cattle than his son. While he respected his father's toughness and willingness to apply himself to hard labour, it was not a life any young man dreamt of. No, Z had dreamt of fast cars and posh houses. He wanted to be a rich businessman, and property was where it was at. He had possessed no money so had got himself a job in real estate. Eventually, he planned to save enough to buy a first property of his own – a flat, most likely, in a nice area. Buy cheap and sell high, that was the name of the game. Look for the desperate sellers, the stupid seller, those with no idea where the market was headed. His agency's clients were just pound signs to Z, and it was all practice for when he went it alone and made his fortune. Then his father would have had no choice but to marvel at his success.

And choke on it.

No chance of that now though. There were no more clients, no more banks, and no more use for money or fortune – only morning, noon, and night. Seconds ticking by on a clock. Nowadays, you measured success by survival. Every day Z got through in one piece was a win, separating him from those already dead. In the new world, he was a rich man just by being alive.

But am I really alive? Is this life? I thought about food and water, but I wish I'd brought books. I wish I'd brought anything that would help me pass this time. How much longer can I keep doing this?

"I might be the last man on Earth," he said to himself, chuckling. "I finally have the big house, but there's no one left to envy me."

Z spent a few minutes staring out the back windows at the rolling fields sloping down behind the house. Part of him suddenly broke, like a spring snapping past the point of no return. "A-ți lua inima 'n dinți, Z. It is time to do something. I would rather die than stay here another year. Papa would despise my laziness. I must work."

And just like that, Z packed a bag and walked out the front gate. He kept himself company by whistling as he strolled down the overgrown country road. Every second he failed to meet a demon gave him hope, while every second he failed to meet another person caused him despair. No matter what, however, he was free. Free in a way that big houses and fancy cars could not make him. He had no burdens beyond taking his next breath and his next step.

When he reached a restaurant called the Coach House at the end of the road, he envisioned finding it full of people. They would tell Z that everything was fine, and that he had been hiding out in Samdean Cottage for nothing. Then they would all share a good laugh. That wasn't the punchline he discovered though. The punchline was the number of demons amassed in the Coach House's car park. It was like they'd been waiting for him.

Z slowly put his bag down at his feet. He opened his arms wide and made sure all the demons saw him. "Okay, *dracu*, let's negotiate. You want this, you'll have to come in with your best offer."

The demons sprinted at Z, making his bladder leak into his

briefs. He wanted to run, but the only place to go back to was Samdean Cottage. Even if he could make it, he would rather die than hide out there any longer. He had come to the UK to live fast and die young, not to cower and starve.

The first demon was fast and tiny, possibly a child in a former life. Z threw a punch and almost knocked its rotten jaw off, then threw another hard right at a second demon, which only glanced off its forehead. When it attacked again, Z saw an undead woman with a missing eye. A third demon collided with him and bit a chunk out of his arm. Z didn't allow himself to scream. He head-butted the demon and sent it sprawling onto its back. "*Sare din lac in put*," he said, then translated out of habit. "Out of the frying pan and into the fucking fire, no?"

The child demon lunged at Z's legs, causing him to stumble. The undead one-eyed woman wrapped its arms around his shoulders and squeezed. He fought to break free but was unable to move his arms as the monster bit into his neck. Terror surged inside him as his blood spurted out. He couldn't run from the fear, he could only use it. He snapped his arms free of the undead woman's grasp and jammed a thumb into its remaining eye. It stumbled backwards, blind, and didn't see it coming when Z booted its legs out from under it.

Next, he dealt with the child, dodging about and wrapping an arm around its throat. It was remarkably easy to twist its neck and snap its spine. Its frail body collapsed to the ground like a rag doll. That left only the third demon. This was the largest, an obvious male. Its burnt face oozed pus. The demon grabbed Z by the wrist and wrenched until something snapped. This time, the pain was enough to make Z cry out. His voice garbled, and he realised his throat was full of blood. His vision throbbed, colour coming and going, edges fuzzing. With his right wrist broken, Z couldn't hit hard enough to take out the large demon, nor could he snap its neck. With no rational plan, he acted on impulse, lunging at the demon and sinking his teeth into its neck. Rancid flesh squelched between his teeth. Z tasted pus on his tongue but kept on biting, kept on chomping down with all his remaining strength. Eventually, he struck a cluster of fragile bones and crushed them one by one until the demon finally tore itself away. Its head lolled against its shoulder and it staggered like a drunk. Z tripped it to the ground and stamped on its skull, satisfied when it broke apart like a watermelon.

The blind woman snarled and lashed out at the empty air surrounding it. Z kicked it over and stamped its head to mush as well. Then he collapsed to the ground, panting and spluttering. His body had turned cold and it was hard to breathe, but he felt good. He studied the three dead demons, in awe of his own savagery. In this new world, he was indeed a very rich man.

Less than an hour later, Z's fortune ran out as he bled to death where he lay.

2

All remaining Hell gates close, blinking out of existence across the globe in a single second. For many – those holed up some place or surviving as a militia – it spells victory. Men, women, and children cheer, believing the end of the world to finally be over. Demons caught by the shockwaves are obliterated. Others further away are left isolated and vulnerable. The threat to mankind's existence has suddenly and inexplicably gone away.

Salvation has arrived.

But the joke is on mankind.

As those many thousands of gates close, a single one opens – a mammoth, sky-swallowing lens that spews forth a great demon army along with its magnificent leader.

Crimolok crashes onto wet ground, cloven feet carving through the earth. The tattered human vessel that held him prisoner lies nearby. The months of entrapment are mere seconds to a being such as Crimolok. Soon, he shall be the oldest creature in existence. The universe shall be his, corrupted and twisted in his image. No more mankind. No more Heaven and Earth. No more God.

Crimolok's chattering hordes gather, the vilest of former

humanity among them, the most twisted murderers and fiends. Mankind's small victories have succeeded only in postponing its own inevitable destruction. Despite Crimolok's infinite wisdom, he underestimated humanity's desire to live. He had thought to destroy it en masse, but that only split the large rock into many pebbles. The proper action all along was to gather his minions like this and peel the flesh of mankind away one glistening strip at a time. Mankind will collapse beneath the weight of his crushing advance.

The end is coming, and it is I.

Crimolok sends forth his legions to purge God's Earth of every scrap of life, to blot out the sun itself, and to bathe in the blood of chaos.

It shall be glorious.

GENERAL THOMAS CLIMBED onto the stage in the centre of Portsmouth's dockland. Speaker systems had been set up throughout the city because the civvies needed to hear him as much as the servicemen. This was the moment Great Britain rose from the ashes. The rebirth of a proud, unmatched nation.

Colonel Cross lingered beside a microphone stand and stood to attention when his superior arrived. "General Thomas, everything is ready and awaiting you."

"The speakers are live?"

"Your voice will reach the entire population of Portsmouth, sir. Thirty thousand people."

"Thank you, Colonel. Dismissed."

Colonel Cross saluted, turned on his heel, then briskly exited the stage. Thomas positioned himself behind the microphone, taking a moment to observe the crowd. These were his people. With that insubordinate female, Amanda Wickstaff, out of the way, there would be no civil war, no infighting or divided front.

Portsmouth would face the enemy as one united people. There were only a few dissenters to worry about now.

The crowd directly in front of the stage represented Thomas's most loyal forces – his officers and specialists. Further out were his regular forces, along with the soldiers who had served Portsmouth before his arrival. In the ruins of the city and the quieter parts of the docklands were the civilians. It was they who most needed to hear his words. Their weak hearts needed emboldening.

Thomas cleared his throat, leant forward, and began. "People of Portsmouth, this is General Thomas addressing you. Some of you do not know me well, but I would like to express my gratitude to every citizen of this remarkable city. I am grateful that you fought with tooth and nail to survive. I am grateful that you refused to give in to fear, that you were unyielding to the brutality and violence designed to cow you. Each of you is a warrior, and I call upon you now to keep that warrior spirit alive. Continue fighting. Continue refusing the enemy at every turn. Do that, and I promise you victory. Do that, and we shall one day stand triumphant. We hail from many different places, but today we stand as brothers and sisters of Great Britain."

There was a brief cheer from the gathered forces, but it was not as loud as he'd hoped. While his long-standing troops were proudly British, those who had served under Wickstaff seemed to have shed their national identity. It would take some time to restore their patriotism, especially in those who hailed from foreign climes. Nonetheless, he was duty-bound to try. "Our enemy is wounded, and we must be merciless. We must show our foe the same savagery it showed to us. We must not relent. We must not stop. The fight can only end once our homeland is wholly liberated. There will be battles to come, I assure you, for the enemy will now do the only thing it can. It shall rally its remaining forces and attempt, one last time, to annihilate us. We must ready our daggers to plunge into the heart of that dying beast, and to do so we must stand together. No longer shall there be soldiers and civilians. From this day forward, we are *all* soldiers. All shall be trained. All shall receive their duties with courage and conviction. We must fight as one and for each other, or we shall surely die."

Muffled dissent spread through the far edges of the crowd. That they even dared to consider the veracity of his words inflamed Thomas greatly. His heart pounded in his chest. "What I speak of is not optional. Portsmouth will become a well-oiled machine of war. Anyone impeding its efficiency shall find themselves unwelcome within its walls. Burdens will not be tolerated."

"Murderer!" someone shouted.

"Long live General Wickstaff!" yelled another.

Thomas's cheeks grew hot. He searched the crowd – whoever had shouted would be shot – but he couldn't identify the offenders. The sheer number of bodies packed together ensured anonymity. His rage spilled out, but he forced himself to contain it. This was not the time for blunt force. "I understand the loss many of you are feeling. Amanda Wickstaff was a hero in the truest sense of the word. She fought alongside you, risking death and injury when she could have sat back and sent others to their deaths. She led Portsmouth to victory after victory in the absence of any established authority. No doubt she was the finest of women and the bravest of souls, but she was also tired. Upon my arrival in Portsmouth, Amanda expressed her relief to me. She was grateful to hand over the mantel and rest. Unfortunately, she never got the chance. The enemy took her from us. Please know that I am not seeking to replace Amanda Wickstaff, only to protect what she has built. As long as Portsmouth stands, she will never be forgotten. She will be the first and most revered saint of our new world. Future generations shall praise her name. For those of you who resent me being here, please know that Amanda Wickstaff welcomed me. So I ask you – no, I beg of you – to please move forward and focus on our true enemy. Let's wipe those demon bastards off the face of the Earth." He hated to use the D word – it reeked of hysteria – but he knew the reaction it elicited in people. Their mutual hatred and fear of their enemy galvanised them and made them family. By using the word, he was one of them. He also hated having to indulge the hero worship of his ignorant predecessor, but it was a necessary evil. If Portsmouth had remained in Amanda Wickstaff's charge, it would have become a mass grave. The woman had been soft, as all women were, and had cared about her people far too much. The only thing that mattered was the survival of the human race, and he, General Thomas, was the only person willing to lead with that sole purpose in mind.

Let people think me callous or uncaring. At least they will live.

Thomas's words had the intended effect. The crowd directly in front of him pumped their fists and cheered. Those further afield – those struggling with past loyalties – seemed more supportive too. That was how easy it was to gain a man's loyalty. Mere words could do it.

General Thomas turned and marched across the stage. He couldn't help but notice the guilty flicker in Colonel Cross's eyes as he passed the man. There had been many disappointments in the last few days, but Colonel Cross's failure to apprehend General Wickstaff's aide-de-camp, Maddy, was amongst the most grievous. The woman had gone missing, and the only way it could have happened was if somebody had helped her.

Was it you, Tony? Can I trust you?

Of course not. No one can be trusted.

Thomas sincerely hoped Colonel Cross was not a traitor, because it would be a shame to shoot such a useful man. But such things happened in war.

GENERAL THOMAS FINISHED his speech at around midday, which meant the sun was still shining when Tony entered the train carriage at the far end of the commercial docks. It was Commander Klein's unofficial office, and while its nights were reserved for poker and drinking, clandestine meetings took place during the day. General Thomas knew of its existence but was yet to risk action. Commander Klein had six nuclear warheads on his submarine. That made the German commander a sovereign nation.

Tony encountered a scruffy guardsman at the carriage's sliding door. The uniformed stranger was larger than Tony and put up a thick right hand to bar entry. "State *ze* business, *freund*."

"Give over, pal! You know who I am, and you know Commander Klein is expecting me."

The guardsmen continued to glare, but then a cheeky grin broke his impassivity. "I kid you, *ja*? Go inside now."

It sounded like an order, but Tony knew better than to take offence. The German language was far more direct and efficient than wishy-washy English. He nodded to the guard and then went through the sliding door. The carriage's interior was mostly uninhabited, bar Commander Klein and a single companion sitting at a table halfway down the aisle. Tony joined them. "Commander Klein, Diane, it's good to see you both."

"And *vy* is that?" asked the commander, blonde hair framing his face like a schnauzer's muzzle.

"Because I keep expecting a bullet in my head every time I take a step. General Thomas ain't no fool."

"That's exactly what he is," said Diane, "and he's going to die."

Commander Klein reached sideways and patted Diane's hand on the table. "Such fire for a tiny *fraulein*, but revenge is a wide arrow that often misses *ze* target, *ja*?"

Diane ignored him and turned to Tony, almost frothing at the mouth. "How can you stand to be around that monster?"

Tony sighed. Diane was operating on rage, and rage didn't appreciate reason. "I understand what General Wickstaff meant to you – meant to a lot of people – but if I go against Thomas, he'll have me shot. I want to see him punished for what he did, believe me, but we need to be smart about it. Whether we like it or not, he's the only leader Portsmouth has right now. Lives depend on him. Last thing we want is a power vacuum."

"He's a murderer and a tyrant, and the longer he stays in charge, the harder it'll be to get rid of him. If we act now, thousands will support us."

Tony nodded. "And thousands won't."

"It *vud* mean war," said Klein. "Thousands would support your crusade, Diane, *ja*, but General Thomas arrived with loyal men. The killing would be many. Whoever survives *vud* be at *ze* demon's mercy. I am sorry, Diane, but Tony is correct. General Thomas needs to remain in charge until he can be peacefully removed."

"And when the hell will that be?"

"As soon as we ready his replacement, *ja?*"

Diane nodded petulantly across the table. "Tony, you should lead Portsmouth. Thomas's men respect you, and so will everyone else once we reveal the truth about Wickstaff. You're the only choice."

Tony pushed himself back from the table and shook his head. "General Thomas already suspects me. If I make overtures towards power, he'll realise it right away. Supplanting him is going to take timing and finesse, neither of which I have. I'm heading out of Portsmouth tomorrow morning."

Commander Klein leaned back against the bench cushion and gasped theatrically. "Heavens, *vy?*"

"To go find this Mass character that everyone in Portsmouth seems to regard so highly. He's been away for more than a week, so Thomas has ordered me to go and find him."

Diane rolled her eyes. "He's hoping you'll die out there."

Tony wished he could disagree. "My orders are to execute Mass and his men as soon as I find him. My death'll probably come soon after. Two birds, one stone."

Diane rose from her seat, fists clenched. "Your orders are to do what?"

"To kill Mass."

Klein eased Diane back down onto the bench and told her to calm herself. Then he stared at Tony beneath his thin blonde eyebrows. "I assume you *vill* disobey *zis* order to kill Mass?"

"Of course. I'm not in the business of murdering local heroes."

"*Vy* does Thomas consider Mass a threat?"

Diane answered the question. "Because he's a badass, and when he finds out about Wickstaff, he'll come at Thomas like a force of nature. I can't wait to see it."

Tony nodded. Diane was exactly right. "Thomas has heard the same things we all have about Mass. That he and his Urban Vampires are the best of the best. A dozen of them are currently furloughed in Portsmouth. I'm going to ask them to come join me on the road. If we find Mass, they can take him north to meet up with Maddy. The only problem will be the men Thomas selects to go with me. They're not going to like the change of plan."

Diane was wringing her hands on the table, clearly unhappy and still operating in rage-mode. Her words came out like poison. "I still don't hear anything that ends with General Thomas choking on his own blood."

"Survival is our mission," said Klein. "Portsmouth needs to stand ready against *ze* remaining demon forces, but we three also need to think about our own skins, *ja*? Diane, see me now when I tell you *zat* I was fond of General Wickstaff. She demanded nothing of men but bravery and compassion. *Zis* General Thomas is a man who lacks faith in anything but himself, and I have no time for arrogant men. Their actions stain our history books."

Tony let his head tilt back and closed his eyes. It was only late afternoon, but he was exhausted. Every night for a week he had lain awake, anxious that his door was going to be kicked in by military police or – even worse – hitmen. He lowered his gaze and sighed. "I used to dream of having a wife and children, of opening a little corner shop in some sleepy village where everyone knows each other. Now all I want to do is to lie down in the middle of an empty field and stare up at the sky without fear of being torn apart by monsters. I want a moment's peace before I die. That's all."

Klein nodded. "I *vud* like to see my home again. I spent my life at sea, expecting to return in old age. Now my final years have arrived and I find myself further away *zan* ever."

Tony glanced at Diane. He wanted to help the girl see past her rage. "What about you, Diane? What do you wish for?"

She seemed surprised by the question, and her eyes flickered with sadness. She opened her mouth to speak but then changed her mind. Without uttering a single word, she stood from the table and exited the carriage.

Klein raised his eyebrows. "*Zat* girl frightens me more *zan* a leaking hatch at *ze* bottom of the sea."

"She's angry," said Tony. "I don't blame her. Wickstaff was a saviour to a lot of people. Now that she's dead, she's become a martyr."

"A dangerous *zing*."

"Keep an eye on her, Klein. While I'm gone, I mean."

The German officer chuckled. "I keep an eye on everything, Tony, don't you know? Take care on your trip. I enjoy your company."

Tony stood and offered a handshake. "I'll send you a postcard."

"*Auf wiedersehen*, Colonel. I hope you return in good health."

"Don't count on it."

MASS SPAT BLOOD on the floorboards, awaiting his death – a death that had been hounding him for a week now, a death that would not stop chasing him. He knew the moment it had all gone wrong. It had been one week ago. He'd been huddled in the rear of an overturned coach with Addy, Tox, Smithy, and a dozen screaming women – chattel rescued from a monster named Naseem hours earlier.

They'd have been better off if I'd left them at the farm. Some hero I turned out to be.

I never wanted to be a hero.

Back then in the coach, Mass had searched desperately for his handgun, which had fallen under the seats, but try as he might, he could not find the damn thing. Only Smithy had a weapon – but there was no way to fire it inside their cramped confines without deafening themselves.

Demons surrounded the upturned coach, their crooked faces pressed against the cracked windows, their shadows melting into the nearby undergrowth. The coach was a henhouse surrounded by foxes, and Mass and his companions were the hens.

"What's the plan, big man?" Smithy managed to sound unconcerned by their imminent deaths. Unflappability was his Smithy skill, even with a massive gash bleeding on his forehead. "You have a plan, right? A good one I'll bet. Come on, tell us how you're gonna save the day. Please?"

"I don't have a plan. We need to get the women out of here."

"Too right," said Tox, covering his ears to drown out their screaming. "They're driving me insane."

"They're afraid," said Addy, pushing against one of the windows that was starting to crack. "Who can blame them?"

Smithy threw down his hunting rifle, knowing it was of no use, then rummaged beneath the seats and around the window ledges.

Tox grunted. "What are you doing?"

"Looking for a solution. My mum always told me that the worst thing you can do in a crisis is nothing."

Tox sighed, but his displeasure went ignored. Addy joined Smithy in his search, getting down on her belly and looking under the seats for something to help. There was little chance of an apache helicopter appearing and blasting them a way out, but maybe they could find *something*.

The first thing Mass spotted was a handheld fire extinguisher mounted against the coach's fire escape. He grabbed the small red canister in both hands and examined it. "We have a chance," he muttered, not fully knowing his own thoughts until the words were out of his mouth. "Smithy, get the door."

Smithy frowned but did as asked. He stood by the fire escape and wrapped his fingers around the handle. Addy seemed on board with whatever they were about to do as well. She had known Mass long enough to trust him. "I'll gather the women," she said.

Tox stopped grumbling and asked what he could do too.

"You can jump out when I do," said Mass. "Shove any demons aside long enough for the women to make it onto the road."

"That's suicide! The demons'll tear us to shreds."

"Not if they can't see us. Okay, Smithy, after three. One… two… three!"

Smithy shouldered open the fire escape. It opened diagonally, hinges twisted and bent. Demons immediately tried to get inside, but Mass threw his colossal bulk through the gap and collided with them. He took them by surprise and bought himself enough time to plant his feet in the uneven ditch and quickly pull the tab on the handheld fire extinguisher. He squeezed the handle. Part of him feared a harmless jet of water coming out, but it was exactly what he had hoped for – a thick cloud of white smoke. "Move, move, move!" he shouted as bodies shoved by him. The women whimpered and screamed, but they knew this was life and death. They had no choice but to make a run for it.

Tox appeared beside Mass, planting a boot in the centre of a small demon's chest and sending it backwards into the weeds. Meanwhile, Mass sprayed the smoky powder into the air, aiming for eyes and snarling mouths. The demons spluttered like sickly children.

Tox shoved aside another demon, this one half-blind and clawing at its own eyes. He pointed to the women halfway up the embankment and about to make it to the road. Addy was right behind them. "It's working," he said. "They're getting away."

Mass threw out a hand and waved. "Smithy, go with the women. Get them out of here."

But Smithy ignored him. He bent to pick something up and swung his arm, bringing down a fist-sized rock on the back of the half-blind demon's skull. It cracked open like an egg. Smithy hissed through his teeth. "Jesus, did you see its head go?"

Mass pivoted and sprayed a pair of burnt men reaching out for him. Tox placed a hand on his shoulder, using him for balance, and kicked at a third. Miraculously, they managed to gain enough space to make it up the hill.

The three men fought their way up the clumpy, uneven slope while the demons stumbled around in the ditch below. Before long, they had made it to the road. They were all hurting from the coach crash, covered in bruises and cuts.

The women huddled together like sheep while Addy circled them like a border collie. When she saw Mass, she nodded.

Good work.

They had made it out of their coffin in the ditch, but the demons were quickly recovering. Whatever powder had come out the fire extinguisher was unfortunately harmless.

Mass clenched his fists. *Pity it wasn't full of acid.*

Smithy searched around. "Now what?"

"We make a run for it," said Tox. "It's the only chance we have."

Mass shook his head. "We're hurting, and the women will slow us down even more. The demons will hound us until we drop."

"But we can't fight them," said Smithy, still holding his gore-encrusted rock. "Caveman kung fu will only get us so far."

Mass reached to his belt and pulled out a heavy knife he'd taken from the body of a dead soldier he'd found slumped on the stairs of a supermarket's escalator. "If we rely on guns to save us every time, what're we gonna do when the bullets run out?"

"They already have," said Tox, pulling out his own knife.

Addy grabbed hers next, a machete longer than the others.

Smithy peered down at the bloody rock in his hand. "This is gonna suck."

The demons climbed the hill, using their claws as anchors in the mud. Some were still disorientated from the powder, but others growled like hungry wolves.

Mass rotated his wrist, getting a feel for the weighty combat knife in his hand. "Addy, get the women back."

"No way! I'm in this fight too."

"Move them back and come join us."

Addy corralled the women to the far side of the road. They were a burden, unable to focus on anything besides their own fear. Addy, though, was a woman as tough as any man – probably more so. Would she have turned out differently if she'd spent the last year at Nas's farm instead of becoming an Urban Vampire? Was there any hope for the women they'd rescued?

Addy rejoined them in the centre of the road, machete at the ready. "Let's get to work."

They lined up, shoulder to shoulder, as Smithy shouted, "Sparta!"

Addy rolled her eyes. "You're such a pain in the arse."

To perhaps dispel the notion, Smithy was the first to attack, lunging in with his rock and braining a burnt man in a ragged yellow T-shirt. It acted as a starting pistol, and Addy, Tox, and Mass joined the fray, slashing with their knives and throwing punches against mottled demon flesh. Their enemies bled, but nothing short of death would deter them from attempting to fall upon their prey and trap it in an unholy embrace.

Mass grabbed a burnt man around the neck with one hand so he could plunge his knife into its eye socket with the other, but when more demons came up the embankment, his courage suddenly wavered. After so long fighting, he was rapidly reaching a point of mental and physical exhaustion. The effort of lifting his fists was becoming too much. Even so, he managed to swipe his knife and slice open a demon's face. It wasn't a killing blow, but it crippled the monster's eyes and sent it away blind.

"There're too many," said Tox, clutching his ribs. "We can't take them all."

"We have no choice," said Mass. "We're in no fit state to run."

"We're in no fit state to take on a dozen demons with three knives and eight fists."

"Don't forget my rock," said Smithy, bashing it against the skull of another demon. "And there's one less now."

Addy gritted her teeth and slashed her knife. "No more talking. If we live, we'll have a story to tell our grandkids."

Smithy chuckled. "That's some wishful thinking, Addy."

"Better than complaining." She side-eyed Tox and then threw herself forward in a scissor kick that caught a child-sized demon right in the face. She landed awkwardly, left ankle twisting and causing her to stumble right into a demon's grasp. She cried out as its decaying jaws clamped around her forearm and her machete fell from her grasp.

"Addy!" Tox buried his own blade so deeply in a nearby demon's temple that it wouldn't come out again, so he shoved the dead monster aside and abandoned the weapon. Unarmed, he threw himself in Addy's direction, grabbing at the demon that was trying to eat her arm. That left Smithy and Mass outnumbered as three demons attacked the two of them.

Smithy didn't have a knife, so Mass stepped up and tried to take the demons out by himself. He buried his knife in a burnt woman's throat and twisted. Chunks of dried blood erupted and spattered his face. A piece went in his eye and affected his vision. The other two demons grabbed him, their weight bearing down from either side. He pushed back with his forearms, trying to keep from being bitten, but they overwhelmed him. Smithy attempted to peel the demons away, but one of them swung around and smashed him in the face with a bony arm. Smithy hit the dirt.

Mass tried to retreat, but his legs twisted and he went down, both demons landing on top of him. He cried out as piercing needles tore into his trapezius muscle, and the pain travelled right up the back of his neck. He tried to shove the demon away, but his arms were pinned. Rotten teeth sank deeper and deeper, extracting a bellowing scream from his lungs. This was it. His death had arrived.

I didn't want to die screaming. I didn't want to die lying on my back like this.

Smithy grunted, engaged in a battle of his own as he staggered to his feet. Tox and Addy were somewhere out of sight, maybe even dead. Mass couldn't give up, though, even if it was useless to try. He was a fighter, and that was how he would go out. He whipped his head up and managed to headbutt the demon biting into his shoulder. It wasn't enough to dislodge it, but it shifted its weight enough for him to free his arm, which he then used to finally shove the demon away. Able to move again, Mass rolled onto his side and leapt up, but another demon tackled him and knocked him right back down. This time he ended up face down – totally defenceless as demons fell on top of him. "You better hope I don't meet your ugly asses in Hell," he grunted, face pressed against the road.

Claws sliced at the back of his neck, opening him up. He felt a huge weight crushing the back of his skull, smushing his face against the unforgiving ground. He could barely breathe, barely move. It took everything he had to just turn his head and gasp.

A high-pitched feminine scream pierced the air, and from out of nowhere the women from the farm enveloped the demons pinning Mass down. They stomped and kicked, screaming hysterically. Mass crawled away in shock, not knowing where he was hurt or how badly.

Smithy fought nearby. The lad had a demon in a chokehold and was slowly rattling the life out of it. Addy and Tox, however, were in dire need of help. Four demons surrounded them, and they were visibly near exhaustion. Mass was bleeding all over, but he had to help his friends. He climbed to his feet and threw himself at the demons, sending two tumbling back into the ditch. The other two merely stumbled in the road. Suddenly, the humans outnumbered the monsters. They had a chance.

"Take them down, quick." Mass tackled a burnt man and dropped it onto its back. As soon as it hit the ground, Smithy jumped on its head with both feet. Addy and Tox took care of the other demons, and within minutes, their misshapen corpses littered the road.

One of the women bent over and vomited, causing Smithy to leap aside and swear. Once finished, she straightened up and wiped her mouth. "I-I can't believe we just did that."

Mass was bleeding badly from his neck. He had to place a hand over the wound and press down as he approached the young woman. She had dark brown hair tangled in knots and smooth olive skin streaked with scratches and cuts. "What's your name?"

"Maria."

"Well, Maria, you and your friends just saved our butts."

"You saved us from Naseem and his bastards. It's nice to repay the favour. We've been victims for so long that it feels good to finally fight back."

The women behind her, who had also calmed down, nodded in agreement. They hadn't fought to save Mass and the others, they'd fought to save their own souls.

Addy bent over and spat blood from a bust lip. "Naseem's farm is behind you, but we need to make it back to Portsmouth if you have any chance of being safe."

Maria nodded to show she understood.

Smithy threw his bloody rock down on the ground and shook his hand gingerly. "We need to warn everyone about that boss-level gate that opened up."

Mass glanced down the road in the direction they'd travelled. Something bad was coming, and it was a consequence of his actions. He never should have killed Vamps and set Crimolok free. The giant gate had appeared because of what he'd done.

I had no choice. I couldn't let Vamps suffer any more. He was my brother.

"We need to rest," said Tox. "I ache all over."

Smithy nodded. "I think I bruised my arsehole."

Mass stared at the blood on his hands and had to agree. He didn't know the damage done to his neck, but he felt weak and feverish. He wanted to puke. "We'll need somewhere to hole up for tonight. In the morning, we can head off, and be back to Portsmouth in less than two days."

But they had never made it back in two days. In fact, they didn't make it out of the small cottage they found shortly after leaving the dead demons in the road.

3

Ted stood in the guard tower watching the world go by. It'd been weeks since they'd last encountered demons, but a scouting party had returned yesterday with reports of the enemy amassing south of Carlisle. That men and women could even make it that far and back in safety was something he would have thought impossible only a few short months ago, but things had changed at Kielder Forest Park. Kothal Castle was at the centre of it all – the new hub of British civilisation.

What had once been a crumbling manor house was now a labyrinth of wood and stone. Ted had personally overseen the construction of timber and plasterboard buildings, providing warm and dry meeting places, dwellings, and workshops. At the bottom of the hill, tents and hastily erected huts surrounded a lodge-style activity centre. The small settlement had popped up after a large group from a nearby supermarket, as well as multiple stragglers, had arrived. Ted didn't know the exact number of people now settled in the forest – they didn't have time to conduct a census – but he was confident there were at least a thousand. Maybe more.

And they had an arsenal.

Damien's arrival, alongside a small group of American

soldiers and several crates of weapons, was a welcome, if concerning, event. Concerning, because one of the young man's companions was a demon. Sorrow, it called itself. A monstrous thing with sharp horns and leathery black wings. It was the demon to which Ted now paid attention. The thing was evil, and it was only a matter of time before it turned on people.

Frank had been standing nearby, and he came over now. The short man – but don't call him a midget – tiptoed so he could see over the guard tower's wooden railing. The structure abutted the rooftop of the castle and, being the highest point, was where most of the lookouts stationed themselves.

"You nay trust that one, do ya?"

Ted gave Frank a pained sigh. "He's one of *them*."

"He ain't done us no harm, kidda. W'out him, we wunt have built half the stuff we 'ave. Fella's strong as ten men."

Ted nodded. It was true. Sorrow had made himself an asset since arriving, no doubt about it. The demon could carry ten-foot logs as if they were broom handles, and his tireless runs up and down the fortifications had sped things up monumentally. Sorrow was a one-demon lumberyard.

But he was still one of *them*.

Right inside their camp.

But there was an even worse threat that plagued Ted's mind. A fallen angel existed somewhere beyond the forest, a giant beast intent on destroying mankind. It had appeared on that dreadful day, months ago now, when a gate had appeared beneath the surface of their lake. A young boy, Nathan, had saved everybody by throwing himself into the water, but not before a massive creature had emerged and then retreated to lick its wounds. One day, it would be back, Ted knew it. He could feel a fight coming – felt it in his bones – and it was going to be bad. He'd been no soldier in his former life, but nowadays he was on constant high alert, always sensing danger and predicting attacks. If the people at Kielder weren't ready to fight when the time came, they would all die.

And that'll be on me.

Ted turned to Frank, who had recently taken to chewing twigs to ease his smoker's cravings. The camp still had cigarettes, but they wouldn't last forever, so a two per day rule had been implemented. Ted was glad he'd never caught the habit based on how many twigs Frank gnawed each day.

Folding his arms to show he wanted an honest answer, Ted asked, "Frank, how prepared do you think we are?"

Frank shrugged, an odd gesture with his slightly offset shoulders. "None of us are born fighters, Ted, but we *are* survivors. Everyone'll step up when the time comes. Death has lost its horror after so much of it. There ain't no cowards here."

"You think we have a chance then?"

"Are yow kidding me? We're more prepared than ever. We 'ave weapons, walls, manpower. We even have our own demon, which I personally think is bostin! Whatever happens, there's nowt more we can do about it. Maybe it's our fate to die, but last time we sent the buggers packing, dint we?"

Ted nodded silently.

Frank saw his sadness and frowned. "What's got into yow, kidda? Yow's a fella with practical solutions, not a worrier like this."

"All I do is worry, Frank. I feel like everything is on my shoulders, and if we don't make it, it'll be because all my planning, all my big ideas weren't good enough. People look to me to keep them safe, but the truth is I don't think I've done anywhere near enough."

Frank gave him a firm pat on the back. "Yow've done more than most. If anyone has better ideas, they can speak up, can't they? I would soon tell you if I had something on my brain."

Ted tittered. "Yeah, I can always rely on you to speak your mind, Frank. Thank you for that."

"Yow's welcome. Oh, bugger it, I forgot to say, Doctor Kamiyo wants to speak with yow at the infirmary."

"Okay, d'you know what about?"

"Nah, but he seemed hot and bothered about something. Yow best be quick."

Ted nodded and got going. Quick wasn't something he would've managed a year ago, not with his age and substantial beer gut, but nowadays he was a lean, wiry, grey-haired man of action. He liked who he'd become, but it pained him that his daughter, Chloe, wasn't alive to see it.

You would have loved this place, sweetheart.

Ted headed out of the castle and through the sally port in the inner wall. A wooden palisade dissected the steep grassy hill halfway down, and Ted had to wait while a pair of sentries opened the gate from above. One of the sentries was Scarlett, the demon's ward. Sorrow seemed to be her bodyguard, and for the first couple of days at Kielder, he had refused to leave her side. Only recently had he relaxed enough to give her some breathing room.

The girl waved to him. "Hey, Ted, Doctor Kamiyo was looking for you. He's in—"

"The infirmary, yeah. Thanks, Scarlett. Um, are you okay today?"

"Yeah, I really need to pee, but I think I can hold it a bit longer. You've got this place really buzzing. Any demons are gonna have a hard time taking us in a fight."

"I hope you're right. Your, um, friend... Will he be willing to fight against his—"

Scarlett smirked. "His fellow demons? Yah, no problem. I've seen him do it before. He's a badass, and he's ours. You can trust him."

Ted passed no comment and headed through the outer gate. Despite the girl's assurances, he didn't think he could ever trust a demon. Especially not one with jet-black wings the length of two minibuses. Even his name was evil – Sorrow. How much of that had it caused serving in Hell?

It was done now though. The demon had ingratiated itself with the population. The children loved it, asking Sorrow to perform feats of strength or perform magic. Women, too, were under its thrall. Someone had to remain suspicious, even if it was only Ted.

I won't ever trust that thing. It will never be one of us. It doesn't understand what it is to be human.

The infirmary was located inside the activity centre, chosen because the upper floor contained multiple bedrooms, each with open fireplaces. It would be the only way to keep the sick healthy during the harsh winter months now rapidly on their way. No one knew the current date, but it felt like late October to Ted – those drizzly, chilly weeks that led into the freezing festive season. It would be the first true test for their community. They had planted crops under the supervision of a pair of ex-farmers, but no one really knew if the produce would survive the ground frosts. No one knew if the people at the camp would manage to keep warm. It all remained to be seen.

Whatever happened in the days ahead, death to some degree was certain. Even if the demons disappeared, humanity had been knocked spiralling into a new dark age. Cut off from each other and with limited resources, things would never again be the same. Medicine was rare, food was dwindling, and Kamiyo was their sole doctor. If he died, the entire camp would have to get by on the four ex-nurses who lived there. Most of the world's doctors had been too involved in the initial rescue efforts during the invasion to still be alive a year later. Kamiyo never spoke about why he hadn't been one of them, and Ted wouldn't ask.

It's his business. We all have a past we're trying to forget.

Ted said hello to various people on his approach to the activity centre. The building was designed to look like a woodland lodge, with thick brown logs and planked flooring. It was a cluttered space, stacked with supplies and people. The lower floor was used as a school for the children, a useful way to keep track of them during the day. Twenty-six were under the age of fourteen, and their laughter was the biggest boost to morale in Kielder. They were the camp's mascots – a treasure that must be protected at all costs. To lose the children would be to lose all hope.

Dr Kamiyo was rushing across the landing when Ted started upstairs. When he saw Ted, he skidded on his heels and waved a hand to follow. "I've been waiting for you to turn up. Follow me."

Ted frowned as Kamiyo hurried to the room at the far end of the landing. The door was closed, but he shouldered it open easily, standing aside so that Ted could enter. "Our patient is awake. I wanted to wait for you to question them."

Ted stepped inside and was greeted by the smell of medicinal alcohol and bleach. The woman lying in bed was indeed awake, but she appeared groggy and unwell. Twice, her pudgy jowls bulged as if she might vomit, and she showed no recognition of where she was. Yet neither did she seem afraid. The scouts had found her a week ago on the outskirts of the forest, unconscious in the middle of the road. She'd been stuck in an endless sleep until now.

"Hello, miss, my name's Ted. We found you in trouble and brought you to our camp. You're safe and among friends. There's no reason to fret."

The woman frowned. Middle-aged, and a little on the heavier side, she was not entirely unattractive, but something about her seemed harsh and unappealing. "What camp?" she asked in a phlegmy voice.

"Kielder Forest, do you know it?"

She shook her head. "I'm not really an outdoorsy type of bird."

"What's your name? Do you remember what happened to you?"

"Vaguely."

"Okay, why don't we start with your name then, and how you ended up in the road."

The woman pushed herself up a little higher on her elbows. She blinked as if trying to wake up fully. "The name's Angela, former minister in the Church of England and drinker of vodka. I went to Hell for being a dyke. Anyone got a cigarette?"

THE WEATHER WAS COOLING. Nowhere was that more apparent than from the deck of *The Hatchet*. The sea seemed to leap up on purpose, aiming with the precision of a child's catapult and hitting Maddy with its icy spray. The only colour was grey – grey boats, grey sky, grey sea. Grey mood. Maybe, once dawn broke, the world would bring back its colour.

Maddy was surprised that tragedy could still affect her, that she could still grieve when there had already been so much death, yet she grieved fully. She'd fallen in love with Amanda Wickstaff. That son of a bitch Thomas had taken her away; a week ago now, but still heavy in the pit of her stomach.

One day, I'll kill him. I promise, Amanda, he'll pay for what he's done.

"We're here," said Tosco, putting a hand on Maddy's back and making her jolt.

"Where is *here*?" she asked.

"About twenty miles north of Newcastle. The demon messenger that Mass sent to Portsmouth spoke about a group of people hiding out in a forest west of here. Kielder Forest Park. We've delayed long enough. It's going to be dangerous, but everyone is rested up and raring to go."

Maddy chuckled. Tosco's attempts at pronouncing English locations was jarring – New Castle. Ports Mouth. She still couldn't believe he'd abandoned Portsmouth to help her. The American had been in charge of half the fleet, respected and admired, but now he was drifting in the dreary North Sea, searching for a group of people who may or may not be hiding out in a forest.

"I hope they're still alive," Maddy muttered, "and willing to receive visitors."

Tosco leant on the railing and gazed across the water to where

England's east coast waited to meet them. "Portsmouth can't be the only place. There has to be more."

"Is that why you came? To find out?"

He turned to look at her and seemed to struggle with something for a moment. "I came because you needed someone on your side, Maddy. I respected General Wickstaff, and I let her down. You warned me Thomas was a threat. I should've fought him the second he arrived."

Maddy sighed, feeling exhausted; so tired of talking, so tired of breathing. "You're not to blame for this, James. Only Thomas is."

"Perhaps you're right. Perhaps not. We'll drop anchor in thirty minutes and take a boat to shore. Most of the men will stay here with *The Hatchet*, but we'll remain in radio contact."

Maddy pointed towards the blue and grey helicopter perched on the rear deck of the ship. "Can't we use that to get where we need to?"

Tosco shook his head. "We don't have a lot of fuel. I figure it'll be more useful pulling us out of a fire than taking us into one. If we need rescuing, someone will fly the bird to come get us. We also have the big guns on deck if we need to bring forth Armageddon."

"We're a little late on that."

Tosco smirked. "Yeah, you might say we missed the boat."

"You Americans aren't famed for your clever sense of humour."

"Hey! We made *Frasier*. That's like the smartest comedy ever." He started singing in an unexpected baritone. "Tossed salad and scrambled eggs."

"I was always more into *Friends*, but I withdraw my comment. Thank you, Tosco. Thank you for doing this."

"James, please."

She put a hand on his arm and squeezed. "Thank you, James."

"I'll let you know when everything's ready. Go visit the latrine, grab a bite to eat, and wrap up warm."

She saluted. "Yes, Commander."

"I'm an outlaw now. *Captain* will do."

Maddy chuckled and leant over the railing, staring out at the north of England, wondering how many people were still alive out there.

Please, let it be thousands, all armed to the teeth and fearless.

And let them be good.

THE HATCHET DROPPED anchor thirty minutes later just as Tosco promised. The frigate lurched slightly, but you could've missed it if you weren't paying attention. Maddy had peed, eaten a protein bar, and was now togged in a thick US Coast Guard parka a friendly sailor had given her. She was warm, but she would've liked a pair of gloves.

Tosco waited for her in the launch bay, standing beside a large dinghy with an outboard motor. He handed her a weapon, telling her it was a "P229R-DAK. Forty-cal. Full clip in the grip, but no spares. Don't fire unless your life depends on it."

Maddy had trained with guns at Portsmouth, but this nondescript handgun was a new one for her. She eyed the slide and checked the safety. Then she shoved it muzzle first into the waistband of her jeans. "Thanks."

"James! I want to come. You can't leave me here." Alice appeared in the launch bay, looking as pissed off as teens were supposed to. Her blonde hair was tied up in a short bun, and she wore an oversized parka like the one Maddy had on.

Tosco turned to the girl and sighed. "I'm not going to change my mind, Alice. It's too dangerous."

"I can do dangerous. What I can't do is being cooped up on this boat for days. I want to come."

"I promised your father I would keep you alive. Once I know

it's safe, I'll send for you. Your days aboard a boat are coming to an end, I promise."

Alice looked like she might hiss at him, but she kept calm. "Be quick, or I'll jump overboard and you'll never see me again."

Tosco rolled his eyes. "Don't be so dramatic."

"It's the end of the world. I'm allowed to be dramatic."

"Good point." Tosco wrapped his arms around the girl and they embraced like father and daughter, which was heart-breaking in a way. Maddy wondered if Guy would have been happy or sad that his junior officer had taken his place in more ways than one.

Alice left, and Tosco waved a hand at several men standing near the dinghy – as well as a single blonde woman who had a long, thin scar on her left cheek. "Our embarkation team," Tosco explained. "The best *The Hatchet* can spare. You've likely already met."

Maddy nodded hello to each person. She recognised them all, having spent the last two days on board with them, but she hadn't exchanged words. Too wrapped up in her own grief and anger.

I should have made more of an effort. These people are risking their lives for me.

No one chatted as they climbed aboard the dinghy, all serious, all professional. Maddy felt ashamed that they were being forced to leave their safety. There could be a hundred thousand demons on the coast, ready to tear them apart as soon as they landed.

Tosco sat himself down at the front of the dinghy, while Maddy sat between a man and the other female on the team. They exchanged glances but said nothing. The launch bay doors opened. The sea spray flew in and battered their faces.

"Okay," Tosco yelled over the howling gust, "launch!"

Four more sailors appeared and grabbed handles on either side of the dinghy. They heaved the tiny boat forward, shoving it down the steel ramp that led right into the sea. The movement began slowly, but the dinghy picked up speed, sliding faster and faster.

And then it splashed down.

The boat ducked beneath the waves for a second, only just staying afloat. Then it leapt up and surged forward as the pilot gunned the motor. They sped away from *The Hatchet*, rising and dropping as the frigid grey sea rolled back and forth. It was exhilarating in a way Maddy was no longer used to – she was having fun. It felt wrong, but also liberating.

She sat and enjoyed the ride until they reached a small rocky beach where they tied the dinghy to a large section of driftwood before covering it in seaweed and branches, which was probably unnecessary, but Tosco said it would make him feel better. By the time they finished, it looked like a disgusting sea creature had washed ashore.

"Okay," said Tosco, "I brought a compass just in case, but the plan is to follow the roads. We're close enough that we should find signs pointing to this forest. You have them in the UK, right? Signs for tourist attractions, *et cetera*?"

Maddy nodded. "I think they're brown. Wouldn't it be safer to stay off the roads though? We don't know what the area is like."

"We'll take things slowly. If it looks like an area is hostile, we'll move into cover and try to find the way via our own devices. Let's hope this group in the forest is large enough to have taken care of most of the threats. Wishful thinking, I know."

Maddy trudged along the pebbly beach. "Being hopeful never hurt anyone. Maybe we'll find a fully stocked bar at the end of this beach."

Everyone chuckled, and it brought a little warmth to Maddy's mood that she had managed to spread some mirth. Wickstaff was dead, yes, but she – and other people – were still alive. It wasn't the end of the road for her yet.

Might as well laugh while I can.

They reached the end of the beach and found a sandy ditch abutting a narrow country road. A large green sign peeked out from an overgrown hedge and seemed to indicate a roundabout.

A roundabout was a good starting point. Maddy pointed. "I say we head that way."

Tosco pointed his rifle left and right, surveying both directions. "I see no reason to disagree. Everyone, keep your eyes open and don't engage unless I give the order. We don't want to announce our presence."

One of the sailors ducked, alerting everyone and causing them to do the same. Even Maddy crouched and produced her handgun. What had the sailor seen?

Tosco crab walked into the ditch at the side of the road. "What have you seen, Taylor?"

The sailor pointed. At first Maddy saw nothing, but then she spotted movement in the hedges near the road sign. Everyone sighed with relief. Some even chuckled. Maddy joined them in their quiet laughter, but not because of anything funny. It was because of what had spooked them.

The zebra had no business roaming the English countryside, but in a world full of demons, watching it stride casually from one side of the road to the other felt like a good omen – a sign that nature was reclaiming the land and refusing to be corrupted.

"I guess there must have been a zoo nearby," said Tosco, lowering his weapon and grinning.

Two more zebras appeared to join the first. Maddy stood in awe for several minutes until they eventually disappeared back behind the hedges. It was only Tosco tugging at her arm that got her moving again.

"Come on, we need to go."

She nodded. "Okay, I'm ready."

———

DAMIEN HACKED off a branch and threw it onto his sled. He estimated around thirty in the pile now. It was getting harder to pull his load.

The chippies can make a hundred arrows with this lot. Not bad for a day's work.

After all the fighting, it seemed incredible that he was doing something as mundane as collecting sticks, but he knew it was merely a calm before the storm. He was here for a reason. The fighting would begin again soon.

It'll only stop once one side has been destroyed.

Damien pulled the sled through the treeline into the open meadow. He heaved his way towards the castle, which was more of a modern art structure these days. Various timber platforms and wooden shacks surrounded the ancient keep, many built into the stonework itself. People scurried around like busy worker ants, working together for a common cause, something the old, self-serving world had been in short supply of. One good thing to come out of the apocalypse was the demise of greedy corporations and wealth-obsessed consumers. People were just people again: neighbours, friends, farmers, and builders. If mankind survived, it had a chance of staying pure like this, but Damien feared it would quickly resume its trek along the rapacious road of progress.

Perhaps things would be different this time. Mankind now knew, unequivocally, that there was a Heaven and Hell. In fact, if mankind had been better behaved, Hell's army would have only been a fraction of its current size. The invasion might not have even happened. Humanity's sinful behaviour had stocked the enemy with troops.

Damien spotted his people – those he and Nancy had brought from Indiana – and headed over with his heavy sled. Sorrow could make himself useful and take the sled up the hill to the castle for him. While Damien was lean and healthy, his previous life of working at a bank had created a specimen averse to hard labour. Perhaps, once the memories of his previous life had fully faded, he would evolve, but right now he still pictured – and longed for – the days of sitting behind a computer screen sipping hot cappuccino. Mankind might have found purity, but that didn't mean you stopped missing all of the sin.

Sorrow noticed Damien approaching and smiled – which was an obscene gesture for a demon. His jagged fangs dripped saliva, and his leathery wings ruffled at his back. "Path walker," he boomed, "how do you fare?"

"I, um, fare well. How are you, Sorrow?"

"I fear for the safety of my ward. The enemy seek to tear Scarlett limb from limb and feast on her organs. I do not like that."

Damien wiped sweat from his brow and looked around for Scarlett, who wasn't there. "Yeah, well, it's not all about Scarlett, you know? Everyone's life is at risk."

"It is most definitely all about Scarlett. She must live."

Damien nodded. There was no point arguing with the demon. He was programmed like a Terminator to care only about his objective. Luckily, a side effect of Sorrow's objective included killing any demons that showed up at camp.

"Why did you come here if you want to keep her safe?"

Sorrow's wings unfurled, creating a breeze. "I brought Scarlett to this Earth to save her life. On her home Earth, there is a curse upon her. A curse that will give her less than one year to live. She is a being known as the Spark – a padlock placed upon the magics of the world – but here she is just a girl. A girl I must protect, even if I have to destroy everything else in existence."

Damien winced. "Let's hope it doesn't come to that."

"Let us indeed hope."

"Sorrow, do you have any *sense* of what the other demons are doing? Are we under threat?"

"Absolutely, but I sense no demons in our immediate vicinity. The people here make preparations, and that is good, Path walker. I like it."

"Can you call me Damien, please?"

"But you are more than a name. You are a powerful being, one of few remaining. Your survival is also important. *Not* as important as Scarlett's."

Damien frowned. It was nice to hear that his death should be avoided, but he didn't think he deserved to live more than anyone else. "Why is my survival important?"

"Because path walkers hold everything together. For this reason, there were once many of you, but with Crimolok's assault on God's creations, few of you remain. You might even be the last."

Damien was about to ask more, but Scarlett interrupted them by skipping in their direction, singing *"Get the Party Started".* Sorrow's wings fanned out like a bird catching water. He even waggled his bottom. "My ward is here. Do not dare harm her."

Damien rolled his eyes and waved a hand. "Hiya, Scarlett, you all right?"

"Just got off guard duty, because I'm, like, totally a soldier now. Just call me GI Jean."

"You are my ward," said Sorrow, "not a soldier."

"And it's GI *Jane*," said Damien.

Scarlett tutted. "Lighten up, you two. Sorrow, it's okay to think about something besides my safety, okay?" The large demon attempted to argue, but she raised her voice and cut him off. "Seriously, relax. Oh, and Damien, Nancy wants to talk to you at the castle. Leave the sled with Sorrow; he'll take it up for you."

Sorrow bowed in agreement.

"Okay, cheers. I'll see you both around." Damien trudged up the hill towards the castle. He and Nancy had been in the thick of it for months now, helping to reclaim the entire state of Indiana from the demons before stepping through a gate and arriving in northern England. Lately, she'd been drifting away. Without the constant threat of violence, she'd grown distant and brooding. Damien understood why. Fighting was a distraction, and now that it had stopped...

Thinking sucks.

Damien passed through the castle's portcullis, getting that same tingling down his spine he always did whenever he walked beneath its metal spikes – an irrational fear that the gate would suddenly drop and impale him. Next, he headed through the courtyard towards the castle. The Great Hall inside Kothal was a meeting place, a collection of benches and chairs assembled in front of a broad, always-lit hearth. It was a safe place for people when the anxiety became unbearable or the spectres of the past got a little too loud. Nancy hung around there a lot lately, as if she dared not be alone. When she saw Damien enter, she smiled, but it was half-hearted.

"Nance, you wanted to see me?"

"I thought we could go for a stroll. I want to talk."

"Oh. Is something wrong?"

"No more than usual." She took his hand and led him back out of the castle. It made him chilly to step back into the autumn air after experiencing the warmth of the hearth, but he soon adjusted. They cut their way through the various huts and carpentry projects, passed through the sally port, and headed down towards the ten-foot outer palisade that had been constructed over the last few months.

Damien looked at Nancy as they walked. "You wanna tell me what's up?"

She glanced around the no man's land between the inner and outer walls and grew teary. "Sorry," she said, wiping her eyes. "It's just... this place."

Damien couldn't help putting a hand against her cheek. "What's wrong with this place?"

"The children. I can't bear it."

It made sense. It did. "The children remind you of Alice and Kyle. That must be difficult."

"When the war first started, I thought there was no hope for any of us, but then we saved Indiana. Then we came here and found even *more* survivors. We lost so many people, Damien, but this place is proof that more made it. What if... what if...?"

"What if Kyle and Alice are still alive?"

She nodded, her eyes wet but no tears falling. She wouldn't allow herself that weakness. "I'm leaving."

"What? Nancy, you can't leave. The demons are still out there – God knows how many. Our only chance is sticking together. That's how we won in Indiana."

"Indiana was my fight, my victory. England is your home, Damien, not mine. My kids are my home. I have to look for them. I have to know."

Tears spilled down Damien's cheeks. Nancy was much older than him, with a life already lived, but they'd been as close as two people could be during the last year. They were soldiers in arms, fellow survivors, and lovers. "I can't lose you, Nancy. Not after everything we've been through."

"That's why I want you to come with me. Alice and Kyle were in London when the gates opened. If they survived, they're most likely in the south. Come with me, Damien. Help me find my family."

Damien leant forwards and kissed her mouth. She might have been twenty years older than him, but she was beautiful. Her eyes were a piercing green that he could stare into forever. "I understand that you need to know if your kids are alive. I get it."

She smiled, this time genuinely. "Then you'll come?"

"I'm sorry, no, I can't. I would give my life to save your children, but I would give it to save the children here too. I need to be wherever I can do the most good. This is where I have to be. Like you said, it's my home. I need to save it."

Nancy looked at him and swallowed. Eventually, she reached out and took his hand. "I hope you get to meet Alice and Kyle some day, Damien. Stay alive for me, okay? Stay alive, and I'll do the same."

He eased her back and studied her face, knowing it might be the last time. "I love you, Nancy."

4

Crimolok senses the warm flesh cowering inside the tower. That such worthless creatures have survived so long is one of God's so-called miracles. It would be undone now.

The human structure reaches as high as Crimolok's middle, an ugly grey block with blacked-out windows framed in rotting wood. It yields easily to his massive fist, bricks and steel showering the ground below. A second impact removes the roof entirely.

The screaming begins. If ever there was a sound so pure, it is the screaming of tortured cattle. Human faces appear at the windows, distorted with terror. Some leak out of the tower's base but are dealt with by Crimolok's legions. His demonic foot soldiers leap upon the fleeing humans and tear flesh from bone as they babble in agony.

Crimolok hammers his massive fist on top of the crumbling tower, smashing apart a floor section and the rooms beneath. He uncovers more humans, hiding like lice beneath a rock. Many are already bleeding to death, crushed by debris, but those attempting to flee are still his to enjoy. He plucks a breasted human into the air and pulls off its legs, then tosses the torso with its flailing arms to the ground thirty feet below. His legions devour what's left.

Boredom soon arrives. Crimolok raises a foot and stamps on what remains of the structure. It explodes in all directions – glass, wood, steel, and flesh. A fun distraction, but merely a stopping point on route to his destination. Blood will flow through the streets of Portsmouth. Humanity will reach its end.

Crimolok sneers, spotting a human hiding behind a large red vehicle. It calls out for God's mercy as Crimolok crushes it into dust.

TONY ASSEMBLED the soldiers General Thomas had allocated him and tried to hide his distaste. They were ambitious young men who would do whatever it took to gain favour. He didn't trust any of them, which made it all the better that he'd arranged his own protection. Known only to him, a dozen Urban Vampires were going to join them on the road. Mass's people were still loyal to General Wickstaff, even in her memory, and Tony wanted to get them out of the city before Thomas turned his wrath on them. Tony's allocated team would bristle at the unexpected arrivals, but the Urban Vampire's current leader, Cullen, had a story prepared. He'd claim to be looking for Mass too, and while Tony would act suspicious at first, he would eventually have no choice but to accept the additional manpower.

It'll be tense, but it'll work. At least, I sodding hope so.

The hard part would come if they discovered Mass alive. Tony had strict orders to kill Wickstaff's most decorated soldier, but no way was he going to do it. He refused to kill an innocent man just to solidify Thomas's illegitimate claim on Portsmouth.

Tony checked his ammo pouches, ensuring he had enough clips and magazines. He also filled a hip bag with loose rounds to make sure he had enough ammunition to obliterate anything he might encounter. He still carried the worn SA80 he'd had since leaving the US Air Force base in Turkey. It hadn't let him down yet. To think his journey had started a year ago on the Iraq–Syrian border, only to end up back home in England. He'd never expected to ever have to fight on home soil.

Tony's men assembled in a line and snapped to attention. Tony turned to see General Thomas approaching in full army dress – medals and all. The skeletal-faced old man marched across the tarmac on the outskirts of the docks, toecaps tapping an ominous rhythm. The regimented click-clack was a sound Tony had once enjoyed, but today it felt like a ticking clock.

Tony stood to attention and saluted just lazily enough not to get reprimanded. Thomas returned the salute and stomped to a halt mere inches away, close enough to make Tony uncomfortable. "Colonel Cross, are you ready to depart?"

"Yes, sir! The men are kitted out and mission ready."

"And what about you, Colonel?"

Tony frowned. "Sir?"

"Are you ready to carry out your orders?"

"I understand what needs to be done, sir."

General Thomas stood in silence, studying Tony's face. When Tony refused to give anything away, Thomas relented. "You're a good man, Colonel, which is why I have provided you the very best men Portsmouth can spare. This mission must succeed, and I have the utmost confidence I can trust you to do the job. Your service to me these last few months has been invaluable and you shall be properly rewarded upon your return."

Tony nodded curtly. Thomas's subtle attempt at bribery meant nothing to him. As a colonel, Tony was already several tiers higher than he'd ever planned to be. All he desired now was the chance to sleep a night in peace. His head was so full of nightmares that he wondered how he even managed to keep sane. "Thank you, sir. I'm grateful."

General Thomas saluted. "Then you should get going. Sooner you leave, sooner you get back."

Tony turned to his men, still standing at attention. "You heard the General. On the double. Move, move, move!"

The men formed pairs and marched towards the defensive wall that ringed the docklands. Tony snapped off a departing salute to General Thomas and joined them. He didn't look back, but he felt the old man's stare. Thomas didn't trust him, which meant the twelve men he'd sent would have orders to shoot Tony if he did anything off the books – maybe even if he followed his orders to the letter. It was only because Thomas lacked concrete evidence of Tony helping Maddy escape the city that he didn't just hang him. He couldn't deal with the PR disaster that would follow a colonel's execution one week after the death of a ranking general. Thomas was a despot dressed in democratic robes. He needed the veneer of fairness.

Tony shouted a cadence, hustling the men along. The bastards could suffer a little. "'Eft-'ight, 'eft-'ight, 'eft...!"

The men picked up speed, heading towards the city and the dangerous countryside beyond. Tony took one glance back towards the sea, certain he would never see it again.

Diane shadowed Thomas as much as possible, always dropping off reports here or checking supplies there. Whatever she did, she always made sure to do it close to the general. The only problem was keeping her hands off him. Every second she spent breathing the same air as Thomas filled her with an almost uncontrollable rage. She wanted to claw out his cold grey eyes. She wanted to force her hand down his throat and yank up whatever rotting innards she could find. She wouldn't rest until he was dead. For General Wickstaff and for Maddy.

And for Portsmouth. We deserve someone better after all we've been through.

Diane missed Maddy terribly. She was the only other survivor from their original group in Crapstone. No more Rick. No more Keith or Daniel. Their loss was a staple beneath her thumbnail, a constant dull pain, but losing Maddy was like hot coals in her stomach, a searing agony burning up her insides.

So far, Thomas, the sonofabitch, hadn't seemed to realise what Diane was up to. Her true purpose for shadowing him was to see who was loyal to him and who was not. She could tell those who disliked the general by the strained expressions they wore as soon as he turned his back. Diane was in the business of recruiting those people. Nineteen had already agreed to take up arms against Thomas when the time was right, and many more would soon join. Wickstaff had inspired all those around her, so finding people willing to fight in her name was easy, but she had to be cautious about who she approached. Some men were only out for themselves. Some men placed their loyalties wherever it would help them most. Trustworthiness could never be assumed.

It made recruitment a slow process.

If Diane gave a rebel yell from the rooftops, she knew several thousand men and women would scream allegiance to Wickstaff and take up arms. The flaw in that plan was that it wouldn't be enough. General Thomas had brought more than fifteen thousand troops with him from the continent, and it would be impossible to retake Portsmouth without persuading at least some of them to join the cause. Tony Cross was the lynchpin to converting many of those forces, but Thomas had shrewdly sent the colonel away on a fool's errand. Mass dead, that much was obvious – he'd never been away this long. Tony Cross would most likely never return from his mission.

I'm running low on allies.

Commander Klein was in favour of General Thomas's removal, too, but the German was a law unto himself, preferring to stay out of things until forced to act. She couldn't rely on him. Maybe he would help her once enough people had been recruited. That was why she was heading to speak with a guardsman named Tom, her next recruit.

Tom was a good guy who'd gone to bat for General Wickstaff several times in the past, including a time when Thomas had directly challenged her authority. He was popular – someone other men instinctively seemed to like – and Diane was certain he would join her cause. Tom stood up for what was right.

And what I'm doing is right.

Diane found Tom sitting on a crate by the edge of the quay. Four others sat with him, all playing cards. It was hard to tell if they were on duty because only Thomas's men wore uniforms. The original Portsmouth inhabitants wore whatever suited them.

"Hi, Tom. You busy?"

He looked up at her and smiled. "Does it look like it?"

"Depends how good your hand is."

Tom threw down a trio of cards – a four of clubs, a two of spades, and a ten of hearts. "As good as tits on a donkey." He stood up and moved further along the quay, motioning for her to join him. In a conspiratorial tone, he asked, "What's going on around here, Di? Me and the guys are getting nervous. People are saying Maddy had something to do with Wickstaff's death."

Diane sneered, wanting to slap him for even saying such a thing. "You know that's bullshit!"

"Of course I do. It's no secret how close Maddy and Wickstaff were."

Diane didn't comment on Maddy's relationship with the general, but it didn't surprise her to learn that Tom – and most likely others – suspected the two women had been more than colleagues. Would it affect people's loyalties? Were people still judgemental, even now?

"Thomas murdered Wickstaff and would've killed Maddy too if she hadn't escaped."

Tom nodded, glancing aside to make sure no one was listening. He whispered, "I guessed as much. Commander Tosco is missing too. I assume he was the one who got her out of the city? Both were a huge part of what we built here. Portsmouth is their home. We can't let Thomas get away with it."

As Diane suspected, Tom didn't need convincing. "We won't let him get away with it, but I don't have a plan yet. I need to know who I can trust."

"You can trust *me* – and a dozen others I know would leap at the chance to rid Portsmouth of Thomas. The guy's an arsehole. A *murderous* arsehole."

Diane chuckled. She went to say something, but their eyes locked for a moment and made them both blush. She finally spoke. "Hey, um, if you're not on duty, you fancy going for a walk or something? I could use a friend."

"A walk? Um, yeah, a walk would be nice."

Diane motioned with a nod and they started walking along the quay. Tom bid his mates goodbye and moved close enough that their arms brushed together. He glanced at her. "So, did you ever see yourself becoming leader of *La Resistance*?"

She laughed, the sound making a seagull take flight from a piling. "To tell the truth, when the demons first invaded, I was a trembling mess. People kept dying around me, but somehow I kept surviving. For a while, I thought it was luck, but then I realised it was something else."

Tom smiled gently, his brow lowering with concern. "What?"

"I was being punished, forced to watch everyone die while I cowered. They got to escape the nightmare, but my own hell kept getting worse and worse. Surviving is my punishment."

"You make dying sound like a good thing."

"Not good, but... easier. My fear got people killed, so I gave myself a talking to. I stopped being a pussy and got my shit together." They both chuckled, but Diane's smile quickly faded. "The problem is that people still keep dying, no matter what I do. They keep dying and I keep surviving. It's filling me up, all this... *anger*."

Tom put a hand on her back and rubbed. He removed it a second later but didn't appear embarrassed. "People have always been dying, Diane. That's what makes us human. What matters is how much we fight while we're alive – and you're fighting harder than anybody else – but be careful, okay? What you're doing is dangerous."

"I'm not doing it alone. Everyone who agrees to help me is risking their lives."

"Then you must be worth the risk."

They reached the end of the quay, an area occupied by several empty warehouses. Portsmouth was a big city with only a fraction of its former residents, not to mention the many people who now lived on boats instead of dry land. There was a lot of wasted real estate. Coming to a halt, Diane turned to Tom. "Are you sure you want to do this? It could all end terribly."

He smiled. "Do you know why I joined the navy? It wasn't to fight bad guys or be a patriot. I just didn't want to work in a supermarket or factory. I never took the job any more seriously than I had to. But then things changed. The demons came and suddenly I was watching civilians leap into the sea and drown rather than face the horror at their back. I watched mothers throw their children from burning buildings, fathers torn apart trying to defend their families. We helped as many as we could, but by the time our ship retreated, the sea was red with blood. After that, I took the job seriously. Mankind doesn't just have to survive, Diane. If it has any future at all, it needs to survive with the right people in charge. Thomas has to go, and if whoever takes over is half as decent as Wickstaff, we might have a chance. We'll make it happen, Diane. No matter what, okay? We'll make the bastard pay."

Diane shook her head, not out of disappointment but out of shocked admiration. "How can you be so sure this is the right thing to do? How can you be so sure about *me*?"

Tom averted his eyes and looked down at his feet. It was cute, but only because he was normally so confident. "Wickstaff was sure about you, Diane. You and Maddy were the two people she trusted most, and if she trusted you, then so do I. Not to mention, you're pretty intimidating. The guys say you have the biggest pair of bollocks in Portsmouth."

It shocked Diane to hear that people talked about her. She had assumed herself invisible. It was part of what made her so effective as a bodyguard, until she had failed dismally by allowing Wickstaff's murder. She placed her hands on her hips and felt a little pissed off. "You think I have a pair of bollocks?"

Tom blushed. "What? No! Not literally. You're all woman. I mean… look at you…"

Diane glared a moment longer, but her irritation had already disappeared. Now she was just having fun. It wasn't the first time she'd spoken with Tom, but with Maddy and Wickstaff gone, she realised how much she missed having someone to joke around with. By agreeing to help, Tom had become her friend. There was trust between them.

I can trust him.

Diane reached out and clutched the front of Tom's shirt. She walked backwards, pulling him along with her. "I'll show you what's between my legs, and I promise it's not a pair of bollocks. Come on."

Tom turned bright red and his eyes went comically wide. It didn't stop him from following her into the abandoned warehouse.

———

MORNING BROKE and Diane awoke with a smile on her face and an aching in her back. The aching was caused by the rickety cot bed she had slept on in a small office inside one of the civilian customs buildings. The smile on her face was due to having had sex last night. Rain had come to the desert.

Hallelujah!

Tom was lovely. A spark had hit her out of nowhere and suddenly she was into him, a teenager with a crush. She wasn't embarrassed though. Tom was an upfront kind of guy, which meant she was in no doubt about the fact that he liked her too. There were no games being played. It was okay to be vulnerable. At least a little.

Last night, they had hung out in the abandoned warehouse for three hours, having sex, chatting, laughing, and kissing, both of them naked and shivering. For a moment, life had felt ordinary, but in the dawn of a new day, things weren't quite so bright. She was still a member of a post-apocalyptic society with a despot in charge. Despite that, she'd formed a connection with another human being, and it meant she could open her heart to more than hate and anger. It was enough to keep the rage from overtaking her completely.

I can keep a little piece of myself for Tom. I can feel something other than a need for revenge.

Diane couldn't let herself be distracted too much by lust and love. Thomas still needed dealing with, and her life was in danger every second he lived. For the first time in a long time, anxiety began to strike her with its venomous fangs. Part of her wanted to run away with Tom, to find somewhere isolated and safe, but that frightened part of her had no place in this world. That Diane was an echo of an unacceptable past.

It was time to get up and go. While Thomas hadn't reassigned her duties since taking charge of Portsmouth, he hadn't relieved her of them either. Most days she went through the motions of maintaining security, pretending to safeguard Thomas, while actually plotting his death. For today, she would take a break and make herself useful around Portsmouth. If she pursued her agenda too often, she would give herself away. Now and then, she had to carry out her duties and nothing more. It allowed her to remain invisible – a knife Thomas would never see coming.

She put on clothes, shivering while briefly naked, then

drank from the gallon jug she topped up with water every night before sleeping. Several of the larger boats had desalination facilities on board, and they kept a regular flow of processed seawater coming onto the docks. People had to fetch their own supply, but there was enough to go around. They also caught as much rainwater as possible on days when it was wet, and you couldn't go ten feet without passing some sort of catcher or butt.

She left the customs office five minutes later and entered the muggy atmosphere of the civilian docks. The air was thick with a fishy stench. A majority of the daily catch came from the several dozen fishing boats along the coast, but some preferred to catch their own supper from the civilian docks. Diane had been learning the ropes from a couple of the older guys, but she rarely found time to cast a line.

Along with the odour pollution was noise pollution. It came from the military wharf – the busiest part of the docks. This morning the noise was particularly loud. She heard shouting and jeering, like a protest was happening. Too many buildings stood in the way to see what was happening, so she decided to ask a fisherman named Mitch. The old man was working nearby, cutting up some mackerel to use as bait for something larger. He noticed her and smiled through a gap in his fuzzy white beard. "Morning, Diane. You look fresh as a daisy."

She smirked, struggling to hide her naughtiness at having had sex. "Hi, Mitch. Hey, um, what's going on over at the military wharf?"

"I would've thought you'd have known all about it. General Thomas has found the rotten apples what plotted to kill Wickstaff. Maybe he's caught that murderous wench, Maddy."

Diane's fists clenched, but she willed them back open. Mitch was a good guy at heart, but not a thinker. He would happily eat up whatever news was spoon-fed to him by those with larger intellects. If people whispered that Maddy had killed Wickstaff, Mitch's simple mind would accept it as fact.

"Maddy wasn't involved in Wickstaff's death, Mitch. Trust me, okay?"

"Then why'd she scarper?"

Diane sighed. There would be little point in explaining. "I don't know. Anyway, what are you talking about? Who are they saying plotted to kill Wickstaff?"

"Don't know. Keep to myself, don't I? Hope they string the bastards up, whoever they are. I liked Wickstaff. Everyone did."

At least they could agree on that. "I'll see you later, Mitch. Good luck fishing."

"I'll share my catch. You look like you could use a good meal, lass."

"You're probably right." She left Mitch with his mackerel guts and headed for the commotion. Ten minutes later, she was close enough to hear the hatred in each individual voice. Something bad was happening, and sure enough, when she rounded the final corner, she saw what it was. Half of Portsmouth had assembled in an area known as the 'parade square'. General Thomas stood on the wooden stage he'd had erected soon after Wickstaff's death.

His little propaganda platform. What is the sonofabitch up to now?

Diane picked up speed, walking fast enough that her shins ached. Her heart fluttered in her chest. She didn't like not knowing what was happening. For nearly a year she'd been in Wickstaff's inner circle, privy to everything going on in Portsmouth. Now she was on the outside looking in – another clueless spectator.

It took her another ten minutes to reach the military wharf. A concrete wall had once stood between the civilian and military areas, but it'd been knocked through and a gate added. The gate was currently open, as it usually was, but guards stood on either side of it. Fortunately, they recognised Diane and nodded. Both were Thomas's men, and it seemed that lately more and more of every security position was being filled with people who had crossed the channel with the general. Wickstaff's forces had been redeployed to scouting missions or menial tasks. Many had been sent out to protect the small farms set up in the surrounding countryside. Bit by bit, there were more and more foxes in the henhouse.

"Shoot 'em!" she heard a woman yell in an American accent. To Diane's horror, she recognised her as a survivor brought in by *The Hatchet* long before General Thomas had arrived in Portsmouth. Diane was certain the woman had been a 'kindergarten' teacher before. Now she was part of a baying mob.

Diane shoved by the woman and passed several other jeering individuals. A line of people slumped on stage with Thomas and several guards stood behind them. They were half-conscious, their beaten faces bloodied. Despite the damage, Diane recognised every one of them; all original citizens of Portsmouth. People she knew. People she had recruited.

Thomas moved behind the lectern on stage and spoke into a microphone. "Citizens of Portsmouth, today I bring you justice. I bring you closure for the death of Amanda Wickstaff. These immoral fiends kneeling before you plotted and carried out the assassination of the woman who saved so many of you. It is my duty to bring her murderers to justice, along with all those who conspired to help them. I will fulfil that duty today."

The crowd bawled with anger. Many spat and threw things, splattering the beaten men and women on stage. One kneeling man attempted to plead his innocence, but a guard struck his skull with the butt of a rifle and silenced him.

Diane felt sick to her stomach. This wasn't right.

These people are innocent. Thomas is the monster. He's the one who murdered Amanda. Why doesn't anyone see that?

Diane wanted to shout at the top of her lungs. She wanted to inform the people of Portsmouth that it was Thomas who they should condemn, that it was *he* who they should spit at. If she did that, though, violence would break out, and it would quickly swing in Thomas's favour. Portsmouth was being guarded by his people, and enough propaganda had spread that many who had loved Wickstaff now supported him too. Shouting the truth would do nothing but get good people killed.

She could do nothing but watch.

Thomas went on, thumping the lectern like an apocalyptic Hitler. "Today, these vile cowards will forfeit their lives, but first they will witness the futility of their crimes. Guards! Bring him here."

A pair of soldiers shuffled from the back of the stage, dragging a badly beaten prisoner between them. The hooded stranger was frogmarched to where the other prisoners were slumped. Thomas glared at him balefully, and Diane knew the hatred's true source was not the death of Wickstaff but the disloyalty towards him. Thomas was rooting out his opposition.

I can't do it. I'll never be able to make him pay. He has all the power.

"This man," Thomas barked into the microphone, "is responsible for convincing others to work against the common interest. He is a traitor to us all, serving only himself and his own agenda."

The crowd roared. Fists pumped the air. More spitting.

Thomas gave the guards a nod and they whipped the hood off of the prisoner, revealing a face swollen and bruised. Diane gasped, not because of the grievous injuries, but because of who it was.

Tom.

No... No, please, no.

Diane lost control of herself, desperate in every way. She shoved her way through the crowd, trying to get to Tom – trying to save him – but someone grabbed her and pulled her back. She didn't recognise the shaven-headed man, but before she could shove him away, he whispered in her ear, "You can't help him, Diane. Stop."

"What? Who the hell are you?"

"Damien. You're Diane. He's Tom. I know a lot, which is why I'm telling you to keep calm and not do anything stupid."

"Calm? That sonofabitch needs to be stopped. Those people up there are innocent. He can't do th—"

"They're not innocent. They're casualties of war – acceptable losses if you want to win this. You do want to win this, don't you?"

Diane peered at Tom. He could barely stand, so badly beaten was he. Even his hands were bruised. He must have put up a fight. She had to help him. "It's not an acceptable loss to me."

"You speak out and you'll end up right next to him. They beat the shit out of him, Diane, but he didn't give them your name. Don't let his suffering be for nothing."

"What the hell do you expect me to do?"

"Whatever shit you're feeling, shove it down and shape it into something useful. Once it's sharp enough, you can shove it in Thomas's throat, but only when the time is right."

Diane's vision blurred. The stranger seemed to sense her weakness because he reached out and steadied her. His hands were freezing, but it helped bring back her alertness. Although she would've preferred unconsciousness over having to witness this.

Tom...

Please...

Thomas moved in front of the prisoners and faced Tom specifically. "I'll have you shot for your crimes, son, but first I'm going to give you the opportunity to redeem yourself. Reveal the rest of your co-conspirators and I'll spare the lives of these other criminals. Tell us who else has been acting against the common good and you may die with a clean conscience."

Tom seemed to glare at Thomas, but it was hard to tell because his eyes were so swollen. His lips were split and they trembled as if he were preparing to speak. But he didn't. Instead, he spat bloody saliva right into Thomas's face. Diane beamed as the tyrant recoiled, the old fucker's bony face growing redder than the blood on his cheeks.

Take that, you piece of shit! Good on you, Tom.

Then Thomas whipped out a handgun and shot Tom point-blank in the face.

Before Diane could scream, Damien grabbed her and pulled her into a hug, keeping her from seeing her lover's body hit the ground. She sobbed into his ice-cold chest, but not loudly enough to block out the noise of further gunshots being fired, and further sounds of bodies hitting the stage.

She was alone.

5

D amien shuddered, but he wasn't sure why. An uncomfortable feeling had come over him, making him want to curl up into a ball. Nancy must have noticed his unease because she asked him what was wrong. "I'm not sure. Just got the jitters for a moment. You still sure you want to do this?"

Nancy looked around, glancing up and down the main road. It was jam-packed with wrecked and abandoned cars, but there was no apparent danger. That didn't make what she was doing any less reckless. "I have no choice," she said. "If there's any chance my kids are alive somewhere, I have to find them. Are you sure you won't come?"

"I'm sorry, I can't. You'll have your guys with you though."

Nancy looked over at the four Americans who had followed her all the way from Indiana. They were tough men who had fought side by side with her. Damien felt better knowing she wouldn't be alone on the road. They were twelve miles south of Kielder Forest, but he didn't trust her journey would be plain sailing from here.

Nancy chewed the inside of her cheek, then said, "I'm really hoping this isn't the last time we see each other, Damien."

"Promise me you'll do everything you can to stay out of trouble. We might have kicked demon ass back in Indiana, but this place is different. You don't know the land."

She placed a kiss on his cheek. "Trust me when I say I'll do everything I can to stay alive, but you do the same, okay? Whatever happens here, survive."

Damien felt tears coming. "You should go. You're wasting light."

"Look who's in a hurry to be rid of the ol' ball and chain. Got your next chick lined up?"

"There's no one else. I'll be waiting for you."

Nancy grabbed his hand and squeezed, holding onto it as she turned away and keeping contact until the last second, when their fingertips slid apart. Damien watched her walk away, wondering if her gait had ever been feminine and gentle instead of strong and powerful. In a previous life, they would never have got together. Damien had been a young banker, frequenting pubs by night for a pint and a shag. Nancy had been a mother of two on her second marriage. In this new world, they were soldiers bound by blood and pain.

Damien thought Nancy would look back, but she didn't. She joined her escorts and started shimmying between the cars and vans that blocked the road. The morning sun was dazzling, sending shards of light across the fading metal paintwork. At first, Damien thought it was those shafts of light that caught his eye, but then he realised it was something else – something moving. A shadow ducked and dived between the stalled vehicles, getting closer. Then it wasn't just one solitary shadow but many.

Damien yelled at the top of his lungs, "Demons!"

Nancy and her bodyguards raised their rifles. Damien didn't see who fired first, but once it happened, the chorus of war began in earnest. Damien added to the cacophony, firing blindly ahead and hoping to hit something.

The first shadow revealed itself, leaping up onto the wide, round bonnet of a silver saloon. It was a demonic primate, a creature so twisted and perverse that it was more beast than man. It glared at them and snarled.

"Fall back," Nancy bellowed. "There're too many of them."

Damien fired off an entire magazine in less than three seconds, hitting the primate on the bonnet and the one that immediately leapt up beside it. Nancy took one out as well, but as she'd said, there were too many of them – two dozen at least. They had to retreat.

Damien waited for Nancy to fall back in line, but as she did so, one of her escorts tripped on a fallen wing mirror. The stumble was all it took for a primate to leap across the roof of a smashed-up Porsche and land on him. His screams lasted less than a second, his throat quickly torn open.

"Where the hell did they come from?" Nancy's attention darted left and right as she fired several shots. "I thought this area had been cleared."

Damien had that bad feeling again, but this time there was no mystery behind the cause. "This is what we've been preparing for. Whatever the demons have been planning, it just kicked off. We've been ambushed."

"I'm never going to find my kids. These fucking monsters. I hate them. I hate them so fucking much."

Damien wanted to argue – to tell her that everything would be okay – but when he spotted more demons racing towards them, he couldn't deny the truth. There was no way out of this. They couldn't run, they couldn't fight. All they could do was take down as many of the bastards as possible to make sure those back at the castle had a slightly better chance of survival.

"It's been an honour fighting with you folks," said one of Nancy's escorts, a thick-necked old boy named Norton. He'd run an Indiana textile factory in his former life with two sons who were both now dead. Perhaps that was why the old guy was so brave; he was eager to rejoin his family. "I'll buy you some time to make it to the treeline."

Nancy shook her head. "Norton, don't!"

But it was too late. The brave American had moved forward, picking his shots and catching the attention of every demon. The two remaining escorts bolted for the treeline, and Damien was about to take off after them, but Nancy didn't move at all. She aimed her rifle and fired, rooted to the spot. Damien grabbed her and yelled. "Come on, we have to go!"

"I'm not leaving Norton."

"He's made his decision. It's too late to change it." And that was the truth. The demons had already surrounded him. Damien fired a shot and hit one of the demons in the thigh, but it was hopeless. More monsters emerged from behind the wrecked vehicles. Who knew how many would eventually present themselves?

Damien pulled at Nancy again. This time, to his relief, she let herself be moved. She turned and picked up speed, rushing for the trees. The two escorts hadn't yet fully retreated, and they fired their rifles to provide cover.

Then the worst thing happened.

The two escorts fell at exactly the same time, wailing first in shock and then in agony. Burnt men appeared behind them in the trees, twenty at least, forming a wall and blocking any chance of escape. Damien's knees deserted him and he collapsed onto the road. His rifle struck the ground and discharged accidentally, the round ricocheting into the air, seeking clouds. "We're fucked," he moaned. "Totally fucked."

"They've cut off our retreat," said Nancy in disbelief. "We're idiots."

"We couldn't have known. This area was clear."

Nancy knelt beside him. "I'm sorry. I'm sorry, you're going to die because of me."

Damien shrugged. "I would have happily died for less."

They fired their rifles until they were empty, tossed them aside, and then embraced. Finally, they waited for it all to be over. It didn't take long.

THEY'D MADE GOOD TIME, travelling fifteen miles according to Tosco, but Maddy's feet were throbbing and she was ready to rest. Her watch told her it wasn't even noon. "When can we take a break?" she complained.

Tosco raised an eyebrow, a cheeky smirk on his face. "Surely you're not ready to quit?" She glared at him, but he only laughed. "I was planning to make camp at the twenty-mile mark. I know we've pushed hard today, but it's nice to take in some new scenery. Most of us spent the first months of the invasion on the water, and we've barely moved since reaching Portsmouth."

Maddy had spent the first months of the invasion on foot, desperately trying to stay alive. The thought of being on the road again didn't exactly thrill her, but she understood that Tosco and his men must have been suffering with some pretty harsh cabin fever. Watching them now, she saw their sharp intakes of breath and wandering eyes. They were enjoying being out in the open – if out in the open meant a deserted village with smashed-in shop windows.

"So far so good," said Tosco. "Maybe I *should* have brought Alice along. Poor kid's been stuck on *The Hatchet* way too long."

"We still don't know how safe it is out here," said Maddy. "When we last saw demons they were aggressive again." She was, of course, referring to the temporary stupor the demons had entered, which had seemingly ended with their recent attack on Portsmouth.

"Alice is tougher than she looks," said Tosco, "but I'm trying to keep her safe. I don't know if it was the right thing bringing her along with me. She had friends in Portsmouth. Now she's a fugitive surrounded by coast guards and mechanics."

Maddy gave him a sympathetic smile. "Once we reach this camp in the woods we can send for her. She'll be on dry land again soon. She'll make new friends."

Tosco nodded, but he seemed genuinely guilt-ridden. He'd

become a surrogate father to the young American girl and Tosco was clearly trying his best to fill Guy Granger's shoes.

The sole female sailor in the group prodded something up ahead with her boot. She looked back and grimaced. "Whatever this belonged to, it's as fresh as airborne pigeon shit."

The chunk of pinkish meat could have been from a pig, but it could also have been human. Maddy grimaced. "Maybe a lion escaped the zoo along with the zebra."

Tosco nodded and added his own theory. "Dogs. There're packs of them everywhere. We need to stay alert."

Everyone raised their weapons and reordered themselves in a line. They moved through the abandoned village slowly, edging along the paths and road. Cars and debris blocked their way, and they passed with caution.

Maddy found another chunk of bloody flesh. It gave off a smell, rotting ever so slightly. Whatever had died had been alive not so long ago. "It's a hand," she said, stomach lurching. It wasn't the sight of oozing flesh – that she was more than used to. It was the shock of coming across it so unexpectedly.

Tosco stood over the disembodied hand with a grim expression. "Damn it. There were people here. What if this camp in the forest has been attacked?"

"I'm sure it has," said Maddy, "multiple times, but we know nothing until we get there. Let's not panic."

"You're right. With the way things are, it would be a miracle not to find a few corpses here and there. It still could've been dogs. I don't see any signs of demon activity."

"Pity," said the female team member. "I wanted something to shoot."

Maddy didn't see any threats either. Demons usually meant blood, and not just in pools, but everywhere. They bathed in it, spread it everywhere. "I say we keep moving. Sooner we reach this camp, the better."

Tosco gave everyone the nod and they resumed their advance. It didn't take long to find more flesh on the road, and this time there was no way to dismiss it. Four bodies littered the landscape, arms and legs strewn about and mixed together. Cracked and half-eaten skulls grinned up at Maddy and forced her to avert her gaze. The bodies weren't fresh, but they weren't old either.

"This is bad," said one of the men. "I say we head back to *The Hatchet*."

Tosco looked back the way they'd come as if considering the option. How could he not be? They were here to find sanctuary, not walk into the midst of a demon lair. But what would retreating achieve? They were a species at war. You could only avoid fighting for so long. They had come here for a reason.

Before Tosco shared what he was thinking, gunfire alerted the team. Everyone threw themselves into cover and raised their weapons. Maddy lifted her handgun and looked for something to shoot. "There are people alive out here," she cried. "We need to help them."

"We could be walking right into a losing battle," said Tosco.

"It could be the group we're looking for," said the female team member, apparently arguing for Maddy's side. The woman knelt nearby, peering down her riflescope. "They're the whole reason we're here, boss. Would be stupid not to lend a hand."

Tosco grunted. "You're right. Let's move. Weapons ready."

Maddy nodded appreciation to the woman and noticed a fine scar running the entire length of the left side of her face. It made her look fierce. "What's your name?" asked Maddy.

"Sarah."

They got moving, risking an ambush every time they passed a car or blind alley. The village ended abruptly, small thatch-roofed cottages giving way to a lone church, a small green, and then an empty country road lined by tree-lined embankments on both sides. The gunfire came from their left. Tosco took point and worked his way into the trees. The fight was close, maybe in the woods themselves, or maybe just on the other side. Maddy wished she had a rifle like everyone else, and she suddenly hoped Tosco hadn't provided her with a handgun for any sexist reason.

The thought seemed an absurd one to be having right at that moment.

The woods were sparse, not much more than a buffer between the village and a highway. The highway must have been the scene of the battle because the gunfire was too close to be coming from anywhere else. Maddy spotted people amongst the trees.

But they weren't people.

The figures standing just inside the treeline were demons – men and women burnt to a crisp in the fires of Hell. They were looking the other way, towards the dual carriageway.

Tosco threw his arm up and shouted, "Fire at will!"

The line of sailors, with Maddy in the middle, pulled their triggers and lit up the gloomy wood. It took the demons unaware and they lurched forward as bullets struck them in the back. Tosco's team was too capable to miss, and within seconds they had taken down over a dozen burnt men. The fighting on the dual carriageway continued, was slowly ebbing. Too few guns. A losing battle.

Maddy broke into a sprint. "Come on, hurry!"

"Maddy, slow down!"

She reached the edge of the woods and hopped over a half-dead burnt man with a bullet wound between its shoulder blades. Then she finally spotted humans – two dead men lying on the embankment, their bodies torn to shreds. If not for the gunfire, she would've assumed the demons had killed everyone, but there were two people still alive on the dual carriageway – a man and a woman. They were kneeling in the road and embracing while a dozen demons approached them hungrily, taking their time to surround them.

Maddy fired a shot, but a handgun was no long-range weapon, so she stuffed it inside her waistband and grabbed a rifle that was lying next to one of the two dead men. The weapon wasn't one she was used to, but thankfully it chattered excitedly as soon as she pulled the trigger. With the attached scope, she found her targets.

Tosco and the others lined up on either side of Maddy and discharged their own rifles. Once again, the demons were blind-sided and fell like rag dolls on the dual carriageway. A few turned and raced towards the treeline, but there was too much distance to cross. A few seconds was all it took to take them down.

The two people in the centre of the road raised their heads from each other's shoulders and looked around in confusion. When the male of the pair saw Maddy standing on the embankment, he gave a small, disbelieving wave.

Maddy waved back.

Tosco had his team clear the area before he allowed them to enter the dual carriageway. When they did, they formed a semi-circle and closed in around the two strangers, who were still on their knees. Both appeared utterly stunned.

"W-Who are you people?" the man asked.

"I'm Maddy. This is Captain Tosco and his team."

Tosco lowered his rifle and nodded. "We're searching for a group of survivors in a place called Kielder Forest."

The man's eyes widened. "We're from there. Well, recently we are. Before that, we were in Indiana. My name's Damien. This is Nancy."

The woman nodded. "Indiana was my home."

"Good to meet you, miss," said Tosco. "How on earth did you make it all the way here from all the way over there?"

"Long story. How did you get here? You're American too."

"I came by boat. I was a coast guard before this."

The woman gasped. "My ex-husband was US Coast Guard based out of New York."

"You're kidding me? What was his name? Perhaps I knew him."

"Captain Granger. First name, Guy."

Tosco stumbled. Even Maddy was gobsmacked by the coincidence. What the hell were the odds? The world had become a large and empty place, so to find his deceased superior's ex-wife was close to a miracle.

Tosco struggled to speak. "I-I was Captain Granger's second in command aboard *The Hatchet*. You're Nancy, right?"

Nancy got to her feet slowly, like she was moving through water. "Y-You *knew* him? You knew Guy? Where is he?"

"I'm sorry."

Nancy's eyes teared up, but she nodded as if she accepted it. "He was a good man. Brave."

Tosco seemed to tear up a little himself. "I learned a lot from Guy. When the war first started, we butted heads many times over him coming here to find his—" He put a hand to his mouth and spluttered. "Jesus Christ! Nancy, I have Alice on board *The Hatchet*. It's anchored at the coast."

Nancy's legs folded, and Damien had to leap up to steady her. Once he got her steady, he looked at Tosco and shook his head. "This is insane, but we shouldn't be discussing it here. Come on, we have a van parked less than a mile away. We should head back to Kielder and figure things out."

"Alice," said Nancy. "I need to go to her. I need to go right now."

"She's safe," Tosco assured her. "I have fifty sailors back on *The Hatchet*, and enough weaponry to break off a chunk of England. As soon as I know it's safe, I'll radio in and have her brought to you."

Nancy's eyes rolled. It looked like she might pass out as she mumbled to herself, "Alice, my sweetheart, you're alive." Then she gathered her wits to look at Tosco sternly. "What about Kyle? Is he on board *The Hatchet* too?"

Tosco peered at the ground. "I'm afraid Guy never reached him in time. I understand he died in London trying to escape with his sister."

Nancy lurched forward and vomited. Damien held onto her and looked at Maddy. "Help me get her out of here."

THE VAN WAS PARKED down an alleyway between a pair of small factory units. One had been a woodworking business. Shavings and half-finished carvings covered the ground, having spilled out from beneath an open shutter. The unit next to it was a shot-blasting firm.

"Okay," said Damien, "into the van."

Tosco and his squad piled into the back of the nondescript white vehicle while Damien hopped up front. Maddy helped Nancy climb into the passenger seat beside him.

"There's enough for three," said Damien. "Hop up."

Maddy obliged, sliding in beside Nancy and slamming the door closed. She went to pull on her seatbelt, before remembering that traffic collisions were a thing of the past. "You have many vehicles?" she asked.

"Five or six," said Damien, leaning forward to start the engine. "The problem is finding petrol. For a while we siphoned it from all the wrecks, but it seems like it's going bad or something. Nothing we get running lasts very long." As if to prove his point, the van's engine coughed and spluttered before catching. Once it was rumbling though, it sounded perfectly healthy. Damien glanced at her as he pulled onto the main road. "The guy with you is American, but you're not. Where you from, Maddy?"

"Reading. I was a paramedic. Still don't know how I survived. Suppose I fell in with the right crowd. I ended up in Portsmouth a few weeks after everything started."

"Portsmouth?"

"There are thirty thousand people there. We've been fighting the demons for months, and we've been winning, but..."

"But it isn't over. Yeah, people feel that here too. Something bad is coming. Don't ask me how I know, but the demons are rallying for one last clash. If we're not ready…"

Maddy sighed. There was no need to finish that sentence.

Nancy began sobbing quietly. Damien rubbed her back with his gear-shifting hand, but he split his focus between Maddy and the road. "So, you planning to get everyone south to Portsmouth?"

"No! Portsmouth was safe once, but now it's a lit firework. There was a woman in charge named Amanda Wickstaff, who locked down Portsmouth before it was overrun. Thousands survived because of her."

"So what happened?"

"A tyrant murdered her and took over. He would've killed me, too, but Tosco and his men got me out. We came here looking for sanctuary."

Damien's knuckles clenched around the steering wheel. "Nothing's changed then? Greedy men are still willing to kill to get what they want."

"Listen, Damien, if you want peace and unity, then General Thomas is your enemy. The woman he killed was a hero. He's an arrogant, dangerous piece of work."

"I'll take your word for it. Everyone thinks their side are the good guys; don't mean it's true."

Maddy rolled her eyes. "Yeah, and what makes *you* such a moral authority?"

Damien half glanced at her and chuckled. "I'm a path walker, maybe the last one in existence. I didn't even realise there were more of us until there wasn't. It's like a part of me got severed. I don't think there are many of God's worlds left."

"What the hell are you talking about? Are you trying to say you're some kind of saviour?"

"No, nothing like that – I'm just a nobody from Sutton Coldfield – but I can create gates. If things don't go our way, I'm the last chance of getting us out of the fire."

"You can open gates? Like those that brought the demons?"

"Similar, yeah, except my gates open across the tapestry. The demon gates only connect to Hell."

"Huh?"

"The tapestry is like a web. It connects all of God's worlds to each other, and to Heaven and Hell. Path walkers can traverse the tapestry. Sometimes they can see things from other worlds too, or see back and forth along a single strand."

"You can see the future?"

"No, but others like me could. I just have the gate thing. My powers are stronger whenever I'm near totems. Oh, totems are people who exist on other worlds too. They're like copies. Path walkers are the same, except we have powers."

Maddy had to laugh, even though the world had moved beyond the scrutiny of the supernatural. Science clearly hadn't known everything. "How did you learn about all this?"

Damien manoeuvred them onto a country road and shrugged at her. "It just came to me suddenly. I think it came from other path walkers, those who died. It's like I gained their knowledge or something. Do I sound crazy?"

"Yes! You sound insane."

Damien chuckled. "Yeah, I would have thought that too, not so long ago. Anyway, I'm just a part of things. Maybe you are too."

"Then we need to help each other. There's not enough of us left for any other option."

"I agree." Maddy knew she was being unreasonable by taking offence. This young man didn't know her from Adam. Of course he wouldn't risk his people just to keep her safe. That might change over time, but right now it was too early to ask a stranger to go to war.

Although I did just save his life.

Twenty minutes went by in silence while Maddy watched the ruined scenery pass by. Skeletal corpses littered the landscape. Dogs roamed the roadsides, staring like hungry ghosts.

Damien broke the silence a short time later when he announced, "We're here."

Maddy straightened in her seat and stared ahead through the grimy windscreen. The country road they'd entered was little more than a dirt track now, with thick woodland on either side. The trees thinned out after a while, revealing ragged stumps where they'd been felled.

"Everyone at Kielder has worked to clear a perimeter around the camp," explained Damien. "They needed the wood to build, and the space gives advance warning if anything tries to come at us. We've dug moats and put up other defences. All in all, we're not an easy target, if the demons even manage to find us."

Maddy's mouth fell open as the van hopped and wobbled over the uneven ground. The trees continued to thin out, until the van entered a massive stretch of open ground punctuated by wooden spikes, trenches, and other fortifications. At the end of the killing field was a grassy hill with a castle.

This wasn't Portsmouth.

"Home sweet home," said Damien, switching off the engine. "Hope you like fish."

Maddy turned her head and saw a massive lake surrounded by people fishing. Further back was a village with dozens of wooden huts and twice as many tents. It was a second dark age, but it was beautiful.

"I can't believe this place. It's paradise."

Damien chuckled. "Let's see what you think when it's your turn to empty the latrines."

Maddy got out of the van. Hundreds of strangers came to greet her.

6

The cottage had been near the road, obscured by thick privet hedges and overgrown bushes, a small place that looked to have been abandoned long before the end of the world. The timber frames were rotten but still intact. The thatched roof was patchy but more or less whole. Mass and his companions had staggered inside almost a week ago, leaving behind a trail of blood.

Mass had collapsed onto the dusty wooden floor, causing Addy and Tox to drag him into an old rocking chair in the corner. The gentle rocking had made him nauseous, but it was better than the floor. "I-I'm hurt bad," he had said.

Tox was hurting too, but his concern was all for Mass. "We need to stop this bleeding. Damn it!"

Addy started searching the cottage, shoving aside the women who had returned to their frightened inactivity. The only one still alert was Maria, and she went to Mass and started examining his wounds. "I'm a nurse."

Mass chuckled. "Must be my lucky day."

"Your shoulder is a mess. I think the arteries are still intact, but there's significant damage to the smaller blood vessels. We need to get this wound closed before you pass out and die."

"Yeah, we should definitely do that."

Addy returned from her search, swearing. "There's nothing here. The place is empty."

Tox limped towards the door. "I'll head out and find supplies."

Mass put a hand up. "No, you're hurt too. We need to rest."

"If we do nothing," said Maria, "you might die."

Mass studied her. She had tanned skin and dark hair. "Only *might*?"

"I'm a nurse, not a doctor. There's no excess blood, which is a good sign, but the damage is bad and you could still bleed out slowly. Then there's the massive risk of infection. We need alcohol, a sewing kit, anything we can use to sterilise and close your wounds."

"I'm heading out," said Tox, opening the door.

Mass continued arguing. "I can't have you risking yourself for me."

"That's the job description, boss. We risk our arses for the good of others. I won't let a bad day at the office affect me. I may be hurt, but I'm not dying. I'll hit the nearest village and raid the pharmacy. Failing that, I'll find the nearest pub or restaurant and grab some whiskey and a first aid kit. I'll be back before you know it. Piece of piss."

"I'll go with you," said Smithy. "Just in case you need a hand."

Tox shrugged. "I don't plan on being long."

"I don't like being cooped up. I'd prefer the fresh air."

Mass sighed and waved a hand to give permission. "Don't go far, you two. It's not worth the risk."

Tox and Smithy closed the door behind them and left.

That had been a week ago.

Tox and Smithy hadn't returned. Mass was now too weak to move. The people in the cottage were hungry, exhausted, and injured. The only reason they had survived the week was because the cottage had a blessedly full hot water cylinder, and its garden was littered with spoiling-yet-edible apples and plums that had fallen from a pair of trees. The women had cleared up a little and made the place a home, but the only one left with any fighting ability was Addy. If demons found them, they would have no chance of survival. That Tox and Smithy hadn't returned suggested the enemy was nearby. They had waited too long for their return. If they had left after a couple of days, Mass might've had the strength to travel, but now...

"I have to get the women out of here," said Addy. She'd been saying the same thing for the last two days. Despite Mass telling her to leave, she hadn't.

"You need to leave today, Addy. No more waiting on me. I'm not going to get any better."

"You just need to rest a little longer."

"Addy! I'm done, and if you wait for me to die, you'll just increase your chances of joining me. Leave now. That's an order."

She raised an eyebrow at him. "An order?"

"Inside this cottage, I'm still team leader. I'm the one with the biggest bollocks."

"Yeah, you look very manly slumped in grandma's rocking chair."

He managed a smile and thought it would probably be his last. "I went down fighting, Addy. I'm okay with that. We've lost a lot of guys, but the Urban Vampires are alive and kicking so long as you're okay. Go, Addy, seriously. When you get back to Portsmouth, you and Cullen can fight over who's in charge."

"But—"

"Go! Get out of here before I throw you out. My runtime's over and I want to be alone. End of movie."

Addy opened her mouth to argue but turned away. She shouted at the women to get moving, then yanked open the front door without turning back. She was finally leaving him to die. Mass was relieved, even when he caught the glint of tears in Addy's eyes. Walking through the door was a goodbye that neither of them wanted. All the same, she opened the door wide.

A stranger stood on the doorstep.

Addy only had her knife, but she produced it in no time at all, slipping it out of her belt and placing it under the stranger's throat. The stranger didn't flinch. In fact, the peculiar man stepped inside the cottage without the slightest concern. "I do not seek to do you people harm. Weapons are unnecessary."

"I'll be the judge of that," said Addy.

"Addy! Put down the knife." Tox limped inside the cottage. Smithy was with him, helping him along. "This is Rick. He saved us."

"Dude's a bit weird," said Smithy, grinning, "but he's a good egg. It's good to see you guys."

Mass struggled to see, his vision blurry, but he vaguely recognised the stranger with Addy's pressed knife against his throat. "You entered the gate with Vamps. Rick... Rick Bastion?"

"Things went badly for your friend. Vamps was brave, but no match for Crimolok."

Mass nodded dismissively, not wanting to talk about such things. "I know what happened to my friend, but what are you doing here?"

"I'm here to help mankind win this war."

"Yeah, okay, fair enough."

SMITHY EXPLAINED the events of the past week so rapidly that he had to start again. "So, yeah, we, um, found this pub a couple hours after we left the cottage – Nailor's Arms, it was. Nice place with loads of guest ales and a specials menu behind the bar. Anyway, inside we found a pair of first aid kits, dishcloths, and as much alcohol as we could carry. It was a perfect score, man."

Tox nodded. "It was. We expected to be right back here with everything we needed."

Smithy continued, excitement in his voice. "Then this hobo with a shotgun appears from out of nowhere and shoots Tox right in the shin – almost takes his leg off at the knee. I almost puked, I swear."

"I was bleeding out fast," said Tox, grimacing at the memory, "and the fucker would have shot me again if Smithy hadn't brained him with a bottle of Irish cream."

"It was Tia Maria."

"Oh, I thought it was Baileys."

Smithy shook his head. "Nah, it was definitely Tia M—"

"Not important," said Mass. He glanced at Tox's leg. His friend was limping, but his limb was intact. His jeans were ragged and covered in blood. "How did you survive a shotgun blast?"

"I wouldn't have," said Tox. "The gunshot attracted demons and they surrounded the pub. They would have got in, but they all vanished."

"Vanished?"

Smithy and Tox both looked at Rick, who gave no response. After a moment, he acknowledged that they wanted his input and sighed. "This body can only endure so much," he said, "but I can exorcise nearby demons to Hell. It is... draining. As is the act of healing. I helped your friend, but it took a lot out of me. I needed a day to rest."

Mass slumped in the rocking chair, his head moving closer to his knees. He was so tired. So cold. His words were slow and soaked with saliva when he spoke. "I wish I could say it all sounds like... like nonsense, but I'm talking to a guy who's been to Hell and back. Tox, how come it took you a week to get back here?"

Tox leant against the wall, taking the weight off his leg. "That was my fault. Rick kept me from dying, but my leg didn't get better straight away. It was like accelerated healing or something, not instant. Each day my leg hurt a little less and looked a little better until, eventually, I could walk again."

"What about the old guy who shot you?"

Smithy chuckled. "Bryan. We tied him to the pub's fruit machine until he calmed down, which took about three bloody days. We asked him to come with us when we left, but the guy's missing the marble from his Screwball Scramble – a complete loon. We left him alone at the pub. I reckon his plan is to drink out the last of his days in peace. Not the worst idea." He looked at Tox wistfully. "I miss Bryan."

Tox sighed. "Yeah. Yeah, me too."

"We came back as soon as we could," said Smithy. "I could have come alone sooner, but I didn't want to leave Tox behind with Jesus mark two."

Rick looked at him, the slightest of frowns upon his face. "You did not trust me?"

"No offence, but you're a tad emotionless, the kind of guy who would work at McDonalds and piss in the milkshake machine when nobody was watching."

Rick shrugged, uninterested.

"Anyway, we're back now," said Tox. "I was worried we took too long. I thought for sure..."

Mass could barely keep his eyes open. "You made it back just in time to say goodbye. I'm glad... I'm glad you're okay. Now... go."

"Not without you, man. I got the thing you need." Tox gave Rick an assenting nod and the former pop star approached Mass with his hands outstretched like he was coming in for a grope.

Mass shifted, almost falling forward out of the rocking chair. "W-What are you doing?"

"Helping you. I'm afraid this will hurt a lot."

It hurt worse.

ANOTHER DAY PASSED. An agonising stream of time, punctuated by Mass's healing body crying out as the cells in his body stitched themselves back together. It was an otherworldly experience, happening so fast that he could swear he saw his flesh knitting back together before his very eyes. The pain was immense.

Everyone sat around anxiously, watching Mass, soothing him and holding him, telling him that everything was all right. He felt like a smackhead being nursed through recovery. His brow sweated, he begged constantly for relief, and yet nobody could do a damn thing to help except bear witness to his soul-destroying agony. "Can't you do anything?" Mass heard Addy demand of Rick several times, but each time the peculiar man said no.

Smithy always seemed to be sitting close by, most often on the second step of the cottage's rickety staircase. His knee juddered up and down ceaselessly, his chin resting on his hand. Concern or boredom, Mass was unsure. The constant, jittery movement was annoying either way.

When Tox and Smithy had returned with Rick, they had brought food and water from the pub. The pork scratchings, salted peanuts, and plain crisps had kept everyone going, but morale was low. Mass's pain was bringing everybody down. Their isolation in the middle of nowhere was sending them insane. Mass thought constantly about what he had released when he had killed Vamps. He thought about the giant gate and what monstrous being might emerge from it. Perhaps a devourer of worlds like the giant squid monster he'd once read about in a dreary old book – probably the last book he'd ever read, the one to put him off the activity altogether.

Lovecraft. That was the dude. Boring old shit. I should have stuck to gangster novels.

Mass wasn't exactly sure when it happened, but he suddenly felt better. After so much pain, the lack of it came like a mirage in a white-hot desert. He almost didn't believe it at first, but then he realised he felt okay. "I-I'm better."

Everyone in the room jolted, and he realised it was because he had barely spoken since Rick had laid hands on him. It was Rick who replied. "Good. We must go soon. Crimolok will be planning mankind's demise."

"Yeah, okay, Batman," said Smithy. "Let the poor bastard catch a breath before we ask him to jump out the nest. Mass, you look better, but don't rush it, okay?"

Mass took a deep breath and tried to get a sense of himself.

There was a sharp pinch in his trapezius, but it wasn't debilitating. His chest was a little tight, like he had asthma or a twenty-a-day habit, but there was no pain. "I-I think I can stand. Someone, help me up."

Tox came forward, no longer limping. He offered an arm. "I got you, brother."

Mass pulled himself up and felt light on his feet, not as if he had lost weight, but more as if his body had been filled with helium. He took a step and stumbled, but then got his balance. "I'm ready to get out of here," he said. "The next face I want to see is General Wickstaff's, followed by a bottle of the strongest booze she has in her private stash. She and I have a lot to talk about."

Addy grinned. "She'd better promote you to top banana after the shit we've been through."

Mass doubted it. They'd done nothing but go from one disaster to another since leaving Portsmouth well over a week ago. They'd made things worse, not better. Mass was just grateful to be alive. It gave him a chance to make up for his mistakes. "Let's just focus on getting back home."

Smithy patted Mass on the back. "Glad to see you back on your feet, big guy."

Mass went to the door and yanked it open. "Everyone, fall out."

TONY and his men encountered the Urban Vampires further along the road than expected, but it only made the plan run more smoothly. The ragtag band of warriors appeared late in the day, claiming to be conducting their own search for Mass. No rational argument existed against combining forces, so after a small show of reluctance, Tony accepted their presence. He tried not to reveal his satisfaction as he exchanged a handshake with the man he'd arranged all this with beforehand. Cullen was ready to do whatever was necessary to ensure Mass's eventual safety – and had promised to keep Tony alive too if his men turned on him. In the meantime, they would assume the roles of uneasy allies.

"We don't have to mix," said Cullen, feigning derision as he spoke with Tony, "but it makes sense to stick close to each other. There's safety in numbers out here."

Tony pretended to mull it over before nodding. "I see no valid reason not to work together, seeing as our mission is the same. I understand that your man Mass was clearing an area south of the Wessex Downs. Is that correct to your understanding?"

Cullen nodded. "We've been working to secure Oxford, along with the areas south and west of it. We were making good headway, which is why it's strange that Mass never made it back. He left Portsmouth armed to the teeth with a dozen Vampires along for the ride. Not to mention our girl, Addy, who's tougher than the lot of 'em put together."

"Addy? That her surname?"

"Yeah, Addison. Urban Vampires don't go by first names. Most of us are running away from who we were, so we give ourselves nicknames. New name, new start."

"I used to be a sergeant," said Tony. "Never thought I'd ever be anything else – certainly not a sodding colonel. I suppose we're all different people nowadays. Probably the only way to keep the past from swallowing us up. We've lost a lot. Everything, really."

Cullen nodded. "Once we find Mass, we can chat about that some more."

Tony side-eyed his men, searching for tells. He didn't know for certain that they had an agenda, and his inherent trust in the brotherhood of fighting men made it difficult for him to condemn them. Cullen could order his men to raise their shotguns and deal with the threat right now, but there was too much risk that some, or even all, of the men were innocent.

"Shall we get going... um, sorry, what was your rank, Cullen?"

"Don't have one. Urban Vampires are a family, not a unit."

Tony detected the eye-rolls of his men, but he couldn't chastise them. "Right, well, shall we make a move? The afternoon's showing us its arse, and I don't want to get caught in the open when night falls."

Cullen waved a hand. "Lead the way, Colonel. We'll trail back a few and watch your tail."

Tony pretended to consider things once again. He needed to act as though he were suspicious of this man and his 'family'. "Not planning on shooting us in the back, are you, Mr Cullen?"

Cullen chortled and shared a laugh with his Vampires. "That might be how you operate, Colonel, but if I want a man dead, I look him in the eye first. I thought we were on the same side. You doubt it?"

"It's my job to doubt, Mr Cullen. The safety of my men depends upon it."

Cullen bowed slightly. "I promise I won't shoot you in the back. I just want to find out what happened to Mass and his team."

Satisfied, Tony got moving, and just like that, he had embedded his own secret bodyguard. It pained him to anticipate a bloodbath, but in war you had to secure the things of most value. Mass, and hopefully Tony himself, was of high value. Thomas's hand-picked men were not, and Cullen was ready to take them down the moment they even hinted at betrayal.

I hope you're everything they make you out to be, Mass, because my bollocks are on the line trying to keep you alive.

Hopefully, Diane was busy taking care of things back in Portsmouth, but no matter what happened in the days ahead, Thomas had an army behind him. It would take a lot of effort and luck to bring him down.

And how was Maddy doing? Had she made it to Kielder Forest? Was she still aboard *The Hatchet*? Was she dead? Tony hadn't known the woman long – and was under no doubt that she and Wickstaff had been an item – but he liked her a lot. Their brief exchanges had been the only times he'd felt more man than soldier. Maddy reminded him there was more to living than fighting to stay alive.

I hope you're okay, lass, wherever you are.

The road ahead opened up. Wrecked vehicles cluttered the verge, most likely shoved there by Urban Vampires on prior missions, but the way forward was mostly unimpeded. Because of Mass's previous hard work, Tony and his men were able to march at a decent clip without any of the fatigue uneven ground would have caused them. Tony considered rustling up a pair of vehicles but then reconsidered. Far easier to track a target on foot, and too easy to miss clues when whizzing by in a vehicle. It would also give his men too much scope to lose their tail, speeding away and leaving Cullen's contingent in their dust. No, slow and steady would win this race. They needed to comb the land cautiously, seeking signs that Mass and his men had been through this way, as well as searching for the reasons they hadn't returned. The last thing Tony needed was a demon ambush striking at their arses. They needed to keep all dangers securely ahead if they were to retain the ability to leg it back to Portsmouth.

As if to cement Tony's concerns, they encountered a demon around the very next bend. It was alive, but injured. The burnt man staggered along the road, right arm flapping uselessly against its hip. When it spotted the humans, it gave a zombie-like moan and called out, "Eat shit. Eat shit. Eat shit!"

The men chuckled. Demons often shouted things or mumbled this and that. In Portsmouth, people laughed about such things while playing cards or sharing a beer. Theories went that the demons spouted memories of their former selves. It made a certain sense. Tony had heard them call out all kinds of things, including a few Latin words, which he was mildly familiar with only because so many British Army mottos employed the language. The old Sandhurst brass had also enjoyed their dead languages, especially to share private jokes between themselves after a night in the officer's lounge – and usually at the expense of whichever poor squaddie was trying to please them. Tony missed many things, but thoroughbred officers wasn't one of them. Men should earn their promotions on the field. You had to earn the right to send other men to their deaths.

Tony gave a hand signal to his squad sergeant – a man with thick black stubble named Pearson – and ordered him to gun down the solitary demon. A single shot leapt from Pearson's rifle and the demon collapsed on the road. No one rushed to check it was dead, but when they passed, Tony gave it a nudge with his boot. The shot had taken the demon right through the heart. Pearson was an excellent shot. Thomas had sent his best men.

Tony looked back and threw up his hand, signalling to Cullen, a hundred metres back, that everything was okay, no reason for twisted knickers. Then they resumed their march, rounding the bend and finding the next stretch of road clear of further monsters. No vehicles littered the verges on this stretch either, yet several dark patches stained the tarmac.

Bodies.

"What do we have here?" Tony muttered. "Stay alert, lads."

Tony assumed the bodies were human, but once he got closer, it became clear they were actually dead demons, seemingly bludgeoned to death. Had Mass and his men been through here? Who else could have taken down a dozen demons in hand-to-hand combat like this? A bloodstained rock the size of a melon lay nearby.

No sign of Mass though.

Tony scratched at his forehead, peeling off grime with his fingernails. He voiced his thoughts. "Cullen said Mass's team left armed to the teeth, so why are none of these demons shot?"

"Hey, Colonel, eyes on this!" Pearson pointed down the embankment on the right-hand side of the road. "We're looking for a bus, right?"

Tony approached the sergeant and peered down the embankment. In a ditch at the bottom lay a muddy white coach. It was lying on its side and its windows were cracked and caked in gore. Bloody smears marked the bodywork and obscured whatever lettering had been printed on the side – the groping of demons trying to get in. Tony told his men to stand ready while they waited for Cullen and his team to catch up. They should see this. A demon named David had said Mass was in a 'fallen wagon.' Could this bus be it?

Cullen approached a moment later with his shotgun raised, eyeballing Tony suspiciously. "Everything good?"

"There's a coach in the ditch. Is it one of your vehicles?"

Cullen peered into the ditch and then shook his head. "I've never seen it before. Mass set out in a van, not a bus."

"The intel we received about Mass said he was trapped inside a bus. I'm afraid this could be it." He started down the embankment, wanting to check things out further. "We need to take a look."

"I'll come with you," said Cullen, lowering his shotgun.

At the bottom of the ditch, the two of them positioned themselves behind the overturned coach and began a whispered conversation while they peered inside the broken windows. No one was inside. No bodies.

"How're things going?" asked Cullen. "Still reckon there's a price on your 'ead?"

Tony sighed. "Used to be I could read a man in the time it took to lace up my boots. Lately though, I don't know a fart from a flute. It disappoints me, after all we've been through, that men like Thomas can still make pawns of us all."

Cullen shrugged one shoulder and pulled a face. "The world has changed but people haven't – maybe they never will. There'll always be good guys and bad guys, and we have a part to play in which side wins."

"I'm glad you've got my back, Cullen. If this coach belonged to Mass and his team, we might be getting close. There're no bodies inside, which means there's still hope of finding Mass and his team alive. Let's get back to the road. We'll make camp and resume our search at dawn."

"Roger that, Colonel."

Cullen trudged up the embankment and Tony followed

behind. He glanced back at the smashed-up coach several times, wondering what had become of the people who had been inside it.

CRIMOLOK SENSES FRESH PREY. Although he is a being above such petty emotions as joy or excitement, he is savouring the methodical, merciless hunt of mankind. His desire to rid the universe of humanity is coming to fruition, but there is no rush. To Crimolok, time is a glacier.

A nest of humans festers nearby, their stink unmistakable. Already, his legions are drenched with death, deformed bodies covered in chunks of gore and filth. Their hunger is endless. With Crimolok's tendrils deep inside their minds, they are bestial.

Crimolok senses something else besides human meat. Something ancient – as ancient as he. The sickly scent of an adversary washes over him, a creature from the other place – the place where Crimolok was born at the beginning of time.

MASS HAD NEVER EXPECTED to ever take another breath outside again. He'd been certain of dying inside that dreary old cottage, but instead he'd been saved. Rick Bastion, once a cheesy one-hit pop star, had appeared and healed him like a modern-day Jesus. And Mass didn't just feel healed, he felt renewed, as if brand new cells had replaced the old. He'd been reborn. The women were doing better, too, which was good to see. For all he knew, they could have been playthings for Nas and his sick followers since day one. He had to get them back to Portsmouth. They deserved to be safe.

"Maria," he said to the woman who'd become the unofficial spokesperson for the rescued females, "keep the ladies in the middle while we march. I'll take the lead with Rick. Addy, Smithy, and Tox will take the rear. You'll be safe."

Maria nodded, but who knew if she believed him or not. They had no weapons and no vehicle. If any more demons stalked the vicinity, they'd be forced to fight hand-to-hand – and he wasn't sure they could pull off a miracle for a second time. While Mass felt renewed and energetic, everyone else was clearly fatigued. They'd eaten, but not enough. They'd slept, but not enough. And now they were back on the road, miles from safety.

"We'll go as far as we can make it today," he told everyone, "and then find someplace to rest for the night. Any luck, we'll reach Portsmouth by tomorrow evening."

"Luck is an empty notion," said Rick, but everyone ignored him.

The women smiled and exchanged glances with one another, while Addy and Tox closed their eyes as if imagining their return. Smithy chuckled. "Can't wait to visit the arcades and get an ice cream. Hey, do they still have those grabber machines with the teddies? Shitting things are fixed if you ask me."

"Portsmouth's changed a lot recently," said Addy, "but the seagulls still steal your chips."

They formed up on the road and reached a steady pace. Their footsteps echoed quietly. Trees swayed on either side of them. It was getting colder as winter closed in, but today was mild bordering on pleasant. Growing up on the streets of London gave Mass an appreciation of everything green, and perhaps his happiest childhood memory was going to London Zoo with his mum. Until that point, he'd thought life was only paved and covered in graffiti. Regent's Park had blown his mind. It pained him that he wouldn't ever raise his own family and take them to a zoo. He'd lost things he hadn't even realised he'd lost.

We've all lost so much.

He focused on the road ahead, but they didn't make it half a mile before the group halted in the middle of the road.

Smithy looked around with a confused look on his face. "Did anyone else feel that?"

Mass had definitely felt something, like the ground itself had shifted beneath his feet. Even now he could sense a mild thrumming in the soles of his boots.

The ground shook again. It wasn't a full-on quake, more a subtle wavering. If they hadn't been marching in silence, they might never have noticed.

The ground shook a third time.

"Okay," said Smithy, "I feel like a T-Rex is about to burst out of the trees and fuck us up. The ground is shaking, right?"

The ground shook again.

Mass looked around, worried by the threat he didn't see. "We don't know what's happening, but it doesn't change what we need to do. Move!"

They resumed marching, this time at a quicker pace, but the tremors kept on coming. In fact, they seemed to grow more intense. Was something getting closer? Something that had spewed forth from the giant gate Mass's actions had summoned?

The question answered itself.

Maria was the one who screamed first. She pointed down the road behind them, to where the tarmac met the sky.

Smithy's eyes opened wide. "Holy shitting Cheerios!"

Mass's blood ran cold. This was all his fault. This was the consequence of his actions. The word 'colossal' came to mind. The beast on the horizon was massive, and it moved like something out of a CGI-dominated monster movie. It was impossible to comprehend. Beautiful and terrifying at the same time.

"I-I read this thing about Godzilla once," said Smithy, a hand over his mouth in an expression of shock. "It said gravity makes giant creatures impossible because they would be too heavy to move their own limbs. What a crock of shit. Look at that thing."

"It's Crimolok," said Rick in a voice devoid of emotion besides an underlying, loathsome hatred. "The fiend has escaped its mortal prison and arrived in its true form. We are not prepared for this confrontation."

"No shit," said Smithy. "That thing's ball sack could crush a Ford Fiesta. We need to get the hell out of here."

The magnitude of what Mass had done rooted him to the spot. How many people had he doomed, or at the very least endangered, with his actions? This monstrosity had arrived because of him. Because he had freed his friend Vamps.

Was this what you were holding onto? This is the thing that was tearing you apart from the inside?

The ground shook with every step the giant took. The trees swayed. Hedges rustled. Birds fled. Demons swarmed into view. The monster had brought an army.

Smithy grabbed Mass by his biceps. "Come on, man. We need to get out of here. Must go faster, yeah?"

The group got moving, each of them sprinting down the road despite their exhaustion. The ground shook like the surface of a drum. The wild screeching of murder-thirsty demons filled the air, getting closer. Portsmouth had never felt so far away.

"Into the hedges," shouted Addy, hustling the women along. "We need to lose them."

Mass nodded. "Everyone, move!"

The demons were three hundred metres away, but gaining fast. The primates at the front of the pack were too quick to outrun over long distances. Addy was right, their only chance was losing the demons in the hedges, but even that might not be enough. They were thin, merely a border between the road and adjacent fields. In the distance there seemed to be some kind of industrial yard, with cranes and heavy machinery, but they would never make it there in time.

"Damn it!" Tox looked around frantically and picked up a fallen tree branch. It wouldn't save his life, but at least he could go down swinging. The first demons broke through the hedges and entered the field, whipping up a whirlwind of twigs and crunching leaves.

Mass started gathering the others. "Everyone, group together. Maria, get the women behind us."

"We're fucked," said Tox. "Every time it looks like we might catch a breather, things get worse."

"Keep calm," said Rick.

"And carry on," said Smithy.

Mass planted his feet and prepared to meet the enemy. "When has it ever been different, Tox? Life was a marathon with two broken legs and a bent neck before the demons even got here. I've been fighting my entire life."

"If the world has always been shitty," said Smithy, "what's the point of trying to save it?"

Mass eyed the hedges, waiting for more enemies to emerge. "Because for every piece-of-shit drug dealer and gangbanger that used to be on the estate, there was a Mrs Gardner or a Mr Zebrowski."

Smithy raised an eyebrow. "Weren't they *Postman Pat* characters?"

"Mrs Gardner was my Year Nine English teacher, who sat with me during detention and finally taught me how to read like all the other kids. Mr Zebrowski was the window cleaner on our estate. Whenever he saw me getting my ass handed to me, he would step in and chase the fuckers off, even though he was just this skinny Polish dude that barely spoke any English. He taught me what bravery was – risking yourself to help someone when you could just as easily look away. Those are the people I'm fighting for, Smithy. You feel me?"

Smithy nodded, serious for once. "Yeah, man, I feel you. For Mr Zebrowski, right?"

Mass gave his friend a fist bump and prepared to meet his fate. The demons broke through the hedges, ferocious and unstoppable.

Rick stepped forward and threw up a hand. A primate made a beeline for Tox, but then it folded in on itself, its malformed spine arching backwards and snapping. A plume of jet-black smoke erupted from its mouth and spiralled upwards, knocking aside branches and leaves like it had physical substance. Then Rick swept his arm horizontally and summoned a gale, sweeping everything up in its path. Half a dozen demons went tumbling through the air.

Rick glanced back at his companions. "I shall hold them here while you make it back to the road and escape. It is unlikely to work, but I will do my best."

Smithy shook his head. "Man, you're insane. You can't fight them all on your—"

Rick's eyes crackled, and something akin to electricity flowed through them. "Go or die!"

Another wave of demons crashed into the field. Rick threw out both hands, causing the demons to twist and transform into black vapour. Hundreds more came. Mass ordered everyone back to the road, giving Rick one last glance before bolting. The strange man was busy conducting a supernatural orchestra, hands directing back and forth.

What the hell is he? He's not human.

I don't even think he's Rick.

They were back on the road in seconds, while the demons continued swarming into the trees, not realising their prey had changed its course. Miraculously, the road was clear, and the only visible threat was the gigantic monstrosity stomping along the horizon. Its casualness was its weakness. If it hurried, it would've spotted their retreat.

Mass urged everyone to run, and they didn't need convincing. The road was long and straight, which was less ideal than a twisty one with branching paths. It meant that even after outdistancing Crimolok by a quarter-mile, they still weren't in the clear.

A primate spotted their retreat. It spilled out of the trees and back onto the road, its screeching alerting its brothers.

"They're coming," said Tox. "They're back on the road."

"Thanks for nothing, Rick," said Tox. "Goddamn Harry Potter wannabe."

Addy shook her head resignedly. "Hey, at least we got to see a magic show before we died."

"I'd have preferred a lap dance," said Smithy.

Mass planted his feet and stopped running. "Maria, you and the women keep going. Soon as the road bends, try to get out of sight."

Maria thanked him and fled with the women. Once again, Mass stood shoulder to shoulder with his Urban Vampires, ready to do what they all knew needed to be done. Dying was part of the job.

The massive creature on the horizon seemed to sense their location. It turned slightly, massive eyes gazing in their direction like unlit spotlights. The number of demons multiplied, spilling out of the trees in their dozens. They gathered rapidly, filling the road and creating a wall of gnashing teeth and ripping claws. Then, as one, they let out a bloodcurdling screech.

Mass and the others covered their ears, trying to keep from being deafened. Perhaps it was intended to distract them, because at the same time the demons began their charge, rapidly closing the fifty metres of space left between them and their prey. Mass felt like a Roman legionary facing down hordes of barbarians – but Rome had fallen to ruin.

Mass forced himself to stand his ground. His bladder loosened and he only just caught it in time. No doubt he would piss himself soon. He looked left and right, wondering if his companions were experiencing the same terror and numbness in their veins that he was. It made him proud that none of them ran. They faced the monsters together.

The demons came in a deranged sprint. It was insane how much Mass hated them – far more than he'd ever hated the bastards who'd battered him as a kid on the estate. These were the monsters who had taken everything from him – his friends, Ravy, Gingerbread, and Vamps. Mass couldn't believe he'd outlasted them all, and he would welcome his death if it meant seeing them again. He just wanted to take down as many demons as he could first.

"Fuck this!" Mass broke away from his friends and charged the incoming enemy. He heard Tox shout after him, but then, to his surprise, his companions followed his lead. Suddenly, the four of them were charging down a hundred demons. It was Mass's proudest moment and a great way to die.

THE WORLD EXPLODED. The sky turned red. A coppery scent grew into an unbearable stench.

Mass threw himself at a primate but missed as it flew backwards out of his grasp. A flaming hole had erupted in the side of its head. Confused, Mass recovered and swung his fists, but his next target slumped to the ground before he could even make contact. More demons fell, not one at a time but in twos and threes. The vile horde wavered, gaps opening up in the onrushing multitude as bodies hit the road. Mass stood like a statue, covered in bloody mist and pieces of meat. For a moment, he thought God had rained thunderbolts from the sky. Then he recognised the mocking chatter of rifle fire and the angry bark of shotguns.

"Soldiers," said Smithy, putting a hand on Mass's shoulder and yanking him out of the fray. "Mofos came out of nowhere like the shitting riders of Rohan."

Mass looked. Twenty, maybe thirty soldiers had lined up across the road. Professional and fearless, they fired their shotguns and rifles as quickly as they could, and they reloaded proficiently without the slightest of fumbles. Some men, those dressed in military fatigues, were complete strangers, but others Mass knew well. He briefly made eye contact with Cullen and the two of them nodded.

The Urban Vampires had arrived – and they were packing heat.

7

General Thomas gave Colonel Cross a passing thought. Was he still out there, searching for that imbecilic thug with the ridiculous name, or was he dead in a ditch somewhere with a bullet in his head? No matter which, the troublesome colonel was out of the way. Either Tony would return alive and well, recommitted to what Thomas was trying to achieve – the liberation of Great Britain – or he would die out there and never be heard from again.

The enemy was on the ropes. Wickstaff had defeated a great number of their foe, but it was Thomas's duty to mop up what remained. Only a fool would allow their enemy time to regroup. Not that Thomas was naive enough to consider a scattered enemy an easy prospect – the Yanks had learned that lesson in Vietnam. Sometimes, letting two amassed armies fight it out to the death was worth the risk. To the victor go the spoils, as they say. The demons – if he must call them that – were disorganised, and deadly because of it. Unlike humans, an isolated group of demons did not lose hope or seek safety from battle. Each would die happily if it meant butchering a human first. Portsmouth could not sit idly by and await a death by a thousand cuts. Every day, patrols discovered the bloody remains of an incautious soldier or foolhardy civilian. Recently, the demons had even been so bold as to attack a supply team returning from a supermarket distribution centre south of Oxford. Those demons had been quickly dispatched, but two good soldiers had lost their lives. If Portsmouth continued to operate with an enemy on its doorstep, a war of attrition would ensue. Losses on both sides would be constant and devastating. That was why Thomas would do what the German Confederation had done in the Middle East and Eastern Europe. Defence would turn to attack.

Time to hunt these bastards down once and for all.

In the forty-eight hours since Colonel Cross had departed, Thomas had been making preparations. Portsmouth was under martial law, and every single citizen was either a trained soldier or a hardy survivor. While Wickstaff had lacked standards, her people were brave and motivated – he had to give the woman that. It was a necessary evil to include them in the battles ahead, unwise to leave them behind in Portsmouth while his more loyal men departed for war. It was a balancing act. On the one hand, too many of Wickstaff's people at either Portsmouth or out in the field would threaten discipline and security. On the other hand, if he had to send men to their death in a fight against the demons, he would prefer it to be Wickstaff's people. Eventually, he decided to leave five thousand loyal veterans behind to police and protect Portsmouth, while the other ten thousand would go to war. Of Wickstaff's people, he took only five thousand and left behind ten thousand: the women, children, the weak, and the old. They would make good hostages if any kind of insurrection occurred in the field. He had tasked several dozen men with returning to Portsmouth upon his death to share the means and manner of such a tragedy. Any foul play, and Portsmouth would become a bloodbath.

No war has ever been won without contingencies.

To help manage the population, both military and civilian, Thomas had promoted several men to positions of high command. He was travelling to go and meet with them right now.

His orders would be concise, for time was of the essence, but everyone would be on the same page. A great army was to depart Portsmouth at first light tomorrow, setting out to reclaim their homeland. Great Britain would be reborn.

DIANE DIDN'T KNOW why she'd been summoned to what Thomas called the 'war room', but her strange new friend, Damien, assured her that everything was okay. Tom hadn't given up her role in the planned coup, nor had he shared her name with the people he'd recruited on her behalf. However, someone Tom trusted had clearly betrayed him, and despite Damien's assurances, Diane feared she was walking into a trap.

"Stop worrying," said Damien for the umpteenth time. The more she got used to his face, the more she noticed the tiny details. A thin scar dissected his right eyebrow and another sliced his bald head. His right wrist was ringed by a line of thickened flesh, like his hand had been cut off and reattached.

"Who are you, Damien? Where did you come from?"

"I'm a fighter like you, but if I told you where I came from, you wouldn't believe me. Not yet, anyway. The only thing you need to know is that the guy I work for disappeared and left me stuck here with nothing to do. I've spent the last couple of weeks in Portsmouth, trying to see where I fit in. I know what you've been doing, Diane, and I want to keep you alive long enough to succeed. Thomas doesn't have anything on you, so don't give him reason to think of you as anything other than a harmless girl. Just go in there and see what's on the cards."

"And what if it's bad?"

"I wish I could say I'd pull your arse out of the fire, but I didn't bring an army with me. Keep your cool, and be smart. It's your only option."

Diane tried to shoo the butterflies in her stomach, but they refused to retreat. In fact, they laid eggs and gave birth to caterpillars. Thomas had paid her zero interest since Wickstaff's death, but now he was suddenly summoning her to a meeting, and only a few short hours after executing Tom and his friends.

This can't end well.

If it looks like he's going to have me shot, I'll do everything I can to slice his throat open first.

She took a deep breath and tried to keep from shaking as she walked down the long hallway inside the port administration building. She entered by a door on the left and was surprised to find several people already inside. Commander Klein stood at the back of the room, and seeing his friendly face was a relief. The brief smile he gave her settled her nerves more than anything else could have. She approached the German and asked him why he was there.

"*Ze* answer alludes me also, Diane. Perhaps *ze* general wishes to have us all shot."

"Not funny. You saw what happened yesterday?"

"*Ja.* Let us not speak of it. Young Tom was a fine canasta player."

General Thomas entered the room through a separate door. Everyone – four men but no women besides Diane – stood to attention. She was no soldier, so she failed to salute the general. It earned her a glare. A bad start to whatever this was.

"Thank you for your presence," said Thomas, eyeballing each of them in turn. Klein behaved as if he had some place better to be. "I am sure you are wondering why I summoned you here. Each of you is now part of my executive cabinet. Commander Klein, I understand you don't like to acknowledge orders, but as you have possession of our only nuclear capabilities, it felt prudent to include you."

Commander Klein said nothing.

Thomas went around the room introducing the middle-aged white men one after another. "Colonel Wanstead is in charge of defence at Portsmouth. He will take control of security, law and order, et cetera."

Wanstead raised a hand briefly to say hello. He was a chubby man, which was a rarity these days with rationing in effect. Diane had seen him around base before, making himself heard whenever Thomas wasn't around. He always spoke slowly, each word perfectly pronounced. "It is an honour to receive such an important duty. I shall endeavour to carry out my obligations in an exemplary fashion."

Thomas pointed to the next man, thinner and taller than Wanstead, with a long nose that seemed custom-made for snobbishly probing the air. "Commander Morrissey, you shall command our navy. Your immediate orders are to appoint your own sub-commanders and separate the fleet into domestic and operational. You will also inherit the small fleet previously commanded by that treacherous Yank, Commander Tosco."

Morrissey sneered, making his already harsh face even harsher. "Less said about him the better, if you wish to hear my opinion, sir."

"Indeed."

Thomas turned to the remaining man, whose face was leathery and old. His eyes were a piercing grey. His lips were thin and pale. His neat brown hair suggested he held high standards for himself even during the apocalypse. Thomas spoke to him a little less abruptly than the others. "Colonel Livingstone, you are a veteran of countless skirmishes, more than I can name. Many would think you unkillable, and it is without question that you should take operational command of Portsmouth's ground forces. You will answer directly to me in the field."

Colonel Livingstone saluted. "It's an honour, sir. Might I enquire as to Colonel Cross's role in the battles ahead?"

It was a good question. Diane had been wondering herself why Tony hadn't been mentioned already. Wasn't he General Thomas's second in command? Thomas nodded as if he also considered it a good question. "Colonel Cross is conducting an important mission on behalf of Portsmouth. Upon his return, he will most likely work alongside me in executive planning.

Without him being here, however, I cannot confirm his place in events to come."

Diane didn't like the ambiguity of the statements. She knew Tony had left to search for Mass, but there was no way Thomas would want the Urban Vampires back in Portsmouth. Mass was a tough son of a bitch who wouldn't swallow Thomas's brand of bullshit. She suspected Tony's mission was intended to fail.

Thomas waved an arm. "Okay, men, dismissed."

The men began to file out of the room, which sparked Diane's anxiety and made her speak up. "Um... can I ask why you summoned *me* here, sir?"

"Ah, yes, Diane, I almost forgot you. You acted as General Wickstaff's head of security, yes?"

Diane nodded, which prompted Thomas to frown at her and tilt his head as if trying to hear her. "Y-Yes, sir. I was her bodyguard and head of security."

"Needless to say, you failed," said Colonel Livingstone, a smirk escaping his lips.

"She is just one woman," said Commander Klein, not bothering to make eye contact with anyone. "It is a miracle she protected Wickstaff as long as she did. I doubt anyone here would have done better, *ja?*"

Livingstone's smirk turned into a distasteful scowl. He was about to reply to Klein, but Thomas cut him off. "It is true, Diane had an impossible task. We live in the most dangerous of times, which is why I will take care of my own security from now on."

Diane swallowed. "Then why am I—"

"I wish for you to use your skills in another way. You know Portsmouth and its people, and you have a certain knack for remaining unnoticed. Why, you're just a tiny waif of a girl, aren't you?"

She wanted to kill him, but Damien's words kept echoing in her head. Don't give Thomas any reason to see her as anything but an unimportant girl.

"I-I will be useful wherever I can—"

"I want you to find those plotting rebellion. As you've undoubtedly seen, I dealt with several traitors yesterday, but I am under no illusion that there are more. The weeds must be yanked if Portsmouth is to ever truly flourish. You were close to Wickstaff, which means those loyal to her will instinctively trust you."

Diane's mouth was dry, and her voice came out in a croak. "I-I suppose so."

"May I ask you a question?"

All eyes in the room were on her as she nodded meekly. Inside, she was a cauldron of bubbling hatred.

"Diane, are you loyal to Portsmouth? Are you loyal to me?"

Every cell in her body yelled *no,* but if that word came out of her mouth, she'd catch a bullet in the skull. "You can trust me, sir. I swear."

How's fuck you, bastard, for swearing?

Thomas stared at her for a moment, then nodded. "Good. If you are truly loyal, then I expect a list of names in due course."

"Of course, sir."

"Dismissed."

Diane turned to leave, but Thomas called her back. "Understand me, young lady, Wickstaff might have been relaxed about a very many things, but I am a different breed of animal. When I dismiss you, I expect you to salute."

Diane had never given a salute in her life. She wasn't a member of the military, even with her recently gained ability to use a variety of firearms. Playing along was the smartest option, though, so she gave in. "I apologise, General Thomas." She snapped off her best attempt to emulate what she had seen others do. "Permission to be dismissed, sir?"

So I can go back to plotting your death?

Thomas nodded, and Diane left the room in a hurry, followed by the small group of middle-aged white men. She picked up speed and left them behind, not wanting to chat or even make eye contact. Considering how quickly she exited the port administration building, it was a surprise that Commander Klein caught up with her. He grabbed her arm and pulled her back a step. "Your anger is showing, Diane. I suggest you *verk* on that."

She glared at the German and shrugged her arm free of his grasp. "That piece of shit! That skinny, stuck-up piece of shit. He made me salute him, when all I want to do is shove a blade in his throat."

"War is a game, and Thomas has made his move. Now you must take time to consider yours." He put a finger to his lips to shush her. General Livingstone walked past, smirking at Diane and sharing a chuckle with himself. Usually, she would've asked him what he was fucking laughing at, but Klein gave her a warning stare not to do so.

Once they were alone again, Diane glared at Klein. "What's to consider? Thomas can piss right off if he thinks I'll rat out the people who want him dead."

"Then you shall be dead, *ja?* Do you not understand? Thomas has manoeuvred you into a situation you cannot *vin*. You either give up *ze* people you recruited, or turn up empty of hand and reveal your disloyalty. Either way, Thomas's enemies die."

"I'll say I couldn't find out who they were."

Klein rolled his eyes at her like she was a silly girl. It made her furious. "Thomas *vill* know you are lying. I suspect he already knows you are a traitor."

"Then why not just shoot me?"

"Perhaps he *vud* like more evidence before he executes another of Wickstaff's people. Or perhaps your squirming amuses him. I have known many men who enjoy such things."

Diane sighed. "I'm screwed then. I didn't even have a plan, but whatever hope I had of taking the bastard down has just gone up in smoke."

Klein shook his head and smiled at her like a mischievous grandpa. "Perhaps not. A *veek* enemy is still an enemy, and even a parting shot can still hit *ze* heart. Be calm, be patient, and make your move when you see it. You might have only *ze* one shot, so make it count."

Diane thought about it. "You're right. I know what to do. There's a reason I've survived this long when everyone I care about is dead."

Klein nodded and walked away.

IT WAS LATE in the day, and the demon attack had left everyone a little high on adrenaline, so they headed off-road and made camp. Mass had never met Colonel Cross before, but Cullen – a man whom he trusted completely – seemed unsettled by something. Mass needed to know what was going on before he was willing to travel the roads and risk being attacked by more demons. That giant beast still stalked the horizon and was no doubt sending out its hordes to find them.

They had found safety in a nearby field, pitching their tents at its centre. Mass and his companions had no equipment, but Cullen and the other Urban Vampires had brought along spares. The women had been allocated three tents, while Tox, Addy, Mass, and Smithy agreed to double up with other Vampires.

Being amongst his people again lifted Mass's spirits. All he had been doing lately was losing people, so to be surrounded by people he cared about again was an unexpected blessing. It didn't mean they were safe, but sitting in a green field as afternoon gave way to evening, Mass was at peace.

The women from the farm finally appeared hopeful. Until now, Portsmouth could have been a giant lie, but seeing twenty well-armed, well-fed soldiers made it all the more believable that there was a settlement nearby.

Cullen seemed like he wanted to talk, but he hadn't yet found an opportunity to get Mass alone. Colonel Cross and his men had pitched their tents in a semi-circle opposite those set up by Cullen's group. Mass didn't know if he was being rescued or guarded. If they hadn't been so shaken up by the attack, they could've been halfway to Portsmouth by now, but the risk was too great. In a straight chase, the demons would have caught them. And it wasn't only adrenaline that had exhausted Mass. When Rick had healed him, it had left him feeling reborn. Now, he felt heavy and depressed, like he just wanted to sleep.

Rick came and sat beside Mass on the grass. The peculiar man had lingered on the periphery for the last hour, staring off into the trees that bordered the field. Maybe he had demon radar. It wouldn't be surprising.

"Hey, Rick. What's up?"

"You will feel normal again soon," he said, and then added context. "I used life itself to heal you, which is why you felt so virile, but it has worn out your body's reserves and you need rest. Tomorrow, your strength shall return."

Mass nodded as if he understood, though he didn't really. "Thank you for what you did, Rick. We only met the once, and you were a weird dude *then*, but now... you seem different."

"I am different."

"So what the fuck are you?"

"An angel. An angel that brought you back from the brink of death. God's miracles exist, even now."

"An angel? I thought the angels were all a hundred feet tall."

"In their true forms, yes. This is not my true form."

Mass waited for more but received only silence. "Okay then. Good talking with you, man. Maybe when you get a minute, you can—"

"These men plot," Rick interrupted, staring at the assembled tents. "It pains me to see no change in humanity."

"Ain't that the truth."

Rick turned his gaze to Mass. "But you have changed, haven't you? You are a better man than you were. Did you follow your friend's example, or was it always in you?"

"Huh? You mean Vamps? Yeah, maybe it was him that caused me to change, but..." He shrugged. "I dunno, I kind of want to think it was all me. I grew up in a bad place surrounded by bad people. It's like being in prison. You can try to do good, but as soon as you do, you hit bars. Eventually, you stop reaching out and just accept your life inside a cell. If the end of the world did anything for me, it got rid of those bars."

Rick nodded. "I understand. Thank you." He stood up and walked away, back off into the field.

"Weird bloke."

Cullen caught Mass's eye from the next tent over, and his friend mouthed a word. It was unclear, but it seemed like he was saying '*be ready*'.

Colonel Cross appeared in front of Mass, unarmed and alone. "Can we speak for a moment, Mass?"

"Yeah, no probs." He stood with effort, bones creaking. "Shit, I feel like a bus hit me."

"I expect you've been though the mill. We can talk here if you'd like, but I thought it would be best to be away from anybody earwigging."

Mass put his hands on his lower back and groaned. "I doubt you plan on sharing anything good. Let's go over here a bit, but not too far. I don't trust you."

Colonel Cross didn't appear offended. In fact, he chuckled. "I've been told you were smart. Looks like it's true."

"I wouldn't go so far as smart, but I wasn't born yesterday, Colonel, that's for sure."

"Please, just Tony. I'm not even a colonel. I'm a sergeant at heart."

That made sense. Nothing about Colonel Cross suggested *officer*. He was a rough, no-nonsense type who seemed uncomfortable with formality. He reminded Mass of someone: Sergeant Honeywell.

Hope you're somewhere back with your family, Rich.

"Okay, Tony, let's get this over with before I collapse." Tony reached out to help Mass, but Mass waved him away. Slowly, they walked twenty metres from the nearest tent. "So what do you want to speak about, Tony?"

"Amanda Wickstaff."

"First name basis, huh? You must have made quite the—"

"She's dead."

Mass stumbled. Fortunately, Tony steadied him before he fell, which was good because he might not have made it up again. He glanced over at the tents, wondering if anyone had seen his weakness. It seemed like the coast was clear. "What d'you mean, she's dead? She can't be. I don't believe you."

"Your man Cullen will confirm it for you. He'll also confirm that she was murdered by my superior, General Thomas."

"Who?"

Tony sighed. "We can get into that later, but right now you need to know that I'm on your side. The men I brought with me aren't though. They were ordered to find and kill you. They still expect to carry out that mission."

"What the fuck? Why?"

"You were loyal to Wickstaff, and somewhat of a legend in Portsmouth. That makes you a threat to Thomas's leadership."

"A legend? A threat?" Mass shook his head. "I can barely walk. This is unbelievable. Wickstaff's really gone?"

Tony nodded.

"And some old prick has taken over Portsmouth?"

"Yes. Thomas was the commanding officer of what remained of our overseas forces. He returned to reclaim Great Britain."

"So where do you come in? Why are you helping me?"

"Because my days of killing on command are behind me. If I hadn't arranged for Cullen to meet me on the road, you would already be dead. It's created a stand-off, but my men will pull the trigger soon. They're just waiting for the right moment, and then they'll kill me too." He peered at the tents. This time, every man was watching. They were too interested in what should have looked like a simple chat between two men. Tony turned back to Mass. "Thomas blamed Wickstaff's murder on a demon that came to tell us you were in trouble, and about a place up north called Kielder Forest."

"Shit, David. Is he okay?"

Tony shook his head. "Its – *his* – body was cooling right next to Wickstaff's, part of Thomas's narrative that the demons sent an assassin. Can't question a dead demon."

"Nor a live one in most cases," said Mass, wondering how much longer his legs would keep him upright. "No offence, Tony, but you're a right soddin' downer. Do you have any good news? Tell me they've opened up a strip club in Portsmouth. Tell me they reopened McDonalds."

"I'm sorry, pal, but all I've got is bad news. The only good thing is we got Maddy out of the city before Thomas killed her too."

Mass pinched his nose and let out a sigh. "Shit, I didn't even think about her. Maddy and Wickstaff were close."

"Yeah, that much was obvious. Thomas planned on making her go away, but I got her out of there. She went north with Commander Tosco, hoping to find this settlement in the north. Are you aware of it?"

"Aware, but not convinced. David spoke about it – said there was a bunch of people holed up in some castle. I hope he was right, but me and my team never made it much further north than where we're standing now." Mass took a breath to summon strength, then told Tony about Nas and the farm they'd stumbled onto after being ambushed. He had lost most of his team but rescued a group of abused women. It wasn't a total loss.

Tony shook his head in disbelief. "Even now, bad men can't help themselves. That's why it's so important for you to survive, Mass. You and your people are the good guys. Take your men and get out of here. Go north and look for Maddy and this settlement in Kielder Forest. There needs to be a force remaining besides General Thomas. He's a tyrant that cannot go unopposed."

"No way, mate. I'm heading straight to Portsmouth to take his ass out."

"That would be extremely foolish. Thomas arrived with fifteen thousand of his own troops, and I imagine he is already politicking to gain the loyalty of Portsmouth as a whole."

Mass clenched his fists, and even that hurt. "He needs to pay. Wickstaff was no friend of mine, but I respected the hell out of her. She earned her place as leader, and I won't let some old-world elitist claim her place because he thinks he's entitled to it."

"I'll handle General Thomas," said Tony. "Diane and Commander Klein are both on board with removing him, but it's a long game and we need to be smart about it. Your talents are more of the—"

"Shooting things in the face variety?"

Tony put his hands up. "Hey, I'm not knocking it. My nature is no different, but I have direct access to Thomas; I need to be a little smarter than I'm naturally inclined to be. You can live to fight another day, Mass. If Diane and I fail at ridding the world of Thomas, there needs to be somebody left to oppose him."

Mass sighed. Tony could be right. All the people Mass cared about were here, more or less, so why shouldn't he leave? Did he really want to take them into danger? If a group existed in the north, then finding them was important enough to delay a reckoning, at least for a while. There was a bigger picture to think about.

That didn't stop me from killing Vamps and opening a giant gate. I'm not a big picture kind of guy.

Mass hadn't yet explained about the giant demon, and incredibly no one had asked. Things had just happened so quickly. He decided to explain now, but Tony held up a hand and stopped him. "We can talk things over and over, but right now, there are twelve men who are planning to shoot you. When they realise I'm not going to give the order, they'll go into business for themselves. You and I need to make a plan before then and be ready.

"Okay, if you have a good plan, I'm ready to hear it."

Tony nodded. "I do have one, but it's not foolproof."

"Then I guess we're a bunch of fools. What are you thinking?"

Tony told him. "How sneaky are you?"

TONY LAY IN HIS TENT, wide awake. His watch told him it was after ten, but no one really knew the time any more. He was knackered, having walked many miles that day, but the real deadweight was Mass. The muscled young man seemed exhausted to the point of coma.

After speaking with him earlier, Mass had become inexplicably weak, and Tony had needed to help him back to camp. Cullen and the others had taken him into their care, and he was now sleeping in a guarded tent. Eventually, Tony had ordered his own men to bed down for an early start, designating four sentries to keep watch in two-hour shifts. Eight hours of rest in the open was dangerous, but also peaceful. Birds chirped in the nearby trees, and somewhere a fox gave a demented mating call. Nature was alive and well, and so were they for now. The demons hadn't found them hiding, which suggested they had continued down the road. Were they heading to Portsmouth? Was that giant monstrosity bringing war?

Of course it is.

During the camp's brief downtime before bed, one of Mass's guys, Smithy, had told Tony about a massive gate opening, and the giant beast that had come through. The lad had been reluctant to share more, ending the conversation with, "Just demon funny business, ain't it?" Whatever the cause, a giant gate was bad news. The demons were back in force, and they had a leader. In the Middle East, the enemy had always been at its fiercest whenever led by one of the fallen – large, terrifying beasts that some claimed to be former angels. The one Tony had seen earlier on the horizon had been three times as big as any he'd ever seen. And it was likely to be a lot more than three times as dangerous.

Tony heard snoring from the nearby tents. Not from every man, but a few. The only people not in sleeping bags should be the guards on duty, but Tony could sense creeping footsteps coming from several directions. It might have been Cullen and his men – they were free to do as they wanted – but he doubted it.

This was his own men sneaking around. They were preparing to make their move.

No one had built a fire – it was mild, and they didn't want to risk giving away their location – but despite the lack of firelight, a shadow slid over Tony's tent. It was cast by the unobscured moon. He held his breath as someone pulled down the zipper. A face appeared in the gap. It was Sergeant Pearson.

"Colonel, you're needed outside."

Tony sat up as much as his small one-man tent would allow. "What's going on?"

"You need to come outside, sir. We've spotted a threat."

"Demons?"

"Yes, sir."

Tony shuffled out of his sleeping bag and crawled out of his tent. For a moment, it was pitch-black, but then his eyes adjusted and revealed the shapes of several men. His entire team was awake, rifles at the ready. "What's going on?" he demanded. "Why is everyone—"

"This way, sir," said Pearson. "Right over here. There's something at the treeline."

Tony hurried between the tents to the edge of the camp and searched for the trees, but it was too dark to see. No one had spotted a threat. It was a lie. Tony froze, not daring to turn around. "Sergeant Pearson, you have a rifle pointed at my back, don't you?"

"Nothing personal, Colonel, but I have my orders – and they supersede yours."

"Thomas ordered you to kill me?"

"Only if it seemed like you were planning to spare our target. Mass is still alive, sir, last I checked. You've disobeyed orders. I don't understand why, exactly, but that's none of my business."

Tony kept looking forward, but he risked a dismissive chuckle. "A dozen Urban Vampires joined us on the road. The mission got risky. What would you have done, Pearson? Drawn weapons and gunned them all down before they had a chance to react?"

"Exactly, and that's what's about to happen. I just wanted you to see the job done properly before I shoot you in the head. Turn around, Colonel. Slowly. Hands on your head."

Tony turned, fingers laced behind his skull. A rifle pointed at his chest, but he tried to ignore its presence. "This is a mistake, Pearson. We shouldn't be taking each other out. Thomas is a danger to us all, and you're doing his bidding."

"I'm just following orders. If we don't obey the chain of command, we're no better than the demons."

"I'm your superior officer, Pearson. Obey *me*."

Pearson sneered, his thick black stubble now almost a beard. "You might call yourself a colonel, but we both know it's a sham. Now, be a good boy and pay attention."

Tony watched, a grim feeling in his guts as the mutineers moved between the tents, pointing their rifles at the canvas walls. They planned on killing Cullen, Mass, and the rest of the Vampires in their sleep. Tony could shout a warning, but it would make no difference.

Pearson kept his eyes on Tony and gave the order. "Fire at will, lads."

Muzzle flashes lit up the night, illuminating the camp and tearing up the darkness. Tony saw shadowy lumps inside the canvas tents and winced at the damage being caused. He called out, begging Pearson to stop. Eventually, the sergeant put up a fist and called a halt. "Enough! Check the tents for anyone still alive; we'll have some fun with them."

Tony flexed his fingers behind his skull, scratching at the back of his neck, so angry that he needed to claw at flesh, even if it was his own. "You're a piece of shit, Pearson. I didn't know for sure that you would actually go through with it, but you did! You'll regret this butchery."

"Really? When will I regret it, exactly? After you're dead and I'm pissing on your corpse?"

"I think you'll regret it sooner."

Shotgun blasts lit up the darkness at the edges of the camp. Pearson's men – for they had never been Tony's – panicked as two of their number collapsed to the ground with gunshot wounds. Wraiths emerged from the shadows, blindsiding the men and making them panic. Within seconds, Pearson's soldiers were lying on the ground moaning, unconscious, or dead.

Tony yanked the 9mm semi-auto he'd tucked into the back of his collar and, at the same time, shoved away the rifle pointed at his chest. Before Pearson could react, Tony had the handgun placed under Pearson's chin. "Drop it, Sergeant, or I'll drop you."

Pearson ground his teeth, but he did as he was told, tossing the rifle down at his feet. Someone tried to get up a few feet away, but a vicious kick put them down again. Tony looked around, genuinely surprised at how smoothly things had gone. "Cullen? You there?"

Cullen stepped out of the darkness with a satisfied grin on his face. "I thought you said these were Thomas's best? Are you okay, Colonel?"

"Call me Tony. I've officially resigned my commission. Thomas can shove it up his arse."

Cullen chuckled. "The Urban Vampires are a little low on numbers, fancy interviewing for a job?"

"Interview? Don't I automatically qualify?"

"Yes," said Mass, limping into view. The guy looked half-asleep, but at least he was standing. "Welcome to the family, Tony. Now, what should we do with these naughty children?"

Pearson put his hands above his head, but he scowled at Tony as he did so. "Put a bullet in my skull if you have to, but you don't need to kill the boys. They were just—"

"Following orders," said Tony. "Yeah, I get it. The thing is, we're doing things differently now. Mankind can't only survive extinction, it needs to earn the right to keep existing. Killing a bunch of innocent people because your boss told you to ain't gonna fly no more. We all need to take responsibility for our actions."

Pearson sneered. "Fine. How did you even pull this off? At least give me that before you kill me."

Tony raised an eyebrow at Mass. "Yeah, I'm still not quite sure how you did it? I never heard you leave your tents."

Mass shrugged his massive shoulders. "Told you I would handle it. We have a magician on the team. He can pull a rabbit out of a hat, heal a dying man, and make us invisible."

A familiar-looking man stepped out from behind a tent. He seemed uninterested in what was going on and spoke in an oddly detached manner. "I made no one invisible. I simply clouded the minds of those who might see. Mass and Tony, you are both needed in the battles ahead." He looked at Pearson and wrinkled his nose. "You, however, are unimportant. I am dismayed to take part in this ruse, but it was necessary. Good men need to live."

Pearson seemed confused, but when he turned back to Tony, he was defiant. "So you're throwing your lot in with a bunch of weirdos and rejects, huh? I thought you understood what was at stake here. Portsmouth needs to survive at any cost. Bad things happen in war, and the only thing that matters is which side you're on."

Tony pulled the trigger under Pearson's chin and blew the top of his head off. The sergeant's body slumped to the grass. "I'm on this side."

The men on the ground that were still conscious tried to make a run for it, but Smithy fired his shotgun and frightened them back down. The blast left tiny flames flickering on the ground. "Sit still, kiddos, or teacher will get angry."

"You don't have to do this," one of the men begged. "You have a choice."

"You're right," said Tony. "I can either shoot you in the face, one after the other..."

The man trembled. "Or?"

"Or I can assume your actions were misguided and spare your

lives. In exchange, I want your word that you will never again act against me. You will obey my orders and no one else's – not even those from Thomas himself."

"Bad idea," said Mass. "Once a traitor, always a traitor."

Tony looked at the younger man with sadness on his face. "I'm disappointed to hear that from you, Mass. Isn't your entire unit built on second chances? I thought the Urban Vampires were a family for those looking for a new start."

Mass went to argue but stopped himself. Shrugging his shoulders, he simply said, "Your funeral."

Tony knelt beside the man who had begged for mercy, trying to speak directly to whatever conscience existed. "What you did tonight was bad. Now, you can keep doing bad things until you eventually pay for it, or you can open your eyes and see what's real. Forget orders, forget careers, this is the survival of the human race. General Thomas murdered General Wickstaff, and he ordered you to murder a dozen innocent people in this camp. Do those seem like the actions of a good man?"

The soldier shook his head. "No, sir."

"Not sir, just Tony. I'm just a man trying to keep things going. My question is, will you help me?"

The soldier nodded. "I swear."

Tony stood, taking in the faces of the grounded men. There was no reliable sign of whether or not he could trust them. It would be an utter and complete risk. "Okay, this is what's going to happen. Mass and his people are heading north to find a group of people who have been surviving in a forest. Meanwhile, I will be heading back to Portsmouth, where I will most likely be a dead man walking, but on the off-chance that Thomas believes my story, I'm going to take the sonofabitch down. Portsmouth needs to survive, but with Thomas at the reins it will all be for nothing. If you care about your fellow man, you dishonourable slags, you'll help me in the days to come. You'll fight for what's right, not for what's easy. You can damn well earn your forgiveness."

The soldier who had already agreed loyalty to Tony spoke up

again. "What are you going to tell General Thomas if we go back?"

"That we carried out our orders to the letter and eliminated Mass and his followers." He looked down at Pearson's almost-headless corpse. "Unfortunately, a gunfight broke out and there were casualties. That's war for you."

The soldier nodded. "Pearson said our orders were to kill you only if you disobeyed orders. If General Thomas thinks Mass is dead, then..."

"Then he might just trust me again. Especially if I have you fine men backing me up."

Mass groaned. "You're committing suicide, mate. Soon as you step through the gates, these guys'll rat you out. They ain't worth shit."

Tony sighed. "Perhaps you're right, but I want to believe they're good men. I want to give them the chance to prove me right. If I'm wrong, then at least I'll die knowing I tried."

Mass limped over to Tony and offered a handshake. "Like I said, it's your funeral. Good luck, Tony. I hope our paths cross again."

"I'm sure they will. Maybe I'm as unkillable as you."

"You are both mortal," said the strangely familiar man. "Mass would have died without my assistance."

Tony nodded. "Yeah, thanks for that, pal."

"Yeah, cheers, Rick," said Mass.

Tony clapped his hands together. "Okay, we've probably blown our cover after all this shooting, so let's strike camp and get a move on. We'll have to march tired." He turned to Mass. "Can you manage? You're looking a little better."

"I can move, slowly, but I'm getting stronger by the minute. We'll keep to the fields and try to avoid a fight."

"Not so easy these days, my friend. You have a safe journey."

"You too, Tony."

Tony pulled a face. "It's not the journey I'm worried about. It's what happens when I arrive."

8

God's wretched sun rises overhead as another beautiful slaughter commences. Crimolok's legions never sleep. They feed only on flesh, and they are ravenous. Their minds burn with ferocious insanity, placed there by Crimolok's ulcerating presence. They have just finished feasting on a mother and son, both having survived inside a long boat floating on a narrow river. Demons detest water, but with Crimolok's insistence they had swum the river and boarded the boat. The mother's startled shrieks had echoed off the concrete embankments for miles while monsters ate her child.

It was disappointing losing the humans on the road yesterday, but with their weapons and numbers, they must have come from the city. No doubt they have scurried back there like vermin. Their fates will come soon. There is no rush. No risk of failure. Crimolok will enjoy mankind's last gasps, for he has spent an eternity in the deepest of hells. He has brought that hell with him, despoiling every inch of God's creation. It would be a waste not to savour every moment.

Every drop of blood.

Dawn broke, lingered, and scurried away. The sun hung high in the sky. Assembled at Portsmouth's gates was one of the largest gatherings of human beings left alive. There might be other populations surviving on the continent, or in America perhaps, but right here was the heart of civilisation. No empire had ever been so great as Great Britain, and it swelled Thomas's chest with pride to ensure its ongoing legacy. This time, the empire would not shrink and fade, but it would grow and expand until it one day smothered the globe. That might be beyond the scope of his remaining years, but the foundations of that everlasting victory would be laid today. The rebirth of a nation.

Reports indicated that the demons were reforming and growing bold again, but they would crumble beneath the unrelenting force of Thomas's army. He had designated his leaders, laid out his strategy, and assembled a force to be reckoned with. Now he just had to pull the pin and wait for the explosion.

Thomas climbed on top of an articulated lorry that blocked Portsmouth's northern gate. A guard waited up there and handed him a megaphone. It hissed excitedly with feedback as he placed it to his dry lips. For a moment, he feared he couldn't speak. A twinge of doubt struck his ribs so suddenly that he almost doubled over. Tens of thousands stood before him, waiting on his orders. What if he was doing the wrong thing? What if his time had come and gone and he was no longer the leader he thought himself to be?

I almost retired because of that populist tart. She had me believing I was past it, but what if she was right? What if I did the wrong thing getting rid of Amanda Wickstaff? No, my only option now is to succeed. Doubting myself is not helpful.

Thomas took a breath, focusing on the life inside his expanding lungs. He had been a great general long before he'd come to Portsmouth. These people needed him to be at his best and that was what he would give them. He was the only one who could do this, the only one who could lead them.

"People of Portsmouth, we are a family, and as a family, we

must sacrifice and provide for one another. Today, we face our fears for the final time, knowing that nothing that can come can be worse than what we have already faced. Mankind is a unique and unmatchable animal, superior since the day it first stood on two legs and reached out to the sun. Unlike God's other creations, we clothed ourselves and warmed ourselves beside fires. We built temples and cities, roads and mines. We are special, for we do not live for the sake of living. The demons shall not steal what we have taken millennia to build. They will not take what our families, ancestors, and bygone heroes gave to us. Mankind has beaten the odds every step of the way, and today it faces yet another obstacle it shall surely overcome. We will send our enemy packing, straight back to Hell."

Fifteen thousand people cheered. Thomas handed the microphone back to the guard and hurried down the ladder, then gave the order for the driver to back the lorry away from the gate. The door to Great Britain was unlocked. Thomas's army stepped through.

Thomas climbed onto a horse that had been found and tamed for him. His designated commanders and junior officers joined him on mounts of their own, each grinning with pride and anticipation. Thomas smiled too, enjoying the determination on their faces. There would be no sympathy for the enemy this time, no empathising with motives or sympathising with beliefs like the adversaries of old. The demons were vermin, and he would put them down with the snapping of fifteen thousand rifles.

Let our enemy despair, for its days are numbered.

All the doubts Thomas had momentarily experienced melted away. This was what his entire life had been leading up to. There was no way he could fail. Absolutely no way.

THERE WAS a time when the start of a new day brought a depressing grey feeling, signalling morning commutes, frosty construction sites, and the odd hangover. Now it meant mankind had survived another night. Ted welcomed the dawn and the tasks ahead. Walls needed building, apprentices needed teaching. Work was no longer a window of hours each day, but a constant state of being. Hard work meant staying alive.

Caution was almost as important as hard work, but it was that the camp lacked. People were too eager to accept newcomers, which had led to Kielder Forest becoming inundated with them. It had started with the group from the supermarket – necessary due to them having a fully stocked pharmacy. Then smaller groups had come out of hiding, creeping out of the trees with fear in their eyes and hunger in their bellies. No one possessed a heart cold enough to turn them away. Lately, however, their newest residents were not vulnerable or needy, but dangerous and suspicious. Besides the American soldiers who had appeared via a gate, there was now a group of American coast guards in camp. Add to that the demon, Sorrow, and various other shady characters that Ted suspected had survived the apocalypse through less than savoury means, and things no longer felt quite so safe at Kielder. It was important not to lose sight of mankind's capacity for evil. Sometimes it exceeded that of the demons.

Then there was the ex-vicar, Angela. What was her deal?

Ted was on his way to meet with some of the newcomers now. He had met with the American coast guards briefly last night, but it had grown late and the excitement of camp had made things chaotic. In the calm of a new day, and after a night's rest to consider things, Ted could now question the strangers properly.

As was the case with all visitors, the newcomers had been allocated the guest cabin built at the rear of the castle's courtyard. Ted had built the place himself with a small team. It was right in the crossfire of several archers standing on the various wooden platforms. It gave visitors the illusion of freedom while retaining the option to fill them full of arrows. It wasn't fun being suspicious, but there was no other way. In the last few months, Ted had started to see the grey areas of leadership. It was impossible to think of himself as good or bad any more. Being good didn't always keep people alive and being bad sometimes saved lives.

Dr Kamiyo had left his post at the activity centre and was waiting by the guest cabin. He had his hands on his hips and was staring up at the early morning sky. When he sensed Ted, he lowered his gaze and smiled. "Morning! Looks like we might get rain. Winter's on the way."

"We're ready for it. Long as nobody does anything stupid."

Kamiyo chuckled. "That might be a problem, because people can't always help themselves when it comes to being stupid."

Ted patted his friend on the back. Along with Frank, Dr Kamiyo was one of the few people he fully trusted. They were each committed to the survival of the camp at whatever cost. "Good thing we have you to patch up all the idiots, Doc. Are our guests inside?"

Kamiyo nodded.

The guest cabin was a rickety structure covered in tarps. The nearby supermarket had sold flatpack sheds, which had come in useful. The only problem was their small size. Ted had needed to fashion half a dozen of them together to make the guest cabin. It had a felt roof and raised floor, which counted as luxury these days.

"They're still inside," said Kamiyo. "Far as I know, they slept all night through, but Nancy woke them at sunrise."

Ted shook his head and pinched the bridge of his nose. "I heard something about her daughter being alive. Is that true?"

"From what I've been told, the girl's aboard a ship parked on the coast near Newcastle. It would be really something, huh? Nancy came all the way from Idaho to get here and her daughter just turns up."

"Indiana," said Ted, suddenly a little grumpy. While it was truly a blessing if Nancy's child was alive, it filled him with jealousy. His own daughter, Chloe, hadn't made it, even with him there to protect her. How could a mother still have a daughter after a year of absence? It wasn't fair. "If Nancy's daughter is alive, we'll do everything we can to reunite them. We can always use more children."

Kamiyo smiled. "Couldn't agree more. Hey, you know Tammy's pregnant, right? Can you believe we've come that far?"

"People feel safe. The irony is that it puts them in more danger. They need to know that they're still only a split second away from jeopardy. You and I both saw what came out of the lake."

Kamiyo flinched and looked away. The mere memory of the giant creature emerging from the lake was terrifying, and they rarely spoke of it. "Have we had any sightings? Any at all?"

"Not one. The few scouts that know about it have been searching everywhere, but it's like the thing vanished."

"Let's hope it did. That's what happened to the demons near the lake."

Ted blew air out of his nose and headed for the guest cabin. "Come on, I want to know what these newcomers are all about. Hey, have you found out anything about our other guest?"

"Angela? Not a lot. She says she's here to help us fight, but she hasn't said a lot else. She keeps asking for a drink."

Ted frowned. "So give her one."

"No, I mean she keeps asking for a proper drink. Whiskey. She got quite arsey about it actually."

"I'll talk to her later. One thing at a time."

Despite being the unofficial leader of the camp, Ted's manners forbade him from entering the cabin unannounced, so he knocked. It was Nancy who appeared to bid him inside. White as a sheet, she had a desperate look in her eyes. Ted hadn't known the woman long enough to trust her, but there was no doubting a mother's misery.

"Nancy, any news about your daughter?"

"Alice, and yes! She's safe. I can hardly believe it. If only I could get to her."

Ted tried not to think about his Chloe. "Amazing."

One of the Americans spoke up at the back of the cabin. "If

you can spare a vehicle, and some people who know the safest way back to the coast, we can get Alice here today."

"First things first," said Ted. "Who are you people?"

The man gave a casual salute. "Captain Tosco. I served on *The Hatchet* with Nancy's ex-husband. He died handing the demons a great defeat in one of your cities to the south. Portsmouth."

Ted nodded. "There's a settlement there?"

"Thirty thousand strong."

The figure seemed impossible. The number of survivors at Kielder was a feat of pure human determination, but thirty thousand was miraculous.

"The problem is," said an attractive brunette in her thirties, "that the whole place is under the control of a power-mad old man. It puts us all in danger."

Captain Tosco nodded. "Maddy's right. General Thomas might not be a threat to you yet, but if he ever deals with the demon problem, there'll be no stopping him from taking control of the entire country."

Ted thought for a moment and ended up shrugging. "If some general wants to wipe out the demons and bring back some authority, I can't see it being anything but an improvement. We're hanging on by a thread here, and every battle might be our last. I really don't care who's in charge so long as the people here live. You've had a wasted journey if you're hoping to stir up some kind of opposition."

Tosco raised his palms. "We're not here to incite anything, but we do request asylum."

Ted huffed. "Asylum?"

"Yes, we request to stay here at Kielder under your protection. We'll work hard and help you face whatever threats may come."

Over by the door, Dr Kamiyo cleared his throat. "By the sound of things, the biggest threat to Kielder would be letting you people stay."

"I agree," said Ted, nodding to his friend. "This General Thomas wants you all dead, I presume?"

The woman, Maddy, glared at Ted, which was a little brazen considering her position. "The bastard planned on killing me in my sleep before I had a chance to tell people how he murdered Portsmouth's true leader. Captain Tosco gave up everything to help me escape. We came here because we hoped you were decent people."

"We are," said Nancy, "and you're welcome here."

Ted raised a hand. "Hold your horses. I don't think you're in any position to be making promises, Nancy. You only just got here yourself."

Nancy rolled her eyes at him. "You might think yourself the mayor around these parts, but this place belongs to everyone. Every man, woman, and child at Kielder has fought to stay alive and build this place. Nobody has a right to rule them. I came here with Damien to help protect Kielder from monsters *and* men."

Ted was flabbergasted, and he let it show on his face. "Is that some kind of threat? I knew you and your misfits couldn't be trusted."

"Let's calm down," said Kamiyo. "Maddy, you're right, we are good people. That's why Ted has to be extra careful to keep everyone safe. You're welcome here, of course, but your problems are not more important than Kielder's survival. I think it's safe to say that we can't make you any promises if this General Thomas makes trouble. As for you, Nancy. You might think Kielder belongs to everybody, but no one has done more for this place than Ted has. Show some respect."

Nancy averted her eyes and turned away. Dr Kamiyo was a mild-mannered young man, which was what made his judgement so damning.

Maddy moved in front of Ted and put her hands together, almost like she was pleading. "I promise we didn't come here to cause you people any trouble. We just want to be safe."

"We're decent people, too," said Tosco, "and so are the people of Portsmouth. We only left because General Thomas gave us no choice."

Ted sighed. As much as he didn't like it, he'd already made up his mind to let these people stay. "You'll need to do your fair share of the work around here... do you hear me? Any nonsense and you're gone."

Tosco nodded respectfully. "You have our gratitude more than you know. With that decided, we have another pressing issue to discuss."

Ted nodded. "Nancy's daughter?"

"I need to go get her," said Nancy, almost hopping on the spot. "I want to leave right now."

There was no stopping a desperate mother, and Ted didn't care to try. "You can take a vehicle and get going right away. I assume you'll take your own people with you as protection? I'm sorry to hear you lost some of them on the road yesterday."

There were tears in Nancy's eyes, and she was a bundle of emotions. "They were good men, but they died well. I'll return here as soon as I can to help keep this place safe, but I can't bear the thought of Alice being so close. I have to bring her here."

Ted smiled. "I look forward to meeting her."

Nancy beamed, then quickly exited. Kamiyo left, too, citing several patients in the infirmary that he needed to check on. That left Ted alone in the presence of strangers. "So, you all came here by boat? How many men do you still have on board?"

"Not enough to threaten you," said Captain Tosco, "if that's what you're asking. *The Hatchet* is fully armed but low on fuel. We took all we could from Portsmouth, but it might be the last we ever get. It'll stay where it is for now, and with your permission, I'll rotate teams back and forth between here and there. I'll keep a skeleton crew on board to man the guns. They might come in handy should we ever need them."

Ted raised an eyebrow. "Your guns can reach here?"

"No doubt. We outfitted our boat with several long-range mortars, but the aim won't be precise enough to avoid casualties. If we find any demons in the surrounding areas, however..."

"You're right, that might be useful. You'll have to tell me more about it later. For now, make yourselves at home. Rest, if you want, or make yourself useful with one of the work crews. They're easy enough to spot."

"I'll be heading back with Nancy," said Tosco. "I'll leave my team here though, if that's okay? They deserve a rest."

Ted nodded and exited the tent. Having a bunch of armed sailors, along with whatever ship was berthed nearby, might end up being a well-needed advantage, but he couldn't help worry about the ire of whoever this General Thomas was. He had images in his mind of rolling tanks and whizzing helicopters storming Kielder Forest. How much of what Captain Tosco and Maddy had said was true? All of it? None of it?

I suppose we'll find out.

Right now, he needed to go see an ex-priest about some whiskey.

"I COME BEARING GIFTS," said Ted as he entered the last bedroom on the activity centre's upper floor. When the woman saw the whiskey bottle she lifted herself up in bed until she was sitting upright. She licked her lips and said, "Bless you, sir. Miracles still exist. What do I have to do?"

Ted frowned. "Nothing. Dr Kamiyo told me there was a risk of you killing someone if you didn't get a drink. Usually, I wouldn't indulge someone with a booze habit, but you're a guest, and I imagine you've been through a lot recently. Is the whiskey medicinal or habitual?"

"Both. Now give it!"

Angela was clothed and lying on top of her covers, so Ted didn't need to avert his gaze as he approached her. He offered the whiskey and she snatched it from his grasp, wasting no time in taking a hearty swig. With a gasp, she thanked him in a gravelly voice. "Ah, that burns. Cheers."

Ted plonked himself down in the chair to one side of the room. "To your health. So, Angela, tell me, what led to us finding you, alone and unconscious, on the road? You said you'd been through Hell."

"No, I said I'd been *in* Hell. I was speaking literally. I suppose I ended up there on account of being a muff diver. The church always warned me. I can't say it didn't."

"You're saying you went to Hell because you're gay?"

She shrugged. "Them's the rules apparently. Tell you the truth, I didn't think God would be that petty. Then again, there were plenty of other reasons I might have ended up in Hell. Anyway, the place went kind of empty recently, and I found myself wandering around with nothing to do. Then a big window opened up in front of me and I could see the Earth. I threw myself through it, and the next thing I know I'm waking up here. Thanks, by the way."

"Say that I believe you – and to be honest I might as well – what did you mean when you said you came here to help us fight?"

"Exactly that. I picked up a few things in Hell. Me and a few other misplaced vicars had a club there. We called it the Reservoir Dog Collars. There was Gay Allan and James the tithe thief, along with a few others. In Hell, you stick with your own. It's a protection thing."

"You mean like prison?"

"Yeah. You wanna see the North Korean gangs – a right strange bunch. They think Hell is paradise. Oh, and the guys that did nine-eleven keep asking where their virgins are. They don't seem to get it. It's a colourful place, overall."

"So you picked up some tricks from a social club in Hell?"

"Yep. You gotta learn how to handle yourself down there or you're gonna have a bad time." She took another long swig of whiskey.

Ted leant forward, finding this mad woman both intriguing and insane. "So tell me, what tricks did you learn?"

Angela removed the whiskey bottle from her lips and grinned. "Just point me at the nearest demon and I'll show you."

"I'm sure that won't be a problem." Ted chuckled. "It's nice to meet you, Angela."

Angela nodded and took another swig of whiskey.

9

Maddy went for a walk, enjoying the sight of trees after so long in Portsmouth. It still hadn't sunk in that this place was real – an oasis hidden in the remnants of a shattered world. People, alive and well, deep in a forgotten forest. It made her wonder how many other people might still be alive somewhere, eking out an existence. The hope she had lost in leaving Portsmouth was starting to return. A little.

Most breathtaking of all was the castle. Augmented by wooden scaffolds and rickety structures, the stone keep was an impressive sight. The archers peeking through the crenellations made Maddy feel like a peasant in some fat lord's service. Next, they would all be riding out on horses, dispatching demons with their lances.

Tosco exited the guest cabin and joined Maddy in the courtyard. "Some place, huh? One thing America doesn't have is castles. I've never seen one before."

"Can't say I've seen one up close like this, either, but if you think about it, what safer place is there to be? We should go round the country snapping them all up. We could even build catapults."

"Ha! I quite fancy myself as a knight. Sir Tosco the brave."

Maddy smirked. "You're definitely brave enough. Not sure about the chivalry though."

"That's the knight's code, right? It means being a gentleman and rescuing damsels in distress? I think I've covered that."

Maddy realised he was right. She had most certainly been a damsel in need of rescuing, and Tosco had been there for her without hesitation. "I suppose you do qualify. I wouldn't be here without you, James. Thank you, I mean it."

He reached out and squeezed her arm. "My pleasure. It all has to mean something, right? You know, before this, I wasn't a man to be proud of. The only thing that mattered to me was my career. The whole time I served under Guy, I was eyeing his position. It nearly came to mutiny when he stole *The Hatchet* to go and find his kids." He pinched the air with his thumb and forefinger. "I was this close to putting him in the brig and taking command."

"So why didn't you?"

"Maybe I wasn't bold enough to go through with it. I kept telling myself to seize the opportunity, and I kept meaning to, but the right moment never seemed to arrive. Now I'm glad I didn't. If this horrible existence has given us anything, it's time to think about who we were and who we want to be. Guy Granger was a good man, and I'm proud to have helped him find Alice before he died. Today, I'm proud to help Nancy in the same way. If I had taken *The Hatchet* from Guy, things would have been different. I still don't know why I didn't, but maybe it was fate."

"Not fate, James. You didn't betray Guy because, when it came down to it, you weren't that man. Thinking about something – even planning on doing it – doesn't make it a reality. Actions define us, and you supported your superior officer and helped him find his daughter. That's what you did, that's who you are. You gave everything up to help me too. When people need help, you're always there."

Tosco looked at her and seemed to consider her words. A variety of expressions crossed his face, but it was a complete shock when he leaned in to kiss her. Maddy stepped back and dodged his affection. "I-I'm sorry, James. That's not what I..."

Tosco's cheeks were already red, and when he looked at her again, he turned into a stammering boy. "I-I'm so sorry, Maddy. I-It was just the moment. The things you just said about me..." He shook his head, like he was trying to get a hold of himself. "I won't ever do that again, I promise."

"No!" She reached out a hand to stop him from fleeing. "You don't have to promise that. It's okay that you... Jesus, I feel like a teenager. Look, James, I started the end of the world with a husband who I loved very much. I lost him, and it took a lot for me to open my heart again to... to..." Tears filled her eyes.

"Amanda. It's okay, Maddy. You can say it."

Maddy swallowed, a lump pulsing in her throat. "I'm still confused about the whole thing, to be honest, but I know I loved her. Then I lost her. Whatever happens next, it's too early to—"

"I'm sorry, Maddy. It was unsympathetic of me. I suppose, with the way things are, taking things slowly feels like a risk. All the same, I never want to do anything to make you uncomfortable."

Maddy hugged him. "You're the only person left who means anything to me, James, so please don't think you don't matter. I don't want to lose you too."

"You won't."

A crack of gunfire alerted them both. They ducked, but their weapons were stowed inside the guest cabin. More gunfire sounded and the archers on top of the castle started shouting. There was no ambiguity about the situation. Demons.

"Shit," said Tosco. "This place was supposed to be safe."

Maddy had a terrible thought. "You think we led them here?"

"Damien drove us here after we saved his ass. If demons followed, it's not on us. Come on, let's make ourselves useful."

The men Tosco had brought with him from *The Hatchet* exited the cabin, all brandishing rifles. One man handed Tosco his weapon, and Sarah, the female sailor, gave Maddy her handgun. Tosco shouted commands and everyone headed off in the direction of the gunfire. It didn't take long to find out what was happening.

To Maddy's surprise, a dwarf – although she knew that wasn't the appropriate word – started barking orders at everyone in a broad accent. "Get on them walls, the lot of ya. Get on them walls."

"We're new," said Maddy. "What can we do to help?"

The small man glared at her. "Didn't yow hear me? Get on them walls!"

The wall he was referring to was actually a wooden platform erected along the edge of the original stone structure. It was accessed by ladders, and Maddy hurried up one of them, with Tosco and his team following. Sarah took a stand beside Maddy and quipped, "Trouble seems to follow you around, Maddy."

Maddy didn't know how to respond at first, but she could only agree. "I guess I just like to party, Sarah."

"Stone. Everyone calls me Stone."

"Why?"

"It's my surname."

"You're not American like the others. You're British."

The tough woman nodded. She was pretty and blonde, with smooth pink cheeks ruined by that long, thin scar on the left side of her face. "I served with Colonel Cross in Afghanistan years ago. He rescued me during an ambush – saved my goddamn ass. He knew I owed him a favour, so he told me what happened in Portsmouth and put me on Tosco's boat to keep an eye on you."

"Wow, that's... Thank you."

She shrugged. "One place is as good as another. Just give me demons to shoot and I'll be happy."

"I don't think that'll be a problem. Here they come."

Maddy looked over the walls, and what she saw wasn't as bad as it could've been, but nor was it good. A horde of demons sped towards the castle, but they were spread thin and caught out in the open. The tree clearance, along with multiple fortifications, pits, and booby traps, slowed their approach to a crawl. Those defending the walls with modern weapons peppered the demons with gunfire while those with bows rained down arrows. Demons staggered towards the walls like porcupines, thin wooden shafts sticking out of their bodies. Others limped along, bleeding from multiple gunshot wounds. Maddy didn't expect to hit anything with her handgun, but she emptied a full clip to show her support.

While those on the battlements were calm, others panicked in the courtyard below. Kielder had been preparing for war, but many of its people were clearly yet to be battle-tested. The small man was pacing the platform with a large shotgun in his arms. He shook his head at those cowering below. "We ain't had time to stiffen 'em up yet," he said, as if addressing Maddy's unspoken concerns. "They spent the last year skulking in holes before we found 'em."

Maddy sighed. "They'll fight once they realise they have no choice. I've seen it enough times."

"The name's Frank. Here, take this. I'm too short to make much use of it."

Maddy took the long-barrelled shotgun and immediately felt empowered. "Thanks! I'm Maddy."

"Nice to meet you. Get shooting, lass.'"

Maddy turned and leant over the wooden railing, holding the shotgun tight against her shoulder and squeezing the trigger. The weapon bucked like a bull, and flames erupted from the spout. To her astonishment, she struck a demon fifty feet away, buckling it at the knees. It wasn't dead but could only drag itself along like a baby. She pulled the trigger again but nothing happened. She searched around for Frank, but he had already raced down the other end of the platform. She spotted a bucket at her feet, full of red and blue cartridges. This would be the first time she had ever loaded a shotgun, but she muddled through and eventually managed to fire a second shot. It hit nothing but the muddy ground. Beside her, Sarah Stone fired her combat rifle with far greater precision, and in the space of a few minutes, the woman had taken out a dozen demons. Stone was a warrior.

"How'd you get the scar?" Maddy shouted over the roaring gunfire.

Stone side-eyed her, still picking out demons with her deadly aim. "Shrapnel from an IED. Almost took out my entire team, but we spotted it just in time. Made the bastards pay afterwards."

Maddy shuddered. "You scare me."

"Sometimes I scare myself. Now, concentrate."

Eventually, the gunfire became less frantic and more measured. Only a handful of demons still raced towards the castle walls, and it was staggering how quickly their brethren had been taken out. The open ground, paired with the fortifications, made the castle even easier to defend than Portsmouth's docks. What these people had done here was amazing.

But it was under threat.

A fresh wave of demons broke from the treeline.

THE FIGHTING CONTINUED for several hours, until the archers grew too tired to pull their bows back fully. The modern ammunition was being depleted every second. Great Britain had not been a gun-toting nation, and its small number of arms were becoming increasingly useless. It reaffirmed Ted's belief that having Captain Tosco and his people would do more good than harm. So far, they had valiantly manned the south wall along with everyone else. Their help had been on the right side of needed.

Not a single demon had fled the slaughter. Each had assaulted the castle until its death, and Ted estimated well over a hundred of their corpses now littered the open ground. Their stink made it almost unbearable to take a breath.

He waited an hour before venturing out to deal with the aftermath, and he did so now only with a small team. A team with which he was not entirely comfortable, but with which there was a certain amount of sense. Sorrow was twice the size of a man and able to snap lesser demons in two. If any threats leapt up off the ground and attacked, the behemoth would have no issue protecting itself. Captain Tosco and Maddy were eager to make themselves useful, so why not let them? Then there was the mysterious ex-vicar, Angela. If Ted was going to risk people out in the open, he would rather it be people he barely knew. A cynical way to operate, but he could see no better way. The last person in the group was Damien, who Ted also knew little about. Again, better to lose a near-stranger over a friend.

Damien carried a pike fashioned from elm, and he used it to pierce the chests of the seemingly dead demons. Several times, bodies thrashed and wailed, and in one instance a pair of demons even tried to tackle Damien, but the young man remained calm, simply stepping back and spiking the demons until they were properly and permanently dead.

"There're so many," said Maddy. "Everything was fine and then they just swarmed out of nowhere."

"It shouldn't be a surprise," said Tosco. "Portsmouth was attacked in the same way. They're smart enough to know that their advantage comes with numbers."

"But still, what made them suddenly attack this place?"

Ted prodded a dead demon with his sledgehammer. "The last time they attacked us like this was when they were being led by a larger demon. We took care of it, but a gate opened right beneath our lake and something came through. I think that's responsible for this attack."

Sorrow flapped his wings. "Lord Amon. I sensed his influence in the broken minds of these demons. Lord Amon sent them to attack this place."

Ted huffed. "There you go then, I was right."

Tosco, clearly unsettled by the ten-foot demon stood next to him, shook his head and appeared confused. "You know other demons? What? Did you used to throw keggers in Hell?"

"Like you wouldn't believe," said Angela, kneeling over a

burnt man and giving it a slap on the cheek. She straightened up and shrugged. "It *was* Hell, after all."

Sorrow studied Tosco with his usual deadpan expression. "I do not understand your words, human. I speak many languages, but you appear to speak one partially unknown to me. What is *keggers*?"

Tosco raised an eyebrow. "I was asking how you know this Lord Amon, or whatever his name is."

"He is a brother. One of Hell's most wicked and vile. We fought side by side in the Wars of Heaven. When I fell into the pits, it was Lord Amon who raised me up into salvation."

"Sounds like you're good buddies, so what the hell are you doing out here with us? Shouldn't you be on Lord Amon's side of things?"

Sorrow snarled, a predator's warning. "Amon sides with Crimolok, who seeks to undo all of creation – including my ward, Scarlett. Lucifer opposes him and so do I."

Tosco seemed to waver between horror and disgust. He held a rifle, but fortunately he didn't raise it. "The devil's real?"

Maddy huffed. "Did you have any reason to doubt it at this point?"

"I guess not."

"I never met the devil," said Angela, "but I had a run-in with his bastard offspring. Snot-faced little shite."

Now that Sorrow was talking, the demon seemed inclined to carry on. That was fine, because Ted was interested in what the demon had to say. "Lucifer led a war against mankind because he refused to bow down to humans. Many of us joined him, not out of hatred for humanity but for our love of Lucifer. He was the best of us, the most beautiful and pure. When the war was lost, and many of us fell, Lucifer regretted damning his brother to the pits. In penance, he gave us dominion over Hell and the freedom to do as we wished. After our servitude in Heaven, this was a great gift, but it was also a mistake. Many of my brothers grew callous and bold without God's love to guide them. They filled

Hell to bursting with humans they blamed for their imprisonment, torturing them for all eternity. Lucifer's mourning at the mess he had made lasted millennia, and he preached the error of his ways to all who would listen. I listened."

Angela spoke up. "What's the deal with homosexuality? Why does that get you a ticket to the bad place? Love is love, right? Who cares which genitals get squashed together?"

Sorrow's wings ruffled. "Such a thing does not damn one's soul."

"Then why did I get sent to Hell? Don't tell me it was an admin error."

Sorrow stared at Angela in silence, his black wings continuing to ruffle. Eventually he nodded slowly, as if confirming something to himself. "June 2007, you drank an entire bottle of whiskey and got in your car to buy more. When you backed up, you killed your neighbour's cat. You never admitted to your crime, even as they wept on your doorstep. August 2008, you defiled your grandfather's gravestone after drinking cider in a graveyard."

"He was a dickhead."

Sorrow didn't acknowledge her and continued with his list. "March 1997, you wrote Geri Halliwell a highly sexualised email suggesting she was by far the most talented Spice Girl and that she should go solo. She later followed your advice, which did not pan out well for her or anybody else. Later, you–"

Angela threw up a hand. "Okay, okay, I get it. I wrote my own ticket. Please stop."

Sorrow nodded. "As you wish, gay priest."

Ted had intended to stay silent, but he couldn't help himself now. He wanted to go back a few steps. "Sorrow, were you trying to tell us Lucifer is a good guy?"

"Lucifer loves humanity. He has walked among you since the days of Jesus, who showed him the error of his ways. At first, I sensed him here in this place, but now he is gone. Where, I do not know. I miss his presence. It is like the disappearing of the sun."

Tosco opened his mouth, and it didn't seem like he was going to say anything nice, but Damien got in first. "It sucks to lose people, Sorrow, but I'm glad you're here with us now."

Sorrow stared at Damien for several seconds, almost like he didn't understand the words that had been spoken to him. Then he moved away, swiping off the head of a demon when it got up off the ground and leapt at him.

Tosco curled his upper lip. "It's stupid keeping that thing around. It's a demon. It's one of them."

"They're not all bad," said Angela. "There was this one who used to whip me on Tuesdays that told the dirtiest jokes. Hey, what do you get when you cross a baboon with a journalist?"

"I don't care," said Tosco. "I'm just saying it's stupid to trust a demon."

Ted surprised himself by speaking in Sorrow's defence. "He fought amongst us today when the demons came. He was one of us."

Tosco sighed, clearly unconvinced.

"It's just a shock," said Maddy, "but it was a demon who came to Portsmouth to tell us about some of our people being in danger. Angela's right, they're not all bad."

"I suppose they're just like people," said Damien. "The weak get manipulated by those in power."

"Lord Amon," said Ted, "was a fallen angel that came out of the lake, and he's out there somewhere, controlling the demons. We need to be ready. This won't be the last time we have to defend ourselves."

"We'll get started on more arrows," said Damien. "This battle used up a big part of our ammo. There's still some left in the crates, but it'll go fast."

"My ship has a supply," said Tosco, "but again, it won't last forever. I'll bring them back when I take Nancy to her daughter."

Ted shook his head. "You can't go. It would be stupid now that we're under attack."

"I don't think I have a choice." Tosco turned and pointed up at the wooden firing platform above the stone walls. Nancy stood there amongst the spectators. There were tears in her eyes, but also determination.

"There are only a couple of things that scare me," said Damien, "and Nancy's one of them. If I were you, Ted, I'd let her go."

"It's suicide."

"I hate to say it," said Tosco, "but it might be necessary. If you want the men and supplies from *The Hatchet*, I need to go get them. Give us all the vehicles you can spare and I'll set off immediately. This is probably only the first wave – sent to test our defences – which means we might get a short reprieve before more come."

Ted didn't like it, but the truth was he didn't have the right to tell any of these people what to do. If Nancy wanted to risk her life reuniting with her daughter, then that was her decision. Maybe he didn't even blame her. "Okay," he said, slamming his sledgehammer into the skull of a half-alive demon. "You can all leave, but I can't guarantee you'll be able to find your way back inside. In case you didn't notice, we're at war."

A demon leapt up off the ground and raced towards the group. Angela stepped in its path and raised a hand. She mumbled something incomprehensible and the demon exploded.

Ted wiped blood from his face and gawped. "W-What the hell did you just do?"

Angela had blood all over her too, but she seemed amused as she gave a shrug. "That's what you might call a pro-vicar move."

Sorrow flapped his wings, shedding chunks of demon meat. "This pleases me."

Ted nodded. "Yeah, it pleases me too."

TONY REGRETTED his decision more with every step. He'd placed his life in the hands of men who had already tried to kill him. If Thomas put them under the slightest of pressure, they would betray him again – there was no doubt. Once Thomas knew Mass was still alive, he would put a bullet in Tony's head. The only thing keeping Tony moving ever closer to his own end was the fact that he couldn't do anything differently. As much as he regretted his foolish decision, he would regret executing nine unarmed men more. If this was his time to die, perhaps he could do so with a soul slightly less tarnished.

Maybe it's enough to earn a little peace. If such a thing even exists.

Not wanting to encounter the demons on the road, Tony's team had taken a sweeping curve through the countryside. One of the men had grown up locally and kept them from becoming lost as they skirted the odd village and highway-adjacent retail park. Eventually they found themselves only a handful of miles north-west of Portsmouth, but it didn't make Tony feel any better. That demon horde was out there somewhere with a giant beast lashing them onward. Portsmouth wasn't safe any more, and he pictured the city in flames. It might already be gone.

As it turned out, they never made it there, because Portsmouth came to them. Half the city had seemingly taken to the road on foot, fully armed and in good spirits. Tony heard chit-chat and singing, the odd gunshot, and the endless beating of boots on the ground. He even spotted horses.

One of Tony's men spoke, a corporal named Dendoncker. "General Thomas is leading them from the front. What the fuck's going on?"

Tony knew what was going on, because he knew the general. "Thomas is marching us to war."

"But we're safer at Portsmouth. They're going to march right into the demon army we saw on the road."

"Thomas doesn't know about that. He thinks there's nothing left out here but stragglers and weaklings. Damn it, the fool. He should've set up a forward base before moving everyone like this.

He's so arrogant, he expects to mow the enemy down without breaking a sweat."

Dendoncker looked mortified, and he suddenly exposed himself for the young man he was. "W-We have to warn him."

Tony nodded. "We will. Okay, men, double-time. Keep your weapons pointed at the ground and put a hand in the air. Let's not get ourselves shot."

A mile existed between them and the army, and if not for Tony's group coming from higher ground, they might not have even spotted the large mass of men marching briskly along what must have been the M27. Vehicles clogged the road in places, but the hard shoulder and the central reservation offered room for manoeuvre where the road became blocked. When the demons had first invaded, even the oldest of bangers kept in lock-ups had returned to service as people sought safety. The punchline was that there hadn't been any to get to.

As Tony led his men downwards through the fields, something occurred to him. As with most of the country's major roadways, a border of trees and bushes sectioned off the traffic from the countryside. It meant that to reach Thomas's army, Tony's men would need to emerge from the trees and hedges. "Hold on," he said, bringing everyone to a halt. "We can't pop out and surprise them. They need to know we're coming. Okay, all of you wave your hands in the air. Jump up and down if you have to."

Tony pointed his rifle at the clouds and pulled the trigger while his men hopped about.

The massive army on the road kept on marching. The odd gunshot was not enough to alert it. Tony pointed his rifle again and this time yanked the trigger five times, a second between each shot. The rhythmic shooting was not a normal sound of war, and it caused the front lines of the army to take a knee and search their surroundings. Eventually, men spotted Tony's group up on the hill, and while their distant shouting was too far away to discern, at least they didn't start firing their weapons.

"They've clocked us," said Tony. "Let's move, but keep your hands in the air."

The men moved at a slow walk, their equipment rattling free at their sides. A part of Thomas's army broke away – a meeting party. Tony met them in the lower half of the field and they knew right away who he was. "Colonel Cross! Good to see you. General Thomas is nearby. I'll take you to him."

"Thank you. My men have been out in the field for several days. Do you have any water?"

"Of course!" The small meeting party handed over their canteens and Tony's men drank thirstily. Then they got moving again, covering the final ground between them and the army.

General Thomas was visibly surprised to see Tony, which confirmed his suspicions that his superior had not expected him to return. "Colonel Cross, what a relief to see you. How was the mission? I don't see Sergeant Pearson with you."

Tony glanced briefly at his men. Each appeared anxious, and he could only imagine what was going through their minds. Clearing his throat, Tony offered the lie. "We were met with hostility. Sergeant Pearson and two other men didn't make it."

Thomas's grey eyes narrowed. "And what about Mass and his unit?"

"Confirmed dead. They were already in a bad way when we found them. They didn't present a challenge after the initial exchange."

Thomas looked past Tony to one of his men. "You, what is your name?"

The soldier flinched as if slapped. "Me, sir?"

"Yes, you!"

"Corporal Dendoncker, sir."

"What kind of name is that?"

The soldier shifted awkwardly. "My grandfather came from Belgium, sir."

"Well, Belgium no longer exists, so perhaps the name will die with you. You served with Pearson overseas, didn't you? You're quite the soldier, if I recall his words."

Tony noticed Dendoncker had his fists clenched. Was it Thomas or Tony he wanted to punch? How close had he been to the now-dead Pearson? "I served with Pearson in the Fusiliers, sir, then again in the war against the demons. All told, I've known him a good five years."

"He was a good man, yes?"

"A fine soldier, sir. Yes, sir."

Tony's breath caught in his throat, and he tried not to reveal his anxiety. If he made a run for it, he might be able to bolt into the trees and escape, but that wasn't how he wanted to end things. That wasn't the way he wanted to be remembered.

Remembered by whom?

"I'm sorry for your loss," Thomas told Dendoncker. "How did Pearson die, if it's not too painful to ask?"

Tony bit down on his lip. He thought about lifting his rifle and trying to take off Thomas's head before the men gunned him down. At least his death would mean something.

Dendoncker let his head drop, staring at the ground. "He was shot, sir."

Thomas nodded. "By whom?"

Dendoncker looked up at Tony and then back at Thomas. "By one of the men we were attempting to neutralise. Like Colonel Cross said, they weren't happy to see us."

Thomas glanced over at the other men, probably to check if any of them objected to that version of events. None of them did, and it caused the general to snort through his nose. "Very well. Colonel Cross, I expect you and your team to remain close by. I value your input in matters of warfare. Have you met Colonel Livingstone? He's the acting chief of our ground forces, answering directly to me."

Tony had to stop himself from groaning as the leathery-skinned, grey-eyed sadist appeared from a group of nearby men. Tony had fought the demons in Turkey alongside Livingstone when he had been a mere captain and Tony a sergeant. While they hadn't personally come to blows, Tony had witnessed him execute injured soldiers rather than get them to safety, and he had once seen him capture a badly burnt demon and tie it to a post in the middle of camp. His men had thrown rocks at it for days before it expired. Some men thrived in times of war – even enjoyed it – and Livingstone was one of them. Tony fought down his dismay and offered a handshake and a smile. He had expected to be shot, so this was at least a better situation than the one he'd anticipated. "Good to see you, Colonel Livingstone. Congratulations on the promotion."

"And to you, Tony. Sergeant to colonel, that's quite the monumental rise to power."

"I like to think I earned it."

Thomas nodded. "You did, Colonel Cross, and I hope you continue to conduct yourself in the same exemplary manner as you have done previously."

"Of course, sir. That's why I need to tell you to turn this army back, right now."

Thomas spluttered. "I'm sorry, what did you just say? Do you not see what's happening here? We're about to take back our country. The enemy is licking its wounds and we must not give it the chance to recover."

"You don't understand, sir. We encountered a demon army on the road. It can't be more than a few miles away from here, and it's being led by a huge creature, bigger than anything else we've seen."

Thomas was clearly surprised, but he rapidly shrugged it off. "The giant demons are no threat now that the gates have all closed. We can deal with it."

"The gates haven't all closed. A new one has opened. Mass and his team told us about a gate a hundred feet high."

Thomas raised an eyebrow, his pupils seeming to flicker. "How exactly did Mass and his team tell you anything if you ended up shooting them?"

Shit, that was stupid. That was so stupid.

"Because it took a while for Mass to die," said Tony, trying to sound confident, "and I made the best use of that time. It wasn't pretty, but men prefer an easy death over a painful one. I wanted to make sure he didn't have other men in the area. He was built like an ox, so there were plenty of body parts to work with. By the time he died, Mass was begging for his mother."

"You piece of shit! You fucking piece of shit."

Tony turned to see a young woman sprinting towards him. She was bright red in the cheeks and spitting fury. "D-Diane? What are you...?"

"You monster! You fucking killed Mass? How could you?"

Tony moved backwards, genuinely afraid of the rage heading right for him.

"Keep your voice down, young lady," said Thomas, peering around at the many eavesdropping men who were now watching with interest. While it was mostly Thomas's loyalists, there were plenty who worshipped Mass and the Urban Vampires. Hearing about his death would not be good for morale. "What are you doing here, Diane? You're supposed to be at Portsmouth, uprooting traitors."

Diane sneered. "Traitors? You want to talk about traitors? Why don't we talk about how you murdered Wickstaff in cold blood?"

Thomas hissed. "Colonel Livingstone, please do something about this distraction."

"With pleasure, sir." Colonel Livingstone attempted to grab Diane, but Diane whipped out a handgun and shot him in the chest. There was total shock in his eyes. Before anyone could react, Diane spun around and placed her handgun against the side of Thomas's head. It was enough to keep anyone from taking a shot at her. "I'm the one who's been working behind your back, you arrogant prick," she told Thomas. "You think people will just let you get away with whatever you want? You think this is all about you? Portsmouth survived without you, and it will continue to survive when you're dead. You're nothing. There's nothing special about you apart from the fact you murdered a woman who actually mattered."

Thomas's throat bulged and he didn't dare blink, but despite his obvious fear, his words were defiant. "Somebody please deal with this lunatic. She's lost her mind."

Diane ground the handgun painfully against Thomas's temple. "I'm thinking completely clearly. You might have taken everything from me, but at least I'll get to watch you die. That's good enough for me."

"Diane, you are making a mistake."

"You should've seen this coming."

"I *did* see it coming, you foolish girl. Honourable young Tom might not have given you up, but every single one of his friends did. I've known all along who the ringleader working against me was. You're an impressive young lady."

Diane's cold eyes widened. "If you knew, then why didn't you—"

"I wanted to see who you spoke with. Colonel Wanstead is likely already dealing with anyone you've been confusing with your mad lies. Pity you left them to die just to pursue some childish revenge."

"You don't know anything, you piece of shit. If you did, you wouldn't have a gun to your head."

"I meant it when I said I was impressed. If I had had men half as sneaky as you in Iraq, we would have caught Saddam in a day. You can kill me, but it will change nothing. My people are in place. Wickstaff will still be dead."

Diane readjusted her grip on her handgun. "I'm just an invisible little waif of a girl, right? Killing you would be more than enough to give me satisfaction."

"So do it."

Tony couldn't stand this any longer. He peered down at Colonel Livingstone, lying on the ground with his chest blown open, and knew there was no way out of this for Diane. She was a warrior until the end, but something had happened during his absence and she couldn't come back from it. "Diane, stop this. There's an army of demons coming and we need to get these people back to Portsmouth."

Diane spat at him. "You pig. I thought I could trust you. I thought you were a good man. All the times we spoke…"

She was going to blow his cover and take him down with her. Tony could feel the words queued up and ready to spill forth from her mouth. Diane thought he had killed her friend and sided with Thomas, even though the complete opposite was true. There was no way to tell her that though. Not without dooming himself to die alongside her.

Diane's hand began to shake, the gun at Thomas's temple trembling. "You were supposed to help Mass, not kill him. Why, Tony? After you helped Mad—"

"Diane, stop! Stand down now and I'm sure General Thomas will go easy on you." Tony took a step forward with his hands up. His rifle was hanging by his hip. His sidearm was holstered at his belt.

General Thomas gave no indication either way.

"He won't be doing anything for anyone once he's dead. I just wanted him to know it was me who pulled the trigger."

Tony took another step. "You shoot Thomas and I shoot you. There's no way out for you unless you give up."

"I already gave up. This is me giving up."

She was about to pull the trigger. Tony could sense her finger tightening. "Diane. Diane, don't do this. Mass isn't dead, okay? I didn't kill him."

She turned to him in utter confusion. Her mouth fell open but no words came out.

This was his chance.

Tony yanked his 9mm from its holster and barrelled into Diane, knocking her handgun aside so that it discharged harmlessly into the air. Tony pulled the trigger twice, burying two point-blank rounds into Diane's guts and holding onto her as she fell. She let out an *oomph* like she'd been winded, and her eyes flicked back and forth. As they hit the ground, Tony's face hovered right above hers. She was dying, but it'd been inevitable since the moment she'd pulled a gun on Thomas. Tony had kept her from accomplishing her dying wish, but if he hadn't stopped her, she would have doomed them both. At least this way he was still in the game

I killed her to save myself.

Because I have work left to do.

Even though Tony could rationalise his actions, he still felt like the bad guy. He leant forwards, moving his mouth next to Diane's ear. He could feel her bleeding out against his hip as he whispered to her. "Mass is alive, I swear to you. He's alive and so is Maddy." A raspy moan escaped her lips, and he wondered if she was trying to talk. He lifted his head and looked her in the eyes, still keeping his voice low enough so that only she could hear. "I'll give General Thomas your regards when I kill him."

Diane smiled, then closed her eyes. Another good woman dead. The last of Wickstaff's friends gone.

Tony climbed up off Diane's body, feeling a million years old. Her blood soaked his clothes, and its warm kiss seared him with guilt. He had taken away the dignity of her death, so now it was Tony's duty to give it some meaning. Thomas had to die. Tony owed it to her.

Thomas grabbed Tony and turned him around. The general was furious. "Mass," he said, raising a handgun of his own. "You didn't kill him? I think you'd better start explaining, Tony, and it better be good."

10

Tony was still holding his handgun, the muzzle smeared with Diane's blood. He put his index finger through the trigger guard and let the gun dangle harmlessly. He raised both hands. "I was lying, sir. I needed to give her pause for thought so I could get the jump on her. As you can see, the plan worked."

"I've known you a while, Tony, and you've never been one to act quite so ruthlessly."

"With all due respect, sir, I've just spent several days on the road, hunting down a local legend more likely to kill me than I was him, all because my superior officer wanted me out of the way because he doesn't trust me. He doesn't trust me despite my having never done anything but follow his goddamn orders. I'm not in the mood for mercy, General, but if you're dead set on executing me for whatever trumped-up accusation you want to level at me" – he stepped forward and glared right in the old man's face – "then go right ahead. Either that, or fucking thank me for saving your life."

Thomas was even more stunned than when Diane had put a gun to his head. Both of his eyes opened so wide it looked like they might fall out and land on his boots. His ruddy cheeks suggested anger, but the creases at the corner of his mouth slowly increased until he was smiling. "Well, I suppose if you can be honest enough to speak your mind like that, you're honest enough to trust. You have my apologies, Tony. Perhaps I was wrong to doubt you. Thank you for your loyalty."

Tony sighed. His words had been half gamble, half frustration, but he had decided that the only way to convince Thomas was by telling as much of the truth as he could. For a split second, he'd been too tired to give a shit.

But it had paid off.

Whether or not Thomas liked it, Tony had saved his life, and while he might never trust him completely, a new grace period had just begun.

Tony re-holstered his handgun. "Sir, I just want to kill demons. That's all I've ever wanted. When you made me a colonel, things got more complicated than I cared for."

Thomas stared at Livingstone's still-bleeding corpse. "I would offer you a demotion, but I'm afraid I'm running low on officers. Perhaps we can discuss the matter later. What you said about a demon army, it's true?"

"Yes, sir. Until we know what's coming, we would be far better off behind Portsmouth's walls."

Thomas thought for a moment, then nodded. "Okay, give me an hour. I need to consider our options."

"What's to consider? We need to fall back, sir."

"Colonel Cross, I have assembled most of Portsmouth's fighters and promised them a march to victory. Do you know how much morale would plummet if I ordered a retreat before we've even met the enemy?"

"But, sir, I—"

Thomas put a hand up and halted him. "I'll compromise, okay. Give me thirty minutes. Perhaps I'll send out some scouts in the meantime."

Tony sighed. Thomas had taken the threat seriously at least. He might order the retreat if left alone, but if badgered, the stubborn old bastard would definitely push onward. Tony had to accept the half-victory. "Okay, sir, I understand you need to think this through, but I strongly advise a full retreat."

Thomas opened his mouth to speak, but screaming erupted at the army's outer fringes. Gunfire responded, but not the pop-pop of a lone demon or two being dealt with. It was the ceaseless staccato of war.

Tony raised his rifle and cursed. "Your thirty minutes just ran out, sir. Your orders?"

Thomas ran a hand through his short grey hair and growled. "Colonel Cross, kindly find out what we're dealing with, and then do whatever you need to obliterate it."

Tony couldn't help but smile. At least for now, life was about to get simple. He threw up a salute to the man he hated and took off in a sprint. Dendoncker and the other men followed, their loyalty now earned.

I was right. They are good men.

They found trouble at the army's left flank. A horde of demons was funnelling down a junction where the M27 joined the M3. The army had been heading north, but it seemed like they weren't even going to even make it as far as Winchester without a fight.

Tony took a knee and fired. It was too hard to tell if he was hitting anything – he was merely firing into a crowd – but many demons fell as the army unleashed on the incoming horde. As much as the demons had come out of nowhere, this was an army prepared. They survived the first wave with zero casualties, while dozens of demons lay dead on the sloped road. As always, though, more arrived to replace them. Burnt men staggered along, five deep in places. Primates bounded excitedly even as bullets tore into their skin.

"If they ever stopped to think," said Dendoncker, kneeling beside Tony, "they would've leapt out of the bushes further down and ambushed us, not race down an open road like this where we can see them."

"Thinking ain't their thing," said Tony, "luckily for us. Keep the pressure on, lads. Hopefully, they'll run out of bodies before we run out of bullets."

A grenade exploded near the top of the junction, scattering demons left and right. In the Middle East, they had used so many of them that they had been forced to unearth stockpiles of old L2A2s, mothballed at the turn of the millennium. To see a grenade exploding today was a surprise, and Tony assumed some cheeky bugger had smuggled it across the channel. Pity more hadn't done the same.

The demons kept coming, and the army formed a wall of continuous fire, picking its shots and making them count. The fighting was far from over, but so far it was going in mankind's favour. Thomas arrived in the thick of it, grimly satisfied. "We'll have the buggers dead by supper. You see, men, this is what I was talking about. The demons are no match for us."

Tony peered down his riflescope with a grimace. He saw no reason to be confident, and he couldn't help picturing the massive beast that was heading in their direction. Where was it now? How near?

Thomas stood with his hands on his hips, peering at the demon-littered junction as if it were a verdant meadow. "We'll warm ourselves beside the fires of victory tonight."

"We need to fall back as soon as we can," warned Tony. "Whatever's coming is worse than this. We don't want to face it head-on."

"Colonel, we cannot retreat, we must push forward. Look at what you're seeing. Hundreds of dead demons and not one of our own. I promised these men a slaughter, and that's exactly what I've given them. Great Britain rises from the ashes!"

Tony stopped firing. The demons were still coming down the road, but their numbers were starting to thin out. The army must have fired a thousand rounds to kill a few hundred demons. A rapid, relentless massacre, but at such a quick pace they would be throwing rocks before long. "General Thomas, with all due respect, we can't afford to be brazen. There's an army heading our way, and I can't say how big, or how vicious, it will be. We need to get our forces back to Portsmouth where we can bed in. This will still be a victory. We can still bask in glory. Sir, I insist."

Thomas glared. "You insist? You forget, Colonel Cross, that my trust in you is already on shaky ground. I appreciate your concerns, but I intend to face our enemy as promised and wipe it from the face of the Earth once and for all. I can't do that by retreating."

"You don't know what's coming."

"A giant demon? We felled half a dozen of them in the Middle East. Without their gates, they bleed like anything else." Tony went to argue again, but Thomas didn't allow it. "Enough! This army is moving onward to Winchester, where it will make the first of many nightly camps. If it makes you feel any better, Colonel, you can arrange our defences while we rest."

Tony ground his teeth.

No, it doesn't make me feel better. We're heading right into the jaws of the beast.

———

THE DEMONS STOPPED COMING after half an hour. Tony shot one of the last, a redheaded dead man wearing a white work shirt and red tie. He wondered if demons emerged from the gates with the clothes they died in. That would explain why they ran such a gamut of fire-damaged fashion. In the last year, Tony had seen floral-print summer dresses alongside World War One uniforms and nurse's outfits. One time, he had even spotted a demon in a toga. Hell was a seemingly timeless place where tortured souls from every point in history could suffer together as one. Would Tony end up there himself one day? He decided that, yes, he would, and that the day might well be at hand.

Dendoncker acted as Tony's sergeant, ordering men into formation and keeping them moving. He was glad to have the young soldier by his side, and already relied upon and trusted him, which was insane considering he had been planning to murder Tony only the previous evening. War moved relationships along fast. There'd been men he'd served with in Afghanistan he had called brother after a matter of months. If someone fought alongside you, facing down death, you grew to love them pretty fast.

"We're about to enter Winchester," said Dendoncker. "I've never been. Is it nice?"

"Not any more. It's a body-strewn ruin like everywhere else."

"I heard the Urban Vampires reclaimed it." Dendoncker spoke of them reverently, possibly still in awe of the ruse Mass and his men had pulled off last night. The Urban Vampires had indeed cleared Winchester out, and the main road was open, all wrecks and debris amassed at the kerbs. Piles of burnt bodies punctuated every quarter-mile or so, and blood stained the pavements. The air was stale rather than repugnant.

Tony looked left and right as they neared what looked like a picturesque high street. The road had been constructed using stone paving slabs, while three-storey Edwardian terraces created a corridor of shops and eateries. Every front window had been smashed in, an echo of early looting or later Urban Vampire supply runs. It made seeing inside the buildings easier, reducing the threat of hidden demons. That safety, however, made Tony tense. It felt like the eye of a storm. They had left a battle behind them, but there was almost certainly another one ahead.

The army spread out as orders from Thomas were communicated. Orders were given to set up camp in a nearby park, scavenging, if possible, from nearby buildings for provisions. Regular patrols would secure a perimeter, and several scouting parties would go on ahead to set up in the town's north. Their flares would act as an early warning if the enemy came. Tony possessed a marginal amount of hope that when Thomas saw what they were up against he would force a retreat. The only question would be how much the man's thirst for victory could trump reason. Thomas was determined to go down in the history books as a hero of the new world. Not content with being a Field Marshal Montgomery, he wanted to be the next Winston Churchill.

Forget that. He wants to be the next Alfred the Great, driving the unwashed beasts from our shores. Vainglorious fool.

Tony spotted a derelict bakery chain store he had used to love, and he set his men up inside. "Dendoncker, I'll leave you to call the shots. Most of the army will make camp in the park, but I prefer walls and a roof. When the fighting starts, get your arses in gear, pronto, but keep your heads down otherwise. An enemy attack always begins with some poor sod at the edge of camp getting taken out with his knob out. Don't let that be any of you."

Dendoncker nodded. The men got to work. They still had their camping supplies from their earlier mission, and it wasn't long before they had some tuck heating over a pair of portable stoves. Tony ate a mouthful of baked beans and then left them to it.

He had to hand it to Thomas, the general had performed an impressive feat organising such a force, and there were plenty of Wickstaff's people camped out too, showing he'd got a majority of Portsmouth on his side. He was a consummate politician, but that was a problem. Politicians had a habit of sending men to their deaths. Back in the Middle East, Thomas had been reined in by the fact he had needed to work with several other leaders. Before that, he had answered to the UK's war council. Now he answered to nothing but his own ego. He was a successful general with no reason to doubt himself.

But Tony was fearful.

He feared for the thousands of innocent people all around him, setting up in the streets and parklands for a night's sleep that would likely end with torn-open guts and half-eaten necks. Tony wanted to scream and shout for everybody to run and hide, to get themselves back to Portsmouth, but it would be useless. Even if people listened, Thomas would have Tony arrested and shot for insubordination. The only way out of this was to remove Thomas as the man in charge. Then, whether Tony liked the idea or not, he would have to take charge.

"It's time for you to go, old man."

Tony went to find Thomas, deciding he would act as soon as the opportunity arose.

MASS and his team waited until dusk before scaling a wall on the southern area of Portsmouth's docklands. At first he had considered doing what Tony had told him to do -- to head north and find safety – but that wasn't who he was. This was his city. He had fought for it. He wasn't going to tuck his tail between his legs and run. And so here he was, back in Portsmouth.

The civilian area comprised closely built warehouses and offices, which made it easy to slink in undetected. It was a concern, seeing as demons would likely get in just as effortlessly, but there were many guard stations and walls further north that would, at the very least, impede their progress any further.

"So, you really were telling the truth," said Smithy, looking around in awe. "Portsmouth's real."

Tox put a finger on his lips and warned Smithy to keep his voice down. "You doubted us? Why would we lie?"

"You had to keep a carrot on the stick or I might have done a runner. It would've broken your heart to see me leave."

Addy rolled her eyes. "Wasn't keeping you alive enough of an incentive?"

Mass waved his hand to get their attention. "Come on. Let's check the lie of the land."

An old fisherman stood on the docks, attaching bait to his hook. Mass vaguely recognised him, which meant the man had been in the city since before Thomas arrived. It still baffled Mass that an entire army had appeared during his absence, but the multiple strangers he'd already spotted while sneaking inside the city confirmed it. At least this old man was part of the Portsmouth he knew.

Mass didn't want to startle the fisherman, so he straightened up and removed his hood before approaching. The old guy noticed him and waved. "Good to see you back in Portsmouth, sir."

"You know me?"

"Everyone knows you. The mighty Mass."

Mass frowned, not liking that nickname one bit. "Looks like things have changed while I've been away. There's a new sheriff in town."

The fisherman nodded. "General Thomas took over after we lost Wickstaff. You know about her death, I take it? Bloody demons."

"Yeah, demons. So where can I find this new general? I should introduce myself."

"Huh? Didn't you spot the massive army leaving Portsmouth? Thomas headed out this morning to wipe the demons out once and for all. You must have just missed him."

Mass had been wondering why Portsmouth seemed a little quiet. The chit-chat wasn't as loud and there weren't as many campfires. "I took the long way into town," he said. "They headed north, I'm guessing?"

"What other direction is there to go? I'm just glad I got to stay here. Don't much fancy being out there on the road at my age."

Mass nodded. "You're right. This is the safest place. Cheers for the info."

"No problem, friend. Hey, if you see Diane, tell her I've got some lovely steamed pollack set aside, but it won't keep forever."

Mass frowned. "Why would Diane come around here? She lives in the port administration building."

"Not no more she don't. She moved over here to get away from it all. Don't think she gets on with General Thomas, to tell the truth. It must have knocked her nose out of joint, seeing as she was part of Wickstaff's inner circle. It were too much responsibility for a young lass anyway."

Mass put his hood back up, ready to exit the conversation. "Diane's as capable as anyone in Portsmouth. When I see her, I'll tell her how much respect you have for her."

The fisherman put down his bloody tackle and folded his arms. "Now, there's no need to go telling tales, lad."

"Have a good night." Mass returned to the others, who were still out of sight in an alleyway between the warehouses.

Addy looked at him. "Well? Learn anything?"

"Seems like Thomas took everyone out on the road – an entire army."

Addy folded her arms. "So, what... he's declaring jihad on the demons?"

"Sounds like a good plan to me," said Tox. "He could finally end this. Aren't you tired of fighting?"

Smithy placed a palm against his temple. "Are you soft in the head? Crimolok's heading this way with his merry band of demonic dickheads. Thomas is marching everyone right into a smackdown."

"And leaving Portsmouth poorly defended," added Mass.

Tox clearly disagreed, huffing and puffing before he responded. "Thomas must know about Crimolok. How could he not? Portsmouth has scouts all over the place."

"Not that far north," said Mass. "We've come twenty miles since this morning, at least."

Smithy arched his back and groaned. "Yeah, no shit. I'm ready to drop."

Mass turned to Addy. "Go get the others. We'll set the women up somewhere safe before we do anything. Hopefully there're still people around we can count on as friends."

Tox nodded. "I know a couple of guys who look after supplies in this area. I'll go see if they're still around. What those women need is a warm bed and hot food."

Mass nodded and waved. "Go!"

Addy brought forward the women and the rest of the Urban Vampires. Cullen was leading them, but he had a grim look on his face. "The city seems deserted," he said. "Does anybody know why?"

Mass told them about Thomas and his army.

"That's good," said Cullen.

Addy frowned. "Why is it good?"

"Because it means we can take back Portsmouth in his absence."

It sounded good in theory, but Mass doubted it would be that easy. "Thomas wouldn't have left the city defenceless. We'll need more than just us to take over. Even if we manage it, Thomas can easily take it back."

"That depends on what happens out on the road," said Cullen. "Least we can do is make life hard for the bastard if he survives and makes it back. I'm telling you, we should find out who's running things around here and take them out."

Mass didn't like it one bit. A lot could go wrong. It was too difficult a decision for him to make alone. "I... I need to speak with Diane. If anyone knows the situation in Portsmouth, it's her."

"She's dead," said a voice from behind them. It spoke from the shadows.

Mass raised his shotgun. "Who's there? Show yourself."

A young shaven-headed man stepped out of the darkness. "I come in peace."

"We'll be the judge of that," said Tox, and he made a grab for the stranger.

The stranger put up a hand and glared. "If your hand touches me, you lose it."

Tox wasn't usually one to suffer intimidation, but he recoiled and stepped back. Something about the stranger's dark eyes suggested danger, too unflinching, too unconcerned.

"Who are you?" Mass demanded again.

"Damien. I was trying to help your friend, Diane, but I did a bad job. She headed out to kill General Thomas. Even if she gets the job done, I doubt she'll be coming back. For what it's worth, I'm sorry."

Smithy cleared his throat and looked at Mass. "Who exactly is this Diane you all keep talking about?"

Mass ignored him, keeping his eyes on the stranger named Damien. "Why the hell would Diane head out to kill Thomas?"

"You're Mass, right? Lotta people been counting on you being alive. Thomas has been taking care of business while you've been gone, executing people in public, playing games with his enemies. He had Diane's number from the start, but she couldn't keep her head and play the game. I tried to help her, but she was too far gone. Revenge was the only thing left for her. I've seen some things, let me tell you, but that girl scares me."

Mass didn't trust this guy. Something about him was off. "What do you want, Damien?"

"To help. I thought I could do it from the shadows, but it turns out I'm not really the *consigliere* type."

Mass frowned. "The hell does that mean?"

"It means he's a fan of *The Godfather*," said Smithy. He put his fingers and thumbs together and said, "I'm-a gonna make him an offer he can't refuse."

Damien smirked. "It means I'm no good at giving advice. There's only one thing I'm good at."

"And what's that?" asked Mass.

"Fucking shit up."

Smithy tittered. "That's so badass. You should have your own comic book."

Damien glared. "You remind me of someone I used to know. Guy called Jerry."

"Handsome, was he?"

"Dead."

Smithy winced. "Downer. Well, I for one am happy to have a self-described badass on the team. Pleased to meet you, Damien." The two men shook hands, but Smithy ended up rubbing his palm as though it ached. "That's quite the icy mitt you've got there."

"Yeah, sorry about that. A consequence of being dead."

Tox spluttered. "Say what now?"

Damien cleared his throat. "We can go into that later, but right now there's work to do. I heard you all talking, and you're right, there's not enough of you to take over Portsmouth. Luckily, Diane was busy while you were gone. Turns out, Thomas isn't as popular as he thinks."

People emerged from the shadows behind Damien. At first, just a couple, then almost thirty men and women appeared.

"Diane was my friend," said a woman.

"The fucker killed Tom," said a man.

"There's no way that old bastard wasn't involved in Wickstaff's death," said someone else, the anger clear in their voice.

Mass couldn't help but smile. Alongside the people Mass had brought back to Portsmouth, they now had a respectable force. Thomas had made a mistake trying to take over Portsmouth, assuming it to be a city. But it wasn't a city, it was a family.

And families stuck together.

11

The flare lit up the sky like a firework. Tony had been propped against a gnarled oak tree with roots the length of a tennis court. He was only half-asleep, which meant he was, at first, only vaguely aware that something was happening. He didn't truly wake up until the first chatter of gunfire. At that point he bolted upright and grabbed his rifle.

Time's up.

Tony had sought to eliminate Thomas, but the general had been sleeping in a tent guarded by several men. The time hadn't been right. Now it might be too late.

The camp erupted, thousands of men and women spreading out around the playing fields and nearby buildings. Many were set up in firing nests on upper floors, or embedded inside vehicles. Those in the parklands formed a wide circle, covering every angle of approach with their rifles. Reserves stood within and without the circle, taking cover behind trees and inside shop doorways. Tony headed to Thomas, whose tent stood directly in the centre of the main playing field. The general had puffy eyes and grey skin, as though woken unceremoniously from a deep slumber.

"They're here," said Tony. "I warned you they were coming."

"Yes, Colonel, you did, and like before we shall deal with them. The men know what they face."

"No, they don't!"

Thomas rolled his eyes, making Tony want to punch him. "A giant beast, yes. We are more than capable of dealing with it." Thomas pointed to the rear of the circle, where a L118 light gun had been parked and unlimbered. The men called the modern-day howitzer 'Lulu', and it was a veteran of the conflict in the Middle East. Two more existed in Portsmouth for home defence. "That gun has one job and we need only to ensure it has enough time to do it. We took down several giants in the desert with less."

"But this one is bigger, and it could be invulnerable, like the others were in the beginning."

"The gates are all closed, Colonel. That thing will bleed, I promise you. Either way, the fight is upon us, and it's your duty to make sure that we meet it as true British heroes. This is our moment – the turning point of history. Be a part of it, Tony. Stand with me."

Tony tried to swallow, but his mouth was dry. He let out a sigh. Arguing was a waste of time and energy that they couldn't afford. "I'm with you, Thomas, but only because there's no other choice. After this battle is through, you can have my fucking resignation."

With a bullet to the head.

Thomas appeared genuinely hurt for a moment, but he soon settled on anger. "Resignation accepted in advance. I suggest you consider your future wisely, Tony, or you might find you don't have one."

"If things go badly here, none of us do."

Before the general could speak again, Tony turned tail and ran. There was no sign of where the threat was coming from, so he picked a section of the circular firing line at random. As it turned out, the threat came from everywhere at once.

Coughing gunfire met demonic screeching. The men had orders to be conservative with their ammo, but it was hard to pick targets in the dark. They had searchlights pointed at the nearby buildings, but shadowy gaps existed in several places and wrecked vehicles obscured many of the sight lines. More than ten thousand men and women were crammed together, standing in each other's way.

When Tony spotted the first demon, he thought he might have imagined it. The slight flicker of movement, a disturbance in the shadows, quickly grew into an endless flow of monsters. Directly in front of Tony, two dozen at least came clambering from beneath the collapsed awning of a French restaurant.

The battle raged. Tony picked his first shot, taking the head off a primate as two more leapt in behind it. Someone else in the firing line took both monsters out with a long burst of rifle fire.

Amongst the staccato of combat rifles, shotguns roared. Handguns popped. Machine guns rattled, spaced every fifty feet along the circle. Demon blood erupted into the air, coating the masonry of the various buildings and painting them red. Guts and innards slopped on the road. The demons slid and fell in the offal of their own dead. All the while, the firing line continued its assault, bullets hitting flesh a hundred times a second. Tony started to believe they had a chance. The demons kept coming, but they were being massacred. They had to run out of bodies sometime. How many could there be? How many had been hiding during the previous months?

And how many came out of that giant gate?

An almighty crash sounded in the near distance, out of sight but not far away. It sounded like a building collapsing, or two speeding vehicles colliding head-on. It was a chest-shuddering, painfully loud noise that caused every soldier to lose their focus for a moment as they peered around for a cause.

Dendoncker sidestepped until he was standing next to Tony. "The hell was that? Sounded like a goddamn plane coming down."

"I think it was a building collapsing. How are you for ammo, kid?"

"I got a shitload, but there're a shitload of targets too. I don't know which will run out first."

Tony checked his own supply and saw he was down to two magazines. Dendoncker had so many that the curved metal containers seemed to hang off every inch of his belt. Tony was glad to see he was prepared. "Where are the others?"

"Taking up the rear, over there. Demons are coming at us from all sides. I reckon they plan on surrounding us and spreading our fire."

Tony looked back and saw men firing at the circle's rear. "It would be the smart thing to do. It means we have no way out of this fight besides winning or dying. There's no third option."

Dendoncker nodded. "Whatever happens, happens. Can't cheat death forever, right?"

"You're right, this has to end. Let it be today."

"You're a good bloke, Colonel. I want to go out following a good man."

Tony chuckled. "Then I have your final orders, soldier."

"Yes, sir?"

"Go give the bastards hell."

Dendoncker ran off to rejoin the circle. Tony did the same. It was too chaotic to stick together, so he focused only on what he could shoot.

The ground shook.

Another boom clattered the air, echoing between buildings.

Tony lost his footing, the grass becoming trampled and slick. He went down on one knee, his rifle strap yanking at the back of his neck as he lost a grip on his weapon. He quickly got a hold of it again and emptied his current magazine into a pair of burnt men joined at the hip.

Tony shook his head in disbelief.

Siamese twins? What on earth did they do to end up in Hell?

He was about to get back to his feet and reload when something caught his attention. He looked left and upward, seeing something moving behind a multi-storey car park built from shiny beams and carefully sculpted concrete. The three-level structure suddenly turned ugly, clean lines contorting as concrete cracked and crumbled. The shiny beams bent and came loose. Within seconds, the car park came crashing down, and a towering beast, more terrifying than anything Tony had ever seen, appeared amidst the rubble. The creature almost seemed to glow.

Portsmouth's soldiers stopped firing, stunned into inaction. Many of them had fought giant demons before, even helped kill a few, but this was three times the size of any they'd ever seen.

Tony was the first to take a shot at the giant beast. His rifle was empty, so he yanked his 9mm from his belt like a gunslinger and started popping shots at the giant. It was more symbolic than an actual attempt to harm it. He just needed to break everyone out of their stupor. The gunshot was a rallying cry. "Take it down," he yelled, reholstering his handgun and pushing his final mag into his rifle. "Take it down."

Echoing his call, General Thomas rushed back and forth inside the circle, his mouth pressed against a radio. "Take it down, take it down. Gunners fire. AT teams fire. Give the enemy everything you've got."

The chaos went up a gear as machine-gun fire was overruled by the kaboom of the L118 firing. Shells whistled overhead and hit the giant demon with pinpoint accuracy, striking its chest and torso. The beast staggered, crashing against the French restaurant and demolishing it. Falling debris obliterated the nearby demons and scattered many more. The whizzing sound of RPGs joined the fray. Explosions lit up the fringes of the battle. Parts of demons rained down to earth with a splitter-splatter. Rifle fire, shotgun blasts, and handguns barked endlessly. Demons screeched in pain and anger, their bodies shredded and torn. The battle raged and twisted, but never once did it cease.

Until suddenly it did.

The only movement was the grey smoke drifting through the

searchlight beams. No more demons emerged from the shadows. Their leader lay motionless in the rubble.

Did we win? Is it over?

Tony wasn't sure who started it, but the army began to cheer. He couldn't help but join in, but when someone grabbed him from behind, he spun around with his rifle raised, ready to shoot.

It was General Thomas.

The old man was beaming. "We did it! I told you, didn't I? We finished the bastards off once and for all."

Tony had no words. If true, they could finally reclaim the land. They could take back the farmland and factories, power plants and water facilities. They could exit the dark ages.

Thomas was screeching like a lunatic, running back and forth along the lines. "We are victorious. We are victorious. Long live Great Britain. Reborn and everlasting."

The smoke gradually cleared, revealing demon corpses, body parts, and dozens of injured soldiers. It was like something out of a nightmare, as close to Hell as Tony ever wanted to get. Yet they had won. They had faced their end and refused to accept it.

Dendoncker appeared in the centre of the circle, a delirious grin on his face. "Christ, we beat them."

Tony nodded, still unable to speak. He looked around, searching for signs of life. The playing fields were only full of cheering men. There were no gunshots or cries of pain.

It can't be this easy. This doesn't feel right.

Something shifted overhead, just above Tony's view. He tilted his head back, expecting to see a bird, but the small shape flew too quickly across the night sky. It glinted against the moon and rapidly descended.

Tony's stomach turned.

Dendoncker disappeared. One second the young corporal was standing there smiling, the next his body was ten feet away in the grass.

Tony whimpered.

A slither of Dendoncker's skull remained, most of it now plastered to the heavy chunk of cement that had fallen out of the sky like a meteorite.

Men shouted. The gunfire resumed. The giant demon rose from the ruins of the French restaurant, its chest blackened but unhurt by the explosive shells levelled at it. In its hand was another chunk of cement the size of a Fiat.

"Look out!" Tony shouted.

The giant skimmed the debris towards the playing field like a stone across a pond, taking out a large chunk of the firing line. Demons immediately threw themselves into the newly created gap, attacking men from the side.

When it had appeared that the demons were defeated, it had been a cruel lie. Hundreds more – maybe thousands – raced from alleyways and side streets. Men screamed and fell, the firing line rapidly shortening as monsters overwhelmed it.

Tony found his voice, shaking his head at Thomas with a mixture of rage and sadness. "We're fucked."

Thomas looked at Tony, his face stricken with horror. "What?"

"I said we're fucked, goddamn it. We're fucked, and I told you we would be." Tony raised his 9mm and aimed it at Thomas's face.

"Don't you dare point that at me, you insubordinate fool."

"I should have done this long before you made it across the channel. You're a lunatic, Thomas. Look what you've done. Fifteen thousand souls, penned in and fed to the lions."

Thomas's bluster began to waver. "The fight is still ongoing. Tony, see reason, man!"

"The fight is over, you arrogant bastard. Wickstaff would never have been so reckless. I'm going to kill you. It's the least I can do for her."

General Thomas turned ashen, staring into the end of Tony's handgun. "Please."

"It's too late."

Thomas's focus suddenly darted over Tony's shoulder.

Oh shit!

Tony turned just in time to see a primate flying through the air. He tried to get out of the way, but it was too late. The demon crashed down on top of Tony and tore at his neck and chest. He rolled back and forth, trying to bring his knees up, trying to bring up his handgun. He yanked at the trigger frantically, probably hitting his fellow soldiers as much as demons. He screamed in pain as talons and teeth tore at his flesh. This was it. This was the end.

It hurt.

It was humiliating.

And in the corner of his eye, Tony watched Thomas hurry away.

THE SCREAMS of men tore the world apart. The stench of blood and demons corrupted the air. Tony was bleeding and walking, bleeding and walking. At any moment, a demon might appear and take him down. Each stumble seemed like a miracle.

How am I still alive?

The answer was simple, yet hard to understand. One moment he'd been trapped beneath a demon, flesh being torn from his body. The next, that demon was dead in the grass with a dozen smoking bullet holes blotting its torso. Twenty-four hours before, Pearson's men had attempted to murder Tony. Now they were saving his life.

The men helped Tony to his feet, but there was no time for thanks. Demons were everywhere, their numbers increasing until there was barely any room to move. Where terrified soldiers attempted to flee, primates hunted them down, leaping on their backs and biting into their necks. While the army had brought only a handful of horses, the animals' hysterical braying could be heard over the top of everything.

Tony possessed only one thought, and he voiced it to the men who had saved him. "Thomas? Where did he go?"

One of the soldiers pointed. "He took off with some of the other officers. I doubt they made it far."

Tony put a hand to his bleeding neck and groaned. "I had the bastard. I was one second away from pulling the trigger."

No one replied. Now that Tony was safe, the men scattered, fighting for their own lives. Thousands of men and women were still fighting, but they fell by the dozen. The demons were like a wave crashing down, gathering up bodies with unrelenting force. More of them spilled from the side streets, but it was their leader that did the real damage.

Tony watched in horror as the giant yanked up the massive oak tree he had slept against earlier. Its massive roots tore the earth apart. The resulting crater swallowed up men and demons both. The beast then swung the ancient oak as if it were a cricket bat, obliterating a hundred men. Bullets struck the giant like a swarm of angry bees, but they imploded on impact, causing no damage besides sooty black marks.

"It's over," said Tony. "We've lost."

And that was when he started walking. He had no destination, no purpose, he just couldn't fight any more. He was done.

At first, he focused on making it to the middle of the playing fields. Then, he continued until he reached the road. Finally, and miraculously, he left the parklands and entered a side street. The more he walked, the more he wondered if he was dead. Perhaps his spirit had left his body and he was simply roaming the Earth.

The fighting faded behind him, the screams of men almost at an end. Demons screeched and wailed triumphantly, their victory well earned. Humanity had never stood a chance.

Thomas doomed us all.

Or were we doomed from the beginning?

Portsmouth's best men lay dead in a moonlit Winchester playing field, their blood soaking the grass. The demons would continue their purge until they reached the gates of Portsmouth.

There, a diminished mankind would stand no chance of repelling an attack.

He wept as he walked, so loudly that he was sure he would be heard. Yet nothing came. No demons appeared to end his misery.

He walked for hours, right through dawn and into the bright morning. Eventually, he made it out of Winchester and entered the rural area that would eventually lead to the North Wessex Downs and Oxford beyond. It was the area where he'd found Mass.

Had the leader of the Urban Vampires taken his people north to Kielder as promised, or was he dead? Exactly how many people lived up there in the forest? Would they have any chance against the giant demon and its hordes? Tony doubted it. In fact, he wondered if Mass had even headed there. He hadn't seemed like the kind of man to flee.

But he had a duty to warn them about what they were up against.

Tony slumped against a road sign as he passed it. The cold bite of his own blood vexed him along with the chill of morning air. Somewhere down the line he had dropped both his rifle and handgun, and he was now armed with only a knife. Any demons would have an easy time finishing him off, but it would probably be unnecessary. He was bleeding all over. His neck was torn along the collarbone, the skin flapping. A second wound bled on his chest, deep and painful. He located various other cuts on his face and shoulders, hands and wrists, but it was his chest and neck that worried him most. If he didn't find help, he would eventually bleed to death or die of infection. He needed a medic, or enough supplies to take care of it himself.

He lifted his bloody hands and saw that they were shaking. He tried keeping them still but failed. For a moment, he feared he wouldn't be able to walk again, but once he got one foot in front of the other he was able to move at a steady pace.

It would take him a week to walk to Kielder, or longer. As much as he loved a good hike, he didn't think he could make this one. Even if his wounds were taken care of, he was too weak and vulnerable alone in the open. He needed transport, but driving was a reckless pursuit, prone to dead ends whenever the wreckages grew insurmountable. The safest and easiest route was always through the countryside – fields and country lanes. The problem with that, however, was that most vehicles – if you could even get one running – couldn't cope with the terrain. Tony thought about trying to find a tractor or a Land Rover, but then he suddenly found something even better.

A village came into view ahead. The very first building he encountered was an old social club. Two wooden picnic tables stood out front, broken pint glasses littering the pavement at their feet. Propped against one of those wooden tables was a 'scrambler'. The British Army always used to keep a few of the lightweight motorbikes around the bases for fun. They were quick, nimble, and small enough to lift whenever the terrain got tricky. They could get you up a mountain or across a shallow river. The lone scrambler outside the social club was like a gift from the gods.

If the thing starts.

Tony limped over to the motorbike and lifted it away from the table. He wondered who'd left it there, and imagined a young lad seeking safety at the social club. That the motorbike was here suggested the young lad's body might be inside the building. Tony would need to find it in order to get the key.

Except the key was in the ignition.

"You're joking me?"

Whoever had parked the bike had been in too much of a rush to care about removing the key. That person had probably died months ago, but their actions had given Tony a chance of making it to safety.

He turned the key.

The whiny engine came to life. Tony angered it by twisting the accelerator. The scrambler was alive – and ready for an adventure.

Tony's vision blurred, and he had to wait for it to pass. Once he was sure he wouldn't keel over, he straddled the small motorbike and kicked it forward into a roll. The engine throbbed between his thighs, growing warm. Despite the heat, Tony shivered. He was still losing blood and he was now in a race against time. If he drove all day and into the night, he might make it to Kielder in twelve hours. That was if he encountered no demons, no impassable obstacles, and didn't bleed to death en route.

"I always did like a challenge," he muttered to himself, and laughed grimly. "On your marks, get set..."

Tony twisted the accelerator and took off, leaving Portsmouth a doomed memory behind him.

THEY HAD FIFTY MEN. It wasn't enough, but if Mass could strike at the right targets quickly enough, he might be able to convince any responding forces to stand down and join him. From his early morning inspections, conducted from the roof of an empty warehouse, there seemed to be an equal mix of Thomas's and Wickstaff's people. The problem was that the men with the guns were all Thomas's. Wickstaff's loyalists had been disarmed.

The women from the farm had all been fed and housed, surprisingly by the opinionated old fisherman named Mitch. He'd also helped Mass and the others remain hidden while they took a breather. Mitch was a fool with a thoughtless mouth, but he was apparently kind at heart. The women were safe, but Mass suspected they understood the dangers ahead as well as anyone. Crimolok and his army was headed for Portsmouth. The fight was coming. At least for now, the women could enjoy some food and warmth without the fear of assault. If Mass had achieved nothing else, he had at least given them that.

Tox came through on his promise of being connected. The men in charge of the area's stockpiles were indeed his friends, and they had offered Mass and his people as much food and drink as requested, including booze. It would be insane to get drunk, but Mass allowed himself one beer. He'd earned it.

Damien stood on the rooftop nearby, so Mass approached him. "Anyone spotted Wanstead yet?"

General Wanstead was, according to Damien, in charge of Portsmouth during Thomas's absence. That made him their number one target. Mass didn't savour the thought of assassinating someone, but he knew it might come to that. It very much depended on the kind of man this Wanstead was.

Damien folded his arms and peered over the edge of the roof. "He's in the port administration building. I saw some uniforms hanging around there earlier, so he won't be alone."

"Okay, just tell me one more time who I'm looking for – a fat white dude with a posh accent, right? Anything else?"

"I got myself within earshot a couple of times this morning. He seems reasonable enough, I suppose."

Mass nodded. "If Wanstead's a good man, we might be able to persuade him to help us. If we tell him what's coming, he'll want to avoid a fight and prepare for what matters."

"Or you could just take the guy out. You have fifty men. Put 'em to use, innit?"

Mass shook his head. "I can't accept murdering a man unless there's no choice."

Damien frowned. "Having a conscience must suck."

"It ain't great, but it's not something I can ignore. If we're doing this, we're doing it my way."

"Fair enough."

Smithy appeared on the roof, entering through a door that led to the warehouse's mezzanine floor. Sipping from a bottle of water, he swished the liquid around his cheeks for a while before swallowing. He looked at Mass and nodded. "All right, boss, what's occurring?"

"We're going to take Wanstead hostage tonight and hope we can convince him to play ball. If not, we'll make sure everyone is listening when we tell them Thomas murdered Wickstaff, and that Crimolok is coming to wipe us all out once and for all. We can fight each other or we can fight together."

Damien scratched his scalp, appearing unconvinced. "You think that'll work? Thomas's men are the ones with all the guns."

"They can still make up their minds about what they're fighting for. Give a soldier a choice, he'll usually make the right one."

Smithy took another swig of water, then asked, "When do we make our move?"

Mass swigged the last of his beer, hoping it wouldn't be his last. "Soon. We don't have the luxury of waiting."

"Okey dokey." Smithy tossed his empty bottle of water off the roof. It bounced on a pallet of old wiring spools and pirouetted in the air.

Damien snarled. "Fucking litterbug. Be a man, fill the can."

"I think global warming has taken a backseat, mate, but yeah, my bad."

"It'll be getting dark," said Mass. "Come on, let's go and tell everyone the plan."

Tox met them down below. He and Addy were both armed, but they hid their faces beneath baseball caps. Both knew the plan because he'd gone through it with them earlier. Along with Cullen, they were the people he trusted most.

Addy pumped her shotgun. "So are we doing this or what?"

Mass nodded. "We wait until nightfall and catch Wanstead sleeping. I hate having to delay even a few hours, but we're only going to get one shot at this. We need to get it right. Where's Cullen and the others?"

"Gathering supplies and people in case we have to fight to make our point. I reckon we have enough bodies to pull it off, so long as we stick to the plan. Everyone is raring to go except for Rick."

"Where is he?"

Addy shrugged. "He said he had other places to be and left. We can get things done without him."

"I agree. Wanstead's in the port authority building. The place is guarded, so follow my lead. We'll make a move soon. Do what you have to do, then meet back here when you're ready. This might be our last mission, so make your peace however you need to."

Smithy elbowed Addy in the ribs and winked at her. "Fancy making peace together?"

Addy snarled. "I'll make pieces of *you* if you try to touch me."

"Ouch! Just remember that we're on the same side."

Mass walked away to find some silence, the banter of his friends fading behind him. He hoped it didn't fade forever.

NIGHT FELL THREE HOURS LATER. Two hours after that, Mass led everyone through the civilian docks and towards the military area. He had fought with the decision to wait so long, but the risk of encountering guards had been too high during the day.

The port authority building was right behind a separating wall that had originally been part of the civilian docks, but because of its size, Wickstaff had cordoned it off inside the military area. It was a good thing, too, because it meant Mass wouldn't have to lead his team through the heavily guarded military zone. They just needed to make it through a single checkpoint at the end of the civilian docks and then head straight for the building.

Again, Mass was uncomfortable with the task ahead. He didn't know whether to approach the checkpoint in force or have his small team spread out. He was a kick the door down and start blasting kind of guy, so having to follow a plan filled him with self-doubt. Too many of his people had died under his watch. Any more would break him.

They rounded the corner, where a section of the quay turned sharply. The checkpoint lay thirty metres ahead. Two guards were visible, and both clutched rifles against their chests. Tox and

Addy could probably take them both down, if he ordered it, but it would raise an alarm and make it all but impossible to get inside the port authority building quietly. They couldn't risk a gunshot from either side.

"Keep your weapons down," said Mass. "Let's not make anyone nervous."

They approached slowly, but when the two guards noticed their weapons, steel edges reflecting moonlight, they got upset. They raised their rifles and barked a warning. "Civilians are forbidden from carrying weapons."

"We ain't no goddamn civilians," said Tox.

Mass waved a hand to quieten his friend. To the guards, he said, "We're Urban Vampires. Seeing as you're new around here, you might not have heard of us, but Portsmouth's our home."

One guard nodded. "From what I've heard, the Urban Vampires are about the toughest bastards around."

Mass nodded. "You heard right."

"But that don't change the fact you ain't coming through here with those weapons. The Urban Vampires have no authority in Portsmouth."

Tox leapt forward. "No authority? We built this place, you jumped-up little twat."

Addy amended their argument. "Us and General Wickstaff, that is. Pity your boss murdered her. She was good people."

The guard took a step forward, his rifle raised, and pointed. "This ain't a discussion, mate. Walk away and get some sleep. It's late. Too late to be skulking about in the dark like a bunch of rats."

Mass exhaled, shaking his head sadly. "This ain't the way I hoped this would go. I suppose you can take the boy out of Brixton..." He was about to give Tox the okay that he was desperately waiting for, but Damien walked into the firing line and approached the guards with his hands raised. He was the only one of them who wasn't armed.

"Look, geezer, why are we having a pissing contest? We all need to stick together, innit? You boys must have served in the Middle East, yeah? Respect to that. You must've seen some real heavy shit."

The guard eyed Damien suspiciously. "You have no idea."

"I believe it. You know, I always wished I'd joined the army. Would've got me away from my old man for one thing."

The guard nodded. "Yeah, my old man weren't up to much either. Barely knew him, to be honest. Guess it's all in the past now though, so my advice is you get over it and move on before you get yourself shot. Thanks for sharing though."

"Don't be like that, geezer. I'm just saying, we're all the same, innit?"

Mass moved his finger slowly towards his shotgun's trigger. What the hell was Damien doing?

The guard shouldered his rifle, ready to shoot. "Talk all you want, mate, but you ain't coming through."

"Why do you insist on butting heads?" Damien yanked the guard's rifle and planted a horrifying headbutt in the centre of the startled man's face. His colleague reacted, but Damien spun around and dropped him with a roundhouse kick that would have made Jason Statham proud. The guards hit the ground, both unconscious. Damien immediately started jostling their prone bodies.

Smithy pulled a face. "Whoa, what are you doing, man?"

"Putting them in the recovery position. We're trying not to kill anyone, right?"

"That was some impressive kung fu," said Addy, nodding appreciatively. "Where d'you learn that?"

"It wasn't kung fu, but I got it from another Damien."

Smithy frowned. "What does that mean?"

"It means there was a Damien someplace else that knew tae kwon do. He died and all his knowledge passed to me. Now there are only two of us left, and I ain't exactly alive."

Smithy raised an eyebrow. "You're like Jet Li in that old film.

You get stronger every time one of you dies. Shit, I miss blobbing out in front of a good action flick."

Damien looked down at the two unconscious guards, a pained expression on his face. "Not stronger, no. Their memories and knowledge filter down to me, but not their strength. It's sort of like muscle memory. I don't remember how I learned tae kwon do, I just suddenly did one day. Like I know I can ride a bike even though I haven't since I was a kid."

Smithy nodded. "So you can just tae kwon *do* it."

Damien rolled his eyes. "Is there an off button on this guy. Look, you people wanted a quiet way in and I just gave it to you."

Mass patted Damien on the back. It was like hitting a slab of ice. "If I'd known we had Bruce Lee on the team, I might have planned differently."

"Bruce Lee didn't believe in kicking above the knee," said Smithy. "So it's not really a good analogy."

Addy groaned. "Someone is going to kick you in the knee in a moment. Shut up, for God's sake."

"Sorry." He made a zipping motion over his lips.

Mass looked at him and put out his palm. "I want the key."

Smithy made the motion of locking his lips and handing over the key. Mass took it and then waved a hand to get everyone moving again. The two guards remained unconscious on the floor.

12

———

"It's late," Addy whispered as they crouched in a dark alleyway, "but Wanstead could still be awake. Do we wait a little longer?"

Mass nodded. "We can't afford to delay any longer. Every second we take counts against us. We need to take control of Portsmouth and prepare ourselves for an attack before it's too late."

Tox adjusted the peak of his baseball cap. "How? Thomas took two-thirds of the soldiers with him."

"Maybe he'll succeed," said Addy. "Maybe the only thing to turn up at the gates will be a victorious army."

"If that happens, I'll be the first to worship at Thomas's feet," said Mass, "but I doubt any army can succeed against what we saw coming. At least not out in the open."

"Maybe Thomas has a plan we don't know about."

"Yeah, maybe. Let's just—" Mass ducked and put a finger to his lips as a guard appeared ahead in the light of a nearby barrel-fire. It was another man he didn't recognise, holding a military-spec rifle. Addy moved into cover ahead, hiding behind a row of army Land Rover ambulances that must have arrived with Thomas's fleet. They moved up to join her, and then waited for the guard to move out of sight. Mass gave the signal to get going again.

The port administration building was right there. More guards should've been watching the entrance, but the place appeared deserted. All the lights inside were off. It was hard to know what time it was, but it couldn't have been past midnight.

"It's quiet," said Addy. "I know everyone's left Portsmouth, but I would have expected more than a couple of guards."

"Thomas doesn't care about the people left here," said Damien. "He cares about wiping out the demons. For that he needs soldiers. I'm kinda sad I'm not out there with them. It'll be a hell of a fight."

"They'll be plenty of fighting here," said Mass, "I can guarantee it. Right now, this is what's important. Come on, let's get inside."

They sidled along the modern glass walls of the port administration building until they reached the double glass doors housed inside the recessed entryway. They were unlocked, which wasn't unusual; the offices were in use all hours and many people also slept inside. Maybe the lax security had contributed to Wickstaff's death. She could have locked herself away inside and posted guards around her twenty-four-seven, but that wasn't who she had been. Amanda Wickstaff wasn't someone who hid.

Mass held the doors open while Tox, Smithy, Addy, and Damien crept inside. The reception area was dark, bar a single dim lamp in the corner of the room. Magazines were stacked neatly on a coffee table. Comfy sofas surrounded the table.

Mass glanced at Damien and got his attention. "Do you know where we can find Wanstead?"

"No idea, mate. I never stepped foot in here before. Not a big fan of authority."

"Okay, we'll have to check each room as we go. We need to be on the lookout for guards, not just Colonel Wanstead. Remember, safeties on unless there's no other choice. Every man we kill is one less to fight the demons when they get here."

"*If* they get here," said Addy. "Can we at least *try* to imagine an outcome where Thomas obliterates the demons forever?"

Tox grunted. "Since when have you been a woman who looks on the bright side? There're only two outcomes to anything these days: shit and slightly less shit."

"Hate to agree," said Smithy, "but Tox is right. Take me, for example. After spending almost a year on my own, I finally find a place full of people, only for it to fall under threat."

"If we keep talking," said Mass, "we'll screw this up. Come on."

They moved through the open security door and entered the corridor. Wickstaff's office lay at the end, although it was probably someone else's now. Thomas had probably moved himself in before her body had even cooled.

Using hand gestures, Mass instructed Tox to check the door on the left. It was locked.

"Leave it," said Mass. "If it's locked, it's probably empty. Either way, we can't risk breaking in and making noise."

They moved on to the next door, and this time when Tox tried it, it opened. He peered inside, staying low to the ground.

"See anything?" asked Smithy in a whisper.

"It's full of boxes and files. Stuff from before the war."

Mass nodded. "Keep moving."

Tox moved to the next door and found another empty office. There were two more doors to try in addition to Wickstaff's former office. A stairwell led to the building's upper three floors.

Tox tried the two side doors. Both were locked.

"I'll get the one at the end," said Mass. "I want to see what they've done with Wickstaff's office."

Everyone crouched and waited while Mass walked the final length of carpet. He was two feet away from Wickstaff's door when it unexpectedly opened. A pot-bellied man, almost bursting out of his uniform, stepped out with a polite smile. "You must be Mr Mass?"

Mass had already been on edge, but seeing someone step out

of the room with a smile on their face completely disarmed him. He rose up out of his crouch, keeping his shotgun pointed downwards. "W-Who are you?"

"Colonel Wanstead. Formerly a captain in the Adjutant General's Corps, but recently promoted. I take it you're here to kill me? Why else would you be sneaking around in the dead of night?"

Tox and the others joined Mass, equally taken off guard. He looked at them, then back at Colonel Wanstead. "You knew we were coming?"

"Why, of course! From the very moment you entered the ruins in fact. I have men hidden out there, keeping watch for demons." He chortled. "Instead, they found Vampires."

"We're not here to kill you, Colonel Wanstead. We're here to warn you."

"About what?"

"There are demons coming – a shitload – and they're being led by Crimolok."

Wanstead tittered, his large belly jiggling. "Who on earth might that be?"

"Crimolok is the monster behind all this – the cause of the entire apocalypse. He's Lucifer and Michael's brother. I know that sounds crazy, but it's true."

"The devil himself? My, we do live in biblical times, do we not?"

"Yeah," said Mass, "and unless we get moving right now, we're going to see Revelations part two."

Wanstead chewed the inside of his cheek for a moment. Was he actually listening? Thank God if he was. "I understand your concern, Mr Mass, but General Thomas has taken the army to deal with the very threat of which you speak."

"He doesn't know what he's up against. He thinks he's going out to deal with a beaten enemy, but what he's going to find is an enemy general waging war with everything he has left."

"Why, that is marvellous news. Thomas intends to wipe the

demons out once and for all. If their leader is here, the task will be all that much simpler."

Mass ran a hand over his forehead and groaned. People like Wanstead didn't listen to people like him. It had always been that way, but right now it was going to get people killed. "You need to prepare everyone for battle. There's not much time. It's probably already too late."

"Okay, Mr Mass, I shall do as you say. I promise you the people of Portsmouth will be prepared to defend the city. I shall see to it right away."

Mass sighed, relieved to have seemingly met a man of reason. "Thank you, Colonel Wanstead."

"Now, Mr Mass, please disarm. You and your people are under arrest."

Mass's hands went automatically to his shotgun. "What are you talking about? Arrest for what?"

"General Thomas gave explicit instructions to contain any Urban Vampires found in Portsmouth until his return. The curious thing is that when I attempted to round you all up this morning, your people were nowhere to be seen. Where are Mr Cullen and the others?"

"This conversation is over," said Mass, lifting his shotgun and pointing it in the colonel's face. "We're taking over Portsmouth, and you're going to be a good boy and stand aside."

Wanstead seem unbothered by the shotgun. "Guards!"

The sound of locks disengaging filled the corridor, and when Mass glanced back he saw soldiers filing out the three locked side rooms. They were quick and prepared, aiming their rifles, ready for the kill. At the same time, three guards stepped out of the office behind Wanstead, each of them sporting semi-automatic handguns that they aimed at Mass's face.

Wanstead still wore a polite smile. "Time to behave, Mr Mass. I have no personal grudge against you, so please understand that I am merely following orders."

Mass lowered his shotgun, sick to his stomach. "Don't you

care that your orders came from an egotistical maniac? General Thomas murdered Wickstaff to take over Portsmouth. He's been executing people for daring to even speak against him."

"Yes, I suspected his involvement in Wickstaff's death, but such things happen in war. If I don't follow orders, I dare say I'll end up the same way. Do you know, I met the woman once, Amanda Wickstaff, back before all of this started. She was an officer fresh out of Sandhurst, all bright-eyed and bushy-tailed. It was an inter-regimental sports day, if I remember correctly, and even then it was clear that she was a force to be reckoned with. She was captain of the women's junior rugby team, and she had those women moving back and forth like pegs on a string. I wish I had such a talent for leadership."

Mass shook his head, not understanding. "Why are you doing this?"

Wanstead seemed genuinely pained. "Because Thomas has twenty thousand men out in the field, and they need a safe home to which to return. Whatever you are doing here, Mr Mass, it isn't anything good. You're a troublemaker, and I suspect you always have been. All the same, I promise you that your people shall not harmed while under my care."

"Until Thomas comes back and kills us all," said Tox, still pointing his shotgun despite Addy and Smithy having lowered theirs.

"You take us prisoner," said Mass, "and my people will storm this place. You think we're alone?"

"No, I believe there's a second larger group led by Mr Cullen. Ah, you seem dismayed? Don't be, I've instructed my men not to use force unless absolutely necessary. All the same, no one is going to rescue you. Peacefully is my preferred way of doing things. Please do not force me to make a mess."

"We can take these guys," said Damien, leaning up against the wall with his arms folded. "What you reckon, shall we start a ruck? I got this beady-eyed little princess with the pretty mouth."

The guard to whom he was referring growled, and looked desperate for the order to kill.

"Don't do anything," said Mass, holding up his hand to Damien and staring at the angry guard. "We've warned Colonel Wanstead about the threat coming this way. Now it's up to him."

Wanstead nodded. "There's a good chap. Now, your weapons, please, gentlemen."

Mass turned and gave everyone the go-ahead. They placed their shotguns on the ground carefully, but Mass tossed his aside angrily. Things hadn't gone exactly as planned, but it wasn't the worst outcome either. Wanstead seemed a reasonable man – perhaps *too* reasonable. Either way, this felt like a defeat.

Mass put his hands in the air. "Okay, we're going to play nice."

"Wonderful news. I do so hate bloodshed." Wanstead whipped a handgun from his belt and pointed it at Mass's forehead. "I really am sorry, but my orders were explicit."

Smithy gasped. "Y-You lied? We gave up peacefully and you're going to execute us anyway? Wow, that's fucking cold, man, even for a baddie."

"I am no *baddie*," said Wanstead, seeming utterly offended by the word, "but the reverence people have for the Urban Vampires is a concern. We don't want a rebellion fermenting, do we? We can ill afford it."

"You kill us," said Addy, "and you'll make us martyrs."

"I imagine people would have said the same about General Wickstaff once upon a time, but alas, most have gone willingly to fight by Thomas's side. Anyway, my orders are only to execute your leader, so don't fret, young lady, you'll be quite all right." He looked at Mass and sighed. "I'm sorry for this, old chap, truly."

"You fucker!" Tox threw himself forward, a glint of steel flashing as he yanked a blade from an ankle sheath. With surprise on his side, he buried the blade in the colonel's chest just as he fired off a shot.

Tox grappled with Wanstead, trapping him in a bear hug. The knife disappeared somewhere between them. Wanstead cried out in pain. Mass tried to make use of the distraction, but before he could take a step, a guard walloped him with the grip of his 9mm. He stumbled but didn't go down. Behind him, Addy and Smithy put their hands up as the guards aimed their rifles, ready to fire. Damien stood with his arms folded, leaning against the wall as if bored by the entire scene. Mass was just glad none of them were being shot... yet.

Wanstead hissed and gave Tox a vicious shove, forcing him to the ground. The knife was sticking out of the fat officer's chest, though not deep. He removed it and examined the blood on the blade with a curious expression on his face. "I've had worse, I suppose."

Tox was panting on the floor, but he soon went still. A bloody bullet wound marked his chest, a point-blank shot to the sternum. His glassy eyes were wide open and fixed in place.

Mass felt woozy, but his anger kept him standing. He looked at Wanstead, a glare on his face. "I'm going to kill you."

Wanstead looked genuinely upset, but it didn't stop him from pointing his gun at Mass's chest. "That was inhumane, but I must say he brought it on himself."

"You'll die for this." Mass closed his eyes, hoping he would get a chance for revenge in the next life. "I promise you."

"Okay, enough chit-chat. Guards, get this over wi—"

Alarms sounded, a mixture of sirens and air horns. The guard towers were equipped with whatever people could find to make a noise. Gunfire began seconds later.

Wanstead lowered his handgun and frowned. "What the blazes?"

"It's happening," said Mass. "The demons are here."

"But General Thomas—"

"Is most likely dead, which means you're in charge now. Forget your orders and listen to me. This is a fight to the death, and when the dust clears, it'll either be us or them that's left – most probably them. Now, you can kill me, or you can accept the fact that my people are the toughest bastards you have at your disposal. This is about survival, right? Let us fight."

For the first time since their meeting, Wanstead appeared uncertain. An uneasy grimace replaced his polite smile. Slowly, he nodded. "Okay, let's be done with this nonsense and focus on what matters. Guards, let them go."

"Good move," said Mass. "Our grudges can wait."

He bent down, not to retrieve his weapon, but to hold his dead friend. The bullet Tox had taken had been meant for him. Colonel Wanstead would pay.

But it would have to wait.

Mass straightened back up. "Okay, Vampires, arm up. There're demons to kill."

THE DEMONS CAME in waves throughout the night until dawn eventually broke, and Ted looked up at what could be his final sunrise. The tangelo sky was beautiful, and he wondered if it was a gift from God to a dying man.

Where the hell is God? Was He ever even real?

"We're out of ammunition," said Frank, standing on the ramparts beside Ted. "Only arrows left. The troops are preparing for hand-to-hand."

Ted shook his head, desperately sad. "If it comes to that, we're already beaten."

"I know. The kid, Damien, wants a word w'yow."

"Did he mention what about?"

"No idea. He's a bit of an odd 'un."

Ted looked down at his short, hairy-faced companion and chuckled. "Not as odd as some, Frank. I'll speak to him later. I need to be here."

"Been forty minutes since the last lot came at us. Must be more soon, I reckon."

Ted nodded, already spotting demons amassing in the distant trees. Between the forest and the ramparts there looked to be at least a thousand dead bodies – a carpet of demon flesh. Several times during the night, the demons had made it to the walls, but the ancient stone and deep trenches had foiled their every attempt. Sooner or later though, when the arrows finally ran out, the demons would amass at the walls and get inside. Even if they didn't, the people inside would eventually starve, cut off from the lake and the forest. That everyone had even made it inside the castle's walls was a miracle, but it was a lot of mouths to feed on a month's worth of supplies.

"'Ere we go," said Frank, shaking his head in despair.

Ted watched as the latest wave of demons spilled forth from the forest. Like before, there were a hundred at least, possibly two hundred. They sprinted, shrieking and wailing, towards the ramparts. The primates were the quickest, the shambling burnt men further back. Some shouted obscenities that might once have been funny.

Turdy turdies.

Bitches.

Wank socks.

Katy Perry.

Ted gave Frank a nudge. "Keep everyone's head up. We're all tired, but this has to end eventually."

Frank rushed off, barking orders and offering stirring comments along the lines of letting "the bastard's 'ave it" and "don't give up". Ted turned back to face the enemy. By now, the demons had made it into open ground. The wooden spikes were all broken or blunted by bodies. The pits and trenches were filled with corpses. This new wave had a clear run at the ramparts. Ted was useless with a bow, so he could do nothing but watch. When things inevitably grew more intimate, he would happily get to work with his demolition hammer. He'd lost count of how many demons it had claimed, but it remained sturdy and capable. In a strange way, it was his closest companion. There was sadness in that.

The first primate made it to the wall, but an arrow found its head. It stumbled backwards, the shaft sticking out of its eye, then fell down dead. Two more demons leapt over its corpse.

Arrows filled the air in swarms only half the size of earlier ones. Many archers were out of ammo and now stood on the ramparts aimlessly. Others, the most accurate among them, still had sheaves of arrows piled at their feet. They weren't toothless yet, but they soon would be.

The demons kept on coming. The forest seemed to shake in fear of them as they tore through its innards. All the birds had long since taken flight. Accompanying the rustling of leaves and the creaking of the branches was a new noise – a heavy crashing sound like an elephant racing through the wilderness. All the previous waves of demons had been the same, but this one felt different. Several of the taller trees suddenly leaned, as if taking on a life of their own. A few of the smaller ones uprooted and fell over. Fighting men and women surrounded Ted, but when he spoke, he spoke only to himself. "It's here."

The fallen angel that had emerged from their lake months ago now exploded from the forest. It hurled an uprooted tree trunk like it was a toothpick. The length of gnarled wood flew like a javelin and came crashing down on top of the ramparts, shattering the wooden scaffolds erected there. Ted watched a dozen people he knew die in an instant.

Frank began shouting. "Eyes on the big'un, eyes on the big'un."

A swarm of arrows pierced the air. Most came down in the earth or pierced the hides of unlucky demons, but a dozen more struck the beast known as Lord Amon and brought forth blood. The giant released a pained howl that sounded like the Earth itself was weeping. Several deep scars already blotted its body, reminders of its previous visit to Kielder.

"Fire again," Frank shouted. More arrows pierced the sky, and more landed and drew blood. Lord Amon stumbled and swatted the air, catching arrowheads with its arm.

"Again."

More arrows. More blood. The angel was hurt, staggering.

"Again."

More arrows flew, but not so many this time. Only a couple found the target.

"Again."

Even fewer arrows flew. The archers were all out.

"It waited," said Ted, once again speaking to himself. "It waited until we were low on ammo. Now we're defenceless."

The massive beast slowly recovered, standing tall and gingerly taking a step forward. One or two more arrows flew, but they landed harmlessly in the mud. Lord Amon reached down and plucked up the demons at its feet, collecting them in its massive hand like writhing insects. It was unclear what it was doing.

Until it became clear.

Lord Amon hurled the demons into the air just like it had the tree trunk. They sailed through the air almost comically before raining down on top of the arrow-less archers. Havoc ensued. Those armed with melee weapons were down below, not up top, and it meant the archers were defenceless against the thrashing beasts that now tore them apart. Ted rushed across the wooden platform, sweeping up a demon with his heavy hammer and lifting it up and over the wall. The next demon he couldn't get to because a man named Brian was in the way. Brian screamed, batting at the demon frantically with hands that were being sliced to pieces. The primate leapt on Brian and tore out his throat, then Ted crushed its skull.

More demons flew in from overhead, scattering along the ramparts and in the courtyard below. Men fought everywhere, but there was no order or strategy to their defence. This was pure chaos, demon against man.

Frank was on the other side of the ramparts, separated from Ted by the broken section caused by the flying tree trunk. He gave Ted a nod that summed up what they were both thinking. *This is it.*

"Don't let 'em scare you, lads," Frank shouted. "They're just grumpy 'cos their mums never loved 'em. Send 'em back to Hell."

Ted left the ramparts and entered the courtyard just as another round of demons came raining down from the skies. Some landed badly, snapping legs or even necks, but others landed on top of people and began clawing and biting. Ted ducked as a primate almost landed on top of him. It hit the muddy ground at his feet and bounced. He didn't wait for it to recover. He caved in its chest with his hammer.

Dr Kamiyo fretted nearby. He shouted to Ted, but it was out of fear more than reason. The doctor could fight, but he had spent the last few months caring for their sick and injured. Ted's fondness for him forced him to fight his way over. He bashed aside two demons and then a third just as it was about to pounce on the doctor. "Where are the children, Kamiyo?"

Kamiyo just stared at him.

Ted shook him. "Where are the kids?"

"In the Great Hall."

"Go to them. Protect them with your life."

Kamiyo nodded and took off, the man's courage greater than his fear. Ted suddenly missed Hannah.

That kid would've been an asset right now.

But even with Hannah's loss, Kielder still had a secret weapon.

Sorrow charged like a raging bull, swatting aside primates and twisting the heads off burnt men. Demons managed to leap onto his back but were quickly thrown high into the air by the flapping of his jet-black wings. Sorrow was a force of nature – a whirlwind of destruction – and each second he crushed another demon to dust, without a moment's hesitation. There was no sign of Scarlett, but Ted knew she would have been banished to the Great Hall along with the children.

There was an almighty clatter, and bricks rained from the sky.

Part of the castle's original stone wall toppled. The rivets holding the portcullis popped loose and the iron gate flopped onto the shingle pathway. A stream of demons tore their way inside, eviscerating everything in their path. For the first time in history, the walls surrounding Kothal Castle had been breached.

"Ted! Ted, we need to get out of here." Ted turned in the direction of the voice and saw Damien and his small group of soldiers standing at the far edge of the courtyard. They were hacking at demons wherever they could find them, Damien waved a hand at Ted and shouted again for him to get over there. "I can get us out of here."

Ted ran, dodging a burnt man that instead fell upon a poor woman named Jamie-Lee. He made it over to Damien, huffing and puffing. Tosco was there with the woman, Maddy, and the other newcomers from the Hatchet. Maddy grabbed Ted and straightened him up, then fired a handgun into the demonic crowd to buy some breathing room. Tosco was holding a radio and said, "I can level this place, but we need to not be here when I do."

"There's no escape," said Ted. "There're demons everywhere. Where would we even go?"

"That's what I need to know," said Damien. "Give me a destination and I'll get us there."

Nancy appeared, and begged in a voice both fragile and fierce, "We need to get to *The Hatchet*. I need to be with my daughter."

"So that's option one," said Damien. "Ted, do you have an option two?"

He was about to shrug and go with what Nancy had said, but then he shook his head and frowned. "What does it even matter? This is our last stand. We can't escape."

"Yes, we can," said a woman who Ted thought was called Steph. She was dating a guy named Harry, and the two seemed to be friends of Damien's. Damien reached out his hands and they each took one, the three of them linking up in a line. A smell of burning arose. The air seemed to tingle... and then crackle.

"I can get us out of here the same way me and Nancy got here," said Damien, "but we can only do it once without resting, so I need to know where we're heading."

Ted didn't know why he said it, but it was the only place he could think of. "Portsmouth."

Nancy hissed, and it looked like she was going to lunge at him. Damien held her back. "Let him explain."

"There's nowhere else," said Ted. "If we run, we die. Our only chance is to keep fighting. If there are people in Portsmouth, we need to add our strength to theirs. The war doesn't end here." He glanced over at Sorrow, still smashing demons to pieces in a magnificent display. "We have to keep fighting."

Tosco nodded. "He's right. There are many good people in Portsmouth. This place might be lost, but we can still carry on the fight by helping them."

Nancy sobbed, but Damien moved her aside and rejoined hands with Harry and Steph. All of a sudden, it was like the air was being torn apart and the oxygen was dispersing. A brilliant blue light bloomed. A gate appeared right there in the courtyard.

Damien grunted as if in pain. "Now all we need to do is get everyone through."

"Okay." Ted yelled like a drill sergeant. "Everyone, get to the gate. Move!"

Several lives were lost in the moment of confusion that followed. People saw the gate but didn't understand. They stared at it but didn't move, which allowed the demons to leap on them and kill them. Ted grabbed the nearest person he could find and had to literally throw them into the glowing blue circle. The startled man didn't so much disappear as fade away, but it was enough for people to realise it was a way out of this horror. Ted bellowed again. "Get through the gate if you want to live!"

A stampede began, people abandoning the fight to sprint towards the light. Some were taken down from behind while attempting to flee, while others managed to toss themselves to safety. Ted tried to clear a path for them, swinging his hammer back and forth, cracking demon skulls and shattering ribs. People flooded into the gate in their dozens, seeming to zap out of existence, but those on the ramparts were doomed.

Sorrow saw what was happening and hurried over to the gate. "We leave here? I must retrieve Scarlett."

Ted nodded. "Then go! Fetch her and all the others in the Great Hall. The children are inside."

Sorrow took off, his lumbering footsteps heavy like an ox while somehow as light as a rabbit. He bounded across the courtyard towards the keep, charging through demons and knocking them aside. Ted and the others continued fighting to clear a path for the survivors.

Lord Amon made it inside the courtyard, stomping on Kielder's defenders as if they were ants. Dozens lay crushed into the mud as more demons spilled through the gaps in the walls.

Sorrow disappeared into the keep, and it took mere moments for him to re-emerge with Scarlett beneath his arm like a teddy bear. She kicked and protested, but the demon wouldn't put her down. For a moment, Ted feared Sorrow had left without the children, but then the beast turned and shielded the entrance while Dr Kamiyo rushed outside with the elderly and young in tow. The children screamed at the sight of so many monsters, but Kamiyo kept them all moving. Ted hurried to meet them, taking out demons on all sides. Other demons saw the children and gave chase, but Sorrow flared his wings and blocked their path. They climbed on the demon's back, forcing him to put Scarlett down. He bellowed at her to run, but she was surrounded.

"I've got this," said Angela, emerging from amongst the older survivors from the keep. It was unclear whether she'd been hiding with them or trying to protect them. Now, her eyes rolled back in her head and she began chanting.

First one demon exploded.

Then a dozen more.

The space around the castle's front entrance was suddenly drenched with demon blood as limbs and flesh blanketed the ground. Everyone coughed and spluttered, wiping at their gore-soaked faces, but it gave them time to run. Kamiyo led the retreat.

Ted managed to grab Scarlett and shove her towards the gate, but she fought him and turned back "No, I have to get Sorrow. I'm not leaving without him."

Sorrow must have had super-sensitive hearing, because he turned and bellowed furiously, "Scarlett, go! You must live."

"No, I can't! Sorrow, please..."

Nancy and her soldiers grabbed Scarlett and threw the girl backwards through the gate mid-protest. Sorrow flapped his wings at Ted in what might have been a thank you.

The children made it through the gate, the elderly quick to follow. Ted was about to join them but found that he couldn't. Angela continued her chant by the castle, demons exploding whenever they got near. Sorrow turned his back and resumed fighting with his fellow demons, but they quickly surrounded him. He was visibly tiring. He couldn't fight them forever.

Ted groaned in anguish. Sorrow was too valuable to lose. Portsmouth would need him in the battles ahead. More than that, Ted could not abandon the demon to die. Sorrow was a friend.

Or a familiar colleague at least.

Maybe a distant cousin.

Ted cut a swath with his hammer, battling towards the demon that he now considered family. He bludgeoned demons left and right until he was finally able to make it to the keep. With one black wing unfurled, Sorrow fought to dislodge a demon biting into the other wing. Ted swatted the demon away with his hammer and rescued his ally. Suddenly free, Sorrow looked at Ted in confusion. "The gate is over there. You will die now."

"I needed to make sure you were okay. Scarlett needs you and so do we. Get through that gate and help humanity survive."

The demon swung a taloned fist and caved in a demon's face without even looking in its direction. Then he spread out his leathery black wings and formed a barrier to keep any more from interrupting them. "I'll take you with me. Are you tired? Sorrow will carry."

Ted shook his head. "I can't leave until I know everyone that can be saved has been saved. That includes you, Sorrow. Please, just go!"

Sorrow bowed. "Goodbye, Ted. You will die. This displeases me."

"Thank you. It displeases me too."

The massive demon bounded away and leapt through the gate. Ted continued searching for more survivors. Angela stood ten feet away, obliterating demons with her chanting. She was holding her own, but further away a group of people fought back to back to keep the demons at bay. Ted ran in their direction, crushing the demons that were blocking their retreat. When he reached them, panting and covered in demon blood, they merely stared at him, wide-eyed and terrified. He had to yell at them to run. Next, he rescued a couple backed up against the castle's rear wall. He swung his hammer and created an opening. They too made it to the gate.

Ted doubled over, gasping for breath as he looked for more people to save, but all he saw were demons. They surrounded him on all sides, cutting off any chance he had of making it to the gate himself. He peered over and saw Nancy leaping through into safety, sobbing for her daughter who was so close and yet so far away. Damien remained with his friends, Steph and Harry, powering the gate like a trio of batteries. Tosco and Maddy stood beside them, the American yelling into his radio, Maddy popping off shots from her handgun. Ted knew what Tosco was doing.

He's calling in the big guns.

The fact Kielder was about to be razed to the ground broke Ted's heart, but it pleased him that so many demons would die – and hopefully Lord Amon too. It had all gone to shit so quickly. This place that had been home for an entire year was gone – reduced to blood and splinters, and soon to be cinders. It was time to give up.

"Piss off, yow bastards. I'll 'ave every one of yow. Soddin' Villa supporters!"

Ted searched for the voice and couldn't believe his eyes when he saw Frank still alive. His diminutive friend was holding a wooden shield that had once hung on the wall of the Great Hall. It was almost as big as Frank, which made it difficult for the demons to get at him behind it. Ted's weary mind conjured images of a gull trying to murder a hairy crab and he couldn't stop himself from laughing.

Ted had been about to give up, but seeing his friend in peril gave him one last energy boost. He swung his hammer and took out two more demons, their skulls knocking together like conkers, but as he attempted to replant his footing, a primate slashed at his arm. White-hot pain erupted from his elbow to his wrist, and when he looked down he saw his own blood. The primate pounced. Ted brought his hammer around and crushed its sinewy thigh. Several more demons stood between him and Frank, but it didn't matter. Ted kept his hammer moving, even as his shoulders turned to lead.

Frank saw Ted coming for him, and for a horrifying moment it looked like he might leave the safety of his shield and wave. Fortunately, a burnt man collided with the wood and reminded him to stay in safety.

Ted took out another demon and was suddenly standing next to Frank. He swung his hammer at the burnt man attacking the shield and then announced, "It's time to leave, Frank."

Frank grunted from beneath his shield. "How yow doing, mucker? I've had better days to be honest."

"After three, you're going to run towards that gate as fast as your little legs can take you."

"Hey, less of that!"

Ted gave his friend a smile and started counting. "One..."

"Ted, what are you doing?"

"Two..."

"Ted, get out of here. I'll just slow you—"

"Three! Run, goddamn it!"

"Jesus Christ!" Frank bolted like a jackrabbit, letting go of the shield and almost being crushed by it. The burnt man lunged for him and went a pisser, landing on its face. Ted kicked it in the head and swung his hammer at another that was approaching. There were demons everywhere now. Ted had done all he could. He glanced back to check on Frank and saw him waddling for his life. Tosco and the American soldiers saw him coming and fought to clear a path.

Ted considered making a run for safety himself, but too many demons had got around behind him now. Even if he fought, it would only delay the others from leaving. He couldn't risk them being killed while they waited for him to reach them.

Maddy called out to Ted, but Ted turned his back and braced himself to absorb the impact as a pair of burnt men crashed into him. His hammer fell from his grasp, so he headbutted the first and kneed the second. A primate grabbed Ted's shoulder and sliced his flesh. Another slashed his thigh.

He fell to one knee, no more fight left in him.

Time's up.

"*Pater Noster, qui es in caelis, sanctificetur nomen tuum.*"

Ted turned his head and saw Angela gliding towards him. She parted the throngs of demons as if they were mere fronds on a palm tree. Her eyes were still rolled back in her head, yet she seemed to see Ted clearly. She placed a hand on his shoulder, a friendly reassurance.

I'm not alone.

The demons surrounding Ted exploded. He had to shield his eyes from the ludicrous amount of gibs raining down on him. He didn't want to interrupt the woman's flow, so he didn't say anything to distract her. He just grabbed Angela's arm and started pulling her in the direction of the gate. Maybe there was still a chance for both of them to get out of there.

But the gate was gone.

No!

Demons swarmed the area where Damien and the others had been standing, making it clear that they'd had no choice but to leave. No choice but to leave Ted and Angela behind.

They were going to die here.

Angela's chanting continued and more demons exploded. As soon as any got close, they erupted like fireworks. She was a one-woman army. An exorcist during a demon invasion.

Ted was in love.

Angela and Ted huddled together, demons failing to get anywhere near them. Angela spoke in tongues, words issuing like a mad rap. She showed no signs of tiring. Maybe she could keep this up forever. Ted caught his breath, safe within the invisible forcefield Angela had somehow put in place. Nothing could touch them.

But then Angela's words were interrupted.

A chunk of masonry struck her in the centre of her chest and knocked her backwards. She landed in the blood-slick grass, unconscious or dead. Ted tried to reach her, to help her, but a giant hand engulfed him and plucked him from the earth. He felt massive pressure restricting his chest and suddenly couldn't breathe. His eyes bulged.

Lord Amon lifted Ted twenty feet above the ground and glared at him with an expression of undeniable hatred. Ted spat, but there was too much distance to hit the monster's face, so he resorted to swearing. "You sorry sack of shit."

The angel roared, buffeting Ted's face with hot, putrid air. He turned his head to protect his eyes and caught a glimpse of Angela down below. She was alive and dragging herself along the ground. The demons would finish her soon.

Ted was the last man standing at Kielder. It felt right somehow. A captain going down with his ship. The pressure in his chest increased. Lord Amon must have been enjoying the sight of his life slowly leaving him, but he wouldn't give the bastard the satisfaction of seeing him scared. He looked up into the sky, wanting to see that beautiful tangelo sky one last time before he died.

What he saw was beyond words.

Four blackbirds fell from the sky – mortar shells plummeting towards the castle at a hundred miles an hour. Ted cackled, and he didn't stop for three whole seconds. Then the world became fire.

———

MASS HEADED for the walls that surrounded the well-lit military docks. Several guard towers had been erected in the last year, and vans and lorries were parked end to end in the longer sections, providing a second skin and flat roofs to fire from. In the city itself, people barricaded themselves inside old buildings or on rooftops, the entrances cluttered with whatever they had been able to find. With so much of the population having left with Thomas, the defences seemed sparsely populated. The various searchlights and campfires only highlighted the lack of manpower. Fifteen thousand people was a lot less than it sounded, especially when the number included the young, the elderly, and the incapable.

Wanstead had followed Mass outside with his guards. The colonel looked around now as officers and sergeants hurried towards him. He put a hand in the air to get everyone's attention. "This is it, gentlemen. We are the last bastion of mankind, and our enemy is here to have at us. You have your duties, so gather your teams and hop to it."

The officers and guards scattered, all apparently knowing what to do. At least Thomas had drilled them well. Or maybe it had been Wanstead.

Mass turned to his own team. "Smithy, you stick with me. Addy, go find out where Cullen is and tell him join back with us here. Damien, you..."

"I'll do what I want," said Damien.

Mass nodded. "Yeah, you do that. Okay, the rest of us, let's get to work."

"It sounds like we're being attacked on all fronts," said Wanstead, shaking his head in disgust, which was far better than despair. "No matter what we do, it's going to spread us thin. I'll call in the guns."

"There are people living in the ruins," said Mass. "We can't risk killing them."

Wanstead chuckled. "You've been away too long, Mr Mass. Thomas set up several bombardment zones. Civilians have been moved out of the areas and we used abandoned vehicles to form a funnel into those zones. If the bastards have come in force, I guarantee there'll be hundreds of them standing right on top of our big, invisible Xs."

Mass hadn't considered that Thomas could have been competent, but it appeared that he was. It was a relief to hear that thought had been put into Portsmouth's defences. "Okay, do it, Colonel. What are you waiting for?"

"Well, not your approval, certainly." Wanstead produced a radio and called in the order. Then he turned back to Mass. "Now we wait."

It took about fifteen seconds, but it felt longer, as Mass stood silently watching the sky. All the while, gunfire lit up the dark pockets of Portsmouth. The twin streaks that eventually cut a path through the stars were beautiful, more so because of the colossal destruction they brought with them. The resulting whoosh of air reached them a full second before a flash of fire lit up the distance. The inferno grew, lighting up the whole of Portsmouth. For a brief moment it was daylight, and Mass saw the frightened soldiers on the battlements, all waging their own private wars.

"I'm going to go get involved," said Damien. "I'll catch you guys later."

Smithy lifted his shotgun and was unable to keep it from shaking. He looked at Mass. "What's the plan, boss?"

"I haven't seen you afraid before, Smithy. You good?"

"It just hits you, don't it? One minute you're coping, and then the next it's all just too much. I've got this feeling like I'm... like I'm looking down on myself, and I'm like... fuck, it's the end of the world and I'm about to go to war with demons. How do you wrap your head around that?"

Mass put a hand on the lad's shoulder and looked him in the eye. "By sticking close to your mates and remembering we're all in this together. I've got your back, Smithy. All right?"

Wanstead cleared his throat. "You are fine men, and I'm grateful to have your assistance. I trust you'll direct your people wherever they are needed, Mr Mass."

Mass cricked his neck and took a step towards Wanstead. "You and me have issues left to discuss, but first we need to survive. We're on the same team for now, and I'll be doing whatever I can to keep Portsmouth standing. You make sure you do the same, Colonel."

Wanstead nodded, showing neither fear nor offence. "Until later then, Mr Mass. Good luck. Truly."

The colonel took off, barking orders into his radio. Mass grabbed Smithy and pulled him towards the walls. Together, the two of them raced over to a tatty white Transit van and climbed up on top of it, and then onto the wooden pallets piled on top. Peering over the walls was disheartening. Thousands of demons teemed throughout the ruins surrounding the docks. They leapt over abandoned vehicles and emerged from dark alleyways. Men and woman fired from the upper windows of several buildings, inflicting massive casualties. More explosions lit up the distance. It was like the storming of the beaches in World War Two, thought Mass, except they were the Germans and the demons didn't care about losses. There was no way to damage the enemy's morale. They would just keep coming.

And the Germans always lose.

The fighting was too far away for Mass's and Smithy's shot-guns to have much of an effect, so the two of them just stood and watched for now, biding their time. So far, Portsmouth had the best of the fighting. Machine-gun fire rattled off across the city and rifles cracked in their hundreds. Demons screeched and wailed in agony. Already their bodies littered the rubble. What concerned Mass was the darkness beyond the docklands where the searchlights faded and night took over. What existed there, beyond what they could see? Another thousand demons? Another ten thousand? A million? And what of Crimolok? Where was the ancient beast responsible for every single death during the last year? Was it watching Portsmouth fall? Or was it coming to crush it with its own hand?

"Hey," said Smithy, pointing, "is that Rick? I was wondering where's he's been."

Mass looked towards the nearby ruins. There, Rick strolled casually towards the demons. He raised his hands and threw out a bolt of pure white light, striking the centre of a car park a hundred metres away and obliterating a dozen demons. The few parked cars almost tipped over from the blast, before dropping back down and bouncing on their suspensions.

"Not bad," said Mass. "Wonder how long he can keep that up for. Do angels get tired?"

Smithy frowned at him. "You really think he's an angel? Then why is he alone? Why didn't God send a shitload of them to help us out?"

"Politics," said Mass. "I never understood it before and I don't understand it now."

"I hear that."

They watched while Rick continued his onslaught, throwing out bolts of light and sending pieces of demons up into the air. The rifle fire was endless, a constant drone, and the larger guns shook the earth. Demonic screeching howled throughout the city, and a biting wind billowed against the buildings and the people.

This truly is the end of the world.

A primate leapt out of a nearby alleyway within shooting distance. Mass felt a jolt of adrenaline and called out, "Mine!" He aimed his shotgun, pulled the trigger, and the primate flew back into the alley with a screech. It re-emerged a moment later, peppered bloody but still able to move.

"Let me finish the job." Smithy shoved Mass's shotgun away and lifted his own. He aimed, fired, and the primate's skull splattered the wall behind it.

Mass huffed. "I weakened it first."

"This ain't a jar of pickles, dude. I just owned your ass."

"It's gonna be a long night. Don't do a victory dance just yet."

Smithy replaced the cartridge he'd just fired and shrugged. "Fair enough. It's one–nil, then. Ready to play?"

Mass shouldered his shotgun. "Hell yes."

13

A ll great leaders suffered defeats. It was taking those defeats and turning them into victories that sorted the great from the mediocre.

This is my Dunkirk. A necessary defeat.

The enemy had handed Thomas a sound defeat, but he had fallen back with a thousand of his men, ready to fight another day. Disaster was behind them now. D-Day lay ahead. Victory would come.

This isn't the end. It's merely the end of the beginning.

Thomas estimated that the thousand men following him through the fields, combined with the fifteen thousand remaining in Portsmouth, gave him every chance of defeating the enemy. They would stand behind the walls and repel whatever came. The only challenge would be getting these thousand men home. This land had become enemy territory.

The enemy were everywhere, all along the roads and teeming through the countryside. Thomas sought to avoid fighting whenever he could, but it was unavoidable at times. His men had used most of their ammunition pushing their way towards Portsmouth, and they had been moving at an almost constant run, knowing that the bulk of the enemy was still behind them. If they could travel quickly enough, they could make it back to Portsmouth without being cut off from safety. Scant few miles remained; they had been rushing across the landscape for the last three hours. It was possible the enemy was yet to reach Portsmouth, but the more Thomas saw demons on the road, the more he knew it was unlikely to be true.

The enemy army that had attacked Winchester was large and cumbersome. There was no way it had moved faster than Thomas and his men, which meant there was time to warn Portsmouth and prepare for war. Thomas estimated five or six hours before the bulk of the enemy's forces reached the city. He could be there in two.

Tony was right. We should have fallen back.

Self-doubt plagued Thomas, and he kept picturing his former colonel raising a handgun and intending to shoot him in the face. Tony had been a loyal man, but he had slowly turned his back and allowed treachery to overwhelm him. Was Thomas responsible in some way for the man's lack of honour? Had he been a poor leader, or was Tony Cross just a bad man? Regardless of the truth, Colonel Cross had warned Thomas about what was coming.

He warned me and I did nothing.

No, I fought our enemy. There is no shame in that. Defeat is a part of war, not the whole. I must ensure we continue to stand tall. We are humanity's best. We shall survive. I shall lead us.

He knew it in his bones to be true, that this was just a test. Mankind had been given too easy a ride. Now it was being forced to prove its worth. After its eventual victory, it would rise again stronger than ever before. The weak and the lazy were all gone. Mankind had become a warrior race, and forever may it remain so.

Demons congregated in a field ahead, perhaps a dozen or more. Thomas gave the order to fire and his men took them down in a second. The way ahead seemed clear. Portsmouth awaited.

Victory awaited.

CRIMOLOK TREMBLES WITH POWER. With each human life extinguished, God's hold on the universe weakens. The barrier protecting Him weakens. Once this place is cleansed of life, Crimolok will assault his father's domain and take existence for himself. Lucifer, Michael, and all of the other heavenly brothers will be forced to bow to a new god. A supreme god.

I shall be all and everything.

The massacre in the human town had been glorious. Crimolok himself had killed thousands. His legions had killed thousands more. Some humans managed to flee, scattering into the fields, but it will only prolong the hunt, which is acceptable because Crimolok enjoys the hunt.

The great human city lies ahead. Soon its name will join Sodom and Gomorrah. No human will survive there. No child will ever grow up there. Mankind is at its end. The tipping point is at hand.

Crimolok watches his legions surround a group of humans hiding up in a large tree. To expedite the slaughter, he grabs the tree by its highest branches and uproots it from the earth. Humans fall from the trunk and land amongst the demons, and are forced to choke on their own blood as they are eaten alive. Some still cling to the tree, begging for life. Crimolok swings the tree and releases it, sending it a hundred feet into the air. It comes crashing down to earth in the distance, no human on it left alive.

Crimolok marches on towards Portsmouth.

ALICE WAS LOSING HER MIND. She got out of bed and crept outside into one of *The Hatchet*'s many identical steel corridors. She headed inside the breakroom and switched on the coffee machine. She'd never been allowed to drink the stuff a year ago, but since coming aboard her dead father's US Coast Guard frigate, no one paid much attention to what she was doing. In fact, they treated her like an adult most of the time, which was one of the few things she liked about the apocalypse. Little else though.

Just when Portsmouth had started to feel like a home, just when life had found a new kind of normal, everything had gone 'tits up' – to borrow a phrase from the Brits. Wickstaff died and then Tosco was suddenly on the run for something she didn't fully understand. Oh, and don't forget they were all going to go live in some forest like a bunch of elves.

Alice had never known that you could feel so alone surrounded by people. She was trapped on a boat with a hundred sailors, barely able to move without bumping into someone, and yet she felt completely disconnected. While she knew everyone on board, they were all strangers. There wasn't a person left alive she had known for longer than a few months. Maddy had known her longest, but even that relationship was new. The loneliness was painful, and she hated it, but she couldn't help but think about all of her friends back home – other kids who were probably all dead. She thought about her brother, Kyle, her mom, and her dad. She thought about her dad especially. He'd sailed across the ocean to find her, only to die the moment he did. She'd watched both her brother and her dad die, and the memories would stay with her forever.

At least I never had to watch Mom die. I wonder what happened to her. Did she stay in Indiana? Did she stay at home?

Alice was used to having a big bedroom full of clothes, books, and stacks of DVDs. Now she slept in a bunk room with three other people. If it wasn't for all the paperback books she'd brought from Portsmouth, she would have already gone insane aboard *The Hatchet*. As it was, she remained only mildly unstable – frustrated and bored rather than crazy.

Tosco had left with his team two days ago, the morning before last. The clock on the breakroom wall read five fifteen, which meant the sun would soon come up and start day three. They had arrived at the forest safely because Tosco had radioed in to say so, but then she had heard little else. Lieutenant Michaels was in charge of *The Hatchet* while Tosco was away, but Alice didn't like the guy all that much. He seemed irritated by her presence, and seemed to be one of the few sailors who considered Alice a kid. She was fifteen, and while in the old world that might have meant she was still young, in this new world, childhood had been cancelled.

Alice sat down with her coffee and sipped at it. She heard voices from further down the corridor, possibly from one of the other bunk rooms. They were trying to whisper, but sound travelled in the bowels of the ship. Whatever they were talking about seemed important.

Maybe they're talking about Tosco and the others.

Not like there would be anything else of interest.

Curious, Alice left her muddy coffee on the table and crept back out into the corridor. The voices were coming from the officers' cabins at the aft of the ship. Tosco had the admiral's suite, but there were two single-occupant cabins opposite. The voices were coming from inside one of those. She crept down the corridor until she could make out words.

"We haven't had any contact in hours. Tosco called in a mortar strike right on top of his position."

"What? That's suicide!"

"I know. Apparently, Tosco said they would be gone by the time the bombs dropped. He demanded Lieutenant Michaels fire the guns and trust him. He said we were to head back to Portsmouth immediately."

"We just left there!"

Alice had to grab the wall to keep herself steady. Why on earth would Tosco have ordered *The Hatchet* back to Portsmouth? She had got the impression they were wanted fugitives there or something. She had a terrible fear that Tosco was dead. Maddy too.

"And can you believe they found Alice's mom? I mean, what the hell?"

"I thought Captain Granger's ex-wife lived in Indiana?"

"Exactly! How did she make it all the way over here, and in the exact place our commanding officer takes us to? It seems like too much of a—"

It was a massive no-no to enter an officer's cabin, but Alice barged open the door and threw herself inside. There, she found Lieutenant Brooks talking with Ensign Grady. Strangely, Brooks was lying in his bed, while Grady was sitting on a chair to one side of the cramped room. Alice assumed Grady had just finished his shift.

"What the hell are you playing at, Alice. Get out!"

"I heard what you just said. You said my mom is alive!"

Brooks and Grady both stared with their mouths open, and their shocked expressions led her to doubt herself. Had she misheard? Or was cabin fever sending her insane? Of course, there was no way her mom could be alive. No way at all. It made no sense.

Brooks swallowed. Slowly the shocked expression left his face. He ran a hand over his mouth and ruffled the stubble on his upper lip. "Apparently, yes, she was alive. That's what Commander Tosco reported to us yesterday, anyway. It seems like the settlement in the forest was attacked while they were there. We haven't heard anything since."

"We have to go there. We have to go and find out what happened."

Brooks sighed. "Our orders are to return to Portsmouth. I think Lieutenant Michaels plans to set sail at oh-seven-hundred."

Alice clenched her fists and stepped up to the officer's bed. He pulled up his blanket and shuffled against the headboard. Was she scaring him? "There's no way I'm going back to Portsmouth if my mom is here. I'm getting off this boat."

"Don't be stupid," said Grady. "You can't survive on your own."

Alice spun on him. "I would rather die alone out there then be stuck on *The Hatchet* any longer. I'm tired of being a prisoner."

Brooks frowned. "You're not a prisoner, Alice. Tosco brought you on board to keep you safe."

"And now he's missing. What kind of person would I be if I abandoned him as well as my mom? I want to go look for them in this forest. That's why we came here, right?"

Ensign Grady stepped towards her with his hand out. "Come on, Alice. It's early. Let's get some chow and we'll talk about it."

Alice swiped at the man's outstretched hand. She ignored Grady and kept her focus on Brooks. "Help me, Lieutenant, please. Help me find my mom. If not for me, then do it for my dad."

Brooks looked away, almost like he was ashamed. "Captain Granger was a good man, Alice, but I fear his spirit will come back and haunt me if I allow you to get hurt."

"He sailed an ocean to get to me. What do you think he would think if I was unwilling to travel a few miles to reach my mom?"

Grady stuttered. "C-Commander Tosco saved my life on more than one occasion. I would be happy to go look for him with Alice."

Alice turned to the junior officer and wanted to hug him. He couldn't have been much older than twenty, and he looked like a starving fox with his wispy red hair, but he was clearly brave to offer to help her. He was willing to do what was right. "Thank you, Grady."

Brooks threw off his blankets, revealing himself naked aside from a pair of briefs. "None of this means anything. It's Lieutenant Michael's decision, so I suggest we go and talk with him. He might be willing to send a small team to find out what happened in the forest, but I doubt it."

Alice averted her eyes, uncomfortable at the sight of the officer's bulge beneath his well-developed abs. "But you'll help me, right? You'll argue on my side?"

Brooks sighed. "Yes, Grady and I will both argue on your behalf. To be honest, Tosco has earned the right for a rescue mission. If he's in danger, he deserves our help. Now, Alice, will you kindly get out of my cabin so that I can get dressed? I expect a coffee waiting for me when I step outside."

Alice snapped to attention and smiled. "Right away, sir."

My mom's alive.

And I'm going to find her.

14

The demons were starting to increase in number. A majority of the fighting was within the ruins of the city, but it was gradually getting closer. The demons came from the rubble, moving through side streets and main roads. Defenders continued firing from machine-gun nests and sniper posts in the various buildings, but over the last two hours, as dawn arrived, screams had begun to break out. The demons were getting through the barricades and making it up the stairwells. A hundred metres away, Mass saw a man fall backwards out of a third-floor window with a primate on top of him. Both died when they hit the ground. The morning sun made their blood shine.

"They're getting closer," said Smithy. The current score was five–three to Smithy. Mass hated to admit it, but he wasn't as good a shot.

"We're making it hard for them, and that's what counts. The more that die out there in the ruins, the less we'll have to deal with at the walls when the real fighting begins."

"I feel bad for the poor sods out there in the city. They've been fed to the wolves."

Mass grunted. "We've all been fed to the wolves. No one is safe."

"How you reckon Rick's getting on? Dude's like one of the X-Men."

"I saw light blasting from near the Spinnaker. Looks like he's made quite the journey."

Smithy looked towards the bent, broken spire that had once topped the city's landmark building. "Where's he going, you reckon? Is he abandoning us?"

"I doubt it. I'm sure he has his reasons."

A demon leapt out of some rubble and sprinted for the walls. Smithy whipped his shotgun around and hit it square in the chest. "Ha! That's six for me now. Suck my big hairy balls."

Mass shook his head and sighed. "I give up. You're too bloody good."

There was shouting behind them, men arguing or maybe just voicing their concerns. Mass lowered his shotgun and turned to face the group walking towards the walls. It was Wanstead and his officers.

"Wait here." Mass patted Smithy on the back and then dropped down off the top of the van. He stepped into Wanstead's path. "Colonel? What's up?"

"General Thomas is alive. That man is made of iron."

"He's made of blood and guts, I can assure you. So what are you telling me, that he beat the demons?"

Wanstead shook his head sadly. "Alas not. He's returning home with only a thousand men."

Mass had to plant his feet to remain steady, suddenly feeling woozy. "And he left with fifteen thousand? Jesus Christ. Jesus fucking Christ."

Wanstead put up a hand. "Let's focus on action not regret. There are a thousand tired and wounded men stranded outside our walls. We need to go and rescue them."

"Thomas can die out there for all I care. He fucking deserves to."

"Perhaps, but what of the thousand men with him? They are

guilty of nothing but fighting for our survival. How many of your own friends count amongst them, do you think?"

It was unlikely anyone Mass knew had survived whatever slaughter Thomas had led them to. The bastard would have used the original inhabitants of Portsmouth as cannon fodder in order to protect his own, more loyal men. Even so, those thousand soldiers were innocent men who had just been trying to do the right thing.

"What do you plan on doing?" asked Mass.

"We need to send out a rescue mission. Those men are too valuable to leave stranded."

"Also, they're human beings, right? We should rescue them regardless of whether they're useful."

Wanstead smirked, obviously finding the questioning of his morals amusing. "Consider yourself lucky that you can still see things in black and white. I need your help, Mr Mass."

"You want me to take my guys out to rescue the son of a bitch who wants us dead?"

"I realise the irony, but your people know the ruins better than anyone."

Mass stepped up to Wanstead and looked him in the eye. His guards bristled, their hands moving to their weapons. "You send me out there, and I promise you that Thomas won't be coming back, you get me? If you want me to risk my neck saving a thousand innocent men, then my answer is yes, but Thomas isn't part of the deal. I see him in trouble, about to die, I turn my back."

Wanstead took a step forward, reducing the distance between them to almost nothing. When he spoke, he almost whispered. "Mr Mass, have you not considered that I understand that? Portsmouth needs all the fighting men it can get, which makes those thousand men out there precious. Whether or not Thomas returns is of less import."

Mass frowned, trying to figure Wanstead out. Slowly, it became clear. "If Thomas fails to return, and we win this fight, Portsmouth has a new leader. You."

Wanstead nodded, almost imperceptibly. "I'm a good man, Mr Mass. I don't toy with people's lives when I don't have to, and I prefer mercy over pain. Portsmouth could suffer worse fates than my leadership."

"I think you might be a good man, more or less," said Mass, "but you tried to shoot me and killed my friend, Tox. I'll take my Vampires out there to bring back those men, but as for what happens next, you shouldn't get too comfy on your throne. Still want my help?"

Wanstead cleared his throat and stepped back. He'd turned a little pale in the glow of the spotlights. "It disappoints me to hear you hold a grudge, and yet I do understand it. As it stands, Mr Mass, I would still very much appreciate you bringing those men home. What you do with General Thomas is your choice. No one will shed tears, whatever happens."

Mass looked down at his shotgun, dirty and battered. "Okay, Colonel. Looks like I'm heading out then. First, though, I'm going to need something from you."

"And what is that?"

"Guns. Lots and lots of guns."

———

THE HUMAN'S weapons are formidable. Several thousand of Crimolok's legion already lie dead, torn apart by tiny shards of metal and exploding chemicals. It is no matter, for tens of thousands more will take their place. The massive gate to Hell remains open. The damned spill out continuously, blanketing the Earth. This is the second great flood – the flood of blood and flesh.

Noah be damned.

Crimolok strides onward, footsteps crushing the metal wagons littering the human pathways, but then he pauses. He senses something. Something terrible. Obscene.

He looks down.

There stands his brother. Even inside the diseased meat he is wearing he shines like a star, and the beauty of his spirit manages to surprise Crimolok after having lost his true memory of it.

"Michael! I sensed you were here. Did God expel you from his feeble cocoon, or did you flee, knowing His time is at an end?"

From inside the wretched vessel of a deceased human, Michael stares up at Crimolok without fear or awe. "Brother, you are an offence to creation. You were born to build, and yet you destroy."

"Destruction is the essence of creation, Michael. How can I create unless given a canvas? God surely forgives me, for he made me what I am."

"God's forgiveness is forever beyond you, vile one. I came here to stop you. Your atrocities must end."

That God's forgiveness is forever out of reach causes a deep sorrow inside Crimolok, but it serves only to stoke the blazing fury inside his soul. "You should have remained in safety and enjoyed Heaven a while longer. How did you come to be here?"

"Our forsaken cousin Daniel gave his power to the human who owned this body. This vessel is the only one in existence able to hold an angel's essence. It was the only way I could come here and face you. I left the warmth of Heaven because of your arrogant crusade."

"Now you will know only oblivion." Crimolok lashes out, trying to crush his brother's vessel with a swipe of his giant hand. Michael leaps aside and throws out an arm. A bolt of heavenly light slices the air and hits Crimolok's shoulder.

Crimolok stumbles backwards, feeling pain for the first time in his long existence. It is exquisite. His legions surround Michael, intending to tear his vessel apart, but he quickly dispatches them with the purifying flames of Heaven. They are no match for an angel.

"Is Lucifer with you too?" Crimolok demands. "I do not sense his presence."

"Lucifer is somewhere else, seeking atonement for his crimes.

It is not too late for you to do the same. God's forgiveness is beyond your reach, but mine is not, brother. Stop your slaughter and embrace me."

"Embrace you? Where? In the depths of the abyss where our father sent me? Do you know what it is like for a creative being to be trapped in an endless nothingness? I spent an eternity in complete darkness with nothing but my own nightmares." Crimolok sneers in disgust. "You think our father to be a just and merciful ruler? He is a scared tyrant, hiding away while his children burn. I would never abandon my garden as He has done His."

Michael sneered back. "It is because of avaricious fiends like you that he was forced to do so. He chose humanity's suffering over humanity's end. A choice with terrible consequences that could not be avoided, but a pained life is better than no life."

Crimolok sneers again. "It depends on the amount of pain. Allow me to demonstrate."

Michael dodges another attack, an irritating wasp. Once more, he releases a white-hot stream of heavenly light, singeing Crimolok's torso and drawing more of that exquisite agony. It is a feeling like no other – an explosion of the senses.

Michael throws more light, burns more flesh. "Give up, brother, or be extinguished."

"Extinction is the only kindness left to me, Michael. I will prevail or I will not, but I will never again be a prisoner. Enough talk! Let us fight as brothers must."

More of Crimolok's legions surround Michael, closing in on all sides and forcing him to deal with them. Crimolok takes his chance, lunging forward and scooping Michael up in his hand. The fight is over.

Michael squirms in Crimolok's hands, but with his arms trapped, he can summon no more of that heavenly light. Crimolok looks down at his brother and is surprised to feel something other than hatred. "You and Lucifer were my brothers. I loved you, yet you abandoned me to Father's wrath. That sin is greater than all else. That sin is the reason this world, and so many others, burn. I am the Red Lord, the painter of blood, the new father of creation."

"You are lost, brother, as you have always been. Your gift is too much to bear. It puts you closer to God than any of us, but you sear in the heat of his glory."

"Then I shall burn." Crimolok clenches his fist, crushing the weak, blood-filled vessel his brother inhabits. Liquids explode from the orifices and Crimolok tosses the quivering meat to the ground.

TONY COULD HOLD on no longer. He'd rode day and night to get here, and there was no doubt that he'd arrived, but his body was done. The trees deep into the forest had all been chopped down, and the uneven ground tossed Tony's scrambler back and forth until he was no longer able to hold on. His wrists were weak and his hands could no longer grip, so he simply let go of the handlebars and tumbled from the seat. The scrambler continued on until it hit a stump and toppled onto its side. For a while, Tony lay there on his back, staring up at the early morning sun. It was a cold sun, more lukewarm yellow than blazing orange. Winter was on its way, and soon the dead world would frost over.

There's no one left. This place is abandoned.

Tony turned his head and saw a field of flesh. Bodies, not people. A crumbling wall lined a nearby hill, a castle hiding behind it. This was the place he'd been looking for. It was a dead place.

Soon my body will join all the rest.

Tony lay on his back, tired, panting, and waiting to die. The war wounded knew when their time was up. They would find a place to rest and close their eyes, knowing they would never again wake up. He had thought to do the same.

But he wasn't dead. Not yet.

His constant shivering and blurred vision told him there could not have been much blood left in him to lose, and he assumed it was only shock keeping him breathing. All pain had gone. His thoughts were basic, focused only on the present. He was partly dreaming, not knowing fully what was going on. The only thought he could hold on to was that he needed to climb the nearby hill. He needed to reach the top.

I need to know for sure that everyone is dead.

And so he managed to climb back to his feet and continue his journey on foot. There was only a hundred metres left to go until the bottom of the hill. He couldn't lie down and die so close to his objective. His feet felt like lead weights and he had to labour over every step. He made it away from the trees and into the field of the dead, intending to avert his eyes and cast out the images of dead men and women, but what he saw surprised him. The carpet of flesh wasn't human. The corpses belonged to demons – thousands of them. They were mostly burnt, but many were dismembered, arms and legs hanging on by sinew and skin. There were arrows sticking out of the ground and peppering bodies all around. Closer to the hill, the bodies were nearly incinerated. Something had obliterated them – like a giant lightning bolt from the sky.

Tony began to hope. Perhaps the people here were still alive. Perhaps they possessed some fantastic weapon that could do this. What on earth could wipe out a thousand demons in a field like this? Military artillery was the only thing he could think of.

That hope slowly bled away as he climbed the hill, seeking the castle at the top. The ancient stone wall was in ruins, entirely broken down in several places. There was no way this place could ever be defended.

It had fallen.

Climbing the hill was a slow process, and Tony nearly quit several times. Demon corpses littered the slope, and their blood made it slippery. If not for the fact that so many were burned, he wouldn't have made it. Their ashes covered the ground and allowed him to barely keep his footing. Eventually he made it to the top.

His energy spent, Tony fell onto his hands and knees. His journey was still incomplete, so he fought the urge to lie down. He wouldn't die six feet outside the castle walls, so he crawled.

And he crawled.

He didn't stop until he made it inside the walls. Bloody saliva hung from his mouth. His pulse pounded in his eardrums.

The castle had toppled, only its lower section was still standing. Its upper floors, walls, and ceiling were scattered in a hundred places, demon bodies crushed beneath. Everything had been scorched black, as if the world itself had caught fire. The bodies were so badly charred in this area that is was impossible to tell human from demon. This must have been the scene of a last stand. Somehow the people here had pulled the pin on something devastating.

Good on 'em. They went down in a blaze of glory.

There was a patch of unburnt ground nearby, shielded from the blaze by a stack of thick logs. Tony dragged himself over to it, barely able to feel his legs any more. It was a struggle, but he managed to pull himself into a sitting position against the logs. Too tired to hold his head up, he let it lower onto his shoulder. It was then that he saw the most beautiful sight.

Ten feet away was a gigantic foot. Tony allowed his gaze to follow a massive leg until it reached a ruined torso torn almost in two. The humans here had managed to kill a fallen angel. It made their last stand even more heroic. It was an honour to die amongst them.

I always thought I'd die on a battlefield. Never thought it would be this peaceful.

Tony managed to lift his head and look straight ahead. The stone wall in front of him was mostly intact, but a small section had been knocked down, leaving a gap the size of two men standing shoulder to shoulder. Through the gap, Tony could see the sun. Beneath that sun, at the bottom of a long, grassy slope was a wonderful lake. Its waters reflected nothing but sky, and it was untouched by the charred chaos of war. There were even ducks gliding on its surface.

Tony smiled. It was a good place to die.

"You all right, mate?"

Tony turned his head more quickly than he should have, and his vision swirled. Standing before him was a middle-aged woman wearing a cassock and dog collar. He blinked several times, trying to dispel the bizarre ghost.

"Gotta say," said the woman, refusing to disappear from his imagination, "you look like something just shat you out. Where did you come from?"

"W-Who are you?"

"Angela. I'm the only one left here. Sorry if you expected a crowd."

Tony wheezed, struggling to breathe. "They're all dead?"

"What? No, not at all, my friend. They buggered off to Portsmouth."

"Portsmouth?"

The woman nodded. "Yeah, apparently there's a bunch of people there."

Tony started laughing. It made him dizzy, and he kept thinking he would run out of breath and pass out, but he couldn't stop. He kept on until the woman grunted at him and appeared pissed off. "Sorry," he managed to say. "It's just that I came from Portsmouth to find you people, only to find out that everyone went the other way. It's funny."

The woman looked at him for a moment, then smiled. It was a warm, genuine expression that made Tony feel completely at home with this odd, middle-aged vicar. She sat down next to him, leaning against the logs and staring out through the gap in the wall. "The people here were bloody mad on fishing," she said. "The place stunk of fish twenty-four-seven. I hated it, but now it smells too much of fire and blood. Reminds me of a place I'd rather not go back to.

"What happened here?"

"The demons attacked, but before the people here scarpered, they called in a fireworks show. It was quite the event. Reminded me of the civic hall on a Friday night. You ever been?"

He shook his head. "How did you survive what happened here, the bombs?"

"The castle had a dungeon. Seemed like a good place to be, so I threw myself down the steps just as the first bombs hit. Felt like the ground was going to swallow me up, but once it stopped I came back outside and everything was on fire. Can't you feel how hot it was, even now?"

Tony shook his head. "I can't feel anything."

"Yeah, that'll be because you're dying. You Christian?"

"No. Fuck God."

"Okay, no last rites for you, then, but can I say one thing?"

Tony looked at her. "Be my guest?"

"All is forgiven. God – or whoever was running the show – really dropped the ball by letting Hell invade the Earth, so believe me when I say there's going to be an amnesty on damnation. Hell is out of business. There's only one place still accepting lost souls now and that's Heaven. I can't tell you what it's like up there, but I can tell you that this place isn't all there is. There's more, and I think you'll be surprised by what you find."

Tony wheezed. "I-I've killed a lot of people. Before all this... I killed... many."

The woman put a hand on his thigh and squeezed playfully. "Amnesty, remember? You're going to be just fine. I just watched you stagger up this hill with everything you've got. Only a decent man has that kind of determination. Now, rest and give in. You've fought your last battle, so no more struggling. Just lie back and let it take you."

Tony couldn't control his eyelids. They were sliding down, millimetre by millimetre. He wanted to yawn, but his lungs had stopped. The only thing he could feel now was his own thumping heartbeat. But even that eventually stopped. The strange thing was that another thumping had begun – a rhythmic, powerful beating of the wind. It was a sound Tony knew well from his years fighting other men's wars.

It was a helicopter.

"Jesus Christ," said the woman beside him. "Hold on a little longer, fella. I think the cavalry's here."

15

Mass moved beyond the gates, giving a hand signal for Cullen to split off with Fang 2 while he led Fang 1. Addy and Smithy were both in Mass's team. Addy was the last member of the team he'd led out of Portsmouth on that doomed mission several weeks ago now. He couldn't bear to be parted with her. Smithy, on the other hand, was Mass's good luck charm. Since meeting the lad, they had survived certain death on several occasions. He was too good not to have around.

Twenty other men had been spread across the two teams, and Mass knew all of them. They were the last of the Urban Vampires, and they were about to do what they did best: saving the goddamn day.

It was early in the day, which made their mission harder. They couldn't sneak in under the cover of darkness and retrieve General Thomas and his men. There was no choice but to fight. At least Wanstead had come through on the weaponry. Mass felt good about that.

The Benelli shotgun was a sight to behold – a semi-automatic with a handgun grip and collapsible stock. It held eight solid shot cartridges at a time, and was an absolute cannon. Mass felt his balls grow every time he fired it. To think the only gun he had ever held a year ago had been the odd antique passed around pubs between drug dealers. In addition, the other ten Vampires on his team had been kitted out with an assortment of combat rifles and less exotic shotguns.

They had set out an hour ago and had already made it halfway across the city, heading north and fighting for every inch. Fortunately, the demons were focused on assaulting the walls around the docks and only attacked Mass and his team sporadically. It still felt like the early waves of a larger assault. Something worse was coming.

Crimolok.

General Thomas had radioed in his position as being to the direct north of the city at Fort Widley. The old fortification was manned by a small group of guards, ready to send up flares if anything entered the city, so Thomas had likely gone there hoping to find allies and weapons. He would have found both. It was a smart move.

Smithy no longer sported a shotgun. He had swapped it for a matching pair of Sig handguns that he wielded like a maniac, popping off shots left and right before gleefully slamming in fresh clips. Mass would never have thought a person could have a natural talent for killing, but Smithy was some sort of prodigy. He made killing demons a performance. The other Vampires watched him in awe.

"How much further is this fort?" Smithy asked as he shoved both muzzles against a burnt man's eyes and pulled the triggers. "Does it have a gift shop?"

Addy was looking around, searching for more targets, but they seemed to be in the clear for the moment. "It's about another half a mile," she answered. "You'll see it soon. Big, ugly thing."

"It's defensible," said Mass. "It was smart for Thomas to head there. If he decides to try and take us out, we won't stand a chance."

Smithy wiped demon eyeball goop from his face and

frowned. "Why would he take us out? We're coming to rescue him."

"He wants me dead, and seeing a team of Urban Vampires sneaking through the ruins is going to give him a perfect excuse to start shooting."

"It presents an opportunity for us too," said Addy. "I say we kill the bastard as soon as we get a chance. With the chaos going on right now, we can get in and out before anyone knows what's happening. We should make a plan."

Mass replaced the cartridges in his shotgun and thought about it. "I don't have a plan. Shit, I haven't had a plan since the first demons arrived on my block in Brixton. We stick together and don't give up. That's the only plan I've ever followed."

"Friends forever!" said Smithy with a great beaming smile. "Hey, heads up!"

A group of demons emerged from a block of flats. They were covered in blood, no doubt from having killed a group of soldiers camped on the upper floors. Mass peered upwards and saw the torn body of a woman hanging half out of a broken window on the fourth floor.

Addy fired and struck the first demon. Smithy let loose with his handguns and hit the next. Mass obliterated the third with his Benelli. All three demons were burnt men. The number of primates seemed to be decreasing, which was a good thing. The burnt men were slower, weaker, and much easier to deal with in small groups than the frenzied primates. It gave Mass hope that perhaps they were making a dent in their enemy's numbers. Their elite troops were running thin.

Mass moved his team deeper into the city, trying to keep to alleyways and overhangs whenever possible. The quieter they could be, the fewer demons that would notice them. Ammunition didn't grow on trees, although Smithy acted like it did. So far, he had performed a majority of the killing. There were Vampires on the team who hadn't even fired their weapons yet.

"We're almost there," said Addy several minutes later. "Let's keep our heads down."

Mass nodded. "I hear machine guns. They're still fighting at the fort. Come on."

They hurried through the ruins, mindful of every corner or potential hiding place for a demon, but they found the way ahead clear except for demon corpses littering the road.

"I think I see the fort," said Smithy, pointing a handgun. "Is that it?"

Mass peered ahead and saw the red-brick fortification cutting into the hillside in a harsh V-shape. "Yeah, that's it. Reckon we should knock on the front door?"

"You guys have never met, right?" said Smithy. "I mean, Thomas has never seen you before? Why don't you just pretend to be someone else until he lets us inside?"

It wasn't the worst idea, but it was still too risky. "Even if he doesn't recognise me, others with him will. If we lie, he'll have even more reason to shoot at us. Our best bet is to be honest. From what I've heard about General Thomas, he's a politician. He won't murder us in front of a thousand men if he doesn't have a good reason." Mass took a few deep breaths, giving it some final thought. "Okay, we go in peace and play dumb. He won't shoot us with our hands in the air."

"You hope," interjected Addy. She held up a radio and waggled it. "What about Cullen's team?"

"Tell him to set up nearby and stay concealed. We might need backup if things go south."

Addy made the call.

Smithy twirled his handguns like an old-fashioned gunslinger. "Ready, boss?"

Mass nodded. "Follow me."

The team spread out in a line and headed across a main road choked with wreckage. They quickly stepped onto an overgrown verge that led up to a steep embankment. Up close, the looming fort was massive: three storeys high and stretching off to the east and west. Muzzles flashed from a dozen places inside, lighting up the shadows inside the many windows. Machine-gun fire chattered nearby.

"What are they firing at?" Smithy aimed his handguns but found no enemies. "The demons here are all dead."

"The demons must have got inside," said Mass, deciding that was the only explanation. "We need to go and help. Come on."

They hurried up the hill, making use of the paved road that led to a small car park in front of the fort. Several cars were parked there, as well as a large green double-decker bus. The bus was full of petrol and supplies, still roadworthy and well maintained. Mass knew because he had parked it there himself in the early days of the war. It was an escape vehicle for those camped out at the fort. It didn't look like anybody had made use of it though.

The fort's front entrance was managed by a turnstile set into an archway. Mass marched up to it and grabbed the bars. They were locked in place. "Damn it."

"Should we try the back door?" asked Smithy.

Mass cupped his mouth with his hands. "Hey! Hey, anyone around?"

No answer at first, but then: "How's it going, geezer?"

Mass stepped back. "Damien? What...? How did you get inside there?"

"I have my ways, innit? Heard General Thomas was around, so thought I'd see what the bloke was all about."

Smithy shook his head and grinned. "What did you do, man? Just stroll through the city like there isn't a war going on right now?"

Damien shrugged from the other side of the bars. "The demons don't pay me much attention. Guess I'm too much like them. Dead, remember?"

"You're serious about that shit?" Smithy tittered nervously, looking between Mass and Addy as if to check to see if their reaction matched his. "Did you come out the gates with the rest of them?"

"No. I wasn't in Hell, but I *am* dead. If it lends me an advantage, I'm all for it. You guys want to come in?"

Mass nodded. "Yeah. Do you know what's happening inside?"

"Demons got in around the back, but not enough to worry about yet. Won't be long, though, before this place is overrun. Demons don't stop when there's good eatin' to be had."

Smithy winced. "Dude."

Damien chuckled and moved out of sight. Nobody knew what he was doing until a metallic *clunk* led to the turnstile hopping in its grooves. Mass tried the metal bars again and the whole thing swivelled.

They all pushed their way inside.

Damien was leaning up against the wall to their right. He pointed up at one of the long, narrow buildings that ringed the central courtyard. "Thomas is up there with a shitload of men. Most of them are injured. Without help, they're gonna die of exhaustion before the demons ever get to them."

Mass eyeballed Damien. "How'd you manage to find all of that out without being discovered?"

"There were some guys already defending this place when Thomas arrived. He assumed I was with them. I was planning to kill the old bastard and do you lot a favour, but... well, it didn't seem right."

Mass frowned. "What do you mean?"

"You'll see. Anyway, you can get inside the building over there." He pointed to an archway at the bottom of the building about thirty feet away. "I'll be around if you need me."

"All right, cheers."

As the team hurried for the archway, Smithy whispered to Mass, "That dude freaks me out. You ever get the impression he might just decide to kill everyone for the fun of it?"

"I think he's hot," said Addy.

"He just about qualifies as a good guy," said Mass, "but I don't trust him. He plays by his own rules."

Smithy nodded. "Yeah, the dude's playing *Jenga* while the rest of us are playing *KerPlunk!*"

Mass ignored Smithy and eyeballed his team, one after the other. "Everyone be on your guard."

He pulled open the rickety iron door inside the archway Damien had pointed out to them, and then waited for his team to go inside. They entered a cramped alcove with a staircase in it. The stone steps had been augmented with a steel handrail and rubber slip-guards – remnants of a world where health and safety regulations mattered. Mass took point with his shotgun, leading the team up the stairs cautiously, rounding each corner, ready to fire upwards. They passed the first landing but kept on going. Thomas and the others would be higher up, firing from the best vantage point they could gain.

The stairs ended on the second floor, leading them to a dank corridor. The sound of gunfire was deafening, echoing off the brickwork. The fort was a strange mixture of modern and old; not ancient like a castle, but not new either. A couple of old cannons were perched beside window ports, a wooden information board explaining their history.

"This place is pretty cool," said Smithy. "You reckon those guns work?"

Addy tutted. "You see any cannonballs around? Of course they don't work."

Smithy's enthusiasm was undeterred. "Hey, did you know the nursery rhyme *Humpty Dumpty* is actually about a cannon? Absolute truth, I swear."

"Shut up," said Mass. "Shut up and follow me."

They headed through the draughty corridor, seeking company. A few rooms on the upper floor were occupied by soldiers firing rifles from the windows. Others were being used as infirmaries, containing men moaning and crying out for help. The room at the end of the corridor was the largest, packed full of men and women. Only half of them were armed, and when they noticed Mass and his team they stared blankly. Then others began murmuring and whispering. Those who recognised Mass acknowledged him. A few moments was all it took for a hero's welcome to begin.

"You're alive. Of course you are. No one can kill Mass."

"The Urban Vampires are here!"

"Thank God, we need help."

"It's Mass!"

"Looking good, Addy."

Mass shoved his way through the welcome party, taking in all the faces. For a moment, it appeared as if he was surrounded by friends, but then it became clear that they had merely moved to the front of the room to greet him. Two-thirds of those further back were strangers, and they were the ones with most of the guns. "General Thomas?" Mass enquired. "Where is he?"

One of the men Mass knew nodded to the far side of the room, where there stood a group of men in fatigues, huddled together and seemingly deep in conversation. One of the men was older, with a head of shocking white hair. The others looked to the older man whenever he spoke. It was Thomas, no doubt.

Mass kept his shotgun low but at the ready. Even now, this close, he didn't have a plan. Did he raise his weapon and shoot, consequences be damned? Or did he try to handle things another way? He didn't like having to think.

The old man turned, alerted by the chatter rising in the room. What Mass saw was not what he expected. General Thomas appeared weak – ill even. His grey eyes were sunken. His bottom lip was split open and bleeding. His right arm hung limply by his side, his sleeve soaked red. "How goes our defence?" the man asked haughtily, although there was a hint of pain in his voice.

"You're still alive," said Mass, "so I'd say it's going better than expected, wouldn't you?"

Thomas scowled. "What's your name, soldier?"

"Mass, and I ain't no soldier. I'm a Vampire."

The men either side of Thomas went for their sidearms, but Thomas stopped them. He looked at Mass as if he were a ghost. "That's a surprise, seeing as I was informed you were dead."

Mass went to ask about Tony's whereabouts but realised he would be breaking the man's cover if Thomas didn't yet know he had helped Mass. It was worrying that the colonel wasn't present. Mass hoped he was still alive.

Thomas scowled. "Did you hear me? I said, you're supposed to be dead."

"Ain't you heard? I don't die, mate." Mass didn't think, he just acted. Throwing the punch was the stupidest thing he could do, but it was also the only thing too. The right hook crunched against the old man's brittle jawbone and it was only the men standing beside Thomas that kept him from hitting the ground.

Mass rubbed his fist. "That was for Amanda Wickstaff."

Safety levers clicked off all around the room as dozens of automatic rifles and handguns pointed at Mass. He didn't care though; he'd lost too many people to care. His team pointed their own shotguns and rifles, outmanned four to one. Smithy thrust his handguns either side of him like a character in a Tarantino movie. Addy did the smart thing and aimed only at Thomas. If shots got fired, Thomas was going down first.

Thomas rubbed his jaw, eyes open wide. "W-Why are you here?"

Mass shrugged. "To rescue you."

"W-Wanstead sent you? He sent *you*?"

"Another surprise I'll bet."

Thomas pushed himself up straight, removing the helping hands that had been keeping him from falling. When he spoke, it was like he was talking to himself. "I led an army – a great army – to destroy our enemy, and instead it destroyed us. A man I thought dead turns up and claims to want to rescue me. He acts like he wants to do the opposite. What did I do to deserve such unpredictable madness? Where did I go wrong?"

Mass growled. "Sort it out with your therapist. I'm here to get you and your boys back to the docks."

Thomas seemed to snap back to reality. He looked at Mass and nodded. "These men are all I have left. We are wounded and poorly armed, so if you've come to rescue us, I thank you."

Mass glanced back at Addy and Smithy, but neither gave anything away. Once again, Mass was out of his depth. Part of him still wanted, more than anything, to just blow this old fucker away, but that would mean killing a wounded man in cold blood. He realised now why Damien had refused to do the deed. There was a line between a soldier and a killer, and Mass wanted to stay on the right side of it. "The city can be navigated if we stick to the side streets. The demons are mostly moving down the main roads towards the docks. If we move fast, we can get back behind the walls from the south before the main invasion begins."

Thomas reached a trembling hand to his waist. At first Mass feared the old man was going for his gun, but he merely lifted his shirt. Underneath was a blood-soaked bandage. "One of the buggers got me quite badly, I'm afraid. We were right outside the city – home free, I thought. It seems I was mistaken. If I can get my remaining men to safety, perhaps I can atone for some of my failures."

Mass thought about Amanda Wickstaff and shook his head. "You can't, but at least no more men have to die because of your arrogance."

Thomas swallowed, but Mass wasn't sure if it was guilt or something else. He detected a hint of aggression in the wounded old man. "Yes, well, I suppose war makes monsters of us all."

"Sometimes it makes heroes. Okay, what are we dealing with here? I saw rooms full of injured men and women. Can any of them walk?"

"I would say most of them can if there's a promise of safety. Those mortally wounded collapsed on the road before we made it here."

"And how many of your people are armed?"

"With ammunition? I would say perhaps three hundred. We were forced to retreat with what we had on us. Most of our ammunition is lying in a field in Winchester."

Mass shook his head. He wanted to condemn the old man, but he had experienced his own set of failures recently. Being in charge was a thankless task, and blaming Thomas wasn't going to help anything right now. "Okay, Thomas, you have your radio?"

"I do."

"Then put in a call to Wanstead. Tell him we'll be coming in from the south-east. We're going to move wide around the city, avoiding the demons heading directly for the docks. Also, call the boats and have them clear us a path. You still have the authority to call in artillery, right?"

"Of course. I might be at death's door, but I am still the ranking official in Portsmouth."

"Not in my eyes you aren't. Tell your men we're falling out in one hour. Anyone too injured to move is going to need a pair of buddies to carry them, or they'll have to stay here and pray there's someone left alive after all this to rescue them."

Smithy stepped forward. "Um, shouldn't we just stay here? I mean, this place is a fort. Will it really be that much safer back at Portsmouth?"

"This place is a tourist attraction," said Thomas. "The main buildings can't be secured. There are hundreds of windows filled with nothing but air. We can't defend this place."

Smithy nodded. "Yeah, okay, fair enough." He then gave an awkward salute.

Mass turned to Addy. "Put in a call to Cullen and tell him to get back to the docks. We might need help getting back inside if the demons get too thick at the walls."

"You sure you don't want him to join us and help us get these people back?"

"We'll be moving a thousand people with three hundred guns between them. Cullen and a dozen Vampires won't add much to the mix. I want them back at the docks where the real fighting is going to be.

"Understood." Addy moved away, lifting her radio.

Mass looked back at Thomas. "One hour."

THE HOUR PASSED LIKE SECONDS, and before long, a thousand men had filtered out into the courtyard, packed in almost too tightly to move. Those unable to travel had propped themselves up against the upper windows, firing at the demons that were still assaulting the fort's west wall. The crack of nearby rifle fire was a constant noise.

"We need to move," said Addy, "before we miss our only chance."

Mass turned to the army assembled behind him, wondering if they would listen to him. Thomas remained quiet, clutching his wounded torso. The old bastard was dying.

Good.

Mass addressed the army. "All right, you lot. We've already beaten the odds by staying alive, so there's nothing to lose. The enemy is everywhere, but that's a good thing. It means there's plenty for us to kill. Every dead demon pushes things a little more in our favour. This is our chance to be heroes. Let's fight our way back to the docks so we can get behind the walls and help our friends stay alive. They need us."

The men didn't cheer, but a majority of them nodded and made the right kind of noises. Mass wasn't going to inspire them any more than that. They weren't his people. He didn't have their hearts and minds, only a modicum of their trust. He had to make the most of it.

"Everyone move out. Follow your sergeants, and don't stop for anything. If we bunch together and try to form a line, we'll get bogged down. We move, we live. Protect one another, but don't fight for lost causes. Some of us are going to die. Now move!"

Everyone rushed for the turnstiles, which a team of men had managed to remove minutes before for easier passage through the archway. The army filtered through in pairs a half-second apart. It was going to take several minutes to get everyone through.

"This is a farce," said Thomas, unhelpfully. "We're sitting ducks out here. Was this your best plan?"

Mass snarled. "From what I can see, the only other exit is over there. You think that would be better?" The area Mass was talking about was at the west of the fort. A large metal gate there had burst open and demons were spilling through from an access road. The soldiers in the upper windows had concentrated their fire on the entryway, and so far they were keeping the horde at bay. Eventually, the demons would make it through though. Mass grabbed a nearby sergeant. "You! Form a rearguard with thirty men. Do it fast."

Whoever the sergeant was, he did what he was asked, rushing to gather a group and form a rearguard. In less than a minute, thirty men were firing at the demons entering through the rear gate, helping to keep them back. It would buy them a little more time.

"You need to hurry this up," said Damien, appearing from amongst the crowd.

Mass shook his head. "Yeah, no shit. You got a better idea, let me know."

"Not my call. I'm just saying you don't have as long as you think."

"What do you—"

Part of the fort exploded, the building where the injured were housed. Men fell from the windows as the brickwork collapsed around them. Their screams joined the erratic gunfire and the side of the fort collapsed like a sandcastle.

Mass had no words except for some that most would deem obscene. Addy joined him, using words that were even more offensive. Smithy stared up at the sky, his handguns by his side.

Crimolok swept away what was left of the top level of the fort's damaged building. Anyone left inside was now most certainly dead. The entire army, those not yet through the turnstile housing, turned and fired, several hundred rifles cracking together in a deafening assault. Scorch marks covered parts of Crimolok's gigantic body, but the bullets did nothing but ricochet harmlessly into the sky.

Smithy still had his handguns by his sides, but he was shaking his head now. "It's invulnerable. We can't hurt it."

Thomas chuckled like a madman. "Yes, we suffered that quandary last night. I'm assuming no one here knows how to solve it."

Mass shoved Thomas out of his way and bellowed, "Everyone form up. I want to see an organised retreat. I want to see bodies moving through that exit. Go-go-go!"

Smithy snapped out of his daze and began firing. Addy joined him, but she fired at the demons that were now teeming in through the rear gate. The courtyard was being overrun. Men began to panic.

Mass roared over the din, "Don't stop fighting!"

"We are all warriors," Thomas joined in, bellowing in a way belying his skinny frame. "We do not give in to fear."

Everyone stood and fought, but two-thirds of the army were out of ammunition or unarmed. These men could do nothing but cower and pray that their brothers were able to hold the line.

Mass turned, making sure men were still fleeing through the turnstile entrance. They were, but who knew what was meeting them on the other side. The demons were filling the courtyard. Crimolok smashed apart more of the fort, seeking to clear the obstacle and get inside to the courtyard.

Damien moved in front of Mass, getting his attention. "Men are going to have to die. It's the only way anyone will make it out of here alive."

Mass knew it was true. It would take another five minutes to get everyone through the exit. No way did they have that long.

The best they could do was to buy a few minutes to evacuate as many people as possible. "I'll go. Anyone who wants to—"

Damien shoved him, a stiff prod in the shoulder. "Stop playing hero. Without you out there leading them, these men won't make it to the docks. Unless you want to trust Thomas to get them there?"

He didn't trust in that at all. From the looks of him, Thomas wouldn't even make it halfway back to the docks.

Mass approached the old man and placed a hand on his frail shoulder. "Call in the guns and clear us a path. Whoever makes it out of here needs every advantage they can get." Thomas stared at him for a moment and said nothing, so Mass shook him. "Now! Before you're too weak to make the call. I was planning on killing you, Thomas, but it looks like the demons got there first. You want to redeem yourself, this is how you do it."

"Y-Yes, of course." Thomas lifted his radio and gave the order. His hands trembled the entire time.

Mass moved towards the rearguard. The demons were about to collide with the men and women fighting there. Too many were coming in from the access road.

Mass levelled a primate with his Benelli as bricks rained down in the courtyard. Crimolok continued dismantling the fort.

We're all dead. What can we do against this thing but run? I damned us all when I shot Vamps.

Most of the terrified soldiers had realised that shooting Crimolok was of no use, but even against the demons they were doomed to fail. They didn't have enough guns. Several hundred demons were amassed at the gate, having the same problem as the humans attempting to flee. If the gate had been wider, the courtyard would already be overrun.

A few hundred men had made it through the turnstile housing by now, but the opportunity to rescue more was diminishing. The demons made it to the front lines and leapt upon the defenders. Rifles fired at the clouds as soldiers fell backwards, their throats torn open. Immediately the line was down, smashed to pieces by the sheer unrelenting weight of the charging demons. Men screamed, cursed, and choked on their own blood. Those near the turnstile housing turned and shoved each other in a desperate attempt to save themselves.

Damien shoved Mass. "You need to go. Now!"

"I'm not leaving these men to—"

"They ain't men, they're supper, and unless you want to be dessert, you need to move."

Mass wasn't having any of it. No way was he going to run and leave these men to die.

Smithy and Addy grabbed Mass and yanked him away from the fighting. He fought them both, but then Damien reached out and grabbed him by the throat. His glare was icy cold. "Heroes die."

Mass tried to fight, but the hand around his neck was like a vice. His breath deserted him and a chill ran up and down his spine. Before he knew it, he was feeling sleepy. His body went weak, and he was only mildly aware of Damien still talking. "You two get him out of here. I'll make some room."

Mass blinked and tried to see as Smithy and Addy dragged him towards the exit. Damien moved through the crowd like a hot knife, tossing people aside like they were made of twigs.

Mass tried to struggle, his body barely responding. "We have to go back."

"They're dead, Mass," said Smithy, dragging him through the turnstile exit, "no matter what we do. We have to get you out of here, big guy."

They made it into the car park. Several hundred men had made it out, but most were unarmed. A dozen made a run for it, dashing towards the ruins in the city.

There was a whistling sound, followed by a massive explosion as the first of the bombs Thomas had called in landed. It was impossible to know how many demons were trapped amongst the rubble, but a dozen fleeing soldiers were caught in the blast.

"Damn it. I told those men to wait." Thomas stood with his

radio in hand. Two larger men were steadying him to keep him from falling. The last of the colour had abandoned the old man's cheeks, and he had taken on the appearance of a corpse. He looked at Mass and said, "There are more bombs coming in."

"Good work, Thomas, but how the hell did you make it out here?"

"My men dragged me. I told them to leave me, but..." His voice faded. He had to breathe for a second before getting it back. "I did my part, now you do yours."

Mass nodded. He had to get the men out of there. More were flowing from the exit every second, but from their hysterical screams it was clear the demons were killing almost everyone left inside. Crimolok had destroyed a massive section of the fort. The giant would come for them any second.

Mass gathered his people. "The bus," he said. "The bus is ready to go. We can't take everyone, but we can get a hundred people out of here. Maybe more."

Smithy frowned. "What bus? The one over there?"

"Yeah, it's a getaway vehicle. I parked it there myself, months ago. It'll run, I promise you. The keys are in the exhaust."

"I'm on it." Smithy legged it towards the small row of parked vehicles. He rooted around at the back of the bus until he re-emerged jingling a set of keys in his hand.

"Nice one," said Addy. "Everyone, on the bus. Get on that goddamn bus."

The men scattered, but several stayed in place, protecting Thomas. "Leave me!" the old man shouted, but they refused.

"We're not leaving without you, sir," said a man with captain's stripes.

"I'll just slow you fools down."

The demons reached the turnstiles, clawing at one another to be the first to get at fresh meat. Forced to funnel through in pairs, the demons were easy pickings for the men with guns.

"To the bus," Mass shouted, and more followed. Others

remained, carrying Thomas along, trying to get the old man moving despite him looking ready for the grave.

Another missile fell, igniting another part of the ruins. Their path to freedom was waiting for them. They just had to get in the bus.

Crimolok appeared from around the side of the fort, coming from the opposite side of the car park. The massive beast bent down and picked up a tiny Fiat, lofting it into the air like a pebble.

Mass realised he was about to die and time seemed to slow. Some inner sense was able to calculate the Fiat's trajectory as soon as it was airborne. It was heading right for him. He would never move out of the way in time. Neither would those around him.

Damn it, we were so close.

Mass wanted to close his eyes as the car tumbled end over end towards him. He didn't want to watch his approaching death or anticipate the bone-crushing impact. But he couldn't take his eyes off it. Mass laughed, a dizzying high washing over him. Then something knocked the Fiat aside in mid-air, sending it down the grassy embankment, where it cartwheeled before coming to a rest on its buckled roof.

Mass blinked. He was unable to find words.

"Once again I am forced to save your life. Can you please try to remain alive on your own?"

Mass turned to see Rick. Or what was left of him. His body was twisted, ribs sticking out of his shirt. One of his arms hung on by a ragged thread of muscle. His left eye bulged like it was about to fall out of his skull.

"Rick? You look like shit."

"My vessel has almost expired. It requires great willpower to keep it moving."

Mass tried not to stare at a length of intestine hanging from Rick's waist like a belt. "Yeah, I can see that. Thanks for the save."

Rick threw an arm out towards the turnstiles and the whole

thing exploded. The brickwork crumbled from above and filled in the gap. The demons would be forced to find another way around the fort. Not done yet, Rick stumbled towards the car park.

Crimolok appeared from around the far side of the fort. It saw Rick and paused, an expression of pure hatred crossing its beautiful, monstrous face.

Rick continued across the car park, heading towards Crimolok. His mangled form was more hideous than any of the demons, but no one shot at. They just watched.

Rick showed no awareness of the spectators. He continued stumbling towards Crimolok until he was just twenty feet away. Then he threw up both hands, unleashing twin jets of bright white light. Both crackling beams struck Crimolok right in the face, right in the eyes. The massive beast stumbled backwards, bellowing in agony and shielding itself.

Mass hurried to catch up with Rick. "You hurt it. Shit, man, you hurt it."

Rick turned back to Mass. "I am too weak to defeat my brother. I was foolish. Go, Mass. Take whoever you can find and run. As long as you live, Crimolok can never prevail."

"Are you coming with us?"

Rick nodded. "I will do what I can to stay alive, to perhaps heal, but if I hinder you in any way, you must abandon me."

Mass nodded. He had already abandoned hundreds of souls today. What would one more matter?

"Everyone, on the bus," Mass shouted. "I won't say it again. Those who can't get inside can climb on the sodding roof. Just get yourselves on board."

"I can't make it," said Thomas from a few feet away. "This is where I plant my flag in the sand."

Thomas's skin was like ash, and he could have been blown away in a strong wind, but his men still refused to leave him. "We're not abandoning you, sir. We've served with you too long to let you die."

"Go, you fools. You need to live."

Mass growled at the suicidal idiots. "He's a goner. Let him die with some dignity."

The men ignored Mass, determined as they dragged Thomas along the car park. Crimolok stood at the far end, still half-blind and raging. How long before the beast recovered from Rick's blast?

"You're going to get yourself killed," said Mass, flabbergasted to see at least two dozen more men refusing to run for the bus without Thomas by their sides.

"This is wasting time we don't have," said Rick. He limped towards Thomas, prompting the old man's guards to pull their sidearms. He ignored them all and snatched at the old man's skull, striking with both hands like the jaws of a viper. For a second, it looked like he was going crush Thomas's head like a watermelon, but then he threw back his head and grunted in pain. White sparks shot from his eyes. Thomas's entire body bucked as if receiving a massive jolt. No one fired a shot, too confused and too wary of hitting the wrong target.

A few moments was all it took, but when Rick stepped away, Thomas was healed. The old man flexed his arms as if they were brand new. He examined his torso – now healed and pink with healthy flesh. "H-How did you?"

Rick's expression remained flat, but his words held a tinge of emotion. "That was the last of my strength. I can no longer heal this vessel and my time is short. Do what Mass is telling you or I shall take back my gift and allow you to expire."

Thomas seemed offended for a moment, but he didn't argue. Instead, he waved an arm frantically, full of energy. "Everyone, on that bus, pronto. Double-time! Move-move-move!"

The men scattered, leaving Mass alone with only a small group. Addy was shaking her head and chuckling to herself. "Strange days we live in, huh?"

"You don't know the half of it," said Damien, appearing, once more, from nowhere.

Mass grunted. "How the hell do you always seem to arrive just in time to make an unnecessary comment?"

"It's a gift. You heading back to the docks? I'll meet you there."

"No," said Addy. "Rick just said we need to run. We can't win."

"We *are* running," said Mass, looking back at Crimolok, who was now starting to recover from Rick's attack. "We're running back to defend our home. I don't know how, but we're going to kill that son of a bitch. Mankind is going to win this war."

Damien smiled. "Still gotta be a hero, huh?"

"I'm just being me."

"I feel that." Damien offered a handshake.

In the distance, another bomb dropped.

ONE OF THOMAS'S men offered to drive the bus, claiming to have experience of driving logistics trucks for the army. He certainly seemed to know his way around the oversized steering wheel and heavy gear stick.

Before long, they were heading through the city, slowly trying to find a way through the debris. The bombs had cleared a way through the demons but left the roads in worse shape than ever. Mass could do nothing but trust that the stranger behind the wheel would get them where they were going.

Thomas stood at the front of the bus, straight-backed and alert. As weak as the old man had been, he now seemed ten years younger. Mass knew the euphoria of having been miraculously healed, and he took pleasure knowing Thomas would soon feel like a tonne of bricks had landed on him. Conversely, Rick was a broken mess on the back seat of the bus. Addy had managed to clear a space there for him, which was an amazing accomplishment seeing as there were almost two hundred people packed inside and onto the bus. They hung out of windows and sat in each other's laps, just grateful to be on board. Several dozen hadn't made it, forced to make a run for it as the bus left without them. Mass was just glad his team of Vampires had all made it aboard, although they were now scattered throughout the seats.

Mass shoved and cajoled his way to the rear of the bus. He wanted to speak with Rick while the man – the angel – was still with them. He gave no reaction to Mass's approach.

"Rick? How are you feeling?"

"Ashamed."

"Ashamed, why?"

Rick swallowed, his neck bulging unnaturally. "My own pride brought me here to face my brother, but it was not enough to defeat him. It took most of my strength to remain here in this body, but it is rapidly failing."

"You tried, man. That's all any of us can do. Who are you, really? You ain't Rick."

"Michael."

Mass was vaguely aware of angel names, but not enough to react in any particular way. He had just wanted to know who he was really talking to. "So what happened to the real Rick Bastion, Michael? You're wearing his body, but where is his, um..."

"His soul resides in Heaven. His sacrifices were great."

That was good news at least. Mass took a breath and asked another question. "What about Vamps? Is he in Heaven too?"

"Yes."

Mass exhaled with relief. "Good. I'm glad."

"Do not be glad. Heaven shall soon fall. God's barrier is weakened and he will soon fall under attack. Crimolok and those loyal to him will erase existence and reignite it in their own dark image."

"Michael, there has to be some way to stop Crimolok. Tell me what to do and I'll do it."

"There is nothing. He cannot be harmed by any mortal means. Only the power of Heaven can defeat him."

"What about the gate? What if we manage to destroy it?"

Michael groaned and a trickle of blood escaped the corner of his mouth. "His power is not linked to the gate – it resides within the abyss – but if you close the final gate, you will succeed only in trapping Crimolok here on this Earth. He will no longer be able to make an assault on Heaven, but this world would most certainly be doomed. Is that a sacrifice you are willing to make?"

"I would rather something be saved than everything be destroyed. Yes, I'm willing to destroy the gate if it means saving lives – even if it's not our own."

Michael tried to smile, but it appeared as a bloody grimace. "Lucifer was right about humanity. It *is* worth saving."

Mass didn't want to believe it was all over, but if they could stop Crimolok from attacking God and destroying the universe, then at least they could go down with a win. "I'll go through the gate myself. As soon as we get these people back to the docks, I'll head out and find it."

Michael blinked, but one of his eyes remained closed. "I'm sorry I was unable to help this world. You will all perish."

"I accepted that a long time ago, but I have to keep fighting. It's who I am. It's who my friends were."

Michael died. The subtle movement of his chest, the slight flickering of his eyelids, ceased. Mass didn't know what he was supposed to do, so he just stood up and moved away into the packed aisle.

The bus lurched. There was the chatter of gunfire as men fired from the bus's upper floor and out of the windows. The tyres screeched and bodies were tossed one way and then another as the suspension bucked and tilted, but their driver had been true to his word; he handled the bus like a racing car.

Smithy met Mass in the centre of the bus. "How's he doing?"

"He's gone, but before he went, he told me what I need to do."

"What?"

Mass didn't want to tell him they were all going to die, at least not right there in a cramped bus doing forty through a backstreet during the apocalypse, so he patted his friend on the shoulder and told him not to worry. "We'll talk later. I'm going to fuck up Crimolok's plans."

Smithy grinned. "Sounds good to me. Hey, can you believe Thomas? I know Rick healed you too, but it took longer. Thomas is like a new man. Makes you wonder what the comedown's gonna be like."

Mass peered through the bodies in the aisle and caught a glimpse of Thomas, still standing at the front of the bus. The son of a bitch deserved to die, but instead he had been given a second chance.

I'll deal with him later. Right now, we have other priorities.

They careened through the backstreets for another ten minutes, firing at clusters of demons they couldn't avoid. Several times, the bus ran straight over the enemy or ploughed through debris. The suspension was beginning to buckle. The bus was gradually giving up on them.

"Everyone get ready," Thomas yelled from the front. "We're nearly there."

Mass tried to see through the windows but it was impossible. Had they actually made it all the way to the docks? The level of gunfire told him it might be so. He still had his Benelli shotgun, but he couldn't lift it in the cramped aisle. The only thing he could do was ensure he didn't drop it.

The bus came to a sudden stop, throwing everyone forward. Many fell and had to scramble to keep from being trodden on. Mass pulled a woman to her feet after she fell face first against his knee. "You okay?"

The woman nodded, sucking on a bloody lower lip. "Sorry."

"No problem. See you at the docks."

"There're enemies on the ground," Thomas yelled. "We need to fight our way to the walls."

"Great," said Smithy, appearing beside Mass. Addy shoved her way over to join him too. "Nothing's ever easy, is it?"

Mass gave both his friends a steely glare. "Whatever happens, we three have each other's backs, right?"

Both nodded.

The bus's door folded open and men tumbled through the opening. Gunfire rattled immediately, joining the cacophony coming from the docks. Mass still couldn't see through the windows, but he sensed the demons out there. Their screeching confirmed it. He tried to make contact with as many of his Vampires as he could spot, trying to convey the message that they should get ready for a fight.

Mass battled his way to the front of the bus, then wasted no time leaping out onto the road. The rush of sound and sight was overwhelming. Men screamed. Demons wailed. Guns fired and bullets ate flesh. The stench of blood and smoke corrupted the air. Limbs from both sides littered the ground like a scene from a horror movie. Mass's boot came down on something soft, and when he looked down he saw a chewed-off nose. Next to it was a string of sinewy meat that might have been the remains of a brain.

Smithy grabbed Mass by the arm and pulled him away from the bus. "Keep moving, remember?"

Mass raised his Benelli and opened a hole in a demon's chest. The burnt man continued standing for a moment before collapsing backwards. Smithy started popping shots from his handguns, hitting targets like he was at a fairground. Addy took out demons left and right with her shotgun. Slowly, the other Vampires converged on their location, and they became a team again.

The wall around the docks was twenty feet away. The driver had parked them almost on the doorstep. Mass looked for him, wanting to bring him in and keep him safe, but he was already dead. His body lay slumped against the bus's front tyre. The driver had been one of the first out of the door. The guy had been one brave bastard.

Men fired from atop the wall, trying to clear a gap in the line of demons large enough for the two hundred survivors to get through. Thomas led his men in an assault, ordering them to concentrate their fire in the right places and hold their line at all times. He was in his element, and Mass had to admit the old man had courage. It was easy to see why men followed him.

The fighting raged on and men fell in their dozens. The demons were everywhere. The wall was right ahead, only a stone's throw away.

"We're not gonna make it," said Mass. "Damn it, we're so close, but we're not gonna make it."

Smithy still fought beside him. "What should we do? Make a run for it?"

Mass thought about the gate, and his chances of making it there. Could he run now and manage to reach it? More likely he would be dead before he made it half a mile.

More gunfire erupted. It came from behind them, lighting up a shadowy side street. Demons fell in droves, blindsided.

Cullen appeared with the other remaining Urban Vampires. They unleashed hell, putting to use the heavy weaponry Wanstead had supplied them. The demons were hit from three sides, forcing them close up. It made hitting them even easier, and within seconds, a gap appeared in the centre of their ranks.

"Come on," said Addy. "There's our ticket." She turned to Mass, taking her eye off the fight for a single second.

Mass called out a warning, but it was too late.

A primate lunged for Addy's throat.

Smithy shoved her aside and filled the primate full of bullets. He popped off shots with both handguns until the thing was lying in a bloody puddle on the floor, then he blew away the smoke from his barrels. "You can thank me later, sweetheart."

Addy looked sick, but she nodded. "We live through this and I'll thank you twice."

Smithy blushed, but they all got moving. Cullen and the others fought their way in from the side while Thomas led his surviving men from the front. The men on the walls fired continuously, working to keep the gap open. More demons came from the ruins.

Guards threw open a small gate in the wall. If any demons got through, Portsmouth would spring a permanent leak. They could only afford to open it for a matter of seconds, and only while the demons were kept at bay.

We need to move.

Mass hung back and secured the rear as the first group made it through the gate. Thomas disappeared inside with them, surviving yet again.

Cullen and his team reached Mass and they formed up into a team of over twenty. Cullen gave Mass a wink. "Looks like I came just in time."

"We wouldn't have made it without you. Cheers."

"Don't mention it."

The demons began to recover. One of Cullen's men fell as a primate pounced on him. Mass took the demon out with his Benelli, but it was too late to save the Vampire. "Get inside before they close the gate."

Everyone sprinted for safety, forgetting the fight and focusing only on reaching the gate. The question was whether the guards would wait long enough for them to make it through.

Thomas stood behind the guards, a smile on his face as he patted them on the back.

CRIMOLOK REACHES the edge of the city, where the buildings and pathways give way to the sea. Floating vessels wait there, perhaps unreachable, but there are still enough humans left in the city to feast on. Blood stains the city of Portsmouth and it will never again see the sun. Night falls, and this time it will be everlasting.

Humanity's last battle has arrived. Once Portsmouth falls, God's power will finally be at an end. Too few souls remain to keep his barrier in place. The tipping point has been reached.

Only one last push is needed.

And then the universe shall burn.

16

———————

Men screamed for mercy as the gate closed on them, but Mass and his team had made it through. For a moment he had feared Thomas would betray them and leave them stranded outside the wall, but he hadn't done so. A dozen or more had been too late, though, and they now wailed to be let inside. Their pleas ended seconds later.

The fighting continued atop the wall, men slapping in new magazines and firing hundreds of rounds a minute. Portsmouth wasn't toothless yet, but there was no amount of ammunition that could harm Crimolok. Once the giant monster arrived, it was all over.

Mass estimated that a hundred or so had made it back from the fort. As rescue missions went, it was abysmal, yet it still felt like a miracle. Mass and Cullen still had most of their Vampires. Along with Smithy and Addy, there was eighteen of them. Was it enough to get him to the gate? On foot, it would take them two days at least to get there, and probably with demons to fight the entire way. It seemed impossible, but the only thing Mass could do was close the gate. He could keep Crimolok from destroying whatever worlds were left, and from destroying Heaven and all the good souls that had earned their place there.

Mass needed to get to the gate. There had to be a way.

Wanstead arrived to meet them, unable to hide his surprise when he saw Thomas alive and well. "General, your safe return is" – he seemed lost for words – "remarkable."

"A miracle is what it is," said Thomas. "You've done a fine job holding down the fort here, Colonel. How go our defences?"

"We're shelling the city, hoping to thin the demons out, but they keep on coming. Their attacks were lighter at first, but now it's a full-on assault. I'm not sure how much longer our ammunition can last at this rate."

"I shall lead us to victory, Colonel, mark my words. An angel brought me back to life so that I can ensure mankind's survival."

"You're shitting me," said Smithy, rolling his eyes.

Wanstead seemed confused, but he didn't say anything. Thomas glared at Smithy, but Mass stood in front of his friend and took on the ire for himself. "Join the club, Thomas. Same angel healed me, so what does that mean?"

"That you were needed in order to safeguard my return. Without your help, Mass, I would be a dead man, no doubt about it. I am grateful for your courage, but your mission is complete."

Wanstead nodded. "Your mission was, indeed, to rescue Thomas and his people. I see very few of the thousand I hoped for, however."

"You're lucky to get this many," said Addy.

"Enough talk," said Thomas. "I have orders for the men."

Wanstead glanced at Mass for a moment – it was a gesture of uncertainty – but Mass gave him a subtle nod. When Wanstead turned back to Thomas, he spoke nervously. "I'm afraid I must insist you leave the city's defences in my hands, General Thomas. The men are following orders, and to change them now would cause disruption we cannot afford."

Thomas's cheeks reddened. "I beg your pardon?"

"I'm afraid, for now, sir, you are not in charge. I must remain in charge of our defence."

"Ha!" Thomas turned to one of the soldiers who had refused to abandon him back at the fort. Immediately, the man raised a handgun to Wanstead's head. Several others did the same. The guards with Wanstead seemed uncertain of what to do, but Mass noticed something about them that would help. They were all Wickstaff's people. They had no loyalty to Thomas.

Smart man.

Mass whipped his Benelli up and aimed it at Thomas's chest. "Wanstead calls the shots until this is over. He and I have unfinished business after that, but no matter what happens, your time in charge is done, Thomas. You murdered Amanda Wickstaff."

The men with Wanstead looked at each other. Several raised their weapons, pointing them at Thomas's men.

"I did no such thing."

"You murdered Amanda Wickstaff," said Mass again, louder. "You murdered the woman who saved this city so that you could take it for yourself. It's time you paid for it."

Thomas's men were nervous. Their eyes darted back and forth, weighing up the odds. So far it was an even split between them and Wanstead's people, but then the Urban Vampires raised their weapons in support of Wanstead. Those wavering finally raised their weapons against Thomas too.

Mass smiled. "Looks like the vote is in. You lose."

Thomas shook his head, eyes wide, mouth twisted in a cruel smile. "You fools. I've been chosen by God to save us. Any who oppose me shall burn in Hell."

"I like him even less now he's found God," said Smithy.

"I agree," said Addy. "He was less of a prick when he was dying."

"I almost gave up," said Thomas, "but it was a test. I did the right thing and I was healed for my sacrifices. We are wasting time here, Wanstead, so order your misguided men to stand down."

Mass raised his Benelli so it was pointing at Thomas's head.

"You ain't in charge no more, Thomas. If *you* don't stand down, I'm going to blow your fucking head off."

Wanstead raised his sidearm and pointed it at Thomas's face. "I'm sorry to have to do this, sir, but I insist you do as Mr Mass says."

"I shall do no such thing. Lower your weapons now and I promise the matter will go no further."

No one lowered their weapons. Nobody moved. With the number of people involved, no one wanted to be the first to pull the trigger. Thomas's men were outnumbered, but they showed no sign of stepping down.

Mass wanted to shoot Thomas in the face and be done with it, consequences be damned, but that would erase any hope of getting to the gate and destroying it. There were too many guns on him to get out of the Mexican stand-off alive. Thomas might think he was mankind's saviour, but Mass felt like he was the one with the divine task. He had to walk away from this in one piece. He didn't see any other choice. Thomas was too arrogant – or deluded – to give in, and meanwhile Portsmouth was being attacked.

Someone has to be in charge, even if it's Thomas. Goddamn it, I don't want to do this.

But what choice do I have?

The air cracked like a whip, making everyone flinch. Luckily, no weapons were discharged. The hair on Mass's arms rose. Thomas's white mop of hair stood on end. The world seemed to split apart. The air imploded, forming a swirling kaleidoscope of colour.

A blast of air sent everyone for cover. No one knew what was happening.

A gate appeared right in front of them.

"This can't be good," said Smithy.

"Get those handguns loaded," said Addy, crouching beside him.

Demons were about to spawn behind their defences. They

would tear the docks apart from the inside. It was the worst thing that could've have happened.

But Mass was wrong.

A person stepped through the gate, someone Mass recognised. His mouth fell open. The person was Maddy.

Where the hell has she been?

Maddy walked out of the gate and marched right up to Thomas. The old man was shaking his head, utterly confused. "What? How did you?"

Maddy lifted a handgun and aimed it at Thomas's head. She pulled the trigger and splattered his brains all over the men standing behind him.

"That was for Amanda."

THE STAND-OFF RESUMED, Thomas's shocked men drawing weapons on Maddy while Mass's people pulled weapons on them. Wanstead's people took cover and aimed their rifles at the people coming through the mysterious gate that had appeared right inside their walls.

It was chaotic.

Maddy stood over Thomas's corpse, not seeming to care about all of the guns being pointed at her. Commander Tosco appeared behind her and placed an arm around her. He whispered something in her ear, and slowly her body relaxed until she lowered the still smoking handgun to her side.

Wanstead broke the silence. His voice was respectful and curious rather than authoritative or demanding. "You're Maddy, correct? Commander Tosco, I believe we've met several times. Where exactly have you come from?"

Maddy glared. "We just got our backsides handed to us in a fight with the demons. We've come here to make sure the same doesn't happen to Portsmouth."

Everyone panicked. At first Mass didn't know why, but then

he saw that a huge demon had emerged from the gate. It was the real deal, with horns, hooves and wings.

Tosco threw a hand up and barked in his officer's voice, "Nobody do a thing. He's a friend. You can call him Sorrow, but he likely won't respond."

The men looked at each other nervously, but mostly they were confused.

A young girl appeared next, sidling up behind the demon and clutching her stomach like she needed to run to the toilet. She waved a hand and smiled. "Please don't shoot Sorrow. He's a big fluffy kitten really. Also, if you shoot him, he'll kill you all."

The big demon bowed. "That is correct. I will."

The next person who came through the gate shocked Mass. It was Damien. At least... sort of. Same face, same height, a little skinnier, but definitely Damien – or his twin brother. "D-Damien?"

The doppelgänger raised an eyebrow. "Do I know you?"

"In a way. Your name is Damien?"

"Yeah. How did you know that?"

Mass shook his head. "It doesn't matter, but be prepared for a shock."

"Um, okay."

"We need to get back in the fight," said Addy. "Can we sort out everything else later?"

One of Thomas's men pointed at the old man's headless corpse. "She just executed our leader."

"He might be your leader," said Maddy, "but he was never mine."

"Mine neither," said Mass, nodding at his friend. It was good to see her.

"Or mine," said Tosco.

"There's no time to fight each other," said Smithy. "Can't we just get along. For the love of all that's holy?"

Wanstead stomped a foot. "With Thomas out of the picture, I am the commanding officer in Portsmouth. I order everyone to focus solely on the only thing that matters right now – defending the walls and preventing our extinction. Leave your grievances aside and get to it. Now!"

Many of the men scattered, seemingly glad to escape the tense situation. More people were coming through the gate. They nearly all lacked weapons.

Wanstead moved in front of Mass. "I will leave you with these newcomers as you seem to know them. Do whatever you can, I beg you."

"I'll do what I can. Good luck, Colonel."

Wanstead took off, leaving Mass with his Urban Vampires and the people from the gate. They were a right mix. Although there were a few dozen fit, young fighters, most were children or the elderly, the wounded and weak. Now that he looked at them, he saw burdens instead of reinforcements. "These people can't fight."

"Speak for yowself," said a small man in the crowd. His face was almost completely covered in thick black hair.

"Some of us can fight," said Maddy. "The others are who we are fighting *for*. If we have any chance of surviving as a species, these children need to live."

Mass nodded.

Smithy pulled a face at a little girl, but he stopped when Addy elbowed him in the ribs. Mass shook his head and sighed. Seeing the immediate effect the children had on those around them, even during a siege, made him realise that Maddy was right. A world without children was no world at all.

"Okay," said Mass, "we'll keep these children safe. Cullen, you and your team are on permanent guard duty. Protect them with your lives."

Cullen was likely unhappy receiving babysitting duties, but he nodded all the same. "Nothing'll get past us, I promise."

Maddy squeezed Mass's biceps. "It's good to see you, Mass. Still working out, I see."

He chuckled. "Just getting up in the morning is a workout

lately. It's good to see you too, Maddy. Shall we go and kill some demons?"

"I thought you'd never ask."

MADDY COULDN'T BELIEVE how much things had changed in the time she'd been away. Portsmouth was under siege and half its inhabitants were dead, led to slaughter by Thomas. At least the bastard was dead now.

And at my hand. How do I feel about that?

And she couldn't believe Thomas had been the very first person she'd seen after stepping through the gate. She'd been floating in a void, unable to see anyone or anything for so long that she feared it would never end. Then the world had come rushing back and she was staring at the man who had killed her lover. It was like nothing else existed but anger, and she'd been unable to stop herself from doing anything except taking a step forward and shooting Thomas in the face. It was too fine a gift to ignore.

She was glad Thomas was dead, but it didn't bring back any of the people she'd lost. That was why it was so good to see Mass and Addy again. Portsmouth had changed, but there were still plenty of familiar faces. It was her home and she would fight for it.

Now, atop a firing platform on the east wall, she unleashed round after round at the incoming hordes. She had survived countless battles but had never encountered anything like this. The sheer number of demons racing through the ruined city was demoralising; she could see it on the faces of all those around her. No one expected to win. They were fighting only because there was no other choice. There would be no prisoners of war, no signing of peace treaties. This was a war of extermination, and you fought until you died, not just for yourself but for anyone who managed to survive longer than you.

She had to be careful not to hit Sorrow with her shots, for the large demon had scaled the walls to go and fight amongst the enemy outside. He tore apart all those around him, dispatching demons with unparalleled ease. He even seemed to be enjoying himself. Scarlett was atop the wall, firing a handgun, but her focus was only on Sorrow. It was clear that she was worried about losing her friend and protector.

There must have been a thousand demons or more attacking the walls by now. Machine-gun fire and a line of wrecked vehicles parked end to end were the only things keeping them at bay. It wouldn't hold them back forever though.

"I didn't think it would get this bad," said Tosco. "I tried to call in the boats, but they aren't recognising my authority."

Maddy cursed. "Then let's hope Wanstead makes good use of them."

Tosco's radio hissed. He frowned at Maddy and held it up so that both of them could hear.

"Maddy? *Fräulein*, are you there?"

"Klein? Yes, I'm here."

"It's good to hear your voice, *ja*? I understand that the other boat captains refuse to accept Commander Tosco's orders."

Maddy looked at Tosco, who was listening intently. "Looks like he's going to have to wait to have his privileges reinstated."

"*Ja, vell*, I *vish* to inform you that my vessel is ready and awaiting your orders."

Maddy was taken aback. "You don't accept orders from anyone, Klein."

"*Nein*, but I am *villing* to take suggestions from a friend. What do you need, *fräulein*?"

"We need it to rain," said Tosco. "Do you have plotting for the area west of the main wall?"

There was a brief crackle of static before Klein replied. "I could drop a bomb down *ze* toilet anywhere in the city. Hold on to your bottoms, *ja*?"

Tosco shouted for everyone to take cover.

Ten seconds later, a whooshing sound cut across the din. Two seconds after that the world lit up, flames rising upwards and ripping apart the dusky sky. *Three huge explosions*. Three seconds more and it began to rain masonry and demon body parts. A few people got struck on the shoulders and back, knocking the wind out of them, but when Maddy pulled herself back above the walls, she saw that the minor losses were worth it.

The area outside the walls had become a crater, reaching right up to the edge of the wall where they were taking cover. A few feet closer and the wall would have been blown to smithereens. Klein could not have been more accurate. Where a thousand demons had been attacking the walls, there was now only a blackened pit of char. It was impossible to make any of the corpses out.

The radio hissed again. "I can do *zat* only *von* more time and *zen* I have only nuclear warheads. Trust me *ven* I say you do not *vant* me to send those."

Maddy put her mouth closer to Tosco's radio so that the German commander could hear her over Portsmouth's triumphant cheers. "It's taken you long enough to get involved, Klein, but thank you."

"And it took you long enough to handle Thomas, but all ends *zat* is *vell*, *ja*? Good luck, *fräulein*. I hope we can play poker with our friends again soon."

"I'll be happy to take your money. Thank you again, Klein."

"*Auf wiedersehen* for now."

Maddy looked back over the walls at the massive black crater. Maybe they had a chance.

***

Mass, Smithy, and Addy looked at one another in shock. The devastation beyond the walls was absolute. The massive crater had swallowed everything in its midst, a massive swath of demons.

"That was insane," said Smithy. "The demons are all gone."

"Wanstead must have called in the boats," said Addy, "but I didn't think we had anything like that."

Mass didn't know much about boats, but the pure destruction gobsmacked him, and he couldn't believe that mankind had originally built such weapons to kill other humans. They'd been on a bad path, but it was certainly helpful to harness such forces against the demons now. Screw the power of Heaven, mankind had powers of its own.

But it won't be enough.

More will come. This isn't over.

"Yow got any more of whatever that was?" asked the small man who had arrived with Maddy through the gate.

Mass looked down at Frank and shrugged. "I have no idea. Let's hope so."

"I'm Frank. Pleased to meet yow."

"Mass. Thanks for your help."

"What kind of a name is Mass?"

"A nickname."

Frank rolled his eyes slightly, but it was more a humorous jest than an insult. "Yow a cockney, aye? Who'd yow support?"

"Crystal Palace."

"Ha, my condolences."

"And who do you support?"

Frank did a little hop on the spot. "Boing, boing. West Brom all the way, mucker."

Mass chuckled. "Then my condolences to you too."

Smithy put a hand on Mass's back and got his attention. "There're more coming."

"Lots more," said Addy, her eyes narrowed and determined.

At the far edges of the crater, a new wave of demons began to form. The sheer destruction had caused them to hesitate, but none had turned away. In the distance, Crimolok strode through the ruins, pulling down buildings and crushing everything in its way. The barriers constructed across the main roads were brushed apart as the giant beast marched straight through them. Hordes of demons followed in its wake.

From the military docks, howitzers punted shells into the air. They hit the ground around Crimolok, obliterating demons but doing no harm to their master. The giant beast strode through the flames unimpeded.

Frank growled. "Another one of the big bastards. Quite the specimen."

"It's Crimolok," said Mass. "He's the one responsible for all of this. We kill him and this ends. Problem is, he can't be killed."

Frank frowned. "Yow need to close his gate. All the big ones have gates attached to 'em. It's what makes 'em invincible."

"Not this one. The only way to kill Crimolok is to destroy Hell itself. It'll take something a little more powerful than what we just saw to achieve that."

"How d'yow know that?"

"An angel told me."

"Bugger."

Smithy chuckled. "Yeah, mate, bugger. You could have met the guy, but he died on the bus getting here."

"We didn't have any angels on our team, but we do have a pet devil." A look of horror crossed Frank's face. "Shite! Sorrow was out there when them bombs landed. Does anybody see him?"

Everybody looked, but no one could see the big demon with the jet-black wings. He'd been right out there amongst the enemy, but there was no sign of him now.

Frank shook his head, genuine grief in his expression. "God-damn friendly fire. We might have wiped out a thousand demons, but he was worth more than that. Damn, what are we going to do?"

Mass thought about what Rick had told him. "Crimolok came through a giant gate. If I can reach it, I can close it. Maybe it'll change things in our favour." He didn't tell them that it would achieve nothing but trapping Crimolok here and pissing him off.

They didn't need to lose hope. Hope was the only thing that had kept them alive this far.

The howitzers fired again, and this time one of the shells struck Crimolok directly in the chest. It knocked the giant backwards, and he almost fell down, but then he continued his unrelenting march.

"That hurt it," said Frank, hopping. "It almost fell."

Mass shook his head. "It was nothing but a hard shove. Not enough."

"We need to hit it again with the big guns on the boats," said Addy. "Maybe it won't be invincible if we hit it with something hard enough."

Mass aimed his shotgun at the blackened crater, ready to take on the next wave of demons to cross the halfway point. The devastation was truly incredible. Maybe Addy was right. Maybe enough force could hurt Crimolok.

Mass turned to Addy. "Give me your radio."

She handed it over.

Mass put out a call on all frequencies. "Whoever just levelled the city outside the walls, I need you to do it again. The enemy's leader is a mile out from us, right next to Buckland Park. If you have any more of those big bombs left, I need you to drop 'em right now. Anyone else with things that go boom can help too. We need to level Buckland Park right now."

The radio hissed. "The big bombs *vere* mine. I have only *ze* one more left. Who am I speaking to?"

"Mass. Leader of the Urban Vampires."

"Ah, you are alive. That is good. What about my good friend Tony?"

Mass sighed. "Your guess is as good as mine. Wherever he is, I hope he's still kicking."

Another voice came on the line. It was Maddy. "Do what he says, Klein. Drop your other bomb."

There was a slight pause, and then Klein replied, "Affirmative."

Several more voices came over the airwaves, various boat commanders willing to fire their guns as well. They were going to drop everything they had left on the park Crimolok was currently passing through. If they hit it fast enough, and hard enough, they might make a big enough dent. Nothing could be truly invincible – not even an angel.

The final voice on the line was Wanstead. "Everybody pray," said the colonel. "This might be the best shot we get."

Overhead, missiles and mortars crossed the darkening sky.

DAMIEN STOOD on the walls a few dozen metres from where Maddy and Commander Tosco were standing. Harry and Steph stood with him, along with Nancy and Scarlett. Scarlett was sobbing. Sorrow was gone. Nancy, the only mother amongst them, was trying to comfort the girl. Harry and Steph held long-range rifles and were putting them to use on the first wave of demons passing through the bomb crater. Overhead, missiles whistled towards the massive demon moving through a park a mile away. Damien spoke to himself. "Die, you bastard. Please, just die."

The first of the missiles struck the main road beside the park. It engulfed the area in flames. Another explosion tossed up mud and grass from the park itself, as well as demons. Then a line of fire tore through the entire area, consuming everything in its path. Within seconds there was nothing left of the park or anything immediately around it. The resulting fires burned out quickly, leaving behind another massive, char-blackened crater. Several hundred demons disappeared in a flash.

The giant demon was also gone.

There was a brief pause before the men and women of Portsmouth let out a triumphant roar. The wooden scaffolds and platforms shook under their stomping boots, and wolf-whistles pierced the air. Damien had never heard anything like it. "It's gone," he said to himself. "We killed it."

"I wouldn't count on it," said a stranger to his left.

Damien didn't know who would be so negative at such a triumphant time, but he was stunned into silence when he turned to give a reply. He was staring at an image of himself – albeit a far more thuggish version.

His doppelgänger chuckled. "Don't shit yourself, we're on the same side. It's nice to finally meet one of us. I think you're probably the last. We tend to get caught up in things. Such is the life of a path walker."

Damien recovered his wits. "You're a path walker too? We're connected?"

"So you know?"

Damien nodded. "There used to be a lot of us, right, acting like pegs and keeping the tapestry in place?"

The thuggish Damien nodded. "Keeping it from unravelling, I guess. Without us, and the connection between our shared souls, the different strands would drift away from each other. The only reason people make it to Heaven or Hell is because of us, and what thanks do we get for it?"

"Am I really the only one left?"

"On this world, for sure. I was the last path walker left on mine, but it got eaten up by the dead. I joined team Lucifer for a while, trying to lend a hand where I could, but he's gone AWOL and I'm stuck here. I've been hoping you can help me find a way back to the tapestry. There's nothing else to be done here. It's over."

"It can't be. No, I don't believe it."

The thuggish Damien shook his head sadly, making the exact same expression that Damien would. "Crimolok's power comes from Hell. There's no way to harm him here. That's why I want out, and you should come with me. We can head to another world and take up the fight somewhere there's still a chance.

Crimolok is close to challenging God himself. He's going to need all the troops he can get. I can't open portals like you can, but—"

Damien glanced at Nancy, and at Scarlett and the others. "I'm not abandoning these people. Nothing is impossible. We'll find a way to save this world."

"That's what I thought about my own home. Come on, help a brother out."

"We're not brothers."

"Then what are we?"

Damien huffed. "Very different people apparently. I'm not helping you run out on us. You want to survive, then fight with the rest of us."

The other Damien scowled. "I guess you had a nicer life than I did, if you still believe in fairy tales. You can't win this. Look!"

Damien stared off into the distance, struggling to see as clearly now that night was rapidly falling and the air was filled with dust. The charred crater began to tremble. From beneath the blackened earth, something emerged. Crimolok rose, unharmed, unhurt, and undeterred.

"Still want to stick around?" asked the other Damien.

"I'd rather die fighting than run. You can do what you want, but if you and I really are part of the same soul, then I know you will stand and fight with us. What other choice do you have?"

"Maybe I'll go find the giant gate twenty miles from here and pass through it into Hell. It'll beat whatever becomes of this place."

"Then go do it."

The other Damien huffed. "I can't. I learned a lot of things from my old boss Lucifer, but one thing he made very clear to me is that path walkers can never pass through a gate not created by themselves or other path walkers."

Damien frowned. "Why not?"

The other Damien shrugged. "Something about tying the tapestry in knots. I got the impression it would be bad."

Damien looked out at the seemingly indestructible beast marching towards them. "How bad could it be?"

"Good point."

17

Mass slumped against the wall, almost dropping his Benelli over the edge. The sight of Crimolok rising from the moonlit ashes shouldn't have been a surprise, yet some small part of him had *hoped*. Now the last of that hope was gone. It really was all over.

Crimolok was covered in the charred remains of his demons. Hundreds of them had been taken out by the blasts, but thousands more emerged from the ruins of the city. There seemed no end to their number.

Mass put down his shotgun and rubbed at his grime-covered cheeks. "I need to get to the gate. I caused it to open. Now I need to close it."

Smithy looked at him, stricken. "There's no way we're getting out of here, man."

Addy turned her back on the approaching demon army and slumped against the wooden ramparts. It would be the last breather any of them would get. "This is it, isn't it? The big goodbye."

Smithy put a hand on her shoulder, but he kept his eyes on Mass. "Got any tricks up your sleeve, big man?"

Mass could only stare blankly.

Gunfire broke out from the docks as people realised Crimolok wasn't dead. Their cheers turned to dismay. The howitzers resumed their ineffective bombardment, slowing Crimolok down but not stopping him. Even at the giant's leisurely pace, it would reach the walls soon. There was only enough time for people to make peace with themselves before they were sent kicking and screaming into the next life – an afterlife that would no longer exist after Crimolok unmade the universe.

Mass closed his eyes and enjoyed the caress of a breeze against his face. All he wanted was to find a moment's peace before the end. One last experience of being alive. Too bad the gentle breeze became a forceful gust that forced Mass to shield his face. When he opened his eyes, he glimpsed something in the sky. At first, he thought Crimolok had thrown another car, but whatever was overhead, it was far larger than any car. A blinding searchlight lit up the docks.

A helicopter.

Addy aimed her shotgun, but she didn't fire. Instead, she gasped. "Where did *that* come from?"

Smithy hopped excitedly, waving at the helicopter as if he were a kid. "It's the army. We're saved."

Addy rolled her eyes. "It's one helicopter, Smithy. Show me a hundred more and I might cream my knickers."

Smithy grimaced. "That's gross."

"Yeah, well, I'm about to die."

The helicopter came in to land. The defenders on the walls ducked, holding on as a huge downdraught assaulted them. Mass climbed down from the ramparts, desperately curious and also grateful to have something to occupy his mind before the endless hordes of demons reached the walls.

Wanstead appeared with a pair of guards at his side. He stared at Mass as if he expected answers; he clearly had none of his own.

The helicopter hovered a few feet above the ground then dropped down on its skids. It had grey and blue camouflage, reminiscent of the sea. The windows were tinted, but two people were visible in the cockpit, illuminated by the dashboard lights. A mechanical whir sounded and the beating of the propellers slowed to a rhythmic *whomp whomp*. The searchlight dimmed, allowing night to close in a little more.

The sliding door at the side of the helicopter slid open and a small group of people hopped out. They looked like sailors, all wearing the same blue overalls, but amongst them was a young girl, a teenager.

"ALICE!"

Mass turned to see a woman sprinting through the flood-lights. She was vaguely familiar, and he thought she might have come in with the group who had appeared from the gate. The young girl saw the woman and screamed, "Mom? Mom! Oh my God, Mom!"

The woman almost took flight and flattened the young girl when they collided ten feet from the helicopter and hugged each other.

Wanstead approached Mass and leaned in to speak. "Do you have any idea who these people are?"

"Nah, but they're idiots. Portsmouth's finished."

Wanstead sighed. "Yes, I fear it is. I'm going to order a mass retreat. If we move quickly, we can get everyone on the boats. We'll head for the States. If anybody has made a go of this, it'll be the Yanks."

"It won't matter," said Mass. "I don't think Crimolok needs to kill us all. He just needs to kill enough."

"And then what?"

"Then he wins and the entire universe loses."

Wanstead frowned, his large gut expanding with an inward sigh. "All the same, I'm going to order a full retreat. What else can I do?"

Mass nodded. He agreed with Wanstead, even if he saw no outcome other than their eventual extermination. Better to let people do what was natural and flee. It would be cruel to make them stand and face their end.

The woman embracing the young girl finally stepped back. She shook her head in disbelief. "What are you doing here, Alice? How did you get here?"

"We went to the forest to search for our people, but all we found were thousands of dead demons. There was a man and woman still there, though, and they told us everyone had gone to Portsmouth. I came to find you, Mom."

The woman looked at the helicopter, and then at the armed men gathered in front of it. "You did this? You came here for me?"

The girl shrugged like it was nothing. "You're alive, Mom. I can't believe it."

Mother and daughter embraced again.

Wanstead and Mass exchanged glances. Somehow a soap opera had unfolded in the middle of mankind's annihilation. There wasn't time for it, and yet no one stepped forward to interrupt the reunion.

Another stranger emerged from the helicopter, a middle-aged woman. She approached Mass and Wanstead. "You two look like you're in charge. General Thomas?"

Wanstead cleared his throat. "Alas, no. I'm afraid you won't be able to meet the late general. I'm sorry if he was a friend of—"

"The bugger's dead then? Good. Not a nice fella from what I've heard."

Mass frowned, noticing the woman was wearing a dog collar. She didn't act very Christian. "Heard from who?"

"I met a man who said he had come from Portsmouth. I tried to keep him alive, but I'm afraid he died shortly after we got him onto the helicopter. He told us about this place before he departed. We brought his body with us. It felt right to bring him home."

Mass didn't know who the woman could be referring to, so when she beckoned for him to follow, he did so curiously. She led him to the helicopter's sliding door and pointed to a flat area in the back behind the two rows of seats. Mass hopped up into the vibrating aircraft and slid to the rear. There was a body on the floor secured by nylon straps.

Mass groaned. "Shit, Tony. I'm sorry, mate."

He'd barely known Tony Cross, but he had liked the guy a lot. In fact, he was only alive because Tony had gone out of his way to help him. It felt wrong to outlive the man who had saved his life.

"He died in peace," said the woman, peering in through the sliding door. "It might sound impossible in these strange days, but he did. He was okay at the end."

Mass turned to the woman. "Thank you for bringing him home. He did a lot for the people here. This is where his body should be."

"That's what I assumed. I'll help you carry him out. I'm Angela, by the way."

"Mass. You came at a pretty bad time, Angela."

"Yeah, it's all over, I can see that. Crimolok can't be harmed and the demons are bloody endless. Tell you the truth, I always suspected it was a lost cause, but what can I say, I'm a fighter. Also, it beats being in Hell."

"You came from Hell? I have friends who've been there. It's good that you came here, Angela. I'm glad."

"Why is that?"

"Because a helicopter is just what I need."

"It isn't mine, but I'll ask if you can borrow it."

Mass nodded. "Ask nicely, because if I can't borrow it, then I'm stealing it."

IT HURT DAMIEN'S HEART. All of it. Nancy was finally back with her daughter, meaning the woman he loved was finally happy, but in twenty minutes she would be dead. There was no denying what was coming their way. They had levelled a chunk of the city, and their enemy had risen from the ashes no weaker than before. There was no end to the demons coming for the walls.

Damien climbed down off the barricades to join up with Nancy. He wanted to meet Alice before it was too late.

I can't believe she's alive. Nancy knew. All this time, she knew.

Tosco met him on the ground before he reached Nancy. "It's a team from my boat," he said, nodding towards the helicopter. "I can barely believe they made it here. I wish they hadn't."

"You think that chopper can start getting people away from here?"

"No more than twenty at a time. It would be almost pointless. We do need to start getting people on the boats somehow though. There's no time left."

Damien agreed. "Running is the only option. Kielder fell, and now Portsmouth will. There's nowhere left. Not here, anyway. Maybe we can head somewhere else on the boats."

"Most don't have much fuel," said Tosco. "Staying together will be impossible. Still, it's a chance."

Colonel Wanstead was arguing with Mass over by the helicopter. Damien knew little about either man, but he could tell they were the ones who were calling the shots in Portsmouth. He hurried over but didn't interrupt. Instead, he listened.

Colonel Wanstead shook his head. "You can't abandon us in the middle of a fight. We need every soldier we have to hold the line while we evacuate the civilians. We have children to think of."

"I understand," said Mass, "but I'm going. Closing the gate will save lives, even if it ain't ours."

"You don't even know if this so-called giant gate is still there. You could be leaving us for nothing. I can't allow it."

Mass reared up and glared at Wanstead. "I don't recognise your authority, so shove it up your arse. Amanda Wickstaff built this place. You're nothing more than a goddamn guest. Try to stop me and I'll shoot you."

Damien shivered. Whoever this Mass was, he was a badass.

Nothing about his tone or expression suggested he wouldn't do exactly what he said.

And is he talking about closing a gate? The same one Damien – the other Damien – was talking about?

Wanstead backed off a little. "Mr Mass, please?"

Damien couldn't hold his silence any more. "Is somebody heading to the gate near here?"

Mass turned to him. "You know about that?"

"Yeah, I... I kind of told myself about it."

Mass chuckled. "I warned you. Where is Damien Two, anyway?"

"Here," said the other Damien, standing nearby, somehow unnoticed until he announced himself. "Believe me, I would rather be anywhere else. Turns out that the *me* from here is kind of a dick."

Damien rolled his eyes. "If anybody is heading to the gate, I'm coming. We need to close it."

Mass nodded. "That's exactly what I'm doing. You want to come, you're welcome. I need a team to get me close enough."

"You know where it leads, right?"

"Yeah, I know the drill. Straight to Hell for me. I'm fine with that."

I was right. The guy's a badass.

Tosco intervened, having been listening from a few feet away. "Those pilots are my men, and I won't force them to take you anywhere unless they want to. I'll go speak with them."

"Please," said Wanstead, imploring Mass with his hands, "stay and fight. Help me get these people onto the boats."

Mass bunched his hands into fists. "I don't know what to make of you, Wanstead, but no matter what happens, you still killed my friend. Me leaving is the best thing for you, trust me."

Wanstead was breathing heavily. Damien didn't know what events Mass was referring to, but Wanstead grew anxious. "Then I fear, if we meet again, it will be a rather bloody affair."

"It won't be," said Mass. "It'll be quick."

Wanstead nodded. "Who are you taking with you?"

"Just a few of my guys. Cullen will stay and lead the rest of my guys to help with the evacuation. Damien, if you want company, better get it fast. I won't wait for you."

Damien glanced over at Nancy and thought about asking her, but she had just found Alice. They needed to stay together. "I'm only bringing two people," he said. "I just need to say goodbye to someone first."

"Then go do it."

Damien hurried over to Nancy. When she saw him, the smile on her face stretched right up to her eyes. It was the happiest he'd ever seen her, but there was a sadness there too. "Damien, I'd like you to meet someone."

Damien offered a hand to the beautiful young girl who looked so much like her mother. "I've been dying to meet you, Alice. I've heard so much about you."

The girl shook his hand, not shyly as he would have expected, but firmly and confidently. "Thank you for keeping my mom safe."

"My pleasure. Do you mind if I just speak with her alone for a second?"

"Go for it."

Damien had to drag Nancy away. Even then, she kept glancing sideways to make sure her daughter was still there. "You need to get Alice on a boat," he told her. "Portsmouth is finished."

"I really wish this place had stood a chance. We should leave right this second. I have to get Alice to safety."

"You're both getting on a boat. I'll make sure there's a place for you both."

Nancy frowned, clearly noticing his carefully selected words. "What about you?"

"I have some place else to be. Don't worry, okay? You have Alice and that's all that matters. I love you, Nancy. You made the end of the world bearable. Thank you for that."

She reached out and held his hand in hers. "That sounded

like a goodbye."

"Reminds me of not so long ago when you were setting off to go find Alice. That turned out all right in the end, didn't it? Take care, Nancy." He glanced at Alice. "She looks just like you."

He turned away and Nancy didn't stop him. They were both too grown up for that. Loss was the only thing left in this world, and there was no point fighting it.

Damien grabbed Harry and Steph. They were reloading their rifles at the wall.

"We getting out of here?" Harry asked.

"Flying out of here," said Damien. He pointed at the helicopter. "Fancy a ride?"

Steph chuckled. "It couldn't make me any more nauseous than travelling by gate. Where are we going?"

"To try and make a difference."

Harry nodded. "Let's get a move on then."

They joined Mass at the helicopter. The muscle-bound badass already had his team, and it included the other Damien. "Oh great, you're coming too?"

"What else am I gonna do?"

Mass banged a fist against one of the helicopter's rear panels. "Get in and prepare yourself for a bumpy ride."

Damien climbed on board and took a seat beside his doppelgänger. Two minutes later, they were airborne

---

TOSCO WATCHED his helicopter take off. It zipped south before heading north, avoiding the giant beast that was now only a couple of hundred metres from the walls.

Ten thousand people filled the docks. Many stayed to fight, but hundreds began to panic and flee. It was utter chaos – gunfire and screams. People fell in the stampede, but it was heartening to see that none were trampled and all were helped back to their feet.

Tosco found himself with no ships under his command and no men to direct. *The Hatchet* was somewhere on the north coast and no other ships recognised his authority. He wasn't a commander any more, he was just a man standing in the middle of a losing battle.

He saw Maddy and rushed over. "Everyone's evacuating," he said. "We need to help."

She grabbed the radio from his shoulder and put out a call. "Klein, are you there?"

"*Ja*, Maddy. I am here."

"Any room on your submarine for refugees?"

There was a pause, and for moment it seemed like the German wouldn't reply. "A submarine is a cramped place, full of dangerous buttons and serious levers. I can take no more *zan* fifty."

"Fifty is better than nothing. Can you be ready to take people in the next five minutes? The other ships will be loading up too."

"I *vill* see if I can find room to come up. Portsmouth's waters are a crowded place."

Tosco leant into the radio. "I'm sending a young girl and her mother to you. Nancy and Alice. Please, make sure you take them."

"Confirmed. Good luck, Commander."

"It's just James for now. Good luck to you too, Commander."

Maddy gave him a cautious smile. "Alice will be okay. She will."

He wanted to grab her and hold on for dear life – he was so afraid – but there was no time for comfort. Instead of saying anything in reply, he turned and ran, locating Nancy and Alice amongst the furor. He grabbed the young girl by the shoulders and looked her in the eye. "It's time for you and your mother to get out of here, Alice. There's a submarine coming up for air and you have a ticket, okay? If you don't see it, then get yourself on whatever boat you can. Do you understand?"

Alice nodded. Any notion of bratty teenagerdom was gone.

She was frightened and wanted an adult to tell her what to do. "What about you? Aren't you coming?"

"I'll join you later. Some people have to stay and fight a while longer."

"No! Let others fight. You're always putting yourself in danger for other people. James, come with us."

He ruffled her hair, something she would have usually hated. "I'll be along, Alice, I promise. Wait for me, okay?"

She threw her arms around him and squeezed. "If you die, I'll never forgive you. I already lost my dad; I won't lose you too."

Tosco glanced up at Nancy and smiled. "You have your mom now. Things are looking up."

To his surprise, Nancy hugged him too. "Thank you for bringing her back to me."

"My pleasure. She's a brave young woman. You should be proud."

"I am."

Tosco stepped back slowly, not wanting to get pulled into another hug and convinced to stay. Then he turned and hurried back towards the walls. It pained him that he would never see Alice again. The odds of him joining her on Klein's submarine were slim.

But she'll be okay. That's all that matters.

I kept her safe for you, Guy.

Maddy met Tosco at the wall. People were aiming their rifles downwards over the top of it, the demons on the other side. The ground shook, the distant strides of Crimolok getting closer.

Maddy clutched his arm and pulled him closer. "Hey, James, can I ask you a question?"

"Sure? Best make it quick though."

She gave him an odd frown. "Why'd you give me a handgun instead of a rifle when we left *The Hatchet*?"

It was an odd question, and not one he had an immediate answer for. He had to think about it first. "Um, because I didn't want to put you in danger. I wanted you to leave the fighting to me. Can't stop trying to be your knight in shining armour, I guess."

Maddy nodded to herself. "So, I was right. It *was* sexist."

"What? No... no way. I was just... yeah, maybe it was." He ran a hand through his hair and sighed. "Sorry. I just didn't want you getting hurt. Not because you're a woman, but because you're *you.*"

"I can handle myself, James." The way she glared at him turned his stomach. He felt ashamed. When she kissed him, though, he felt confused.

She pulled away and left him spluttering. "W-What was that for?"

"Like I said, James, I can handle myself, but the thought of letting a man take care of me is surprisingly nice. Thank you for caring about me."

"I do! Which is why I would really like you to get on Klein's submarine. There's no way you would agree to that, though, is there?"

She lifted the handgun he had given to her on *The Hatchet* and cocked it. "No way in Hell. Someone needs to stick around to keep you safe."

He grinned. "Thank you for caring about me."

She grabbed him and gave him a forceful yet intimate kiss on the mouth. "I do. Now come on."

———

MADDY JOINED the fight atop the walls. The wooden platforms were rickety, but the cement wall was reassuringly firm. Tosco followed behind, still blushing from their kiss.

I can't believe I did that.

Her head was still a mess. Her feelings for Amanda hadn't gone away, but it was likely she and Tosco were both going to die. She didn't want that to happen without having kissed him at least once.

Or twice.

There were many she recognised on the platforms, including her recent friends from Kielder. Frank ran back and forth, barking orders like he was still back at the castle. Dr Kamiyo was comforting Scarlett, who had lost her pet demon in Klein's initial bombardment.

Maddy leant over the wall with her handgun and searched for a target. She didn't have to look for long.

The demons had made it to the wall. The only thing keeping them back now was the sheer number of corpses piled up in front of them. They stumbled and clambered over a field of flesh, unable to find their footing. Maddy took several shots at them, each round finding a target. There were too many to miss.

Crimolok made it to the crater Klein had created with his initial bombardment. The giant flattened everything in its path. Soon it would reach the wall.

Frank rushed by on the platform. He was too short to fire over the walls, but he excelled in his role as drill sergeant. She grabbed him before he could disappear. "Frank! Everyone is getting onto the boats. You need to get out of here."

"Ha! No way, lass. My buddy Ted died for me back at Kielder. Now it's my turn to die for someone else. I'll be on these walls till they fall flat. My legs are too short for running anyway."

Maddy laughed. There wasn't an ounce of fear on Frank's heavily bearded face. He was a warrior. "Then it looks like we're going to be holding the fort together."

"Just so long as you leave the big bugger to me."

Maddy looked at the terrifying monster striding through the blackened crater. She shuddered. "He's all yours."

Tosco moved up beside Maddy and rattled off several rounds from his rifle. "I've got one more magazine," he said, "then nothing."

"We can always heckle them," said Maddy, firing off the remainder of her clip. It was all she had left, so she tucked her handgun into her waistband and searched for another weapon.

There were none to be found. All along the walls, men and women stood unable to do anything but watch or turn and flee. Portsmouth was almost out of ammunition. The howitzers had fallen silent too. The docks were full of frightened people running for the boats.

Maddy looked down over the wall and saw a throng of demons directly below. They were still clambering over corpses, climbing over each other like rats, but they were gradually making it higher. Without the constant barrage of gunfire, they were amassing faster than they were being pushed back. It was like looking down into an ocean of teeth and claws.

Frank continued running back and forth along the platform, shouting for everyone to fire whatever they had left. "We'll fight 'em with our bare 'ands if we 'ave to. Who do they think they're dealing with?"

Dr Kamiyo started leading Scarlett towards the ladders. He noticed Maddy watching and shook his head sadly. "There's nothing more I can do here. I'm going to get Scarlett back to the boat."

Maddy smiled weakly. "People are going to need you, Doctor, so go. You have time."

Scarlett had stopped crying, but her eyes were swollen and red. All the same, she managed to give Maddy a polite nod that was really a simple goodbye. They would never see each other again.

"Demons on the walls," Frank shouted. "Demons on the sodding walls."

Maddy turned just in time to see a primate bounding awkwardly along the narrow wooden walkway. Tosco grabbed her out of the way and let rip with his rifle. Bloody divots opened up on the primate's clammy chest and it went toppling back over the wall.

Tosco tossed his rifle and groaned. "That's me empty. You okay?"

Maddy nodded. "Fine. I have my knight in shining armour

with me, don't I?"

"Always."

Frank staggered backwards along the ramparts. "Ah, bloody 'ell!"

Two more primates had leapt onto the walls, knocking a pair of soldiers off the platform and onto the hard concrete fifteen feet below. Dr Kamiyo and Scarlett were forced backwards, their route to the ladders cut off.

"They're trapped," said Maddy. "We need to help them."

Scarlett screamed as Dr Kamiyo stood in front of her with only a knife to defend himself with. The young doctor was brave, but he was outmatched.

Frank tried to get the demon's attention by shouting obscenities. It didn't work; they had their eyes on vulnerable meat.

"Get back," Dr Kamiyo yelled, his voice wavering. "Please!"

Maddy picked up Tosco's rifle, knowing it was empty. She turned it around and used the stock to strike one of the demons between the shoulder blades. The demon spun to face her, furious. Its fangs dripped bloody saliva. Maddy then swung for its head, but a swipe of its lethal claws sent the useless rifle cartwheeling over the wall and into the writhing mass of demons below. More and more were nearing the top of the wall, climbing on top of each other like acrobats. Maddy's spine stiffened at the sight of them.

Dr Kamiyo grunted, swinging his knife at the primate and drawing blood from its arm. With a bloodcurdling screech, the demon leapt on Dr Kamiyo, knocking him down and pinning him against the wooden walkway. Maddy was forced back by the other demon, unable to help.

Scarlett screamed for help, screamed for Sorrow.

There was a whoosh of wind, and something dark shot up into the sky. Maddy could only make out a shadow, a bat-like shape streaking through the spotlights that criss-crossed overhead. For a moment she thought it was a new kind of demon – an abominable creature they had yet to see – but then the beast came crashing down onto the ramparts and she realised it was Sorrow.

He survived. How the hell did he survive?

Sorrow flared his wings and knocked the primate off of Dr Kamiyo just as it was about to tear into his throat. The force sent the doctor rolling towards the edge of the platform, but Sorrow snatched his ankle and yanked him back just in time.

Scarlett saw her friend was alive and lost her mind. "Sorrow! Sorrow, you're alive!"

The demon took a step towards the girl, but the other primate leapt onto his back and caused him to stop. Sorrow merely reached back and yanked the demon away. Then, without mercy, he tore the arms off the demon like wings from a butterfly. The way he tossed the armless torso over the wall was chilling. Sorrow was furious.

Thank God he's on our side.

The space between them now free, Scarlett threw herself at Sorrow. The demon embraced her, cocooning them both with his leathery black wings. "Ward, I feared the worst."

"I thought you were dead, Sorrow."

"Merely injured. Your allies hit me with crushing fire. It caused me great anger."

Maddy winced. "I can't believe you survived that."

"How did you?" asked Scarlett, still hugging him, still sobbing with joy.

Sorrow pulled his wings back in and stood straight. "I was forged in flame. No fire may burn me."

Tosco raised an eyebrow. "Good to know."

Kamiyo got to his feet and rubbed at his arm. "Thanks for the save, Sorrow."

"I am happy you live, Doctor, but you will die soon. Crimolok is here."

As if to prove his point, a part of the wall thirty metres away crumbled as Crimolok strode right through it. Men and woman fell, shattering against the concrete twenty feet below.

People stopped fighting and ran for their lives.

FRANK STARTED SHOUTING, but this time, instead of telling people to stand and fight, he yelled at them to get to the boats. Hundreds of people stayed to fight on the battlements while thousands fled. Maddy felt their fear. This was sheer terror.

Further north, the demons were massacring people. Their screaming was the only thing she could hear. All gunfire had ceased.

"We only have a few minutes," said Tosco. His eyes were wide and unblinking. "They're going to overwhelm the docks before everyone can get away."

"The bastards," said Frank, seething.

There was a sudden burst of gunfire as a large group of soldiers sprinted across the courtyard. Instead of running away, they were running *towards* battle. Maddy saw Colonel Wanstead among them, and when he saw her questioning stare, he stopped to explain himself. "Reserves. I wanted to keep something back in case the demons breached the wall. The children and the elderly are already safe, but there are still thousands trying to make it onto the boats. We need to buy them time."

"Good work, Colonel," said Tosco, nodding appreciatively.

"Yeah," said Frank. "Bostin'."

Maddy didn't quite understand the reason in keeping reserves, but slowly she realised that these men would have just emptied their weapons into an endless sea of demons. Now they could deal with the demons that had made it past the walls. Smart move.

Someone handed Tosco a rifle. Then someone else appeared and handed one to Maddy. It was Sarah. "You're still alive then?" she said.

Maddy nodded. "For now. Where have *you* been?"

"Got dragged into a fight nearby. I saw these fine gentlemen handing out guns and decided to tag along."

Wanstead pointed to the broken section of the wall. "Attack those demons before they overwhelm the docks."

Everyone roared like bersekers as thousands of bullets whizzed through the air and struck demon flesh. Even at this range, the assault was devastating. The demons fell in their hundreds, once again creating a barricade of their own corpses. Their progress through the broken-down wall slowed to a trickle. It brought time for people to break cover and race for the quayside. With any luck, they would find boats there waiting for them.

Crimolok stomped at another section of the wall, creating new gaps for the demons to flow through. The giant being seemed in no rush to end the battle. It looked like Crimolok was enjoying it.

Maddy savoured the feeling of a rifle bucking in her hands as she fired round after round. Sarah knelt beside her, once again showing inhuman accuracy and speed. It was as though the woman had been *born* with a high-powered weapon in her arms.

Wanstead waved at the armed men. "Fall back to the warehouses. We can take cover inside and try to keep them at bay for as long as possible."

"We go inside," said Tosco, "we'll never make it out again."

"I understand the consequences, Commander. It's my duty to stay behind, but the rest of you should fight only as long as you want to. Get yourself back to the boats before it's too late."

"Maybe Sorrow can fly us out of here," said Frank, half-serious.

Sorrow flapped his wings.

Everyone fought their way back towards the warehouses. Most of them had been cleared and organised, used for accommodation or supplies. The first warehouse they reached was full of bedrolls and assorted human belongings. Fortunately, it was empty of people.

Wanstead gave orders. "Set up at the windows. Don't pick

your shots, there are too many. Hit whatever you can as quickly as you can. Let them climb over their own dead to get at us."

Maddy pulled aside a makeshift curtain that someone had put up over a broken window, then set her rifle against the sill. The demons came in their hundreds now. Soon, it would be thousands.

They're like locusts. Biblical.

I hate them.

The warehouse was like the inside of a deafening drum as two hundred soldiers fired their rifles at once. Their combined assault pushed the demons back, injuring most but killing many. The beasts clambered and bumped into each other, their clumsiness slowing them down.

Sarah fired out of the window beside Maddy. "These things never get any less ugly, do they?"

Maddy chuckled. "Are you still trying to keep me alive?"

"A soldier without a mission is just a maniac with a gun."

"Good point. I'm glad you have my back, Sarah."

Sarah rattled off a full magazine. "Saw you and Tosco eating each other's faces earlier. How long's that been going on?"

"It's *not* going on. Maybe if we don't all die in the next ten minutes, something might get to go on, but right now..."

Frank yelled in the background. "Make 'em eat shit!"

Sarah nodded. "Yeah, bigger issues. I get it."

The two women fired round after round for so long that it was hard to breathe amongst the gun smoke, but it was a losing battle. The demons advanced relentlessly – a tide that couldn't be held back. Every now and then a primate would make it into open ground and start sprinting. It shifted everyone's fire enough that the larger mass of demons would gain a few yards every time.

"Everyone, spread your fire," shouted Tosco. "I'll deal with any demons that make it into the open."

Maddy was out of ammo, so she headed over to the rucksack that one of Wanstead's men had put down. It was full of ammo, and she grabbed what she needed. Reloading her rifle, she turned to go back to the windows, but a radio hissed and caught her attention. The handset was clipped to the side of the rucksack. She grabbed it.

"Commander Tosco," said a familiar voice, "are you still alive?"

Maddy grabbed the radio. "Klein, is that you?"

"*Ja, fräulein.* It is good to hear your voice. Is James still with you?"

"Yes, he's alive."

"Then please inform him I have young Alice and her mother aboard my submarine. They are safe."

"I'll tell him right now." Maddy turned and headed for the windows. Tosco was busy and hadn't heard the conversation over the din of rifle fire, but she was glad to be able to give him some good news. If nothing else, he would die knowing that Alice was safe. "James! James, that was—"

Maddy was struck from behind. She hit the ground and smacked her head on the concrete floor. She didn't see the demon at first, but she smelled it. Rotten flesh and spilled blood. She tried to get up, but her vision swirled.

"Shit!" someone shouted. "They're coming in round the back."

The deafening gunfire got louder as people turned their rifles inwards, gunfire echoing off the vaulted ceiling. Maddy saw stars, and when a burnt man collapsed onto the ground beside her, she realised someone had just saved her life. Sarah appeared and grabbed her. "On your feet, soldier."

"I'm not a soldier," said Maddy, looking around for her rifle. "A real soldier never loses their weapon for one thing, right?"

Sarah located the rifle and shoved it into Maddy's arms. "You're a soldier whether you like it or not. Get your head in the game, bitch."

Maddy nodded, struck by the other woman's ferocity. "Sure thing."

"We're surrounded," someone shouted.

"We're trapped in here," said someone else.

"No," Frank roared. "The sorry bastards are trapped in here with us! Let 'em 'ave it."

Tosco looked around desperately. "Everyone, head for the side door over there. We can fight our way out of this."

Maddy lifted her rifle and fought for her life. A dozen demons had made it inside the warehouse from a side entrance. She picked her shots and hit headshot after headshot. Maybe she *was* a soldier. Sarah edged her towards the other side of the warehouse, firing her rifle and using her elbows to keep Maddy moving. Eventually, they joined up with the others. So far, no one had been hurt.

But that quickly changed.

With their focus no longer on the demons coming in through the broken-down wall, the primates at the front of the pack were finally able to make it to the warehouse. The first of them crashed through a half-broken window and landed on a woman, twisting her head right around and snapping her neck. The demon started eating her, but Wanstead put a stop to it, shooting the monster in the top of the skull at point-blank range. The colonel then turned to his men and bellowed, "Full retreat. Get to the boats. Stop for nothing."

"Yow heard the man," Frank shouted. "Move your arses."

More demons exploded through the windows and burst in through the side entrance. Shadows surrounded the building, blocking out the glow of the spotlights. Everyone fought for the door at the back of the warehouse as men began to fall, pulled down by burnt men and primates. Within seconds, two dozen men were dead or screaming.

Sarah shoved Maddy. "Move it."

Maddy let off another three shots, but then she was out. The rucksack of ammo was lost in the sea of demons. Others ran out of ammunition too, forced to used their rifles as clubs.

More men fell.

"Damn it!" Sarah backed up against Maddy and fired the last

of her ammunition. Then she threw her rifle at a primate before whipping out a handgun and shooting it in the chest. "Maddy, you need to go. We can't hold them any more."

"I'm not leaving without you."

"I'm not your fucking girlfriend. Go!"

Maddy looked around for answers that didn't involve abandoning people to die. Frank, Wanstead, and a small group of men were surrounded nearby, cut off from escape. Despite that, they continued to fight. Frank continued to shout and bellow. How could she run while they remained behind?

"I can't leave."

A hand wrapped around her elbow and wrenched it behind her back. "Yes, you can!"

Tosco dragged Maddy backwards towards the door while Sarah shoved her from the front. All around them, people died. Maddy looked desperately towards Frank and Colonel Wanstead, but both men were now lost in a sea of demons.

We can't abandon them.

Maddy threw her head back and struck Tosco's face. He grunted and released her, and with both arms free, Maddy shoved Sarah out of the way. She had no idea what she was doing, but she knew she wanted to stay and fight. She wanted to fight like Amanda and Tony and Diane and all the others who had died trying to protect other people.

She caught another glimpse of Frank amidst the demons. He was unarmed, throwing his fists and kicking out with his legs. His awkward movements were hard to predict, and it bought him a little space while the demons struggled to get at him.

Tosco and Sarah shouted after Maddy to stop, but she ignored them and rushed to help. Dying for others was better than living for yourself.

She had no regrets. This was the ending she wanted. Maybe it was the one she deserved.

But when the ceiling came down on top of her, all thoughts of helping others went away.

18

M addy couldn't breathe, couldn't move. She was buried alive. She coughed and dust filled her mouth, choked her throat. She began to panic, unable to see or hear anything. She focused on a pinprick of light that slowly got larger. First she saw stars, then the moon. Was she outside?

A face appeared above hers. It was Tosco. He bled from his forehead and was covered in chalky-white dust. "Maddy, you need to get up."

She reached out and grabbed his hand, holding on to him like a life jacket. The warehouse had collapsed around them, the roof now on the floor in pieces. The walls had shattered. Breeze blocks lay exposed. Steel lintels leant at precarious angles. Men and women lay in the rubble, some dead or unconscious, others moaning and dazed. The demons were in the same state, trapped and clawing to dig themselves out of their concrete graves.

Maddy was lucky to be alive.

What the hell happened?

Sarah was on the ground nearby. She got to her feet groggily and Maddy gasped when she saw the left side of her face. It had been torn wide open. Blood gushed down her shirt.

"Sarah, you're hurt."

She fingered at her face gingerly and winced. Then she shrugged. "I was never that pretty to begin with. What the hell happened?"

Maddy opened her mouth to reply but men's screams cut her off.

Tosco grabbed Maddy and Sarah, pulling them back and cursing. "Look out!"

Crimolok stared down at them from outside the ruined warehouse, a cruel grin spread across his face.

"Oh, yow's the big bastard that caused all this, are ya?" Frank clambered from beneath a pile of bricks, remarkably unhurt. He was furious. "Do yow know how many good people have died because of you, ya bloody piece of shit!"

Maddy called out. "Frank, what the hell? Get away from there!"

Frank pointed a stubby finger at Crimolok, having to crane his neck upwards. "I've had enough of this. All this death, all because of this gobshite!"

Maddy looked up at Crimolok, staggered by the sight of something so massive. Nothing on earth had ever existed like the thing standing before her right now. She didn't know if Frank's words bothered Crimolok, but the giant's face contorted in anger.

Maddy called out again. "Frank, get away from there. Move!"

Frank continued shouting obscenities at Crimolok, red-faced and enraged. He didn't care about anything except venting his fury at the abomination that had wiped out billions of people. Maddy understood his anger. She had almost died for hers too.

Frank didn't move out of danger. He was hysterical with rage.

"Use your legs, you fool." Colonel Wanstead appeared from the rubble and raced towards Frank. He grabbed the smaller man and tossed him so hard that he went airborne.

Crimolok stomped a massive foot and Colonel Wanstead disappeared in an instant, crushed flat like an ant beneath a work boot. Brick and cement shattered, sending up clouds of clogging dust.

Frank scrambled through the debris, trying to get to his feet. Maddy helped him out of harm's way as demons slashed their claws and snapped their jaws, desperately trying to get themselves free of the rubble. Some managed to climb out, and they immediately went on the attack, focusing on the men and woman still trapped or too injured to move. A few dozen soldiers were still able-bodied, but they exited the warehouse in terror, no longer willing to fight now that Crimolok had arrived. It was useless.

Sarah pointed to a section of the back wall that had crumbled. "There! Everyone get through the gap."

Maddy shoved Frank, almost knocking him over. His ranting had stopped; he was oddly vacant. Whatever fury had possessed him was gone. He was broken.

Tosco reached the gap in the wall first, but he waited for the rest of them. Maddy made it there and helped Frank through, then went herself. The gap was narrow and tight rather than a massive hole, which would make it harder for the demons to follow.

Tosco still remained on the other side of the gap. Maddy reached a hand through the gap and yanked at his arm. "James, come on!"

He passed through and joined her on the outside, but he quickly turned back. "Sarah, hurry!"

"I'm coming, I'm coming." Sarah appeared at the gap, her face covered in blood. She slipped one leg through while Maddy grabbed her arm. She had almost made it through when her eyes went wide and she grunted. Her body stiffened, half in and half out of the gap. Maddy pulled at her, but she wouldn't move.

"Sarah, come on!"

Sarah opened her mouth and blood spilled from between her lips, mixing with that already covering her face. She looked like a ghoul, a lost, frightened ghoul.

Maddy cried out. "Sarah, please!" She pulled harder, yanking at the woman's arm hard enough to almost tear it off at the shoulder, but instead of moving forward, Sarah fell back into the warehouse.

Maddy lunged, tying to hold on to the other woman, but the only thing she could see through the gap were demons. Hundreds of them.

A primate leapt into the gap, claws swiping at Maddy's throat. Tosco pulled her back just in time. His expression was grim. "We have to make it to the boats."

Maddy understood. There was no one left to save. She started running, tears staining her cheeks. Behind her, Crimolok was destroying what was left of Portsmouth.

———

MASS FOUND it mildly amusing that he was travel sick. Such a silly thing to worry about on his way to throw himself through a gate into Hell, but he was miserable with nausea all the same. He had taken to breathing deeply, concentrating on keeping the contents of his stomach on the inside.

"You okay?" Smithy asked, raising his voice over the din of the rotor blades. "You don't look good."

"I'm fine. Just battered and broken like everybody else."

"I've never had a helicopter ride before. It's loud!"

"That's because you're not wearing your ear protectors," said Mass, nodding at Addy, who was sitting quietly on the front bench wearing hers. At the rear of the chopper, the undead Damien sat beside Angela. The thrumming of the cabin seemed to relax everyone.

"Neither are you," said Smithy. "Too manly to put them on?"

Mass smirked. "What's your deal, Smithy? Before I met you, I had thirty Vampires, every one of them a total badass, but none as calm and collected as you. Other than the lame jokes, you're a fucking warrior, man. Tell the truth, were you a secret agent before all this?"

"Ha! Nah, I was... well, I wasn't much of anything, really. I didn't really think about anything beyond the weekend. I treated life like a laugh most of the time."

"So what changed?"

Smithy shifted in his seat. "I dunno. I kept surviving at first because I was desperate to find other people. It terrifies me, the thought of being lonely. The worst. I suppose I take risks because I would rather die myself than see everyone around me die and leave me on my own again."

Mass saw the fear in Smithy's eyes. It was clear that loneliness frightened him far worse than any demon. "You're a good bloke, Smithy. I wish I'd known you before all of this. Look after Addy for me, okay? She's not as tough as she acts."

"None of us are." Smithy glanced at Addy, unaware of their conversation due to her ear protectors. "So, this trip you're taking is one way then?"

"It is for me. I wish there was another way, but this is my mess and I need to clean it up. I killed Vamps. I set Crimolok loose."

Smithy pulled a face. "Get out of it with that shit, will you? How long do you think Vamps' body would have held out? He was rotting from the inside out, man. Crimolok was getting free eventually. All you're guilty of is speeding things along. Besides, if we let our friends suffer, then what's the point? We're fighting for the survival of the human race, aren't we? Well, part of being human is giving a shit about other people. You did the right thing, Mass. Stop beating yourself up about it. It's getting old."

Mass's tear ducts erupted and he was suddenly sobbing. He couldn't remember the last time he had let his emotions go, but he made up for it now. Whimpering sounds he wasn't proud of kept erupting in the back of his throat and he couldn't keep his face from scrunching up in misery. He went to turn away, but Smithy lunged and pulled him into a hug. "It's okay, big guy. If ever there was a time to cry, it's now."

Addy noticed the movement and turned her head. She saw Mass's tears and immediately threw off her ear protectors and came over. She joined in with the hug, the three of them holding each other without saying a word.

Mass missed his friends; not just those he'd lost, but those he was *going* to lose. The future no longer existed, causing a massive hole to grow inside of him. There was only one thing to do now: close the gate.

I guess I always knew I would end up in Hell. Brixton boy till the end.

"I think we've found it," said the living Damien, who'd been leaning over the back of the pilot's seats and staring out of the cockpit. His friends, Steph and Harry, were with him, holding hands and silently awaiting their destination. They were an odd bunch.

Mass wiped away his tears and headed up front, holding on to the ceiling straps to keep from falling. At first he saw only the night sky, but when he managed to look down at the ground three hundred feet below, he saw the gate. It lit up everything around it, but not in a beautiful way. It was like staring at a nuclear reactor ready to explode.

Against the autumnal trees and green fields of the Wessex Downs, the gate was an unnatural blight on the scenery. It shimmered and popped, more like a flame than a lens, and every now and then it would shift in such a way that you got a glimpse of what lay beyond. Mass knew he was looking straight into Hell.

Demons were flooding out of the gate, a line of ants from up high but an army of death on the ground. Getting to the gate would be impossible, even with their weapons. The pilots had already informed Mass that the helicopter was an old US Coast Guard rescue chopper. It had no guns, cannons, or missiles, only a winch, harness, and high-powered searchlight. At a push, the pilot had said it could paint a target for something else to shoot at – but they were on their own in this.

"So what's the plan?" the undead Damien yelled from the rear of the helicopter. "Are you going to leap out of the helicopter *Mission Impossible* style, or are we going to land and have ourselves a ruck?"

"There are too many demons on the ground," said Mass. "The best bet is to go down on the harness."

Angela wore a disapproving look on her face. "That puts a lot of trust on the pilots. What if they screw up?"

"Then he goes splat," said undead Damien with a grin. "Embarrassing way to go."

Mass looked at everyone. "Who has a better plan? I'm all ears."

"I don't," said Harry. "Seems the right call to me."

"Anyone else?" said Mass. "Like I said, I'm all ears."

"And biceps," said Angela. "If I were twenty years younger, still alive, and not gay, I would let you use me for a workout. That aside, I don't want to see you throw your life away in vain. We have to make sure you go to Hell, sweetheart."

"Cheers. Look, the gate is massive. If I go down on the winch, it should be easy to swing me into it from above. The demons below won't be able to reach me."

Smithy shook his head. "You sure you want to do this? We get this wrong and you'll be forever known as piñata boy."

Mass shook his head, realising he was going to miss all of the lame jokes. "What's to lose? Crimolok will destroy the universe if I do nothing."

"Good point. Okay, so we're going to do this then?"

Addy nodded. "Sooner we do it, the sooner we give everyone at Portsmouth a chance."

Mass had to swallow his guilt. He couldn't tell them that it was all over for the people of Portsmouth. Crimolok might not be able to destroy the universe, but he would remain in Portsmouth, angry and determined to exterminate all that he could.

Mass exhaled, another wave of sickness washing over him. "Somebody show me what I have to do."

One of the pilots left the cockpit and helped Mass get into the harness. It felt secure, which was good, even though he intended on swinging to his death anyway. He gave everything a tug, making sure the equipment would hold him. He'd lost a little muscle mass recently, but he was still a thick piece of meat. "Okay," he said once he was satisfied, "I'll leave the manoeuvres up to the men with the pilot licences, but the plan is to swing me until I pass inside the gate, right? From what I've seen, that's all it'll take. I've seen plenty of gates close, and it's always instant. Soon as a living soul passes through the lens, *kablooey*."

"Let's hope there's not a brick wall on the other side," said Smithy.

Mass realised that his hands were shaking. "Okay, let's do this before I lose my nerve. No goodbyes, no advice, let's just get it done."

There was a moment's silence. Even that was more than Mass could bear. He grabbed a handhold and pulled himself over to the sliding door. He looked at Addy and gave a nod. She yanked open the door, letting in the wind and forcing everyone to hold on.

Mass moved into the opening and stared at the ground below. It felt like they were barely moving, almost floating above the earth. The helicopter descended gradually, the trees, buildings, and wrecked cars slowly getting larger in the glow of the gate. The mass of demons got larger too. There were thousands of them down there.

The gate was huge.

Mass placed his toes over the edge. His stomach was in knots. Acid burned his throat. The wind lashed at his cheeks. It was time to jump.

Any second now.

Just jump, man. Get it over with.

Okay. I'm going to jump. Watch me jump.

It'll be fun.

Just jump. One step, that's all.

This is embarrassing.

"You sure you want to do this?" Smithy asked. "Like, are you one hundred per cent sure that you want to jump? Stick a needle in your eye sure?"

"Yes, I'm sure! I have to do this. I'm not going to change my—"

Something struck Mass between the shoulder blades and shoved him through the door. As he fell, he realised that Smithy – the sonofabitch – had pushed him.

That git!

Mass's stomach lurched into his throat as he became weightless. He screamed like a terrified baby. Why people had ever jumped out of helicopters for fun, he would never understand. Nothing was fun about falling.

The rope won't catch me.

I'm going to hit the ground.

Mass's free fall was halted by a sudden, painful jolt. The seams of the harness bit into his groin and armpits, threatening to cut him into pieces. He swung back and forth in the glare of the helicopter's searchlight and twirled round and round. Bile leapt up into his mouth, and he spat it at the demons a hundred feet below.

That went well.

Now comes the hard part.

The cable was short, only ten feet long. The rest of it was still coiled around the winch. Once the helicopter got low enough, the pilots would extend the cable.

Then they're gonna swing me around like a vinegar-soaked conker.

Fuck my life.

Vamps, Rave, Ginge, if you can see me now, you better not be laughing.

The gate was directly below. Mass strained his neck to get a look at it. It popped and hissed angrily, almost like it was aware of what was happening. The demons looked up to the sky and screeched. Somehow, they knew Mass was there, dangling in the sky two hundred feet above their heads.

Look all you want, bitches. Unless one of you has a jetpack, you ain't getting this sirloin.

Mass had been given a radio. It was secured inside a pocket at the front of the harness. It crackled and Addy's voice came through. "How you doing down there, mate?"

"Just hanging out. Everything going to plan?"

"We're going to lower you down in front of the gate. I'll stay on the line."

Mass's stomach lurched again as the cable unwound. At the same time, the helicopter descended. It was like free falling again, but this time he had more trust in the harness and the winch.

There was nothing to do but wait, so Mass filled the awkwardness by whistling. It was something he used to do a lot when he was bored as a kid.

Addy chuckled over the radio. "What is that? *Lady in Red?*"

"Was the first thing that came to mind. Got any requests?"

"*We Are the Champions?*"

"Seriously? All right, then." Mass whistled the bits he knew and then fell silent. The gate was right below him now, just slightly ahead. Another ten metres and he'd be directly in line with the top of it. It was almost time.

Am I actually going to go through with this?

Yeah, and that's why I'm so fucking terrified.

The demons beneath Mass thrashed wildly, reaching up at him despite him being massively out of reach. He felt like a chunk of meat being dangled above a horde of alligators.

"It's go time," said Addy. She sounded sad. "Still time to back out."

"Just do what you have to do." Mass reached up and switched off the radio. No goodbyes. No regrets.

Above him, the helicopter swayed to one side, swinging Mass on the cable. At first it was like being dragged, but then the helicopter swayed back the other way and Mass was swinging upwards like a child at a playground. The cable creaked and the harness cut in to his groin once more, but he held on tightly and reminded himself to breathe.

The helicopter swayed back and forth, back and forth. Mass was a pendulum cutting through the air. It was exhilarating, nauseating... and terrifying.

The helicopter banked, and suddenly Mass was swinging towards the gate. His eyes burned from staring into it, assaulted by colours and images that made no sense. A howling wind seemed trapped beneath its surface and it gave off a throbbing heat. It was a portal straight to Hell, and he was swinging right towards it.

Mass closed his eyes.

And passed through the gate.

MADDY SLUMPED against a pile of pallets. She had nothing left. No more energy. Those still alive had been pushed right back to the docks, and the only things keeping the demons at bay were the ship-mounted weapons. Several boats had stationary machine guns, and some were able to direct their lighter cannons at the demons racing from the ruins. It would only keep the enemy at bay so long, but at least it gave people a chance to get onto the boats.

No one was trying to play hero any more. Even Frank had joined the evacuation queues. No one wanted to stay back and hold the line. People just wanted out of there before it was too late.

"We're almost there," said Tosco, standing beside Maddy. He was clearly unwilling to leave her. "Just a little longer."

Maddy shook her head. "The boats should leave now before it's too late."

Crimolok entered the military docks, and those shooting from the boats instinctively shifted their focus to the larger target.

Demons were everywhere.

Sorrow did what he could. With his wings flapping, he rushed back and forth, trying to keep his brethren from making it to the last of the survivors yet to get onto the boats. They engulfed him like ants on a wasp, weaker as a species but more powerful in numbers. Sorrow was eventually brought down beneath the sheer weight of them.

Crimolok marched onward, reaching down and grabbing Klein's train carriage from its resting place at the edge of the docks. The carriage was empty, but it was still horrifying when Crimolok tossed it into the air. The glass and steel tube hit the deck of a Royal Navy frigate like a missile, obliterating a hundred men firing from its decks.

Demons began tackling the men and women shoving their way towards the boats. They died screaming in agony, fifty feet from safety.

Crimolok scooped up an old van parked next to one of the warehouses and launched it at the same frigate he had already hit. The vehicle struck the upper structure of the frigate, taking out the bridge and toppling the conning tower. A fire broke out. Hundreds of people still on deck howled in terror.

Tosco was aghast. "You're right, Maddy. Those ships need to get the hell out of here. The rest of us are doomed."

The noise of metal scraping and engines firing drowned out the sounds of killing as the first of the ships began to move away, its captain smart enough to realise the same thing Maddy and Tosco had.

Tosco put his forehead against Maddy's and held her. "Whatever happens, we stick together."

"We managed to survive for so long, James, only for it to end like this. It sucks."

"Yeah, it does."

Crimolok continued throwing projectiles at the boats and the demons continued swarming. The ships carried on providing support, but more were starting to push away from the docks. There was no other choice.

Maddy saw Sorrow get back on his feet. A pile of demons lay dead around him. Before more could engulf him, Sorrow leapt into the air, wings unfurling like a bird of prey. To Maddy's astonishment, he lunged at Crimolok. The giant roared furiously and swatted at Sorrow as if he were a fly. Sorrow was much smaller, able to dart around and avoid the blows. Several times he made a slice at Crimolok's face, but it did no damage. Sorrow's lethal talons were as ineffective as the ship's cannons. At least Crimolok was distracted for the moment.

On the ships, men doubled down with their machine guns, slicing through the swarming demons. Some of the primates made it to the water's edge, falling upon humans trying to get up the gangways. Many fought back with knives and empty rifles. There were no cowards in Portsmouth, but at the rate things were going, mere minutes remained before everyone not on board a boat would be dead.

Crimolok roared triumphantly, snatching Sorrow out of the air and gleefully tearing off the smaller demon's wings. Then he tossed Sorrow to the ground and raised a massive foot to crush him into the dust.

Maddy couldn't take her eyes away from the scene. Seeing Sorrow torn apart could be the final atrocity before she met her own end, a parting horror before oblivion.

Crimolok paused, balancing on one leg as he hesitated. He seemed confused, almost like he had suddenly realised he'd forgotten something.

Maddy swallowed the lump in her throat. *What is he doing?*

Slowly, Crimolok lowered his foot and turned around. Then, in an inexplicable move, he stomped away, picking up speed until he was sprinting back through the ruins of Portsmouth like a raging bull.

19

Something is wrong.

A part of Crimolok shivers, a sense to which he is a stranger. Something beneath his conscience is crying out.

His tether is under threat.

Something is trying to interfere with his plans. His enemies seek to weaken him while his back is turned.

The gate.

His enemies are fools, not knowing the futility of what they do. Yet they cannot be ignored. He will find them and eviscerate them. They will pay.

Portsmouth is finished. His legions will destroy what is left. Crimolok turns and heads for the gate.

MASS SEES HELL. He sees what Vamps must have seen. Fire and flesh. Burning. Screaming. Oozing blood. Twisted monsters. Cancers and boils grow from every surface. It goes on forever. An eternity of pain and misery.

Then he sees the star-filled night sky. He sees autumn trees and black roads illuminated by the glowing of the gate. He is swinging backwards, away from the lens. Back out of the gate.

Then his movement stops and he is suddenly swinging forward again, speeding towards Hell for a second time.

No, please, I can't!

Mass passes through the lens once more and is back in that place of agony and despair. Somehow it is even more terrifying as he hears the most pitiful of moans. People cry out for mercy, millions of desperate souls. Hooks tear at their flesh. Insects burrow into their eyes.

And then he is out again, swinging through the starry night.

"Nothing's happening," said Addy's voice through the radio on his harness. She sounded confused, desperate. "You keep coming back out. The gate isn't closing."

Mass couldn't take another dose of Hell. He couldn't go back willingly now that he had experienced it. Universe be damned. "Pull me up, pull me up."

Immediately the cable yanked him upwards, the helicopter banking to the left and whipping him away from the gate just as he was about to pass through it a third time.

There were tears in his eyes and his body was trembling. His heart thudded in his chest. He realised he had wet himself.

He didn't understand it. Every time he'd seen a person pass through a gate it had instantly exploded, taking out any nearby demons along with it. He had never seen a person pass in and out before. What had gone wrong? What was he missing?

Smithy came on the radio. "Big man, your plan ain't working."

"I know. Damn it, I know."

"What you want us to do?"

"Just pull me back up. Please, get me out of this harness. I can't breathe."

"Okay, buddy. Hold on."

The cable shortened. A minute later, Addy and Smithy were yanking him back inside the helicopter. Smithy slammed the sliding door shut behind him.

Mass slumped onto one of the benches and vomited. Addy rushed over and rubbed his back. He was quaking. "Mass, what's wrong?"

"He stared into the abyss," said Angela, standing at the rear of the cabin. "No one gets a dose of Hell without at least puking. It gets better after a while, but the first time is always the worst."

Mass straightened up and wiped his mouth. "She's right. It was... No, you don't need to know. I'm glad I'm out, but what went wrong?"

Angela shrugged. "Your guess is as good as mine. Crimolok isn't your regular demon and this ain't your regular gate. Living souls aren't supposed to pass through the seals, but I don't think this gate is one of the seals. It's not a lock like the others, it's a doorway. You can't break a doorway."

The living Damien emerged from the cockpit, his messy brown hair stuck to his clammy forehead. He looked curiously at Mass. "This gate leads to Hell though, right? Whatever it is, it's part of the tapestry. All gates are."

Smithy frowned. "Part of the *what* now?"

"He said the tapestry." The undead Damien stepped forward and scratched the back of his shaved skull. "Think of it like the universe's transport system. During this war, you've gotten pretty good at destroying the odd country road here and there, but this big sonofabitch is a motorway. It's going to take something stronger than a single human soul to put it out of commission."

Mass clutched his stomach, trying not to puke again – trying not to think about the things he had just seen. He would never unsee them. "What will it take?"

The two Damien's looked at each other. The living Damien sighed and said, "The soul of a path walker would probably do it."

Smithy frowned. "A *what* now?"

The living Damien went on. "If a path walker passes through a gate not summoned by themselves or other path walkers, then..."

The dead Damien finished the sentence. "Then shit gets fucked up."

Addy folded her arms and huffed. "Sounds like the best plan we've had all day."

Mass collapsed on the bench and threw back his aching head. "Looks like I'm the wrong guy in the right place. Where do we find a path walker?"

Both Damien's looked at one another. Neither looked happy, but only the living Damien spoke. "You're looking at two of them."

SMITHY WAS STILL STRUGGLING to understand, causing a delay they couldn't afford. "So, if one of our Damiens passes through the gate, it will, like, blow the back end out of the universe?"

The living Damien grunted in frustration. "It'll tie the tapestry in knots, breaking the connections between different worlds. It would make it impossible for Crimolok to ever leave here and attack God. Whatever few remaining Earths that are left would be safe. Heaven would be safe."

Smithy nodded. "But we're screwed either way, right?"

Mass sighed. "We were screwed the moment the first gate opened, man. This mission was never about saving *us*. I'm sorry."

"Hey, at least we had fun, right? We gave the bastards hell. You jumped out of a helicopter and pissed yourself."

Mass looked down at his wet trousers and blushed.

Angela tittered.

"I need to go down on the winch," said the living Damien. "Same movie, different actor."

One of the pilots shouted back, "Better do what you're doing quickly because we're running out of fuel."

Mass groaned. "Typical. Okay – take two. Let's get moving."

The living Damien stood in the middle of the cabin and held up his arms. Harry and Steph helped him get into the harness. "That too tight?" Steph asked him.

"A bit."

Harry grunted. "Man up, soldier."

"Do you want to do this."

Harry chuckled. "I most certainly do not."

"Okay," said Damien a moment later, "I'm ready." He looked at Mass. "Is it really that bad?"

Mass couldn't even give a reply.

Damien took it for the answer it was. "Great, well, hopefully Angela is right and it gets better. Maybe I can get a position on the board and campaign for change." He chuckled at his own joke, but it came out as an emotionally fraught squeak.

"You're a better Damien than me," said the dead Damien, offering a handshake.

The other Damien went to take his counterpart's hand, but Smithy yelped, "Don't! If you two occupy the same space, won't we all implode or something?"

Addy groaned. "They're not time travellers, you idiot. They aren't the same person."

Smithy looked at the two nigh-on identical young men and raised an eyebrow. "Really?"

"We're not the same," said the dead Damien. "Two sides of the same coin, maybe, but still different. As I was saying, this Damien here is a good bloke. I'm better looking."

The two Damiens completed their handshake, and the one in the harness stepped up to the sliding door.

"Ready?" asked Harry.

"Yep! What the hell."

Harry threw open the door.

Damien turned back and eyeballed Smithy. "No one push me, okay?"

Smithy held his hands up and stepped away.

Unlike Mass, Damien wasted no time. He took one step forward and was gone, plummeting out of view. The winch clunked. The cable went taut. When Mass had fallen it had felt like a minute went by before he had felt that life-saving jolt.

Harry got on the radio. "Damien, you good?"

"Never better. I see the gate. It's to my right."

The pilots confirmed their intentions and started to manoeuvre the helicopter.

"Almost there," Damien said through the radio. Just a bit more and I'll be— Oh shit!"

The helicopter lurched. It was as if gravity had suddenly increased tenfold and they were falling out of the sky. The pilots cursed and fought with the controls. Something yanked the cable. The winch groaned and clunked.

Harry shouted into the radio. "Damien! Damien, are you okay?"

There was no reply. Mass rushed over to the open doorway and leaned out. Damien was no longer on the end of the cable. It had snapped and was now dangling weightlessly in the wind. Something had happened. Something had snatched Damien out of the air.

What is happening? Where did he go?

Mass sensed movement to his left, to the rear of the helicopter.

Crimolok raised a giant fist and swung at the helicopter.

———

THE BOATS WERE LEAVING en masse. Only a few remained, their captains either stupid or brave. The demons came in droves, although they seemed unsure since their leader had sprinted away into the distance. Maddy still didn't understand why Crimolok had fled.

Tosco had rallied a group of men together, bringing them into a tight group. Everyone was armed with blades or clubs of some fashion, which were mostly empty rifles. Some had picked up sheets of metal or scraps of wood to use as shields. It was ridiculous, but at least they weren't completely unarmed.

"The closer we push together," said Tosco, "the harder it will be to knock us down. There aren't many primates left. We can fight the burnt men with what we have if we stick to the plan. Shoulder to shoulder, swing and stab."

A demon staggered towards the group and the men put their orders into action. A woman hiding behind a sheet of metal peeked out and planted a long kitchen knife in the burnt man's skull. It dropped like a lead weight. The woman removed her knife and got back behind her shield.

"One down," said Maddy. "Good work. We can do this."

But for how long?

Even without Crimolok guiding them, the demons were everywhere. If Tosco tried to get everyone onto the boats, they would probably be taken down as they ran. The only chance they had was to stand their ground until they were too exhausted to fight. Perhaps a miracle would come and save them.

"How do you reckon Mass is getting on?" Maddy asked Tosco, trying to distract herself from the demons racing towards them.

"I think he made it to the gate like he intended. Why else would Crimolok have turned and ran. He's under threat."

"You think there's a chance Mass might actually do something to help?"

Tosco shrugged. "I have no idea. Everyone, brace!"

A dozen demons hit the small squad of men and women. They held tight, pushing against one another and forming a solid wall. They pushed out their shields to absorb the impact and to avoid being toppled.

"Everyone, swing and stab."

The squad lashed out with their knives or brought down their heavy rifles as best they could one-handed. The demons were pressed up against the shields, so it was easy to slash and bludgeon at their heads and necks. Several fell in the first assault while others tried to recover and attack. The second round of swinging and stabbing dropped several more, which led to the demons losing half their number. They were unable to get past the shields, unable to avoid the knives and clubs slipping from between the gaps and striking them unawares.

The melee went on for ten minutes until the attacking demons were all dead.

More would come soon.

"Good work," said Tosco, panting and dripping with sweat. "Everyone catch their br—" His radio hissed and Klein spoke to them.

"Maddy, James, are you still alive? I was hoping to see you on my submarine by now. Please tell me *zat* you are to come any minute now, *ja?*"

Tosco gave a grim smile. "I'm sorry, Commander, but I don't see a way out for us. You get Alice away from here for me, okay?"

"*Ja,* she will be safe with me. I am sorry for you both. I wished to share happier days with you. Maddy, can I do anything? Anything to get you out of there?"

"You can't help us, Klein, but thank you. Don't stop being you, whatever happens."

"You have my *vord.* Goodbye, *fräulein.*"

"Wait. Klein, there's one last thing you can do. There's a team of people headed north in a helicopter. Can you try to radio them? If they need help, give it to them. Whatever they ask."

The radio crackled. "I can try to hail *zis* helicopter, but without knowing its exact—"

"I have everything you need," said Tosco, and he quickly shared the details of the helicopter's radio frequencies. "Give 'em a call and say hello from me."

"Consider it done, Commander."

"Thank you, Commander."

More demons rushed towards them. They threw themselves against the squad's shields, pushing everyone back. This time, more than two dozen burnt men attacked. It was too many. Maddy's shoulders cried out in pain.

We can't keep this up.

20

The helicopter spiralled in the sky, completely out of control. Crimolok's attempt to swat it out of the sky missed, but his massive hand had glanced off the underside of the fuselage.

The pilots cursed, veins popping out of their necks as they fought the controls. Everybody in the cabin grabbed a hold of whatever they could. Mass almost went flying out of the open doorway, only just managing to grab a handhold beside the door.

The helicopter spun around twice before the pilots managed to correct it. Mass looked out of the open doorway, but he couldn't catch sight of Crimolok. Where had the bastard gone? Was he right behind them, about to smash them to pieces?

"Get us out of here," Mass yelled at the pilots.

"He's on our tail," said the pilot. "I can take us up, but our fuel is gone. Our tanks are ruptured and we were almost out anyway."

"What does that mean?" Smithy asked as he hugged the front bench of the cabin.

"That I can take us up out of harm's way for a few minutes, but then we're going back down whether we like it or not."

Smithy looked at Angela. "Hey, vicar. You think we can power this thing on prayer?"

"I don't think you understand how prayer works."

Now that the helicopter was level, Steph dragged herself over to Mass, grabbed him, and looked at him with a pleading expression. "Damien?"

Mass shook his head. "I'm sorry, he's gone."

Steph turned away and Harry pulled her into an embrace as she broke out into a sob.

The dead Damien – now the only Damien left – groaned. "Damn it, I liked that guy."

The helicopter rose up, Mass felt it in his stomach like getting in a lift.

The pilot turned back to the cabin. "We're out of reach for now but we only have a few— Hang on, there's a call coming through."

Mass frowned. "A call? You mean someone is trying to contact us?"

"I'll open the line." The pilot turned a switch and static hissed from the cockpit speakers.

"Auklet One, do you read me?"

The pilot pulled a wired handset up to his mouth. "Loud and clear, friend. Who am I talking to?"

"Do I really need *ze* introduction? This is Commander Klein. Commander Tosco asked me to assist you in *vatever vays* I can."

Mass leant over the pilot's shoulder. "It's good to hear from you, Klein, but I think we're beyond helping. I passed through the giant gate but nothing happened. The demons are coming out in their thousands – and Crimolok is here. In a few minutes we're going to run out of fuel, and then that's pretty much it for us."

"Is that you, Mass? You truly are unkillable. I am afraid to report that things are finished here in Portsmouth too. Those of us left are departing by boat to seek safety elsewhere. It pains me to leave these shores. They have become a home to me. If Crimolok is truly there, kindly flip him *ze* middle finger, *ja?*"

Mass chuckled, although there were tears in his eyes after hearing that Portsmouth was truly gone. "I'll give him more than the middle finger, Klein. I wish I could smack the bastard in the face and send him right back through the gate."

"Yeah," said Smithy, "and then send a nuke in after him and blow Hell to pieces!"

Mass patted his friend on the back and laughed – but then he fell silent as something formed in his mind. He stared at Smithy until Smithy became uncomfortable. "Um, what's wrong, big man? You just shat yourself or something?"

Mass turned back to the pilot holding the radio. "Klein? You still there?"

"*Ja!*"

"I know you're really protective about those nukes of yours, but do you think you could spare one?"

"Mass, what are you suggesting? The enemy have claimed this place and you *vant* to burn it to the ground? I cannot do such a thing in good conscience. Not even—"

"No," Mass interrupted, "I don't want to scorch the Earth, I want to scorch Hell. The gate is right here. How accurate can you fire your missiles?"

"With perfect accuracy, providing I have prefect targeting. Without precise coordinates, however, I cannot—"

The pilot blurted out, "Commander! We have a laser targeting module on our helicopter. I can paint an X if you can hit it."

"I can, *ja*. I hoped never to send my missiles anywhere, but I will trust in you fine men and do as you ask. I hope it helps."

"It will," said Mass. "Thanks, Klein."

"I'll await your instructions."

Angela grunted. "Why didn't anyone mention earlier that we had nuclear missiles?"

"The guy who has them doesn't like them being mentioned," said Addy.

Smithy moved up beside Mass and looked at him. "You know I was joking about the nukes into Hell thing, right?"

"All you do is joke, Smithy, but sometimes you say smart things too. We're going to send a nuke straight into Hell. If nothing else, it'll stop the flow of demons coming out. How many would die in a nuclear blast?"

Smithy shrugged. "Like a billion-nillion?"

"At least. So let's paint an X on that gate."

The pilots leant forward, pushing down on their control sticks.

"Wait," said Addy. "Ever heard of killing two birds with one stone?"

Mass looked at her. "Huh?"

"If we can lead Crimolok so he's in front of the gate, we could hit him with the nuke and send him back to Hell, just like you said."

"Like we *joked*," said Smithy. "We're taking things very literally here, people. We can't harm Crimolok. He'll just shake it off, so why risk it?"

Mass thought about it. "He can't be harmed by *our* weapons, but he *has* been harmed. Rick hurt him. Maybe Crimolok can be hurt by the right kind of weapon. A nuke isn't the same as a bullet or even a bomb. It's like the power of the universe unleashed in a tiny package, right?"

Smithy shook his head. "I was due to study astrophysics *next* year. This year was home economics."

"We're kind of in a no-lose situation," said Addy. "I say we try it."

Damien crossed his arms and nodded. "Yeah, let's fuck things up."

Angela shook her head. "That kind of language will get you sent straight to Hell, young man."

"Been there, done that."

Mass took a deep breath. "After we do this, there might not be a Hell left."

"THE ENGINES ARE STARTING TO STRUGGLE," said one of the pilots. "We need to get down on the ground."

Mass nodded. "Okay, take us down in front of the gate. Once we're back within reach, Crimolok will come for us. Make it look like we intend to fly right on through. Soon as he's close enough, paint a target on the gate and get us out of there."

The pilot chewed his lip for a moment. "We're not going to survive a nuclear blast. It'll fry our circuits even if we don't get obliterated by the blast."

Mass sighed. "We're not doing this for us."

The pilot nodded; he understood. They all did. None of them were making it through this alive. That wasn't what this was about.

"Okay," said the pilot, "descending."

Everyone held on to the roof straps while the helicopter plummeted. The cabin vibrated, not fully under control after the damage it had taken. The engines made unhealthy noises and several warning lights lit on the dashboard.

Mass felt like puking again, but he held on, knowing there wasn't time even for that. This was a nearly impossible mission, and he held onto that... *nearly*. The *nearly* was hope.

Mass moved to the open doorway and looked out. Crimolok was a hundred metres away, watching them balefully. The giant had been unable to reach them at high altitude, but now that they had descended he came right for them, crushing droves of his own demons beneath his feet. He let out a soul-shattering roar and Mass felt his bladder let go for the second time. The warmth against his leg reminded him he was alive. He could still fight.

"Okay, paint a target on the gate," he yelled to the pilots.

A second passed. "Target painted. Commander Klein, do you copy?"

Another second. "*Ja!* Target acquired. Missile launched. May Heaven take you fine men."

Mass kept his eyes on Crimolok and wondered how long it

would take for a nuclear missile to travel twenty miles. Seconds, he imagined. "Hold our position," he shouted. "Hold it until I say go, and then get us the hell out of here."

Crimolok's enraged sprint tore up the ground and uprooted trees. The roads cracked beneath his feet. It was the most terrifying thing Mass had ever seen, and only his hatred allowed him to face down the charging beast. Annihilation was seconds away – a clash between an ancient evil that thrived on spoiled flesh and mankind's greatest weapon launched by a computer. It was just a question of which would reach the helicopter first.

"Hold!"

Crimolok bounded twenty metres in a single step.

"Hold!"

Twenty metres left, a single second.

"Hold!"

Crimolok swung a massive arm and released an ear-splitting roar.

Mass roared back. "Move! Move! Move!"

The helicopter tipped onto its side and fell. Mass's feet left the ground and he was swinging from the handholds beside the doorway. Through the opening he saw Crimolok's huge fist swipe the air. Then Mass saw the ground, a blanket of flattened demon flesh covering the road and fields. The helicopter's searchlight strobed wildly against the countryside, making the whole thing feel like an acid trip. Everyone inside the cabin screamed, but Mass could do nothing to help them. This was the end, and as much as they were together, they would face it alone.

There was an almighty flash and Mass closed his eyes, but it was like staring into the sun.

The helicopter tumbled and spun.

The pilots yelled at one another, fighting for control. The helicopter's cockpit was a chaos of sounds, warnings and alarms.

Mass didn't know which way was up. His legs dangled in the air as he held onto the nylon roof straps with everything he had left. It felt like his arms were going to tear off. Any second, it would all end. They would hit the ground and explode, or the nuclear blast would eat them up.

Mass's ankles struck the side of the helicopter's cabin wall and bounced. His body rotated and his legs entered a wind tunnel. He was dangling outside the helicopter. The wrist strap tightened around his arm, the only thing keeping him alive.

Why wasn't it over yet?

Why weren't they dead?

Mass's legs crashed back down. His shoulders were on fire. The light began to fade. He dared to open his eyes. What he saw was chaos. Smithy was unconscious sliding around beneath the seats. Harry was bleeding from his nose. Steph and Angela were clinging on in the back. The pilots fought with their controls. Even Damien seemed terrified.

"Hold on," one of the pilots shouted. "Hold on!"

There was an almighty crash, followed by the sound of imploding steel.

MASS WAS UPSIDE DOWN, his knees pressed against his face. He heard moaning but couldn't tell if it was his own. The helicopter's interior had changed. It was smaller now and angled all wrong.

Mass tried to move, but he was numb. His entire body had stiffened. He felt bruised. With effort, he managed to rock himself back and forth slowly until he tumbled over onto his side. He expected it to hurt, but it didn't. The only thing he was feeling was a tingling in his limbs.

Smithy was splayed on his back. The pair of benches were twisted and his legs were tangled up inside their metal supports. His eyes fluttered open and he moaned, "I think we crashed."

"We're alive," said Mass. "How are we alive?"

"Perhaps we ain't. This kind of feels like dying, don't you think?"

No, they were alive. The helicopter was on the ground. It was wrecked, but somehow, the pilots had got them down in one piece.

More or less.

"Addy?" Mass started dragging himself through the wreckage. "Addy, talk to me?"

"I'm still here," said Angela. "In case anybody was wondering."

"I'm alive too," said Damien. "Well, not exactly *alive.*"

"Addy? Addy, where are you? Damn it, talk to me." Mass pulled himself past the twisted benches, noticing the blood that covered Smithy's legs. He kept on moving towards the cockpit. There, he found Steph, her neck angled in a way that she could never have survived. He hadn't known the woman well, but it sucked to see her dead. There was no sign of Harry, but both pilots were still sitting up front. One was slumped backwards, a huge shard of glass lodged in his Adam's apple. The other was alive, but clearly in shock. He was trembling and mumbling to himself, and when he looked at Mass, his eyes were bright red like they'd been held over a flame. Mass feared the man was blind.

Mass panicked. "Addy, where the hell are you?"

"Mass, I'm here. I'm here."

Mass looked around. "Where?"

"On the grass. I'm hurt, but I think I'm okay."

Mass's heart fluttered. Adrenaline coursed through his body, but the relief of hearing Addy alive filled him with joy. He clambered through the wreckage, pulling himself along with numb hands and pushing with heavy legs. The opening in the side of the helicopter was now only half as big as it had been, the sides pinched inwards. There was barely enough space to crawl through, but Mass made it through. He found himself surrounded by a grey landscape devoid of colour. He heard demonic screeching from every direction.

We're in Hell. We must have fallen through the gate.

No, Hell was worse than this.

As he crawled away from the wreckage, Mass felt soft grass beneath his palms and realised that the grey landscape was merely night giving way to dawn. The starry sky had gone away, replaced by a featureless expanse that would soon welcome a morning sun.

Addy lay in the grass ahead, rolled onto her side. She clutched her hand and gritted her teeth, but when she saw Mass she smiled. "I'm going to get a god complex if I keep surviving this shit," she said. "I've got to be the toughest woman alive."

Mass smiled back. "No doubt."

"How are the others?"

"Steph didn't make it. Neither did one of the pilots."

Addy nodded to a spot nearby. There was a body lying there, every limb twisted. "Neither did Harry. Is Smithy okay?"

"I'm fine, sweetheart." Smithy appeared in the gap inside the helicopter and pulled himself through. His left leg was injured, and it dragged behind him uselessly. He was pale but alert. "I could really use a rest after all this," he muttered. "Let's just find a house with a copy of *FIFA* and sit things out for a while."

"Sounds good to me," said Addy. "I get to be *Real Madrid* though."

"Glory chaser."

The three of them sat together on the grass and caught their breath. The demons were nearby, heralded by their screeching and wailing, but they were a little ways away for now.

Damien and Angela emerged from the wreckage next, pulling the blinded pilot along behind them.

"This guy saved your lives," said Damien. "Hey, buddy, you still with us?"

The pilot nodded, a little more in control of his senses than he had been in the cockpit. "T-The blast blew us out of the sky. It wasn't as strong as it should've been, but we couldn't keep from crashing. Is Braggs okay? He wouldn't answer me."

"I'm sorry," said Angela. "Your co-pilot didn't make it, and you appear to be blind."

"I had to keep my eyes open if there was any chance of setting us down. The blast burned my retinas. T-There's a chance I might recover."

Mass nodded. "Good. That's real good. Why the hell were we not all incinerated though?"

"Because the plan worked," said Damien. "Take a look!" He pointed around the side of the crashed helicopter, necessitating everyone to shuffle themselves along until they could see past it. In the distance, the gate was on fire. The lens was still intact, but beyond was a fiery hellscape beyond comprehension. Ash and embers swirled through a realm of melting flesh. Hell had been incinerated along with an infinite army of demons. It was beautiful.

"The gate's still open," said Smithy.

"And the demons already through it ain't dead," said Damien.

Addy dragged herself along and winced in pain, still favouring her hand. "What does that mean?"

Mass stared at the gate, trying to work out if they had won or not. However many demons had been waiting to come through the gate were now ash, but none of those already through were dead. There were still thousands of them.

Something moved inside the gate. The ashes on the ground rose up, embers spilling everywhere. A black mountain grew out of nothing; then that mountain split apart, revealing massive limbs and a huge torso.

Mass flopped onto his side, too weak to hold himself up any longer. He rolled onto his back and groaned up at the grey sky. "Crimolok is still alive."

CRIMOLOK WAS ALIVE, but they had clearly injured him. The giant stumbled on wobbly legs and, as the ashes fell away from his flesh, glistening wounds revealed themselves. Crimolok's entire body had been burnt.

"We need to hit him again," said Addy. "Another nuke may do it."

"You got a radio?" asked Mass, nodding towards the wrecked helicopter. "Because I'm guessing the one in there is broken."

Smithy shook his head. "Damn."

The demonic shrieking in the distance was gradually getting closer. The demons were unsure exactly where the helicopter had crash-landed, but it wouldn't be long before they found it. This time, Mass wasn't even going to fight. It was pointless now. The last of his hope was gone.

"If only we could close the gate," said Addy, "Crimolok would be stuck where he is."

"Even if we could close it," said Mass, "there are too many demons. You'd have to wade through a thousand just to reach the gate."

"I've got this." Damien rose to his feet. Unlike the rest of them, he was unhurt and didn't even appear winded. He was a dead man walking, and that made him more alive than any of them right now.

Smithy tutted. "Yeah, okay, man. I know you're a badass and all, but even you can't fight a thousand demons."

"I don't need to fight them. I'll see you guys later. Don't wreck what's left of the world, all right?" He looked at Smithy. "Put it in the can, man, remember!"

Damien walked away, marching down the hill they had landed on. Mass couldn't get to his feet, but he managed to rise onto his elbow and shout, "Damien, what are you doing?"

Damien turned back with a smirk. "I'm going to go fuck shit up. Like I said, I got this. It was always meant to be me."

"What was meant to be you?"

"Saviour of mankind, innit? Keep it real, Mass, and stop skipping leg day. You look like a goddamn turkey."

Mass chuckled, not understanding at all. The only thing he knew was that Damien was a law unto himself. There was no controlling the guy. All you could do was watch and see what he would do next.

"That guy is about to become a demon McMuffin," said Smithy. "What the hell is he doing?"

Mass remembered something Damien had said to him not so long ago. There was a reason he had made it to the fort so easily when they were looking for Thomas. Mass remembered the exact words Damien had said to him.

They don't pay me much attention.

Damien carried on down the hill. The others dragged themselves to positions where they could watch him. The demons were mostly congregated around the ruined roads. None of them made a move when Damien appeared on the slope and headed towards them. Some looked his way curiously, but they didn't attack. They looked at him the same way they looked at each other. Like he was one of *them*.

The gate was nearby, maybe two hundred metres ahead of Damien. Smouldering, irradiated embers drifted out as Crimolok continued to stumbled around drunkenly. It was like he had never felt pain before and was as confused about that as he was about suffering from it.

The demons were gradually moving towards the hill, spreading out in their pursuit to find fresh meat.

Smithy groaned. "The demons are going to rip us to shreds, and I really want to see what Damien does."

"Leave it to me," said Angela, dragging herself along the ground like a slug. "Christ, every bit of me hurts. I hope I can still do this."

Mass frowned. "Do what?"

"This!" Angela pointed at the closest demons on the hill and began uttering what sounded like nonsense. Then, to Mass's utter astonishment, a dozen demons exploded into a bloody mist. It began to rain, and when Mass looked at his forearm, he saw it was blood.

"I think a demon's anus just landed on me," said Smithy.

"Tastes like chicken."

"Maybe you were licking your own arsehole," said Addy. "Your mouth always has to be doing *something*."

Smithy grinned at her. "Girl, you are so into me."

Addy blushed. "What? I so am not!"

"Yeah, you are. You want me."

"I do not!"

Angela looked back from the edge of the hill. "Sorry, sweetheart, but I think he's right."

Addy glared at both of them, but a smile slowly crossed her face that she failed to fight. "Yeah, okay, maybe I *am* into you. Too bad we're all going to die."

Angela nodded at Smithy and chuckled. "Too bad for him at least."

Smithy blushed. "Can you just get back to exploding demons, please, vicar?"

"No problem." Angela turned and started chanting again. Another handful of demons went up in a bloody mist. It was a neat trick.

Mass turned his focus back to the gate. Crimolok was starting to recover. His wounds seemed to be healing, burned flesh hardening into scar tissue. His once beautiful face was now a craggy mess, but his agony dripped away and anger took over. As he looked around in confusion, it seemed to dawn on Crimolok that he was back in Hell. Then he glared right through the gate, peering back upon the world he had just been blown out of.

Mass's jaw tightened.

Don't you come back through that gate, you sonofabitch. Stay where you are. Please.

Crimolok was still wounded, but he started to stagger towards the gate, seeming to stare straight at Mass. It couldn't be true, but it's how it felt.

Damien continued walking casually amongst the demons. They paid him no attention, some even moving out of his way.

Others, he simply grabbed and shoved aside. He was a slow-moving bullet slicing through a wall of flesh.

Get your arse in gear, mate. Look alive. Hurry!

Mass dug his fingertips into the soil, his whole body tense. Addy and Smithy crawled up beside him while Angela continued chanting to keep any demons at bay. Their exploding bodies were just part of the background now. Several times, the blind pilot asked what was happening.

"He's not gonna make it in time," said Smithy.

"I can't believe he can just walk through them like that," said Addy. "He needs to be careful."

Mass felt the same way. Damien pushed his luck several times, stopping to pat a dead woman on the cheek once, and shadow-boxing whenever he passed a particularly large demon. All the while, Crimolok was making his way towards the gate, intending to escape the nuclear devastation that had befallen Hell and resume his destruction of the Earth.

Mass thumbed the ground. "Come on, Damien. Don't you see? Get a move on!"

Damien continued to stroll along casually, like he had all the time in the world, but he didn't. Time was running out. Fast.

Crimolok gained strength, his wounded gait disappearing. He picked up speed, hurrying for the gate and already roaring in fury.

Damien glanced back towards the hill. He searched for Mass and the others and then shot them the middle finger. If not for the smirk on his face, it would've been cause to worry. Somehow, it was a gesture of respect.

Crimolok bounded for the gate.

Damien turned and sprinted. He dodged between demons, his arms like pistons. He was twenty metres from the gate. Crimolok was the same. It was a straight-up race to the finish line.

Crimolok spotted Damien and glared. He lowered his head and threw himself forward into an all-out sprint.

Damien slid through a pack of demons, grabbing their shoulders and propelling himself forward.

Crimolok was bigger, faster – but still wounded. The giant stumbled, his foot coming down on uneven ash-covered ground. At the speed he was going, Crimolok was powerless to stop himself from crashing down awkwardly onto his massive hands and knees.

Hell shook.

The gate shimmered.

Smithy gasped. "The plonker's fallen over."

"Even gods and angels are imperfect," said Angela, catching her breath while the demons were at bay. "Their biggest weakness is not realising it."

Crimolok clambered back to his feet, but it was too late. Damien sprinted the final few feet and launched himself into the air. His body passed through the lens of the gate and he was on the other side, crashing down into the thick ash.

Mass held his breath... waited.

Nothing happened.

No! Come on. Something please happen.

Damien stood and brushed himself off. He looked back through the gate, peering towards the hill where Mass and the others watched in terror.

"It didn't work," said Mass, shaking his head back and forth, over and over. "No. No, it didn't—"

The lens shimmered. The hellscape beyond it began to skew – a subtle movement like the swaying of grass in a breeze.

Crimolok rose to his feet, glaring down at Damien. The giant, ancient beast seemed confused.

Damien suddenly burst into flames, burning in a raging blue fire. A badass until the end, he made no sound as his body turned to ash. He was gone in a matter of seconds.

Then Hell caught fire. The grotesque landscape twisted in on itself like a piece of paper inside a clenched fist. The lens shrunk in on itself until it was the size of a football, and then it exploded.

Light, noise, and wind took over everything, assaulting every sense. It was a tsunami without water. A volcanic eruption with no volcano. It was pure, unrelenting force.

Mass and his companions pressed themselves against the dirt. If the blast was deadly, they were about to go up in smoke.

The wind came first, buffeting the shirt on Mass's back. Then came a bone-rattling quake. The heat came last.

Mass expected to burn, but the heat never rose above that of a relaxing bath. It summoned memories of sunbathing on Brixton's terraces as a kid, letting the heat increase until it almost burned him. Was his life flashing before his eyes?

Mass dared not lift his head to look at what was happening. If might blind him like it had the pilot. It wasn't until the wind, the noise, and the heat had completely gone away that he dared to raise his face from the ground.

21

I t was time to die. Maddy saw no other option. The boats had left the docks, leaving several hundred men and women behind to face their death. Maddy and Tosco were among those doomed souls. Sorrow and Scarlett were there too. The demon had become enraged that his ward was under such an attack. Did he realise it was useless? Scarlett was going to die no matter what he did. The girl seemed to realise it and was silent.

The demons had pushed them back to the very edge of the quay. For a while, they had managed to hide behind a storage container while Sorrow fought to keep any threats away. They had watched, and listened to, the deaths of their fellow human beings, knowing that it would eventually be their turn.

Now their turn had arrived.

Sorrow battled furiously, slicing apart demons with his talons and sending them tumbling into the water. The problem was that he was getting exhausted. For a long while it had seemed impossible that the demon might give up, but after his near death at the Crimolok's hands, Sorrow had gradually gotten slower and weaker. Now, he gasped and grunted with every movement. More and more demons managed to injure him, slicing into his leathery flesh. Maddy and Tosco had to keep Scarlett from crying out and drawing attention to them, but when Sorrow finally fell to ground, keeping Scarlett from screaming became impossible.

The demons came in force. Three dozen of them racing down the strip of narrow wharf that housed the shipping container. Maybe there was a way inside the steel shell. Perhaps Maddy and her companions could lock themselves inside it – like sardines in a can – but that was a worse death. They would be trapped in the dark, surrounded by monsters, until they starved or suffocated.

Tosco reached out and took Maddy's hand. Together, they grabbed Scarlett and pulled her in close. There was no point in fighting. None of them spoke; final words would change nothing.

A primate broke to the front of the pack, racing right towards Maddy. Its demonic screeching pierced the air, backed by a distant explosion – a petrol station going up in flames perhaps. Dawn was still moments away, but suddenly the day became bright and shining, everything bathed in an orange glow.

Tosco stumbled, yanking Maddy and Scarlett with him as he fought to keep his balance. A gale engulfed the docks, blowing aside everything not bolted down. It howled through the gaps and crevices of the nearby ruins making the whole world feel haunted.

Maddy shielded her eyes, the light getting brighter. "W-What's happening?"

Tosco grabbed her arm. "I don't know."

The primate on the wharf leapt at Maddy, but before it reached her it faded out of existence like an autumn leaf disinte-grating in the wind.

Maddy flinched and then gasped. Thousands of demons had invaded the docks, but every single one of them now faded away. Other than the blood and destruction, there was no evidence they had ever been there. Even the bodies of those slain disap-peared. Only human corpses remained on the docks.

Scarlett broke free and raced towards Sorrow. The large demon was slumped on the ground nearby, having dragged himself over even in his death throes. He was drenched in blood and his flesh was torn, but he was smiling – something Maddy had never seen the demon do before. It was obscene.

Scarlett held her friend and sobbed. "Sorrow. Sorrow, it's okay."

"Yes, it is okay. You are safe. I have... succeeded."

"Yes, you protected me. It's over, you can relax."

"Yes. Relax." Sorrow's flesh began to peel away, tiny slithers rising up into the air. He began to wither, his skin turning grey.

Scarlett shook him. "Sorrow. Sorrow, please stay with me."

Sorrow continued to smile. "Always."

The demon disappeared before their eyes, just like the others had. Somehow, Sorrow had managed to hold on long enough to say goodbye. Scarlett wept quietly over the space where his body had lain in her arms, nothing left to mourn over.

Tosco slumped against the shipping container, looking ready for sleep. "What just happened here?"

Maddy looked out across the water, at the fleet of ships containing thousands of people who were now going to live. "Mass did it," she said with the smallest of grins. "He saved us."

DAMIEN DID IT. He had saved mankind. Mass couldn't believe it, but it was true. The giant gate was closed, and Crimolok was back in Hell where he belonged. They'd even nuked the God damned place for good measure. Mass had expected to die, but instead he was alive and basking in victory.

The demons had all gone. Whatever had happened to them was a mystery to Mass, as he had kept his eyes closed the entire time.

"It's a miracle," said Addy. "Do you think it's just here, or are they gone everywhere?"

Mass shook his head. "I have no idea, but I hope so. Christ, I hope so."

"Did we do it?" asked the pilot, staring blankly. "Are we saved?"

Addy put a hand on the man's thigh. "I think so. I think we're okay."

"I can't even imagine what life will be like if it's actually over," said Smithy, pale and sweaty. "What would we even do?"

Mass patted him on the back. "We enjoy the life we have for however long we have it. It's a gift. After everyone who died, each day we get to breathe is a miracle."

Smithy collapsed onto his back and chuckled. "Well, at least no one has to worry about going to Hell any more."

"Nobody here will ever go to Hell," said Angela, the only one standing, "but nobody will ever go to Heaven either."

Mass looked up at her from the ground. "What do you mean?"

"I mean, if I understand correctly, that we are now cut off from the tapestry – maybe the tapestry is gone altogether – but at the very least, Damien cut our umbilical cord. Nothing can visit our world, and nothing can leave. This place is the beginning and end of our existence. There's nothing to follow after. Not for any of us."

Smithy frowned. "You're still here. Aren't you dead or something? How come you didn't go up in smoke like the others?"

"I'm a wraith," said Angela. "Similar to what Damien was, but not quite. Someone in Heaven must like me, because they dragged me out of Hell to bring me back to Earth. I didn't pass through a gate like I told others I did, I just materialised suddenly outside of Kielder. My release was conditional on me helping to defeat Crimolok. Hopefully this counts as mission accomplished. I suspect I'll be here forever, wandering the Earth like a big saddo."

Addy turned grey. "Will that happen to us, after we die?"

Angela shrugged. "Honestly, I don't know. All bets are off. Whatever rules used to apply to life and death are null and void. Let's just see what happens."

Mass finally felt strong enough to stand. At the edge of the hill, he went and stared at the broken road where the gate had been. Mankind was saved, but the universe was broken. The tapestry, whatever that was, might no longer exist. Crimolok was in Hell, but not dead. Did he still present a threat – if not here, then somewhere else? Would tomorrow arrive safely?

Mass looked up at the dawn sky, enjoying the warmth on his face. After a moment, Smithy and Addy got up and stood beside him. He reached out and placed a hand on each of their backs. With a smile, he had only one thought on his mind.

Forget about tomorrow. Just enjoy today.

22

"All right, yow lot, move it! We ain't got all day."

Mass chuckled. Frank might have been small, but he was mighty, and nobody ever dared chat back to him. It would take a whole lot longer to get things done without Frank.

The last thing Mass had ever expected to be was a farmer, but he found he enjoyed it more than anything he had ever done before. The work was so strenuous that he had packed on hard, slender muscle that was far stronger than the inflated fibres he had grown before in the gym. He was a brute, and it felt good. Even in the drizzling winter rain, it felt good.

It had been three months since the demons had been defeated, and for a while people had lived cautiously, doubting that it might finally be over. They had assumed more gates would open, or that groups of demons would emerge and devour them. But nothing had come. Mass and Cullen had led numerous missions to seek out the enemy, but the enemy was nowhere to be found. The war was over. Mankind was saved.

It had barely survived.

Less than ten thousand people had survived in Portsmouth, leaving the city feeling empty. People were finally able to mourn and feel sorry for themselves, which was why what Mass was doing was so important. He was building a tomorrow. He was creating hope.

The Urban Vampires had put down their weapons and picked up tools. Today, they were building a wooden fence around a field north of the city. The ground was hard and the work was harder.

The population had moved away from the docks and were now living on the coast to the north-west of the city. There were lovely houses for people to live in, and spaces to walk and breathe. Nobody missed the paved ruins that had once kept them safe.

The new wooden fence was necessary to house the twenty-nine cows that the Urban Vampires had managed to rustle during the previous weeks. With the demons gone, wildlife was easier to spot, and cows, pigs, and chickens roamed everywhere.

"Oi," Frank shouted, "get your fingers out your shitter and help us set this pole. Bloody moron."

Mass chuckled again. He was due a break, so he headed over to the old tractor where people liked to sit and catch a breather. They all agreed that its over-stuffed foam seat was the comfiest thing in existence.

When he reached the tractor, he found Smithy and Addy. They were snogging each other's faces off like teenagers. Mass grimaced. "Seriously, you two. If Frank catches you, you're both dead."

Smithy broke away from the kiss but kept both his hands on Addy's waist. "I will fight any man for the right to love my woman."

Addy rolled her eyes. "Frank would eat you for breakfast."

Smithy grinned at her lecherously. "Why don't I eat *you* for breakfast."

Addy shoved him away, a smile on her face. "Okay, I'm going back to work. Good to see you, Mass. We playing poker later?"

"Klein will put out a warrant for our arrest if we don't go."

Addy laughed. "We're still using the old church, right?"

"Yeah, Klein seems to find it amusing to gamble there for some reason. He hasn't got any less strange."

"Strange is good."

Addy left and Smithy went to follow, but Mass put his hand out and stopped him. "Stay and chill for a while. If Frank comes, I'll protect you."

Smithy shrugged and leant against the old tractor's massive back tyre. "Sounds good to me, man. All this work is too much like hard work for me. I think I might open a nightclub or something. I'll just kick back with a drink while the DJ plays."

Mass chuckled. "Luckily, there's an opening for just about every business you can name right now."

"Record unemployment, right? What a world we live in."

Mass folded his arms and leant on the tyre next to Smithy. "You and Addy seem to be moving pretty fast. It's going good, yeah?"

Smithy beamed, no cheekiness in his smile, only genuine happiness. "*So* good, man. I love that woman. Toughest bird I know."

"Don't let her hear you call her that."

"No way. She scares me even more than Frank. Anyway, big man, how are *you*?"

Mass nodded. "I'm all right, yeah."

"Wow, you sound delirious with joy."

"No, it's not that. I'm happy. Of course I am. I can't believe we made it. It's just..." He shook his head and sighed. "I suppose I don't know where I fit in now. Before the demons invaded, I was nothing. Now they've gone, I'm worried I'll go back to being nothing."

"Are you soft in the head? You helped save the world. There's no going back to being nothing after that."

Mass shrugged. "I never did a thing with my life before. One year of fighting doesn't change who I am."

"We were all different people before because the world was different. It controlled us and kept us down. Only people like

Thomas did well in the old world, but tomorrow is up to us. You really think the fighting is over? No way, man. The battles ahead are going to be even bigger than those behind us. We get to help shape mankind. You honestly saying you don't want to be part of that?"

Mass looked over at the two dozen men busily working to erect a fence. They were working hard to make things better, not just for themselves but for each other. How long would they hold on to that? How long before mankind turned selfish again?

"I guess the least we can do is try, right? Who knows what good we might do."

"Exactly. Don't forget to find a little happiness for yourself too, while you're at it? You earned it, man."

Mass huffed. "No argument there."

Someone else walked over to take a break at the tractor. It was Maria, one of the women Mass had helped rescue from Nas's farm. She'd been helping out for a couple of months now, eager to work hard. When Smithy noticed her coming, he gave Mass a sly wink and started walking away. "Like I said, mate, find a little happiness for yourself. I'll get out of your hair."

Mass punched his friend on the arm and then smiled at Maria. Maria smiled back.

DR KAMIYO FELT guilty even for taking an hour to himself, but if he didn't catch some fresh air and scenery, he would go insane. Hundreds had been injured in the battle with Crimolok, and in the early days many had been lost to shock or infection. Then had ensued a period of dutiful watching and regular treatment to help as many people as possible recover from their injuries – which had ranged from broken bones and flesh wounds to damaged organs. A couple of hundred more souls had been lost, but Kamiyo had saved as many as he could with the limited means and medicine at his disposal. It was the worst period of his life, and he was glad to finally be coming out the other end of it.

The small clinic they had cleared out in the village was still full of patients, but few were seriously ill. There was a bout of influenza he needed to keep a close eye on, and a patient with a broken hand, but most of the beds were full of people getting over simple illnesses or minor injuries. For the first time in months, Kamiyo felt able to step out and take a break.

Winter was in full swing, rainy and cold most days. Today was slightly milder, and the rain was only a drizzle. It felt good against his face, a simple pleasure to enjoy. With the demons gone, food was plentiful if you knew where to look, and the village was partially powered by solar panels, batteries, and petrol generators. The elderly and the vulnerable were provided with heaters at night or given homes with open fireplaces. The local pub was open most of the day and part of the night for people to indulge their newfound freedom. Life was still a wretched, vulnerable existence, full of threats and hardships, but it was improving every day. They were building a future together. There were no enemies or rivalries – at least not yet – and for now, peace was total. It was a golden age for mankind, and Kamiyo enjoyed being part of it, despite the amount of death he had witnessed to get there.

Perhaps mankind was better off being reset. Even without the demons, it had seemed to be on a collision course with disaster. This was their chance to do better.

Kamiyo headed to the village square where there was a circle of grass with benches and a rockery. On one side was the pub, and on the other was a small Anglican church. He had been intending to visit the pub – an old coach house called the Hartlebury Inn – but instead his attention was caught by something at the church. It had been opened up as a communal space, and people often gathered there. Not because they wanted to pray or worship, but because a church was an intrinsically welcoming place. It was a relaxing space with lots of happy memories – weddings, christenings, et cetera.

People were gathered in the graveyard outside the church, so Kamiyo went to go see what was going on. Many had been buried in the last few months, but due to the number of bodies, a majority had been burned on pyres. People did their best to make things ceremonial, but the smell always reminded them that death was never beautiful – especially now that people knew there was no afterlife to pass on to. When you died, you just... stopped. It was depressing, and yet at the same time it caused people to appreciate their lives and make the best of things. It was a blessing and a curse. Perhaps it had always been that way.

He found Angela in the graveyard along with Scarlett and a few others. Nancy and Alice were there, too. The mother and daughter were inseparable, and it was nice to see a family intact. When they saw Kamiyo, everyone smiled warmly.

Angela welcomed him. "Doctor, we're just honouring our dead. It would be good if you could join us."

"Oh, yes, of course. I would be glad to."

Scarlett kept mostly to herself these days, so it was nice to see her. She seemed a little less sad today. "You never really knew Sorrow," she said, "but he meant a lot to me. Because he was a demon, his body..." She sighed. "Well, it kind of went *poof*. It's been hard not being able to speak to him any more. For so long, he never left my side. He saved my life, like, a *lot*."

Kamiyo nodded. "I understand."

Angela put a hand on his shoulder. "People need to grieve. They need a place where they can have a conversation with the people they've lost. I told Scarlett that graveyards have never been for the dead. They have always been for the living. Nancy, too, had the same problem."

Nancy nodded, a little sadness in her eyes. "Damien left me to put himself on the line. He died helping to save us all. I never got to say goodbye – or thank you."

Angela waved a hand. "The dead should be remembered whether we have their bodies or not. What do you think?"

Kamiyo looked at where she was pointing and saw several nondescript blocks of stone. They had been roughly carved and etched with messy capital letters. They were beautiful in an understated way. Solemn. Simple. A few of the stones had names on them listed in columns. Two of the stones, however, were reserved for single names. One tombstone read: **Damien Banks. Saviour.** The other read: **Sorrow. Demon. Protector. Hero.**

Kamiyo looked at Nancy and then at Scarlett. He saw the sadness and joy on their faces and realised how much these names carved into simple blocks of stones meant to them. "I like it," he said. "I really like it. I have names of my own I would like to add."

Angela motioned to a large group huddled around several more roughly carved stones at the rear of the graveyard. "So do a lot of people. Let's not forget our heroes just because we have so many."

Kamiyo thought about Ted, Hannah, and so many others. With a smile on his face, he said, "I look forward to building a world where heroes aren't needed, but I never want to forget the people who died so that I can live."

Angela patted him on the arm. "Amen."

———

MADDY RUBBED her hands together and blew on them. It wasn't particularly cold, but she felt a chill. She was stressed, anxious, and entirely unsure of what she was doing. Two years ago, she had been a married paramedic. Now she was in charge of the last human settlement in England – although it was no longer really England. The survivors from Portsmouth were a mixture of regions, nationalities, and race. Old identities were gone. The loss of so much history and pride was sad, but it felt like a step forward for civilisation. Her biggest fear was that, once you accounted for the elderly, there might not be enough people to repopulate. It took more than just Adam and Eve. She was captain of a ship that might sink no matter what she did.

There was a knock at the door. Maddy sat down at her desk. "Come in."

James entered the room and stood to attention. "Ma'am, you requested me."

"Commander Tosco, how is our fleet doing?"

"Fishing yields are up, especially now that our warships have been repurposed towards the task. Our smaller vessels are continuing to scout the coast. Yesterday, they found a small group of survivors hiding out in Bristol – nineteen people. That's over a hundred survivors in the last month."

Maddy smiled. "Gives me hope that there might be more of us out there. We need to bring them all home. This place needs to grow."

"It will. Now that people realise it's safe, they'll come out of hiding."

"*Are* we safe, James?"

He frowned and stood at ease. "Maddy, everything is good here. You're doing a great job, and everyone is working hard to make the best of it. It's time to relax."

"You know I can't do that. Not yet."

"Capri?"

Maddy leant back in her chair and sighed. "I have a call scheduled with him right now. He won't stop until the entire continent is under his fist. Since the demons left, he's gobbled up Portugal and whatever is left of Spain. There's no stopping him."

"We thought that about the demons. Then we kicked their butts."

"This is different. Capri has an army. We don't have a single bullet left. Our ships have swapped their guns for fishing nets."

James strolled forward and put his hands on her desk. He gave her a hard stare. "Maddy, this isn't you. When Thomas took over Portsmouth, you dealt with him – and you'll deal with Capri.

He's just another arrogant old man with an ego as big as his pecker is small."

Maddy cackled. "You do make me laugh, James. We still on for a drink tonight?"

"Of course. Alice and I found a lovely little spot today on our walk. There's a pond there with fish and birds, a perfect place to get rat-arsed."

"Ha! Have you been working on your slang?"

He grinned. "I heard one of the guys say that earlier. Did I use it right?"

"You did – and this pond sounds lovely. I can't wait to see it. Being alone with you is the only time I ever stop worrying."

James stood back at attention. "Glad to be of service, ma'am."

The radio at the side of her office crackled. A green light blinked.

"That'll be Capri." Maddy stood and straightened her blouse. "Here goes nothing."

James reached out and took her arm. "Hey, just remember who we are and what we've done. No one gets to push us around, big or small."

Maddy went over to the radio and accepted the communication. "This is Maddy, spokesperson for New Hope. Who am I speaking to? Over."

A woman's voice replied, clipped and accented. "Chancellor Capri wishes to speak to whomever is in charge. Over."

Maddy rolled her eyes. "That would be me. Put him on the line. Over."

"Please await the chancellor."

Maddy exchanged a look with James and mouthed the words, *Can you believe this guy?*

"*Guten morgen,* spokesman, this is Chancellor Capri."

"It's spokes*woman*," said Maddy. "What can I do for you, Chancellor?"

"I believe we spoke one month ago, and my demands have not changed. Commander Klein, his crew, and his nuclear submarine must be handed over to the German Confederation immediately. An expeditionary force will soon be dispatched to the British coast. He may hand himself over then, peacefully."

"You do not have permission to send anyone here, Chancellor, and I—"

"I do not need permission, young lady. The German Confederation has taken guardianship of mankind's survival. It exists to secure—"

"Your own fucking agenda," Maddy snapped. "New Hope will not become part of your empire, Capri. I consider every part of this island to be sovereign territory. I suggest you stay off our property."

"How dare you speak with such insolence, you foolish girl. You are in no position to make threats. The people of New Hope will not thank you for your truculence. The German Confederation is responsible for their welfare, and—"

"We are responsible for our own welfare, thank you very much. We don't want your help."

There was silence on the line. She had no idea what Capri was thinking – or even what he was like as a person – but she knew he was nowhere near backing down. The game would go on far longer than this.

"Spokeswoman, if you do not comply with the demands of the German Confederation, you will be *forced* to comply. Surely you understand this?"

"I'm afraid you're the one who doesn't understand. You've built yourself an empire, Capri, congratulations. The thing about empires, though, is that they fall. War is fleeting; only peace can make us immortal. New Hope is willing to be a close friend and ally to the German Confederation. In fact, we have already done more for your people than you have done for yourself?"

"Explain this."

"We're the reason the demons are gone. Perhaps you already knew that. I've had my people radioing out to whoever will listen on the continent, telling them how a handful of brave survivors in Portsmouth managed to close the final gate and defeat the demons once and for all. We've managed to speak with several of your ship commanders and many of your fishermen... even the odd hobbyist with a dusty CB. Basically, anyone with a radio knows that we're the good guys. It's really going to confuse them if you attack us."

Capri growled. "I won't be cowed by propaganda. While I respect what you people did in the war for mankind's survival, my people will do as I command. Stories mean nothing to men and women who wish to eat."

"You're misguided, Chancellor. Don't you see that you're taking mankind down the same path it was on before the demons came. Force a man to kneel and all he will do is dream of freedom. Give a man freedom and he will dream of a better world. We can build that better world, Capri. New Hope will not kneel, but it is willing to offer a hand in friendship. My people are brave. They are ferocious. Stick a hand through our bars and we will bite you."

"Even so, you shall be crushed."

"And the stain of that will follow you around for the rest of your life. You'll be remembered as a tyrant who subjugated heroes and warriors. Do you really want mankind to begin again with more atrocity? Have we not earned peace? Can we not work together for something wonderful? What kind of a man do you want to be, Chancellor? What kind of world do you want to live in?"

More silence on the line. Then, "Hand over Commander Klein and I will consider it the start of a new friendship. The German Confederation will not tolerate nuclear capabilities under foreign command."

Maddy sighed. She turned a couple of switches and opened a second line. "Klein? Are you hearing this?"

"Yes, *fräulein*. Capri wishes to be friends."

"If you hand over your nukes."

"*Ja*. Men always seem to want them. It's getting very tiresome."

"I'll bet. Should we hand them over?"

"*Ja!* Activating launch sequence in *drei, zwei, ein.*"

Capri came back on the line. "Wait! Wait, what are you doing?"

Maddy snarled. "Sending you those nukes you want so badly."

"*Nein.* You are insane. What have you done? This is madness."

"You're right," said Maddy. "Killing each other after what we've just lived through *is* madness. It doesn't matter how strong you are, Capri. You're just a man, and you can be killed. If you continue to threaten New Hope, I'll be the one to kill you, just like I killed General Thomas. He, too, thought he was strong. He, too, thought I was weak. Yet I live while his body rots."

"You're a murderer. You just authorised a nuclear—"

"I just authorised Commander Klein to relinquish his warheads into the sea. Right now they are probably headed, unarmed, into the English Channel. There, they will sink harmlessly to the seabed and hopefully stay there for all of time."

"What? You are more insane than I thought. Those warheads were the only leverage you had."

"You're right. I could have kept you at bay with the threat of using them. That's why you've been so eager to get your hands on them. Probably to use them as your own leverage against China and Russia. I hear they've become quite friendly recently."

"*Ja!* And they no doubt have nuclear weapons of their own."

"Perhaps, but that doesn't mean I'm going to try and put out a fire by starting a bigger fire. Klein's nuclear warheads are gone. They will never kill anybody. I'll never be tempted to fire them at you and kill your innocent citizens. I won't be brought down to your level, Capri. New Hope is no threat to the German Confederation. The only thing you have to gain here is an ally, if you want it."

Capri hissed. "Our radars have detected multiple jet signatures over the English Channel. Is it true? Has Klein really disarmed?"

Klein answered, still on the line. "I am glad to be free of the wretched things. They are *zunk* to the bottom of the sea."

"Heaven's above. I can hardly believe what I am dealing with. You people are fools."

"We are people who just want to live in peace, Capri. Will you take that away from us?"

"No. You have proven that you are fiercely independent, and that is no problem providing you remain on your island. The German Confederation offers friendship and alliance to the people of New Hope, and recognises its sovereignty over the former British Isles. Remain peaceful or said alliance will end."

Maddy looked at James, barely able to keep from gushing with happiness. She kept her cool and finished the call. "The people of New Hope thank you. Best health to the German people, and cheers to you, Capri."

"*Ja! Auf wiedersehen.*"

Maddy switched off the radio and threw herself into James's arms. "Commander Tosco, did I really just do that?"

"Spokeswoman Maddy, I believe you just did."

She smothered him in kisses and then stepped back. There was no benefit in getting excited. She had to stay focused. "Do you believe Capri will keep to his word?"

James shrugged. "We'll spread the good news of our newly acquired friendship on the airwaves. Capri needs his people to respect his decisions, so he won't attack an ally without cause. We just have to play nice and be friends like we said we would. Capri's biggest concern is competition, and he has enough of that with China and Russia. He doesn't need any distractions."

Maddy shuddered at the mention of China and Russia, mainly because she knew so little about what was going on there. "Do you think they'll ever go to war? After all that's happened?"

"No, I don't. I think it's a land grab, and eventually the chips will fall where they may. The worst we'll get is a cold war. No man wants to be the first to fire a bullet at his fellow man after we survived extinction. History has taught us too much to see sense in war, and the demons taught us too much to see sense in killing. Whether men like Capri realise it or not, mankind has changed. We are fearless warriors, and yet every one of us yearns for peace. It'll take time for us to figure everything out, but I think you just proved that there's hope for us all."

Maddy frowned at him. "How did I prove that?"

"You just stopped a war with nothing but words. You formed an alliance without giving anything away. You made a friend of an enemy. No one can control the actions of others, but we can decide who we want to be, and you just decided who *we* are."

"And who are we?"

"The good guys. Let's never be anything else."

"Cheers to that!" She rubbed her tired eyes and moaned. Tiredness existed in every cell of her body, and all she wanted to do was sleep, but there would be time for that later. "Okay, James. Take me to this pond you found. I need to clear my head."

James offered his arm. "If the lady would accompany me."

"A lady would be thrilled." Maddy took her lover's arm and they headed for the door. Outside, New Hope awaited them.

WANT FREE BOOKS?

Don't miss out on your FREE Iain Rob Wright horror pack. Five bestselling horror novels sent straight to your inbox at no cost. No strings attached & signing up is a doddle.

Just visit www.iainrobwright.com

PLEA FROM THE AUTHOR

Hey, Reader. So you got to the end of my book. I hope that means you enjoyed it. Whether or not you did, I would just like to thank you for giving me your valuable time to try and entertain you. I am truly blessed to have such a fulfilling job, but I only have that job because of people like you; people kind enough to give my books a chance and spend their hard-earned money buying them. For that I am eternally grateful.

If you would like to find out more about my other books then please visit my website for full details. You can find it at:

www.iainrobwright.com.

Also feel free to contact me on Facebook, Twitter, or email (all details on the website), as I would love to hear from you.

If you enjoyed this book and would like to help, then you could think about leaving a review on Amazon, Goodreads, or anywhere else that readers visit. The most important part of how well a book sells is how many positive reviews it has, so if you leave me one then you are directly helping me to continue on this journey as a full time writer. Thanks in advance to anyone who does. It means a lot.

ALSO BY IAIN ROB WRIGHT

OTHER BOOKS IN THE HELL ON EARTH SERIES

- The Gates (Book 1)
- Legion (Book 2)
- Extinction (Book 3)
- Defiance (Book 4)
- Resurgence (Book 5)

MORE HORROR BOOKS FROM IAIN ROB WRIGHT

- Escape!
- Dark Ride
- 12 Steps
- The Room Upstairs
- Animal Kingdom
- AZ of Horror
- Sam
- ASBO
- The Final Winter
- The Housemates
- Sea Sick
- Ravage
- Savage
- The Picture Frame
- Wings of Sorrow
- TAR
- House Beneath the Bridge
- The Peeling
- Blood on the bar

Iain Rob Wright is one of the UK's most successful horror and suspense writers, with novels including the critically acclaimed, THE FINAL WINTER; the disturbing bestseller, ASBO; and the wicked screamfest, THE HOUSEMATES.

His work is currently being adapted for graphic novels, audio books, and foreign audiences. He is an active member of the Horror Writer Association and a massive animal lover.

www.iainrobwright.com
FEAR ON EVERY PAGE

For more information
www.iainrobwright.com
iain.robert.wright@hotmail.co.uk

Lightning Source UK Ltd.
Milton Keynes UK
UKHW041532210920
370272UK00001B/197

9 781913 523381